DARING and the Duke

The Bareknuckle Bastards Book III

SARAH MACLEAN

AVONBOOKS

An Imprint of HarperCollins*Publishers*

This is a work of fiction. Names, characters, places, and incidents are products of the author's imagination or are used fictitiously and are not to be construed as real. Any resemblance to actual events, locales, organizations, or persons, living or dead, is entirely coincidental.

First Avon Books mass market printing: July 2020
First Avon Books hardcover printing: June 2020

Print Edition ISBN: 978-0-06-269208-5
Digital Edition ISBN: 978-0-06-269199-6

Cover design by Patricia Barrow
Cover illustration by Alan Ayers

FIRST EDITION

20 21 22 23 24 CWM 10 9 8 7 6 5 4 3 2 1

For rebel girls.
Especially mine.

DARING *and the Duke*

Chapter One

Burghsey House
Seat of the Dukedom of Marwick
The Past

There was nothing in the wide world like his laugh.

It didn't matter that she was unqualified to speak of the wide world. She'd never strayed far from this enormous manor house, tucked into the quiet Essex countryside two days' walk northeast of London, where rolling green hills turned to wheat as autumn crept across the land.

It didn't matter that she didn't know the sounds of the city or the smell of the ocean. Or that she'd never heard a language other than English, or seen a play, or listened to an orchestra.

It didn't matter that her world had been limited to the three thousand acres of fertile land boasting fluffy white sheep and massive hay bales and a community of people with whom she was not allowed to speak—to whom she was virtually invisible—because she was a secret that was to be kept at all costs.

A girl, baptized the heir to the Dukedom of Marwick.

Swaddled in the rich lace reserved for a long line of dukes, anointed with oils reserved for the most privileged of Burghsey House residents. Given a boy's name and title before God even as the man who was not her father paid servants and priests for silence and falsified documents and laid plans to replace her mother's bastard daughter with one of his own bastard sons, born on the same day as she—to women who were not his duchess—offering him a single path to a ducal legacy . . . theft.

Offering that useless girl, the mewling babe in nurse's arms, nothing more than a half life, full of the aching loneliness that came from a world so large and so small, all at once.

And then *he'd* arrived, one year earlier. Twelve years old and full of fire and strength and the world beyond. Tall and lean and already so clever and cunning and the most beautiful thing she'd ever seen, blond hair too long over bright amber eyes that held a thousand secrets, and a quiet, barely ever heard laugh—so rare that when it came, it felt like a gift.

No, there was nothing in the wide world like his laugh. She knew it, even if the wide world was so far beyond her reach she couldn't even imagine where it began.

He could.

He loved to tell her about it. Which was what he did that afternoon, one of their precious, stolen moments between the duke's machinations and manipulations—a thieved day before a night when the man who held their future might return to revel in tormenting his three sons. But today, in that quiet afternoon, while the duke was away in London, doing whatever it was that dukes did, the quartet took happiness where they could find it—out on the wild, meandering land that made up the estate.

Her favorite place was on the western edge of the land, far enough away from the manor house that it might be forgotten before it could be remembered. A magnificent copse of trees soaring into the sky, lined on one side with a small, bubbling stream, less stream than brook, if a body were honest, but one that had given her hours, days, weeks of chattering company when she'd been younger and conversation with the water had been all she could hope for.

But here, now, she was not lonely. She was inside the trees, where dappled sunshine flooded the ground where she lay on her back—collapsed after racing across the land, taking great breaths of air heavy with the scent of wild thyme.

He sat next to her, his hip to hers, his own chest rising and falling with heavy breath as he stared down into her face, his ever-lengthening legs stretched past her head. "Why do we always come here?"

"I like it here," she said simply, turning her face up to the sunlight, the tattoo of her heartbeat calming as she stared through the canopy to the sky playing hide-and-seek beyond. "And so would you if you weren't so serious all the time."

The air in the quiet place shifted, thickening with the truth—that they were not ordinary children, thirteen and without care. Care was how they survived. Seriousness was how they survived.

She didn't want that now. Not while the last of the summer butterflies danced in rays of light above, filling the whole place with magic that kept the worst at bay. So she changed the subject.

"Tell me about it."

He didn't ask her to clarify. He didn't need to. "Again?"

"Again."

He swiveled around, and she moved her skirts so he could lie next to her, as he had dozens of times before. Hundreds of them. Once he was settled on his back, his hands stacked behind his head, he spoke to the canopy. "It's never quiet there."

"Because of the carts on the cobblestones."

He nodded. "The wooden wheels make a racket, but it's more than that. It's the shouts from the taverns and the hawkers in the market square. The dogs barking in the warehouses. The brawls in the streets. I used to stand on the roof of the place I lived and bet on the brawls."

"That's why you're so good at fighting."

He lifted a shoulder in a tiny shrug. "I always thought it would be the best way to help my ma. Until . . ."

He trailed off, but she heard the rest. Until she'd taken ill, and the duke had dangled a title and a fortune in front of a son who would have done anything to help. She turned to look at him, his face drawn tight, resolutely staring up at the sky, jaw set.

"Tell me about the cursing," she prodded.

He let out a little surprised laugh. "A riot of foul language. You like that bit."

"I didn't even know cursing existed before you three." Boys who came into her life like a riot themselves, rough and tumble and foul-mouthed and wonderful.

"Before Devil, you mean."

Devil, christened Devon—one of his two half brothers—raised in a boys' orphanage and with the mouth to prove it. "He's proved very useful."

"Yes. The cursing. Especially on the docks. No one swears like a sailor."

"Tell me the best one you've ever heard."

He cut her a sly look. "No."

She'd ask Devil later. "Tell me about the rain."

"It's London. It rains all the time."

She nudged him with her shoulder. "Tell me the good bit."

He smiled, and she matched it, loving the way he humored her. "The rain turns the stones on the street slick and shiny."

"And at night, it turns them gold, because of the lights from the taverns," she filled in.

"Not just the taverns. The theaters on Drury Lane. The lamps that hang outside the bawdy houses." Bawdy houses where his mother had landed after the duke had refused to keep her when she'd chosen to have his son. Where that son had been born.

"To keep the dark at bay," she said softly.

"The dark ain't so bad," he said. "It's just that the people in it haven't a choice but to fight for what they need."

"And do they get it? What they need?"

"No. They don't get what they need, and not what they deserve, neither." He paused, then whispered to the canopy, like it really was magic. "But we're going to change all that."

She didn't miss the *we*. Not just him. All of them. A foursome that had made a pact when the boys had been brought here for this mad competition—whoever won would keep them all safe. And then they'd escape this place that had imprisoned them all in a battle of wits and weapons that would give his father what the older man wanted: an heir worthy of a dukedom.

"Once you're duke," she said, softly.

He turned to look at her. "Once one of us is duke."

She shook her head, meeting his glittering amber gaze, so like his brothers'. So like his father's. "You're going to win."

He watched her for a long moment and said, "How do you know?"

She pressed her lips together. "I just know." The old duke's machinations grew more challenging by the day. Devil was like his name, too much fire and fury. And Whit—he was too small. Too kind.

"And if I don't want it?"

A preposterous idea. "Of course you want it."

"It should be yours."

She couldn't help the little, wild laugh. "Girls don't get to be dukes."

"And here you are, an heir, nonetheless."

But she wasn't. Not really. She was the product of her mother's extramarital affair, a gamble designed to deliver a bastard heir to a monstrous husband, forever tainting his precious familial line—the only thing he'd ever cared for. But instead of a boy, the duchess had produced a girl, and so she was not heir. She was a placeholder. A bookmark in an ancient copy of *Burke's Peerage*. And they all knew it.

She ignored the words and said, "It doesn't matter."

And it didn't. Ewan would win. He would become duke. And it would change everything.

He watched her for a long moment. "When I am duke, then." The words were a whisper, as though if he spoke them in truth, he'd curse them all. "When I am duke, I shall keep us all safe. Us and all of the Garden. I shall take his money. His power. His name. And I shall walk away and never look back." The words circled around them, reverberating off the trees for a long moment before he corrected himself. "Not his name," he whispered. "Yours."

Robert Matthew Carrick, Earl Sumner, heir to the Dukedom of Marwick.

She ignored the thread of emotion winding through her and lightened her tone. "You might as well have the name. It's proper new. I've never used it." She might have been baptized the heir, but she didn't have access to the name.

Over the years, when she'd been anything at all, she'd been *girl*, *the girl*, or *young lady*. Once, for a heartbeat when she was eight, there was a housemaid who called her *luv*, and she'd rather enjoyed that. But the maid had left after a few months, and the girl had been back to being nobody.

Until *they'd* arrived—a trio of boys who saw her—and

this one, who seemed not only to see her, but also to understand her. And they called her a hundred things, *Run* for the way she tore across the fields, and *Red* for the flame in her hair, and *Riot* for the way she fumed at their father. And she answered to all of them, knowing that none was her name, but not caring so much once they'd arrived. Because maybe they were enough.

Because to them, she was not nobody.

"I'm sorry," he whispered. He meant it.

To him, she was somebody.

They stayed that way for a heartbeat, gazes locked, truth like a blanket around them, until he cleared his throat and looked away, breaking the connection and rolling onto his back, returning his attention to the trees above, and saying, "Anyway, my mum used to say she loved the rain, because it was the only time she ever saw jewels in Covent Garden."

"Promise to take me when you leave," she whispered into the quiet.

His lips set into a firm line, his promise written in the lines of his face, older than it should be. Younger than it would have to become. He nodded once. Firm. Certain. "And I'll make sure you have jewels."

She rolled onto her own back, her skirts haphazard in the grass. "See that you do," she jested. "And gold thread for all my gowns."

"I shall keep you in spools of it."

"Yes, please," she said. "And a lady's maid with a particular skill for hair."

"You're very demanding for a country girl," he teased.

She turned a grin on him. "I've had a lifetime to prepare my requirements."

"Do you think you're ready for London, country girl?"

The smile faded into a mock scowl. "I think I shall do just fine, city boy."

He laughed, and the rare sound filled the space around

them, warming her. And in that moment, something happened. Something strange and unsettling and wonderful and weird. That sound, like nothing in the wide world, unlocked her.

Suddenly, she could feel him. Not simply the warmth of him along her side, where they touched from shoulder to hip. Not only the place where his elbow rested beside her ear. Not just the feel of his touch in her curls as he extracted a leaf from them. *All* of him. The even rise and fall of his breath. His sure stillness. And that laugh . . . *his laugh.*

"Whatever happens, promise you won't forget me," she said quietly.

"I shan't be able to. We'll be together."

She shook her head. "People leave."

His brow furrowed and she could hear the force in his words. "I don't. I *won't.*"

She nodded. But still, "Sometimes you don't choose it. Sometimes people just . . ."

His gaze softened with understanding and he heard the reference to her mother in the trail of her words. He rolled toward her, and they were facing each other now, cheeks on their bent arms, close enough for secrets. "She would have stayed if she could," he said, firmly.

"You don't know that," she whispered, hating the sting of the words behind the bridge of her nose. "I was born and she died, and she left me with a man who was not my father, who gave me a name that is not my own, and I'll never know what would have happened if she'd lived. I'll never know if . . ."

He waited. Ever patient, as though he would wait for her for a lifetime.

"I'll never know if she would have loved me."

"She would have loved you." The answer was instant.

She shook her head, closing her eyes. Wanting to believe him. "She didn't even name me."

"She would have. She would have named you, and it would have been something beautiful."

The certainty in his words had her meeting his gaze, sure and unyielding. "Not Robert, then?"

He didn't smile. Didn't laugh. "She would have named you for what you were. For what you deserved. She would have given you the title."

Understanding dawned.

And then he whispered, "Just as I would do."

Everything stopped. The rustle of leaves in the canopy, the shouts of his brothers in the stream beyond, the slow creep of the afternoon, and she knew, in that moment, that he was about to give her a gift that she'd never imagined she'd receive.

She smiled at him, her heart pounding in her chest. "Tell me."

She wanted it on his lips, in his voice, in her ears. She wanted it from him, knowing it would make it impossible for her to ever forget him, even after he left her behind.

He gave it to her.

"Grace."

Chapter Two

London
Autumn 1837

"To Dahlia!"

A raucous cheer rose in reply to the shout, the crush of people in the central room of 72 Shelton Street—a high-end club and the best kept secret of London's smartest, savviest, most scandalous women—turning in unison to toast its proprietress.

The woman known as Dahlia stilled at the bottom of the central staircase, taking in the massive space, already packed with club members and guests despite the early hour. She offered the assembly a wide, glittering smile. "Drink up, my lovelies, you've a night to remember ahead of you!"

"Or to forget!" came a boisterous retort from the far end of the room. Dahlia recognized the voice instantly as that of one of London's merriest widows—a marchioness who had invested in 72 Shelton Street from the earliest days, and loved it more than her own home. Here, a merry marchioness was afforded the privacy she never received in Grosvenor Square. Her lovers, too, received that privacy.

The masked crowd laughed in unison, and Dahlia was freed from their collective attention just long enough for her lieutenant, Zeva, to appear at her side. The tall, willowy, dark-haired beauty had been with her since the earliest days of the club and managed the ins and outs of the membership—ensuring that whatever they wished was theirs for the taking.

"Already a crush," Zeva said.

Dahlia checked the watch at her waist. "About to be more of one."

It was early, just past eleven; much of London only now able to sneak away from their boring dinners and dances, making their excuses with megrims and delicate constitutions. Dahlia smirked at the thought, knowing the way the club's membership used the perceived weakness of the fairer sex to take what they wished beneath the notice of society.

They would claim that weakness and play to it: all while summoning their coachmen to the rear exits of their homes; while changing from their respectable fashions to something more exciting; while peeling off the masks they wore in their world and donning different ones, different names, different desires—whatever they wished, out of Mayfair.

Soon, they would arrive, filling 72 Shelton Street to the gills, to revel in what the club could provide on any given night of the year—companionship, pleasure, and power—and specifically for what it delivered on the third Thursday of every month, when women from across London and the world were welcome to explore their deepest desires.

The standing event—known only as *Dominion*—was

part masked ball, part wild revelry, part casino, and entirely confidential. Designed to provide club membership and trusted companions with an evening catering entirely to their pleasure . . . whatever that pleasure might be.

Dominion had a single, driving purpose: Ladies' choice.

There was nothing Dahlia liked more than providing women access to their pleasure. The fairer sex was not treated fairly in the slightest, and her club was built to change that.

Since arriving in London twenty years earlier, she had made money in scores of ways. She'd sculleried in dingy pubs and dank theaters. She'd minced meat in pie shops and bent metal into spoons, and never for more than a penny or two for the work. She'd quickly discovered that daytime work didn't pay.

Which was fine with her, as she had never been suited to daytime work. After chamber pots and meat pies turned her stomach and metalwork left her palms sliced to ribbons, she'd found a job as a flower girl, racing to empty a basket of fast-wilting posies before dark. She'd lasted two days before a hawker in the Covent Garden market had seen her keen eye for a customer and offered her work selling fruit.

That had lasted less than a week, until he'd backhanded her for accidentally dropping a bright red apple in the sawdust. When she'd come to her feet, she'd put him into the sawdust himself, before sprinting from the market, three apples in her skirts—worth more than her pay for a week.

But the event had been surprising enough to attract the attention of one of the Garden's biggest fight men. Digger Knight had been on a constant hunt for tall girls with pretty faces and powerful fists. *Brutes are one thing*, he used to say, *but the belles win the crowd*. Dahlia turned out to be both.

She'd been taught well.

Fighting wasn't daytime work. It was nighttime work, and it paid like it.

It paid well. And it felt better—especially for a girl from nowhere who was full of betrayal and anger. She didn't mind the sting of the blows and she quickly found her sea legs from the dizziness that came the morning after a bout . . . and once she learned how to see a blow coming, and how to avoid the ones that would do real damage? She never looked back.

Turning her back on flowers and fruit, Dahlia sold her fists instead, in fair fights and dirty ones. And when she'd seen the kind of money that the latter could earn her, she sold her hair to a wigmaker in Mayfair who shopped the Garden wholesale. Long hair was weakness . . . and bad for business for a bareknuckle girl.

The short-haired, long-legged nearly fifteen-year-old had become a legend in Covent Garden's darkest corners. A girl with a lean, sinewy form and, somehow, a punch like oak, whom no man wished to meet on a darkened street, especially when flanked by the two boys who came with her, who fought with a young, feral rage that brought ruin to anyone who faced it.

Together, they made money hands over those fists, building an empire, Dahlia and those boys who quickly became men—her brothers in heart and soul if not in blood—the Bareknuckle Bastards. And the trio sold their fists until they no longer had to . . . until, eventually, they were unbeatable. Unbreakable.

Royal.

And only then did Queen Dahlia build her castle and claim her place, no longer in the business of flowers or apples or hair or fights.

And to her subjects, she offered a single magnificent thing: choice. Not the kind she'd been afforded—lesser of multiple evils—but the kind that let women have access to their dreams. Fantasies and pleasure, made good.

What women wanted, Dahlia provided.

And Dominion was her celebration.

"You dressed for the occasion, I see," Zeva said.

"Did I?" Dahlia replied with a raised brow. The scarlet corset she wore above perfectly fitted black trousers skimmed her lush curves beneath a long, elaborately embroidered topcoat in black and gold, lined with a rich golden silk.

She rarely wore skirts, finding the freedom of trousers more useful while working—not to mention, a valuable reminder of her role as proprietress of one of London's best kept secrets and queen of Covent Garden.

Her lieutenant slid her a look. "Coy does not become you. I know where you've been for the last four days. And you haven't been wearing velvet and silk."

A raucous cheer came from the roulette wheel nearby, saving Dahlia from a reply. She turned to watch the crowd, taking in the wide, delighted smile of a masked woman, anonymous to all but the owner of the club, as she pulled Tomas, her companion for the evening, in for a celebratory kiss. Tomas was nothing if not a willing participant, and the embrace ended to whistles and huzzahs.

No one would believe that to all of Mayfair, she was a shelf-bound wallflower who lost her voice with men. Masks were infinite power when they were chosen.

"The lady is running hot?" Dahlia asked.

"Third win in a row." Of course Zeva was keeping track. "And Tomas isn't exactly a cooling influence."

Dahlia offered a half smile. "Nothing escapes your notice."

"You pay me very well for that to be the case. I notice everything," the other woman said. "Including your whereabouts."

Dahlia looked to her factotum and friend and said, quietly, "Not tonight."

Zeva had more to say, but kept quiet. Instead, she waved a hand in the direction of the far end of the room, where a collection of masked women stood huddled in private discussion. "The vote will fail tomorrow."

The women were aristocratic wives, most legions smarter than their husbands, and all as (or far more) qualified to hold seat in the House of Lords. Lacking the proper robes did not keep the ladies from legislating, however, and when they did, they did it here, in private quarters, beneath the notice of Mayfair.

Dahlia turned a satisfied look on Zeva. The vote would have made prostitution and other forms of sex work illegal in Britain. Dahlia had spent the last three weeks convincing the wives in question that this was a vote in which they—and their husbands—should take interest, and ensure did not pass. "Good. It's bad for women and poor women the most."

It was bad for Covent Garden, and she wouldn't have it.

"So is the rest of the world," Zeva said, dry as sand. "Have you got a bill to pass for that?"

"Give it time," Dahlia replied as they passed through the room to a long hallway, where several couples were taking advantage of the darkness. "Nothing moves as slowly as Parliament."

Zeva gave a little huff of laughter behind her. "You and I both know there's nothing you love more than manipulating Parliament. They should give you a seat."

The corridor opened up on a large, inviting space filled with revelers, a small band of musicians at one end, playing a rousing tune for the collected audience, many of whom danced with abandon—no mincing steps, no careful space between couples, no discerning eyes watching for scandal—or, rather, if they were watching, it was for enjoyment and not censure.

The duo wove through the crowd along the edges of the room, past a sinewy man who winked at them as the woman in his arms stroked over his muscled chest, which looked as though it might burst the seams of his topcoat. Oscar, another employee—his work, the lady's pleasure.

A scant handful of the men in attendance were not employees, each having been properly vetted beforehand, checked and rechecked via Dahlia's far-reaching network—made up of businesswomen, aristocrats, politicians' wives, and a dozen women who knew and wielded the most complex of power: information.

The orchestra rested as a songstress moved to the center of the raised stage where they sat, a young black woman whose voice rose like heaven, big enough to echo around the room, bringing the dancers to an out-of-breath standstill as she trilled and scaled in a bright aria that would bring down any house on Drury Lane.

A collection of awed gasps sounded around the room.

"Dahlia."

Dahlia turned to face a woman in brilliant green, elaborate mask to match. Nastasia Kritikos was a legendary Greek opera singer, one who had herself brought down houses across Europe. With a warm embrace, she nodded to the stage. "This girl. Where did you find her?"

"Eve?" A smile played across Dahlia's lips. "In the market square, singing for supper."

A dark brow rose in amusement. "Is that not what she does tonight?"

"Tonight, she sings for you, old friend." It was the truth. The young woman sang for access to Dominion, where a handful of other talented singers had been catapulted to stardom.

Nastasia cast a discerning eye at the stage, where Eve sang an impossible run of notes.

"That was your specialty, wasn't it?" Dahlia said.

The other woman cut her a look. "*Is* my specialty. I wouldn't call hers *perfect*."

Dahlia gave her a little, knowing smile. It was perfect, and they both knew it.

With an enormous sigh, the diva waved a hand in the air. "Tell her to come see me tomorrow. I'll introduce her to some people."

The girl would be treading the boards before she knew it. "You're softhearted, Nastasia."

Brown eyes glittered behind a green mask. "If you tell anyone, I'll have this place burned to the ground."

"Your secret is safe with me." Dahlia grinned. "Peter has been asking for you." It was the truth. Besides being a proper London celebrity, Nastasia was also a coveted prize among the men in the club.

The older woman preened. "Of course he has. I suppose I can spare a few hours."

Dahlia laughed and nodded to Zeva. "We'll find him for you, then."

That sorted, she pushed forward, through the crowd that had collected to listen to the soon-to-be-famous songstress, to a small antechamber, where faro games routinely became heated. She could feel the excitement in the air, and she drank it in—and the power that came with it. London's most powerful women, collected here for their own pleasure.

And all because of her.

"We'll have to find a new singer," Zeva grumbled as they weaved through the gamers.

"Eve doesn't want to be the downstairs entertainment at our bacchanals forever."

"We could keep them longer than a month."

"She's too talented for us."

"*You're* the one with the soft heart," came the retort.

". . . the explosion." Dahlia slowed at the snippet of

conversation nearby, her gaze meeting that of a maid delivering a tray of champagne to the gossiping group. A barely-there nod indicated that the other woman was also listening. She was paid to, and well.

Still, Dahlia lingered. "Two of them, I heard," came a reply, full of scandalized delight. Dahlia resisted the urge to scowl. "I heard they decimated the docks."

"Yes, and imagine, only two dead."

"A miracle." The words were hushed, as though the woman actually believed it. "Were any injured?"

"The *News* said five."

Six, she thought, gritting her teeth, her heart beginning to pound.

"You're staring," Zeva said softly, the words pulling Dahlia away from the conversation. What more was there to learn? She'd been there mere minutes after the explosion. She knew the count.

She slid her gaze past Zeva and over the crowd to a small door, barely there at the other end of the room—the seams of it hidden in the deep sapphire wall coverings, shot through with silver. Even the members who had seen staff use it forgot the unassuming opening before it had been snicked shut, thinking whatever behind it far less interesting than what was in front of it.

Zeva knew the truth, though. That door opened to a back staircase running up to private rooms and down into the tunnels beneath the club. It was one of a half dozen installed around 72 Shelton Street, but the only one that led to a private hallway on the fourth floor, concealed behind a false wall, which only three staff members knew existed.

Dahlia ignored the keen itch to disappear through it. "It's important we understand what the city thinks about that explosion."

"They think the Bareknuckle Bastards lost two lading men, a hold full of cargo, and a ship. And that your brother's lady was nearly killed." A pause. Then a pointed, "And they're right." Dahlia ignored the words. Zeva knew when the battle wasn't to be won. "And what shall I say to them?"

Dahlia slid her a look. "Who?"

The other woman lifted her chin in the direction of the labyrinth of rooms through which they'd come. "Your brothers. What would you like me to tell them?"

Dahlia swore softly and cast a look over the shadowed crowd—packed several deep. By the entrance to the room, a notorious countess finished a filthy joke for a collection of admirers. ". . . the carrots go in the *rear* garden, darling!"

Peals of delighted laughter rang out and Dahlia turned back to Zeva. "Christ, they're not here, are they?"

"No, but we can't keep them out forever."

"We can try."

"They've a point—"

Dahlia cut the other woman off with a sharp look and a sharper retort. "You let me worry about them."

Zeva lifted her chin toward the hidden door, and the stairs beyond. "And what of that?"

A hot wash came over Dahlia—something that might have been a blush if she were the kind of woman who blushed. She ignored it, and the pounding of her heart.

"You let me worry about that, too."

A single black brow rose above Zeva's dark eyes, indicating that she had legions more to say. Instead, she nodded once. "Then I shall hold the floor."

She turned away and pushed back through the crowd, leaving Dahlia alone.

Alone to press the hidden panel in the door, to activate the latch, and to close it tight behind her, shutting out the cacophony of sound beyond.

Alone to climb the narrow stairs with quiet, steady rhythm—a rhythm at odds with the increasing pace of her heart as she passed the second floor. The third.

Alone to count the doors in the fourth-floor hallway.

One. Two. Three.

Alone to open the fourth door on the left, and close it behind her, cloaking herself in darkness thick enough to erase the wild party below, the world distilling to nothing but the room, its single window looking out over the Covent Garden rooftops, and its sparse furnishings: a small table, a rigid chair, a single bed.

Alone, in that room.

Alone, with the man unconscious in that bed.

Chapter Three

He'd been rescued by angels.

The explosion had sent him flying through the air, knocking him back into the shadows of the docks. He'd twisted in flight, but the landing had dislocated his shoulder, rendering his left arm useless. It was said that dislocation was one of the worst pains a body could experience, and the Duke of Marwick had suffered it twice. Twice, he'd staggered to his feet, mind reeling. Twice, he'd struggled to bear the pain. Twice, he'd sought out a place to hide from his enemy.

Twice, he'd been rescued by angels.

The first time, she'd been fresh-faced and kind, with a wild riot of red curls, a thousand freckles across her nose and cheeks, and the biggest brown eyes he'd ever seen. She'd found him in the cupboard where he hid, put a finger to her lips, and held his good hand as another—larger and stronger—had reset the joint. He'd passed out from the pain, and when he woke, she'd been there like sunlight, with a soft touch and a soft voice.

And he'd fallen in love with her.

This time, the angels who rescued him were not soft, and

they did not sing. They came for him with strength and power, hoods low over their heads keeping their faces in shadow, coats billowing behind them like wings as they approached, boots clicking on the cobblestones. They came armed like heaven's soldiers, blades at their sides turned flaming swords in the light of the ship that burned on the docks—destroyed at his command, along with the woman his brother loved.

This time, the angels were soldiers, come to punish and not to save.

Still, it would be rescue.

He had pushed to his feet as they approached, prepared to face them head-on, to take the punishment they would deliver. He winced at the pain in his leg that he had not noticed earlier, where a shard from the mast of the destroyed hauler had seated itself in his thigh, coating his trouser leg in blood, making it impossible to fight.

When they'd been close enough to strike, he'd lost consciousness.

And that's when the nightmares had come, not the stuff of beasts and brutality, not full of sharp teeth and sharper terror. Worse than all that.

Ewan's dreams were full of *her*.

For days, he dreamed of her touch, cool at his brow. Of her arm lifting his head to drink bitter liquid from the cup held to his lips. Of her fingers, running over the aches in his muscles, easing the sharp pain in his leg. Of the scent of her, like sunshine and secrets, like the smile of that first angel, all those years ago.

He'd nearly woken a dozen times, a hundred. And that, too, made the dream a nightmare—the fear that the cool cloth at his brow was not really there. The terror that he might lose the gentle care for the wound in his thigh as the bandage changed, that the taste of the bitter broth she fed him might be fantasy. That the slow spread of salve over his wounds was nothing but fever.

And always, he dreamed the touch remained long after the salve was gone, soft and lingering, tracing over his chest, smoothing down his torso, exploring the ridges there.

Always, he dreamed her fingers on his face, smoothing over his brows and tracing the bones of his cheek and jaw.

Always, he dreamed her lips at his brow. On his cheek. At the corner of his mouth.

Always, he dreamed her hand in his, their fingers tangled, her palm warm against his.

And the dreaming it made it a nightmare—the aching knowledge that he'd imagined it. That it wasn't she. That she wasn't real. That he couldn't return the touch. The kiss.

So he lay there, willing himself to dream, to live the nightmare again and again, in the hope that his mind would give him the last of her—her voice.

It never did. Touch came without words, care without voice. And the silence stung worse than the wound.

Until that night, when the angel spoke, and her voice came like a wicked weapon—a long sigh, and then, soft and rich, like warm whisky, "Ewan."

Like home.

He was awake.

He opened his eyes. It was night still—night again? Night forever?—in a dark room, and his first thought was the same he'd had upon waking for twenty years. *Grace.*

The girl he'd loved.

The one he'd lost.

The one for whom he'd spent half a lifetime searching.

A litany that would never heal. A benediction that would never save, because he would never find her.

But here, in the darkness, the thought came harsher than usual. More urgent. It came like memory—with the ghost of a touch on his arm. At his brow. In his hair. It came with the sound of her voice at his ear—*Ewan.*

Grace.

Sound, barely there. *Fabric?*

Hope flared, harsh and unpleasant. He squinted into the shadows. Black on black. Silent now. Empty.

Fantasy.

It wasn't she. It couldn't be.

He ran a hand over his face. The movement produced a dull ache in his shoulder—an ache he remembered from years earlier. His shoulder had been dislocated and reset. He made to sit up, his thigh twinging—bandaged tight, already healing. He gritted his teeth against the lingering twinge of pain even as he welcomed it, and the way it distracted him from the other, far more familiar pain. The one that came from loss.

His head was clearing quickly, and he recognized the dissipating haze as an effect of laudanum. How long had he been drugged?

Where was he?

Where was she?

Dead. They'd told him she was dead.

He ignored the anguish that always came with the thought, reached for the low table near the bed, feeling for a candle or a flint, and knocked over a glass. The sound of liquid cascading to the floor reminding him to listen.

And then he realized he could hear what he could not see.

A cacophony of muffled sound, shouting and laughing nearby—just beyond the room?—and a roaring din from farther away—outside the building? Inside, but at a distance? The low rumble of a crowd—something he never heard in the places he usually woke. Something he barely remembered. But memory came with the sound, from a similar distance—from farther away, from a lifetime ago.

And for the first time in twenty years, the man known to

all the world as Robert Matthew Carrick, twelfth Duke of Marwick, was afraid. Because what he heard was not the world in which he'd grown.

It was the one into which he'd been born.

Ewan, son of a high-priced courtesan come down a notch—or a thousand—with a babe in her belly, made one of Covent Garden's finest molls.

He stood, crossing the darkness, feeling along the wall until he found a door. A handle.

Locked.

The angels had rescued him and brought him to a locked room in Covent Garden.

He did not have to cross the room to know what he would find outside, the rooftops filled with angled slate and crooked chimneys. A boy born in the Garden did not forget the sounds of it, no matter how hard he'd tried. He stumbled to the window nonetheless, pushing back the curtain. It rained, the clouds blocking the light of the moon, refusing to let him see the world outside. Denying him sight, so he might hear sound.

A key in the lock.

He turned, muscles taut, prepared for an enemy. For two of them. For battle. He'd been locked in war for months, years, a lifetime with the men who ruled Covent Garden, where dukes were not welcome. At least not dukes who'd threatened their lives.

It did not matter that he was their brother.

Not to him, either, as they had broken his trust—unable to keep the only woman he'd ever loved safe.

And for that, he would do battle until the end of time.

The door opened, and his fists balled, his thigh stinging as he came to the balls of his feet, prepared for the blow that would come. Prepared to deliver a matching one in kind. Strong enough for it.

He froze. The hallway beyond was barely brighter than

the room where he stood—just bright enough to reveal a figure. Not outside. But *inside*. Not coming. *Leaving*.

There had been someone in the room when he'd awoken. In the shadows. He'd been right, but it was not his brothers.

His heart began to pound, wild and violent in his chest. He shook his head, willing it clear.

A woman in shadow. Tall. Lean and strong, wearing trousers that clung tight to impossibly long legs. Leather boots that ended above the knee. And a topcoat that could easily have been a man's, if not for the gold lining, somehow gleaming in the darkness.

Gold thread.

The touch hadn't been a ghost. The voice hadn't been imagined.

He took a step toward her, already reaching for her, aching for her. Her name wrenched from him, coming like wheels on broken cobblestones. "Grace."

A tiny inhale. Barely sound. Barely there.

But enough.

Like that, he knew.

She was alive.

The door slammed shut, and she was gone.

His roar shook the rafters.

Chapter Four

Grace turned the key in the lock with lightning speed, barely able to pull it from its seat when the handle vibrated—an attempt of escape from within. No. Not escape. Pursuit.

A shout came, angry and wounded. And something more. The sound was punctuated by a wicked thud, instantly recognizable. A fist against wood, hard enough to terrify.

She wasn't scared. Instead, she pressed a hand to the door, her palm flat against it, holding her breath, waiting.

Nothing.

And if he had struck it again, what then?

She pulled her hand back as the thought seared through her.

He wasn't intended to be awake. He was intended to have been dosed with enough laudanum to down a bear. Enough to keep him abed until his shoulder and leg were ready for strain. Until he was ready for the fight she planned to give him.

But she'd seen him stand without hesitation, an indication that his wounds were healing quickly. That his muscles were as strong as ever.

She knew those muscles well. Even as she shouldn't.

She'd meant to be as clinical as possible. To tend to his

wounds and mend him enough to send him packing—to give him the punishing he'd deserved since that day, two decades earlier, when he'd destroyed all of their lives, and hers the most of all.

She'd planned this revenge with years of skill and rage, and she was ready to mete it out.

Except she'd made a mistake. She'd touched him.

He'd been so still, and so strong, and so different from the boy she'd left, and yet—in the angles of his face, in the way his too-long hair lay on his forehead, in the curve of his lips and the slash of his brows—so much the same. And she hadn't had a choice.

On the first night, she'd told herself she was looking for injuries, counting the ribs beneath the flat planes of his torso, the ridges and valleys of muscle there. Too lean for his frame, as though he barely ate, barely slept.

As though he had been too busy looking for her.

She didn't have an excuse for the way she'd explored his face, stroking over his brows, marveling at the smooth skin of his cheek, testing the roughness of the new growth of beard on his jaw.

She couldn't say why she'd catalogued the changes in him, the way the boy she'd loved had become a man, strong and angled and dangerous.

And fascinating.

He shouldn't be fascinating. She shouldn't be curious.

She hated him.

For two decades he'd loomed, hunting her. Threatening her brothers. Ultimately hurting them and the men and women of Covent Garden, whom the Bareknuckle Bastards had sworn to protect.

And that had made him her enemy.

So he shouldn't be fascinating.

And she shouldn't have wished to touch him.

Shouldn't have touched him, either, shouldn't have been

riveted to the planes of him, the even rise and fall of his breath, the roughness of the stubble at his jaw, the curve of his lips—the softness of them—

The floorboards of the locked room creaked as he crouched.

She backed away, pressing herself to the wall on the opposite side of the hallway, far enough out of view to ensure that the man within could not see her when he looked through the keyhole. He was the one who had taught her about keyholes, when she was young enough to believe that a closed door was the end of the story.

She stared at the tiny black void beneath the door handle, consumed with the wild memory of another door. Of the bite of another handle in her palm, of cool mahogany against her forehead as she leaned close to it, a lifetime earlier, peering within.

The inky blackness inside.

The feel of the metal casing of the lock against her lips as she whispered into the room beyond. *Are you there?*

Two decades later, she could still feel her heart pounding as she pressed her ear to the mysterious opening, searching for sound where she could not use sight. She could still feel the fear. The panic. The desperation.

And then, from the void . . .

I'm here.

The hope. The relief. The joy as she'd repeated his words.

I'm here, as well.

Silence. And then . . .

You shouldn't be.

What nonsense.

Where else would she go?

If you're discovered . . .

I won't be.

No one ever saw her.

You shouldn't risk it.

Risk. The word that would come to be everything between them. Of course, she hadn't known that then. Then, she'd only known that there'd been a time when she would never have risked on that massive, cold estate, miles from anywhere. The barely-there home given to her by a duke to whom she was told she should be grateful. After all, she'd been another man's bastard, born to his duchess.

She was lucky, she was told, that he hadn't sent her away at birth, to a family in the village. Or worse.

As though a life hidden away without friends or family or future wasn't worse.

As though she wasn't consumed with the ever-present knowledge that she would someday run out her time. Outlive her purpose.

As though she didn't know that the day would come when the duke would remember she existed. And be rid of her.

And then what?

She'd learned early and well the truth that girls were expendable. And so it was best to stay out of sight, out of hearing. *Survival* was her purpose. And there was no room for risk.

Until *he'd* arrived, along with two other boys—his half brothers—all of them bastards, just as she was. No. Not just as she was.

Boys.

And because they were boys, infinitely more valuable than she.

She'd been forgotten the moment she'd been born—a girl, the bastard daughter of another man, unworthy of attention, or even a name of her own, valuable only in that she'd been born at all, a placeholder for a son.

A placeholder for *him*.

And still, she'd risked for him. To be near him. To be near all of them—three boys she'd come to love, each in his own way—two of them, brothers of her heart if not her blood, without whom she might never have survived. And the third . . . him. The boy without whom she might never have lived.

Don't—

What?

Don't leave. Stay.

She'd wanted to. She'd wanted to stay forever.

Never. I'll never leave. Not until you can leave with me.

And she hadn't left . . . until he'd given her no choice.

Grace shook her head at the memory.

In twenty years, she'd learned to live without him. But tonight, she had a problem, because he was here, in her club, and every moment he was conscious was a moment that threatened everything Grace Condry—consummate businesswoman, power broker, and the leader of one of the most coveted intelligence networks in London—had built.

He wasn't just the boy she'd once whispered through keyholes with.

Now, he was the duke. The Duke of Marwick, and her prisoner. Rich, powerful, and just mad enough to bring the walls—and her world—crumbling down.

"Dahlia . . ." Zeva again, at a distance, warning in her lightly accented speech.

Grace shook her head. Hadn't she made it clear that Zeva was not to follow?

What the fuck had she done?

"What the fuck 'ave you done?" Ah. The reason for Zeva's warning.

Grace closed her eyes at the sound of her brother's voice in the darkness, opening them a heartbeat later, even as she turned away from the locked door and her prisoner's eerie quiet, and strode down the narrow hallway, raising a finger for silence. "Not here."

She met Zeva's gaze, dark and altogether too knowing.

Ignoring that knowledge, she said, "The room needs a guard. No one goes in."

A nod. "And if he comes out?"

"He doesn't."

A nod of understanding, and Grace was pushing past to meet her brother at the dark entrance to the back stairwell. "Not here," she repeated, seeing that he was about to talk again. Devil always had something to say. "My offices."

One of his black brows rose in irritation, punctuated by a quick tap of the walking stick hc was never without. She held her breath, waiting for him to agree . . . knowing that he had no reason to. Knowing that he had every reason to push past her and face the duke himself. But he did not. Instead, he waved a hand in the direction of the stairwell, and Grace released her breath silently, leading the way to the top floor of the building, where her private rooms adjoined the office from which she managed a kingdom.

"You shouldn't even be here," she said softly as they made their way through the dark space. "You know I don't like you near the customers."

"And you know as well as I do that your fine ladies want nothing more than a look at a Covent Garden king. They just don't like that I've a queen now."

She scoffed at the words. "That part, at least, is true," she said, ignoring the way her heart pounded, knowing as well as Devil that the conversation was to be forgotten the moment they were inside her quarters. "Where is my sister-in-law?" She'd do anything to have Felicity there now, with her good sense, distracting from Devil's purpose.

"At Whit's, watching over his lady," he said, as they reached the door to her quarters.

She looked over her shoulder at him, her hand stilling on the door handle. "And Whit is not watching over the lady himself because he is . . ."

He lifted his chin, indicating the room beyond.

"Dammit, Dev."

He shrugged. "What was I supposed to do? Tell him he couldn't come? You're lucky I convinced him to wait here while I found you. He wanted to ransack the whole place."

Grace pressed her lips into a thin line and opened the door to reveal the man inside, already crossing the room toward her, enormous and barely hinged.

Once they were inside, Grace closed the door and pressed her back to it, pretending not to be unsettled by her brother's obvious fury. In the twenty years she'd known him, since they'd escaped their shared past and rebuilt themselves as the Bareknuckle Bastards, she'd never known Whit to rage. She'd only known him to punish, cold and deadly, and only after reaching the end of a fuse as long as the Thames.

But that was before he'd fallen in love.

"Where the fuck is he?"

She didn't pretend to misunderstand. "Downstairs."

Whit growled, low in his throat—acknowledgment barely audible inside the threatening sound—like a wild animal ready to spring. Known to all of Covent Garden as Beast, he was strung tight that night—had been for the week since the explosion on the docks—Ewan's handiwork—had nearly killed Hattie. "Where?"

"Locked away."

He looked to Devil. "Is that true?"

Devil shrugged. "Dunno."

Lord deliver her from obnoxious brothers.

Whit looked to her. "Is it true?"

"No," she drawled. "He's downstairs, turning a jig."

He didn't rise to the bait. "You should have told us he was here."

"Why, so you could kill him?"

"Exactly."

She met his anger head-on, refusing to cower. "You can't kill him."

"I don't care that he's a duke," he said, every inch the Beast the rest of London called him. "I'll tear him apart for what he did to Hattie."

"And hang for it," she said. "What good will that do your lady, who loves you?"

He roared his frustration, turning for the massive desk that stood in the corner, piled high with the club's business—current member dossiers, gossip rags, invoices, and correspondence. She advanced as he swiped a hand through a tower of new member requests, sending paper flying through the room. "Oy! That's my work, you lout."

Beast thrust his hands into his hair and turned on her, ignoring her protest. "What do you plan for 'im, then? 'E nearly killed her. She could have . . ." He trailed off, not wanting to speak the words. "And that was after leavin' Devil to freeze to death. After nearly killing you, all those years ago. Christ, you all could have . . ."

Grace's chest grew tight. Whit had always been their protector. Desperate to keep them safe even when he was too small and too battered to do the job. She nodded. "I know. But we are all here. And your lady mends."

He let out a harsh, relieved breath. "That's the only reason why my blade isn't in his gut."

She nodded. He deserved vengeance. They all did. And she intended for them to get it. But not like this.

Devil spoke then, from his place by the door, where he leaned against the wall, deceptively loose, one long leg crossed over the other, "And you somehow remain calm, Grace. Somehow, willing to let him live."

Knowing where he was going, she narrowed her gaze on him. "Women aren't allowed the luxury of anger."

"They say you've been mooning over him."

Anger came then, to be sure, and her fingers tangled in the red scarf at her waist. "Who says that?" When Whit did not answer, she turned to Devil. "Who says that?"

Devil slowly tapped his walking stick on the floor twice. "You have to admit, it's odd you've mended him. Zeva said you did it yourself. Collected him from death's door. Refused to call a doctor." He cast a pointed look to her desk, in disarray. "And the work of the club piling up as you nursemaid."

It was Grace's turn to scowl. "First, Zeva talks too much." When they did not reply, she added, "Second, my desk always looks like that and you know it. And third, the more people who know he's here, the less likelihood he gets his punishment."

That was it. That was why she'd cleaned his wounds. Why she'd set her fingers to his brow, waiting for fever. Why she'd stood in the darkness, listening to the even rise and fall of his breath.

That was all.

It had nothing to do with the past.

"The more people who know he's here, the more of a danger he is to all of us," she added.

"He's a danger to us all as it is," Devil said.

Frustration flared at the words, calm and quiet, as though her brother was discussing the next shipment coming into port. She knew the steady truth in the words was just that—truth. Knew, too, that keeping the Duke of Marwick prisoner on the fourth floor of 72 Shelton was not the most sensible course of action.

"Give me one good reason why I shouldn't be able to kill him after everything he's done. After what he did to Devil. After Hattie. After the shipments he came for. The men he had attacked. The ones who didn't survive. Five men. The Garden is owed 'is blood." Whit's voice went hoarse even as surprise flooded through Grace. She hadn't heard him speak so many words all at once in . . . well, perhaps ever.

Devil's eyes were wide with similar surprise when she

met them, but he recovered quickly. "He's right, Grace. We deserve a crack at him."

She shook her head. "No."

The wicked scar down the side of Devil's face went white as the muscle in his cheek flexed. "Then you'd best have a reason why."

She pressed her lips together, her thoughts wild with frustration and fear and anger and a decades-long desperation for justice. And then she said, "Because he took the most from *me*."

Silence fell, thick and potent, eventually punctuated by a low curse from Whit. She turned to Devil, long and lean, with his wicked scar—put there by Ewan's hand. "Not long ago, we stood together on the docks and you said it, bruv. He took more from me than from you."

Devil watched her for a long moment, his cane tapping against his boot. "And so? What, he gets your care? Tender mending from the woman he loves?"

"Get stuffed," she said. "He doesn't love me."

Twin amber gazes leveled her.

Her heart began to pound. "He doesn't."

No reply.

"What he feels—it's never been love."

It didn't matter that they'd called it that, when they were children, playing at a soft, kindhearted version of the emotion—young and fresh and too sweet to be real. Something they were never destined to see to adulthood.

She willed her brothers to drop it.

They did, miraculously. "What, then?" Whit asked. "He goes free? Back to Mayfair? Over my corpse does that happen, Grace. I don't care what he took from you—we've been waiting for this day for years, and I'll be damned if he gets returned to the life he stole."

"You mistake me," she said. Two decades earlier, when Ewan had betrayed them, they'd vowed retribution if he ever came for them. She'd promised it herself as she'd mended them. "You weren't the only ones who promised him vengeance. I was there, too."

Whit with his cracked ribs, Devil with his slashed face.

And Grace, with her broken heart and worse—her trust, shattered.

"And you think you're strong enough to keep that promise, Gracie?" Whit asked, low and dark.

Grace lowered her hand to the scarf at her waist, her fingers tangling in the fabric there. "I know I am."

A knock sounded, punctuating the vow.

"Revenge is mine." She looked to Beast. "I shall fight you both for it, and you won't like the outcome."

Silence, again, as the two most feared men in London considered the words. Devil was the first to give his agreement. A tap of his stick. A quick nod.

Whit growled, low at the back of his throat. "If you don't . . ."

"I shall," she vowed.

The knock repeated itself, louder and quicker. "Come," she called out, the word still in the air when the door opened to reveal another of her lieutenants, Veronique.

Where Grace kept the finances and managed the business beyond the walls of 72 Shelton and Zeva handled the inner workings and requirements of the clientele, Veronique ensured the entire operation ran safely. Now, the black woman stood sentry in the doorway, her coat hanging open to reveal a linen shirt, tight-fitting breeches, and high, over-the-knee leather boots to match those Grace wore. What did not match was the pistol strapped to one thigh, at the perfect height to be drawn without hesitation.

Still holstered.

Not that it mattered.

Dark eyes found Grace's with urgent purpose. "Dahlia."

Grace did not hesitate. "Where is he?"

Veronique's gaze tracked to Devil and Whit, and then back to her.

What had she wrought?

"He ripped the door off the hinge."

Beast cursed, already moving across the room, Devil drawn tight like a bow. "Where?" Grace asked, putting herself in her brother's path, ignoring the riot of emotion that came with the question.

Beast looked to the other woman. "Is he gone?"

Something like affront came over Veronique's face. "No. We took him down." She met Grace's eyes. "Conscious."

Another emotion she did not care to name surged.

"I wager he loved that," Devil said, his smirk audible.

Veronique turned a wide smile on the Bareknuckle Bastards, the Caribbean in her voice as she replied, "He didn't go without a fight, but we were good for it."

"I've no doubt," Devil said. The 72 Shelton guards were the best fighters in the Garden, and everyone knew it.

There wasn't time for pride, though. "He's asking for Grace." The name was foreign on Veronique's lips—it had never been spoken in front of her, and still, the other woman knew.

And here it was, the past, come for a reckoning.

Beast leveled her with a look. "He's seen you."

She considered denying it. After all, the room had been dark. He couldn't have possibly really seen her. And still, "For a heartbeat."

I touched him.

I shouldn't have, but I couldn't stop it.

"I'm surprised they took him down, then," Beast replied.

"Why?"

"Because you just gave him something to fight for."

She didn't ask him to clarify. She was too unsettled by what he meant.

Veronique filled the silence. "What shall we do with him, Dahlia?"

She didn't hesitate, the name a welcome reminder of her purpose. Of the life she had built in the two decades since she'd left him. Of the dominion over which she reigned. "If he's well enough to take a door off the wall, he's well enough to fight."

"He's strong enough for it; gave the lads a good bout."

She nodded. "Then I get my bout, too. This ends tonight." She crossed the room toward her private chamber, already untying the scarf at her waist.

Devil's words followed her. "I almost feel sorry for the bastard. He won't know what's hit him."

And then, Whit's reply. "Almost."

Chapter Five

She was alive.

Even now, on his knees, hands bound behind his back, blinded by the sack that had been placed over his head when he'd been subdued, muscles straining from the tussle that had brought him down mere feet from the doorway where he'd seen her, he was consumed by that single thought.

She was alive, and she had run from him.

He hadn't been knocked unconscious in the fray—he'd been taken to the ground, then hauled, bound and blindfolded, to a room large enough to echo with quiet—somewhere in the distance was a low hum of unintelligible sound. The people who'd brought him there had checked his bonds and—once certain he could not escape—had left. He'd waited, the boards beneath his knees slick with something that eased his movement, rubbing his wrists raw on the ropes that refused to budge. He'd waited there as seconds turned to minutes, to a quarter of an hour. Half.

Counting time was a skill he'd honed as a boy, locked in the darkness, waiting for light to return to him. Waiting for her to return. And so it seemed as natural as breathing that he would count the minutes now, even as he was tormented by the idea that he might not be waiting for her this time.

He might be giving her time to run.

And still the fear that she might have fled was overshadowed by the sheer, unmitigated relief that she lived. How many times had his brothers told him she was dead? How many times had he stood in the darkness—in Covent Garden, in Mayfair, on the Docklands—and heard them lie? His brothers, who had escaped their childhood home with Grace in their care . . . how many times had they lied?

She'd run north, they'd told him. *Become a maid. Lost touch. And then . . .*

How many times had he been tempted to believe them?

Hundreds. Thousands. With every breath since the first time Devil had told that lie.

And then, when he had finally believed them, how he'd gone mad with grief. He'd wanted nothing but their punishment at his hands, under his boot, in his power. To the point where he'd set the London Docklands aflame, willing to watch it burn as punishment for what they had taken from him.

The only person he'd ever loved.

No longer gone.

Alive.

The thought—and the peace that came with it—altered him at his core. For years, he'd ached to find her. To know that she was well. For years, he'd told himself that if he could only see for himself—prove, without doubt, that she was well and happy—that would be enough. And now, he did know that. She was well. She lived.

That single, perfect thought consumed him as he waited, unable to stop thinking of the dark shadow of her figure in the doorway to the room from which he'd broken free. Unable to stop wondering how the girl he'd once loved had changed. The way she would look at him, now. Again.

A door opened off to the left, behind him, and he turned toward it, his vision stolen by the rough burlap sack over his head. "Where is she?"

No response.

Uncertainty and desperation flared as the newcomer approached, footsteps slow and even. Behind, there were others. Two, maybe three, but they did not approach. Guards.

His heart raced.

Where was she?

He craned his neck, swiveling on his knees, ignoring the twinge in his thigh as he moved. Pain wasn't an option. Not now. "Where is she?"

No answer as the door closed in the far corner of the room. Silence fell, those slow footsteps drawing ever nearer, an ominous promise. He straightened, steeling himself for what might come. Having one's sight and movement hindered did not bode well, and as the bold newcomer approached, he prepared for attack.

Whatever physical blow came would be nothing compared to the mental torture.

What if he'd lost her, just as he'd found her?

The thought echoed through him like a scream. He squirmed, the sack over his head suddenly suffocating, the bindings at his wrists now too tight as he fought and twisted and writhed to no avail. "Tell me where she is!"

The command hung heavy in the silent room, and for a heartbeat, there was no movement, the entire space so still that he wondered if he'd been left alone once more. If he'd imagined the entire thing. If he'd imagined her.

Please, let her be alive. Let me see her.

Just once.

Like that, the sack over his head was gone. And his wild prayer was answered.

He sat back on his heels, his jaw slackened like he'd just taken a blow.

For twenty years, he'd dreamed of her, the most beautiful thing he'd ever seen. He'd imagined how she might have aged, how she might have grown and changed, how she would have gone from girl to woman. And still, he was not prepared for it.

Yes, twenty years had changed her. But Grace had not gone from girl to woman; she had gone from girl to goddess.

There were little hints of her youth, only visible to someone who'd known her then. Who'd loved her then. The bright orange curls of her childhood had darkened to copper, though they remained thick and wild, tumbling around her face and shoulders like an autumn wind. The crooked scar on one brow was barely noticeable—only there if you knew to look for it. He noticed. He'd been there when she'd earned it, learning to fight in the woods. Ewan had put his fist into Devil's face for the infraction before wiping her blood away with the sleeve of his shirt.

And though she revealed nothing in the moment as she stared at him, Ewan drank in the fine lines at the corners of her mouth and at the outer edges of her eyes, lines that proved she knew well how to laugh, and had done it often over the last twenty years. Who had made her laugh? Why hadn't it been he?

There'd been a time when he was the only one who could. There, on his knees, wrists bound, he struggled with a wild urge to do it again.

The thought consumed him as he met her beautiful brown eyes, ringed with black, the same as they had been when they were children, but with none of the openness they'd once had for him. None of the adoration. None of the love.

The fire in those eyes was not love, but loathing.

Still, he drank her in.

She'd always been tall, but she'd grown into her awkward lankiness, nearly six feet of it, towering above him, and with curves that made him ache. She stood in an impossible pool of light—the space somehow cast in golden glow, despite the scarcity of candles in the room. There were others there—he had heard them enter, hadn't he?—but he could not see them, and he did not try. He wouldn't waste a moment looking at others when he could look, instead, at her.

She turned away, crossing out of the light, out of sight.

"No!"

She didn't respond, and Ewan held his breath, waiting for her to come back. When she did, it was with a long strip of linen in her right hand, and another slung over her shoulder. She began to methodically wrap the material about her left knuckles and wrist.

That's when he understood.

She wore the same trousers from earlier in the evening—black and fitted tight to her legs, long and perfect. The boots over them were made of supple, dark brown leather that hugged her calves, ending a half foot above her knees. They were scuffed at the toes, not enough to look unkempt, but enough to prove that she wore them regularly—and did business in them.

At her waist, two belts. No. One belt and a scarf, scarlet, inlaid with gold thread—the gold thread he'd always promised her when they were children, playing at dreams. She'd bought it herself. Above the belt and the scarf, a white linen shirt, the arms cut short, leaving her bare from her fingers to above her elbows. The shirt was tucked in carefully and tied up the middle, no loose fabric to be found.

No loose fabric, because loose fabric was a liability in a fight.

And as she wrapped her wrist carefully, around and around, like she'd done it a hundred times before—a thousand—Ewan knew a fight was what she had come for.

He didn't care. Not as long as he was the one to give it to her.

He would give her whatever she wished.

"Grace," he said, and though he meant it to be lost in the sawdust on the floor between them, the word—her name, his title—carried like gunshot in the room.

She didn't react. Not a flinch, not even a flicker of recognition in her face. No change in her posture. And something unpleasant whispered through him.

"I hear you tore my door off the wall," she said; her voice, low and liquid and magnificent.

"I've brought London to its knees searching for you," he replied. "You think a door would keep me away?"

Her brows rose. "And yet here you are, on *your* knees, so it seems something has kept you from me after all."

He lifted his chin. "I'm looking at you, love, so I don't feel kept from you at all."

A slight narrowing of her gaze was the only indication he'd struck true. She finished wrapping her wrist, tucking the end of the bandage neatly in the palm of her hand before beginning to wrap the second. And only then, only once she'd begun the measured, methodical movement, did she speak.

"It is strange, is it not, that we call it bareknuckle fighting, but we do not fight with bare fists?"

He did not reply.

"Of course, we did fight with bare knuckles. When we came here." She met his eyes then. "To London."

The words were a blow, harsher than any she could have given him, with or without the wraps. A reminder of what they'd faced when they came here. He went still beneath them.

"I can still remember the first night," she said. "We slept in a field just outside the city. It was warm and we were under the stars and we were terrified but I'd never felt such freedom. Such hope." She met his eyes. "We were free of you."

Another blow, nearly knocking him back.

"I stitched Devil's face in that field, with a needle I'd snatched as we left the manor, and thread pulled from my skirts." She paused. "It didn't occur to me that I might need unripped skirts to find work."

He closed his eyes. Christ. They'd been in such danger.

"No matter," she said, "I learned quickly. After the third day of no kind of work that would care for all three of us—no decent food to be had, and no decent roof over our heads, we learned that we had limited choices. But I—I was a girl—and I had one more readily available to me than Dev and Whit."

Ewan sucked in a breath, rage steeling his jaw and straightening his spine. They'd run together, his only comfort in the idea that they would protect each other. That his brothers would protect her.

She met his gaze and raised a dark brow. "I didn't have to choose. Digger found us soon enough."

He'd find this Digger, and he would eviscerate him.

She smirked. "And would you believe there was a market for child fighters?" Grace finished wrapping her wrist. She came closer, and he imagined he could scent her, lemon cream and spice. "That was a thing we all knew how to do, didn't we?"

They had. They'd learned together.

"Digger didn't give us wraps that first night. They're not just to protect your knuckles, you know. The padding actually makes the fight longer. It was a kindness—he thought the fights would end faster for us if we fought bare." She paused, and he watched the memory wash through her, saw her preen beneath it. "The fights did end faster."

"You won." The words came out like gravel, as though he hadn't used his voice in a year. In twenty.

Maybe he hadn't. He couldn't remember.

Her eyes flew to his. "Of course I won." She paused. "I'd learned to fight alongside the best of them. I learned to fight dirty. From the boy who won, even if it meant the worst kind of betrayal."

Ewan somehow avoided flinching at the words, dripping with disdain. At the memory of what he'd done to win. He met her gaze, straight and honest. "I'm thankful for that."

She did not reply. Instead, she advanced, and continued her tale. "It didn't take long for them to give us a name."

"The Bareknuckle Bastards." He paused. "I thought it was just them." Just Devil and Whit, one with a wicked scar down the length of his face—a scar Ewan had put there—and the other with fists that landed like stone, propelled by fury Ewan had sparked on that long-ago night. Just the two boys-turned-men who'd become smugglers. Fighters. Criminals. Kings of Covent Garden.

When, all along, there'd been a queen.

One side of her mouth turned up in a ghost of a smile. "Everyone thinks it's just them."

Grace was close enough to touch, and if his hands were untied, he would have touched her. He wouldn't have been able to stop himself when she was there, tall and towering above him. "We climbed out of the muck and built ourselves a kingdom here in the Garden, this place that had been yours."

She remembered. "I thought about that as I learned the curve of Wild Street. As I scrambled over the rooftops, out of reach of thugs and Bow Street. As I cut purses on Drury Lane and fought for blood in the moving rings of the Rookery."

He worked at the bindings again, too well-tied for freedom.

And then freedom was impossible, because she was reaching for him. She was going to touch him, her fingertips stroking down his cheek, leaving fire in their wake. He inhaled sharply as her nails raked over the several days' growth of beard, tracing over the rough stubble, toward his chin. He stilled, afraid that if he moved, she'd stop.

Don't stop.

She didn't, her fingers curling beneath his chin, tilting his face up to her, her own now shadowed by angles and curls. She stared deep into his eyes, her gaze holding him in thrall. "How you look at me," she said softly, the sound barely there and filled with disbelief.

But she had to believe. Hadn't he always looked at her this way?

Christ, she was moving in closer, leaning over him, blocking out the light. Becoming the light.

Her eyes saw every inch of him, laying him bare with their investigation. And he couldn't stop himself as she drew closer and closer, setting his pulse pounding, until the room fell away, and it was nothing but the two of them, and then he fell away, and it was nothing but her. "They hid you from me."

She shook her head, the movement wrapping him in the scent of her, like a sweet he'd had once and could both remember perfectly and somehow never find again.

"No one hides me," she said. God, she was close. She was right there, her lips full and perfect, a hairsbreadth from his. "I take care of myself."

He strained at the bonds, straight as steel. Hard as it. Desperate to close the distance between them. How long had it been since he touched her? How long had he dreamed of it?

A lifetime.

Her eyes were black with desire, on his mouth, and he licked his lower lip, knowing she wanted him like he knew his own breath. She wanted him as much as he wanted her.

Impossible. No one could want anything the way he wanted her.

Take it, he willed.

Please, God. Kiss me.

"I found you," he said, the words like a prayer.

"No," she corrected him, softly. "I found *you*, Ewan."

His name—the name no one ever used anymore—shattered through him. He couldn't stop himself from whispering her name in reply.

Her eyes lifted to his again, like a gift.

Yes.

"Take it," he said. *Whatever you need.*

Everything you need.

"What do you need, Grace?" he whispered.

She leaned in, and he ached beyond reason.

Two taps, sharp and insistent, from the darkness, instantly recognizable as Devil, his brother by blood.

Hers by something much stronger.

Grace was gone instantly, as though drawn by a string, and the loss of her touch made him wild. Ewan turned toward the sound, a low growl in his throat, like a dog who'd been promised a meal and had it snatched away at the last second.

"He told me you were dead," he said, turning back to her—keen for her nearness. "But you're not dead. You're alive," he said once. Then again, unable to hide the relief from his voice. The reverence. "You're alive."

She narrowed her gaze, unmoved. "You tried to kill him."

"He told me you were dead!" Did she not understand?

"You nearly killed Beast's love."

"I thought they'd let you die!" He'd nearly gone mad with the knowledge of it.

Not nearly.

She shook her head. "That's not enough of a reason."

He lifted his chin, a raw laugh pulled from him at the idea that he might not have torn London apart to avenge her death. "You're right. It wasn't enough. It was everything." He met her gaze, warm and brown—a gaze that had aged like the rest of her. Full of knowledge and power. "I would do it again. Untie me."

She watched him for a long moment in silence. "You know, I thought about you as I walked those cobblestones and learned to love them. As I learned to protect them, as though it had been me born in a Covent Garden drainpipe, and not you."

"Untie me. Let me—"

Let me hold you.

Let me touch you.

She ignored the words. "I thought about you . . . until I stopped thinking of you." She let the words wash over him. "Because you were no longer one of us. Were you, Duke?"

Grace wielded the title like a knife, carving deep enough to strike bone, but he did not show it.

Instead, Ewan did the only thing he could think to do. The only thing he could imagine would keep her with him.

The only gift she would take from him.

He leveled her with his most direct gaze and said, "Untie me, and I'll give you the fight you want."

Chapter Six

A fight *was* what she wanted.

She'd stood on the highest floor of this building she owned, in the world over which she reigned—a world that had once been his—looked her brothers in the eyes, and told them that she longed for vengeance.

It was the only thing she longed for, if she was honest. Everything else—everything she had and everything she was, was a means to that end. It was, after all, the only thing that was fully hers. All else—her home, her business, her brothers, the people of the Rookery, they were all shared. But vengeance was hers alone.

From the moment she was born, nothing had been hers. Her name had been stolen. Her future. A mother who loved her. A father she'd never know. And then, as she'd found the good in the world, those things, too. Happiness. Love. Comfort. Security. Every bit of it, gone. Taken from her.

By the only person she'd ever loved, because the idea of a life with her hadn't been enough. Not when he might have a dukedom.

That had been the promise the boys' father had made when he'd summoned his sons, half brothers, to his estate in the country. They would compete, like dogs, for a title that did not belong to any of them. A title that would bring with it fortune and power beyond measure—enough to change lives.

At first, the competition had been easy. Dancing and conversation. Geography and Latin. The trappings of aristocracy, with only the duke and an endless line of servants and tutors aware of their presence. And then it had taken a turn for the worse, and the challenges had become less about learning and more about suffering. About what the duke called "mental fortitude."

The boys had been separated from her then . . . kept in dark rooms. In the cold. In isolation.

And then they'd been forced to fight each other. All for the promise of power. Of fortune. Of future. Of a name that had been hers, at baptism: Robert Matthew Carrick, Earl Sumner. Future Duke of Marwick.

Few had known that the babe in the nursemaid's arms was a girl—and those who had . . . they were too terrified of the duke to say anything as he broke the laws of God and country.

And it didn't matter, in the long run, as eventually, there had been a boy who took the name. A boy who had won, even as Grace and Devil and Whit had run before he could complete his final task.

They'd tried to forget, building their family and their empire without him. But they'd none of them found peace—at least, not until Devil and Beast had found love.

But Grace had never had peace.

It would come tonight, however, when she made good on her promise to her brothers, and sent the man on his knees before her into the street with the certainty that he would never again come for them. He'd spent years searching for them—for her—and they'd spent years hiding her from him. It was time for him to understand that what he sought did not exist, and hadn't for twenty years.

Memory flashed, Devil and Whit shouting as Ewan advanced on her, blade in hand. She hadn't moved quickly enough. She'd been frozen by the realization that he would actually hurt her. No matter what the monstrous duke had promised him, Ewan had claimed to love her. He'd vowed to protect her. They'd all vowed to protect each other. How many times had the three brothers fought as one? How many plans had the four of them made in the dark of night?

How many promises had the *two* of them made?

Future. Family. Safety. Love.

None of it had mattered that night. Not once the dukedom was on the line. Not once it was in hand. Ewan had won the day, and with it, power and privilege that rendered the rest of them at best useless and at worst dangerous.

And Grace the most dangerous of them all, because she was the proof that Ewan—now Robert Matthew Carrick, Earl Sumner, Duke of Marwick—was a fraud.

As Grace and Devil and Whit had grown stronger—as they had built names of their own from the soot of the Rookery where they still lived and from which they managed businesses that employed hundreds and made them hundreds of thousands—they'd known they were building more than names. They had been building the power to protect themselves from the inevitable—the arrival of *this* man, their enemy, whom they'd known would one day come for them—the only other people in the world who knew his secret . . . a secret that would see him hanged for treason.

All the years of preparation ended tonight. Now. At Grace's hands, as her brothers looked on.

But before she punished him, she'd touched him.

She didn't know why.

It wasn't because she'd wanted to.

And the kiss—she hadn't wanted that, either.

Lie.

She hadn't wanted to want it.

But there, in the darkness of that underground room, the sounds of the party raging above muffled by sawdust, she hadn't been able to resist. He had been a handsome boy—taller than most, whipcord lean, with amber eyes that saw everything and a slow, easy smile that could tempt a body to follow him to the ends of the earth. As they'd all been willing to do.

Ewan. The boy king.

There was no smile now. It was gone in the magnificent angles of his face. All three of them—Devil, Beast, and Ewan—carried the marks of their father in their eyes and their jaws, but Devil had grown tall and rakish, and Beast had become a massive bruiser with the face of an angel. Ewan was neither of those things. He had become an aristocrat, all planes and shadows, a long aquiline nose, clefted chin, hollowed cheeks, a noble brow—and his lips, pure temptation.

Grace was the owner and proprietress of 72 Shelton Street, the most discreet, highest-end brothel for ladies in London, and a place that was known to offer a discerning clientele a bevy of men who were each more perfect specimens of masculinity than the next. She considered herself a connoisseur of handsomeness. She traded in it.

And he was the most handsome man she'd ever seen even now. Even a touch too thin for his frame. A touch too hollow in the cheeks. A touch too wild in the eyes.

So, of course she'd been tempted. Just for a moment. A second. A fraction of one. She would have wanted to kiss anyone with such a face. She would have wanted to touch anyone with such a body.

Another lie.

She'd touched him because there would never be another chance to touch the boy she'd once loved. To look into his eyes, and maybe find a glimpse of him, hidden inside the cold, hard duke he'd become.

And perhaps, if she'd seen him there, she would have stopped it. Perhaps. But she hadn't, and so she'd never know. And when she'd let him go, he'd ended any chance of her knowing.

"Untie me, and I'll give you the fight you want."

The words hung in the air between them as she considered his face, all its soft boyishness gone, disappeared into the hard angles of manhood, thieved by time.

He'd always known what she wanted.

And tonight, she wanted a fight. The long linen strips weren't as comfortable as they usually were, wrapped tightly over her knuckles. They did not feel like second skin, as they had for years, night after night, as Grace had taken to the sawdust-covered floor in makeshift rings in the darkest, dingiest, dirtiest rooms in the Garden.

They scraped, just as they had twenty years earlier, when she'd wrapped her knuckles for the first time. Unfamiliar. Unwanted. She shook out her hand as she walked around him, leaning down to extract a blade from her boot and cut the binds at his wrists.

Once free, he moved, rolling to his feet as though he'd been relaxing on a chaise longue instead of on his knees in the sawdust of the basement ring of a Covent Garden club. He straightened with the ease and skill of a fighter—something that should have surprised her. After all, dukes did not move like fighters. But Grace knew better. Ewan had always moved like a fighter.

He'd always been agility and speed . . . the best fighter among them, able to make a blow look like it would shatter bone and somehow, miraculously, pull the punch so that it landed like a feather. She could see he hadn't lost his skill. But Grace—she had gained it.

He'd trained where gentlemen trained. Eton and Oxford and Brooks or wherever it was toffs learned to fight with their pretty rules.

Those rules wouldn't help him in the Garden.

She tracked his movements as he danced backward, out of the light, shaking his arms, bringing the blood back to his fingers.

Grace Condry had been a winning street fighter since she was a child, but it was not strength that brought her victory—girls could rarely compete in that arena—nor was it speed, though God knew she had that. For Grace, it was the ability to see an enemy's faults, no matter how well hidden. And this duke had faults.

His gait was a touch too long—it would crowd him to the edges of the ring before he knew what had hit him.

He held his broad shoulders too straight—leaving the wide expanse of him open to attack. He should have canted himself, leading with one side, shielding the flat planes of his chest, which wouldn't be able to take a blow.

And then there was his right leg, with its barely-there drag . . . so slight that one couldn't even call it a drag. No one would even notice it, the whisper of a limp that would go away eventually, once the gash on his thigh—sustained when he'd blown up half the London dock and her brother's future bride—fully healed.

It would heal because Grace had stitched him perfectly.

But tonight, it was a liability, and she would not hesitate to take advantage of it. Two decades ago—an hour ago—she had promised herself and her brothers vengeance, and now it was here, in reach.

He turned to the far corner of the room, where Devil and Whit sat in the darkness, invisible. "You let her fight your battles for you?"

"Aye, bruv," came Devil's clear reply. "We cast dice for the honor. She's always been the lucky one."

Ewan looked to her. "Have you?"

She lifted her chin and rocked back on her heels. "I'm in the ring, am I not?"

A muscle in his jaw twitched as he seemed to consider his next move. Grace waited, trying to ignore the long lines of him, the way his dark blond hair fell over his brow, the way his limbs remained loose even as he faced her, preparing for a fight.

He'd been a natural fighter when they were children. The kind every street rat in London ached to be. The kind every street rat in London ached to beat. Grace included.

She took a deep breath, willing herself calm. How many had she fought before now? And with virtually no losses? Her heartbeat slowed along with time in the room. He approached and she raised her fists, ready for the fight as he closed the gap between them.

But he didn't close the gap. Instead, he launched a different kind of attack. One for which she had not been prepared.

He began to disrobe.

She stilled as he lifted his arms, clasping the back collar of the linen shirt he wore, pulling it out of his trousers and over his head without hesitation, and casting it to the side, forgotten in the dust. Her gaze followed the discarded shirt. "A gross mistreatment of the only clothing you have."

"I shall fetch it later."

When she looked back at him, it was to discover that he was closer than she would have imagined. She resisted the instinct to take a step back, refusing to reveal her response to the way he filled the ring. This was different from seeing him unconscious in a bed.

If his face had changed over the last two decades, his body had been revolutionized. He was tall—over six feet, and his broad shoulders tapered to narrow hips via a vast expanse of lean, corded muscle lightly dusted with hair. The trail of hair darkened as it descended past his navel, into the waist of his trousers. If the warm color of his skin was any indication, that athleticism had been honed in the outdoors. In the sunlight.

Doing what?

She might have asked if the scar on his left pectoral muscle hadn't distracted her. Three inches long, a quartet of jagged, pale lines against smooth tan skin. She was transfixed by it—the proof that this man was the boy she'd once known. She'd been there when he'd taken it.

His father had put it there as punishment for protecting her. As a reminder of what was truly valuable. She could remember the bite of her fist tight against her lips, desperate to keep her cries silent as the blade had sliced through his skin. Her cries hadn't been silent though. He'd shouted them for her as he'd taken the pain.

Days later, the letter M still fresh on his skin, he'd stopped taking it.

And he'd come for her.

The thought returned her to the present. To the fight. Her gaze flickered up over his chest and the cords of his neck, to the line of his jaw, the high angles of his cheekbones—and finally, to his eyes, watching her. Betraying nothing.

And then, the bastard smirked. "Like what you see?"

She narrowed her gaze. "No."

"Liar."

The single word sent a hot flush through her. Twenty years earlier, the flush might have been pleasure or embarrassment. A keen understanding that he'd seen right to the heart of her. But now, it was anger. Frustration. And a refusal to believe that he might still see through her. That she might still be the same girl she'd been all those years ago. That he might still be the same boy.

"I felt you," he said, low enough that only she would hear. "I know you touched me."

Impossible. He'd been dosed with laudanum. Still, she couldn't stop herself from saying, "Not me."

"It was. It was you," he said, softly, advancing on her with slow, predatory grace. "You think I would forget your touch? You think I wouldn't know it in the darkness? I would know it in battle. I would walk through fire for it. I would know it on the road to hell. I would know it in hell, which is where I've been, aching for it, every day since you left."

She ignored the pounding of her heart at the words. Empty. Meaningless. She steeled herself. "Since you tried to kill me, you mean," she tossed out, lifting her chin. "I've a building full of decent men abovestairs; I've no need for a mad duke."

A shadow crossed his face, there, then gone in an instant. Jealousy? She ignored the zing of pleasure that shot through her at the realization, instead focusing on his approach. He was within reach now.

He spread his arms wide. "Go on, then."

Perhaps he didn't think she would do it. Perhaps he thought back on the girl he'd known, who never would have hit him. Never would have hurt him.

He was wrong.

She let her right fist fly, packing pure power in the punch. It connected with a wicked crack, sending his head back with the force of the blow. She danced backward as he caught his balance.

Grace let out a breath, slow and even.

Devil's walking stick pounded twice with approval in the darkness.

Ewan met her eyes. "You always could land a good blow."

"You taught me."

She saw the memory cross his face. The afternoons hidden in the glade on the estate at Burghsey House, when the four of them had planned and plotted against the duke who had vowed to steal their futures along with their childhoods. The afternoons when they'd made their promises—whoever won the duke's perverse tournament would protect the others. Whoever became heir would end the line.

They'd been brought together because there was no other possible heir—no brothers or nephews or distant cousins. On the duke's death, the dukedom, centuries old, would revert to the Crown. The trio of boys were his only chance at legacy.

And they would take it from him.

He would never win, they promised. Not in the long run.

Grace saw him remember those afternoons, when they'd worked so hard to choreograph their fights—Ewan's idea, stolen from stage fighters his mother had known on Drury Lane—so they would survive the fights their father forced on them. He could not keep them safe from all the duke's warfare, he knew, but he could keep them safe from each other.

And Ewan did. Until he did not.

The thought set her fist flying again. Years of fury and frustration landed the blow, and a second, at his ribs. He let the third punch push him back, toward the edge of the ring, out of the light.

And that was when she realized he was not blocking her.

She stopped. Stepped back. Drew a line in the sawdust with the toe of her boot. Lifted her fists. "Come to scratch, Duke."

He stepped forward, toward her, but he did not lift his fists.

Anger flared. "Fight."

He shook his head. "No."

She stepped toward him, her voice rising with frustration. "Fight me."

"No."

She lowered her hands and turned from him, crossing the ring away from him. A wicked curse sounded from the darkness, nearly feral. Beast wanted in. She grasped the wall of the ring, the bite of the wooden planks welcome on her bare fingers.

How many of these rings had she claimed? How many had she triumphed in, and all because of this man? How many nights had she cried herself to sleep thinking of him? "I've waited twenty years for this," she said. "For this punishment. For my vengeance."

"I know." He was behind her. Closer than she expected. "I'm giving it to you."

She turned her head at the words, looking over her shoulder at him. "You think to give it to me?" She laughed, the sound devoid of humor, and turned to face him again. "You think you can *give* me what I want? You think you can offer me my vengeance? Your own punishment? Your destruction?" She stalked him back across the ring. "What nonsense. You, who stole everything from me. My future. My past. My fucking name. Not to mention what you took from the people I love.

"What, you think a night in the ring, accepting my blows, will win you forgiveness?" She kept at it, the spark of rage she had at his gift, flourishing into flame. Into inferno. "You think forgiveness a prize to which you have access?"

He was off balance. She could see it. Could read the wild thoughts in his eyes so clearly it was as though she had put them there. "Nah, perhaps you think that if you offer me the hits, I shan't take them." She shook her head. "Becoming a duke has surely addled your brain. Allow me to set you straight, Your Grace." She let the Garden seep into her voice. "If somefin' come free, take it."

He stiffened, and she was there with a smart jab. "There's one for what you did to Whit for threatening his lady." Another. "And there's one for the lady, who you're lucky did not die, or I'd let 'im kill you." A wicked punch to the gut, and he didn't block it. Grace didn't care. "And there's one for Devil's lady, whom you were ready to ruin." And another two in quick succession, her breath coming faster, a sheen of perspiration at her brow. And hot fury to feed her. "Them's for Devil. One for leaving him to die in the cold last year, and the other for the gash you put in his face twenty years back." She paused. "I ought to put one on your face to match."

He took them all. Again and again, and she fed on his inaction, air to her flame. Another blow, this one setting his nose to bleeding. "And that one? That's for the boys no longer in the Rookery because of you. Gone, because your henchmen were out for blood. Because you were on your own mad pursuit of your own security."

That got his attention. He looked up, his amber gaze finding hers instantly. "What did you say?"

"You heard me." She spat. "You fucking monster. Making us all hide from you because it wasn't enough that we'd given you everything you ever wanted. You needed our lives, as well." She turned away from him, crossing the ring.

"Behind!" Beast's warning had her spinning back as Ewan came for her across the ring. Before she could resist, he lifted her by the waist and carried her to the wall, putting her back to it. Not with force—if there'd been force, she might have welcomed it. Might have taken glee in an opponent.

They froze in tableau, their breath coming hard and fast, somehow synchronized. His lips were at her ear, close enough for her to feel the ragged words he whispered. "I didn't come for myself. I came for you. I swore I'd find you. How many times did I promise you I'd find you?"

I'll find you, Gracie. You worry about keeping safe. I'll find you.

A vow, whispered across decades by a boy who no longer existed.

"I never stopped looking for you," he said, his lips sliding over skin. Into hair. She gasped. How did still he smell like leather and black tea? After days upstairs in a locked room? How did he still feel like this? After years of being the enemy?

How did he set her aflame?

"I never stopped missing you," he whispered, his breath hot at her ear.

Making her want.

No. She wouldn't have it.

Grace squirmed in his grip, her fists free enough to bat him about the head and shoulders, but without the angle to do proper damage.

"They told me you were dead." She could hear the ache in the words, and for a wild, unexplained moment, she wanted to comfort him.

"The leg!" Devil shouted from the darkness, pulling her away from the mad thoughts. He'd seen what she had from the start. The weakness. A strong kick to the wound in Ewan's thigh and she would set him to his knees. He'd release her. This would be over.

She dropped a hand to the scarf at her waist. Wrapped her fist in it. "What they told you is true. The girl is dead. Killed by a boy she trusted, who came at her with a knife, willing to do anything to win."

She yanked the scarf, pulling it loose from its moorings and, holding one weighted end, letting the other sail over their heads in a wide scarlet arc. She caught it with her other hand, pulling it taut. In an instant, the straight cloth was at his throat, as dangerous as a knife's point when wielded by someone who knew how.

Grace had spent years learning how.

He reached for the scarf, a natural course, and the wrong one. With a flick of her wrists, his hands were caught in the fabric, cuffed and immobile. He had no choice but to back away, lowering his hands. "Release me."

Instead, she knotted the silk, knowing it would make movement impossible.

"I would never have killed you," he said. "I would never have hurt you."

She narrowed her eyes on him. "What a lie."

"It's the truth."

"It's not," she spat. "You hurt me."

Was the word past tense or present?

He growled his wordless reply, the sound wrenched from low in his throat.

She ignored it. "And even if it were true, you hurt *them*. Whit with a half-dozen ribs broken and Devil with a gash that could have killed him, if not from blood loss, then from fever. Do you forget that I was there? That I saw you turn into this?" She looked him up and down, the way one might look at a rat or a roach.

"I watched you, Ewan. I watched you become this. I watched you turn duke." She fairly spat the word. "I watched you choose the fucking title over us—who were supposed to be your family."

A pause. He met her eyes.

Before he could speak, she did. "You chose it over me. And you killed me then. The girl I was. Everything I dreamed. You did that. And you can never have it back." She paused, refusing to let him look away. Wanting him to hear it. Needing to hear it herself. "You can never have her back. Because she is dead."

She saw the words strike.

Saw the truth of them course through him.

Saw him believe her.

Good.

She turned away, focusing on the ache in her knuckles, the proof that she'd finally taken the vengeance she'd wanted.

Refusing to acknowledge the other aches—the ones that were proof of something else.

Her brothers stood sentry beyond the ring, two men who would protect her without hesitation. Two men who had protected her for years.

They told me you were dead.

The desperation in his words echoed through her.

"Grace!" he shouted from the center of the ring, and she turned back to look at him, bathed in golden light, impossibly handsome even now, even wrecked.

Veronique materialized from the shadows behind him, flanked by two other women with muscles that rivaled those of any Covent Garden strong arm. They approached and took hold of him, and the touch made him wild, fighting to be free even as he refused to look away from Grace.

He had no chance. The women were stronger than they looked, and he was not the first man to be exited from 72 Shelton Street.

Nor would he be the last.

Ewan cursed and shouted her name a second time.

She ignored the sound of it on his lips. Ignored the memory of it there. "You should have chosen us."

She meant the three of them—Beast and Devil and her—didn't she?

He stilled at that, his gaze somehow finding hers in the darkness. "I chose us," he said. "You were to be duchess."

We'll marry, he'd promised her a lifetime ago, when they were too young to know that such things weren't in the cards. *We'll marry, and you'll be duchess.* Pretty promises to a girl who no longer existed, from a boy who had never existed in the first place.

The memory of them should have made Grace sad, but she had wasted enough sadness on Ewan for a lifetime. And so she let the past make her cold.

She spun on him—all present. No longer Grace. Only Dahlia.

"Why would I settle for duchess?" she asked, the night cloaking her in fury and vengeance. "I was born the duke."

She saw the words strike.

"Don't return," she said. "You will not find such a warm welcome next time."

And with that, she turned her back on the past, and walked away.

Chapter Seven

72 Shelton Street
One Year Later

"You're going to want to see this."

Dahlia paused as she passed through the kitchens of 72 Shelton Street to inspect a platter of petits fours headed to one of the club's upstairs rooms. "In my experience, very few good things come introduced with 'You're going to want to see this.'" With a nod of approval for the perfectly turned out cakes, she turned her attention to Zeva.

"This one does, believe it or not," the factotum said, passing Dahlia a ledger sheet. "Congratulations."

She looked to the bottom row of figures, curiosity, then surprise filling her as she scanned the entire document, calculating a long column of numbers to be certain she was reading correctly. One of Zeva's dark brows rose in amusement. "The club's most profitable month ever."

"God save the Queen," Dahlia said quietly, passing through the door to the oval salon, the magnificently appointed centerpiece of the club, checking the numbers once more.

Queen Victoria had been coronated only months earlier, and the crowning of a female monarch had done more than keep London in season for longer than usual—through the summer and into the autumn. It had given the city's finest ladies the belief that they could have anything they desired, which made Dahlia fortuitously lucky, in that she was in the business of providing women just that.

"Yes, well, I shan't go that far," Zeva said. "I've no doubt she'll be as invested in growing the Empire as her uncles, and without thought."

"Without question," Dahlia said. "Power at any price is the only certainty for a leader."

Zeva gave a little huff of agreement as they crossed the large oval room, her rich eggplant skirts shimmering in the light as they brushed against Dahlia's dark blue trousers, shot through with silver thread.

The oval salon of 72 Shelton was one of the lushest in London, appointed in rich blues and greens and boasting champagne and chocolates at every turn—and that was before the clients received what they actually came for.

Dahlia cast a discerning look around the salon, designed to serve several purposes. Members were brought there while rooms abovestairs were prepared, filled with requested food, drink, and various desired accoutrements. While waiting, the ladies had their pick of refreshments—the 72 Shelton Street kitchens were known for a wide variety of delicacies—and Dahlia made certain that the cupboards were stocked with regular clients' preferences.

Every comfort was recorded and replicated, and with the utmost discretion. One lady preferred the green chaise by the window; one had an aversion to nuts; one sat in the darkest corner—terrified that she might be recognized, and still unable to resist the pull of the club.

Not that recognition was easy. Even on the quietest of days, club members were required to wear masks to ensure anonymity. Newer members often selected less complicated masks, some as simple as a black domino, but many were magnificently elaborate, designed to showcase a woman's power and wealth without revealing her identity. There were currently six masked women in the salon, each enjoying the third purpose of the room.

Companionship.

With each woman was a doting male companion, dressed to accommodate the lady's fantasy: Matthew, in his handsome soldier's uniform, entertained an aging spinster in a beaded mauve mask; Lionel, in his dark formalwear that would give Brummell a run for his money, whispered into the ear of an ancient earl's young wife; and Tomas, with his billowing shirt and tight breeches, long hair pulled back in a queue, eye patch a dark slash over his brow, entertained a lady with a remarkably active imagination . . . who knew precisely what she wanted: Tomas.

A laugh sounded, loud and authentic and decidedly more free than its Mayfair twin—Dahlia did not have to look to know it came from a widowed marchioness, laughing with the married baroness she'd loved since they were children. Later, they would take to an upstairs room and their mutual pleasure.

On the far end of the oval, where the windows looked out on the Garden, Nelson—one of the most skilled of the club's workers, and paid well for that skill—leaned low into the ear of a particularly wealthy widow. The dowager countess in question was well into her fifties and only ever came to 72 Shelton when Nelson was available.

They laughed as he made a no-doubt scandalous suggestion, and waved over a footman, silver tray laden with champagne. Standing, Nelson guided her to her feet, taking two goblets in one hand and the widow in the other, escorting her to the lushly carpeted stairs and up to the room that awaited them. Their path took the lovers directly past

Dahlia and Zeva, but Nelson had no attention to spare for the owner of the club—he remained riveted to his lady as they slipped by.

"If I didn't know better," Dahlia said quietly, as the private entrance to staff quarters opened behind her, "I'd say we were soon to lose Nelson to finer fettle."

"I'm not sure you do know better," Veronique interjected from her place behind them.

Dahlia shot her a look. "Really."

"He has made himself available to her every evening this week . . ." Zeva replied, softly. The club's employees were given their choice of clients—and while regular assignations were not uncommon, regular *daily* assignations were something to remark upon.

"Mmmm," Veronique said. "He's been more than willing to . . . raise the sail."

"Mmm," Dahlia said with a sage nod. "And so the dowager has secured her very own admiral."

Zeva snorted a laugh. "You shan't be making jokes when we lose one of our best men."

"Quite the contrary. If Nelson would be happy with the widow, I shall wish him more than well." Dahlia plucked a glass of champagne off a passing tray and toasted the air. "To love."

"Dahlia, toasting love," Veronique teased. "The mind boggles."

"Nonsense," she said. "I am surrounded by love—two brothers in their domestic idyll, and look at this." She waved a hand across the room in front of them. "Have you forgotten that I deal in it?"

"You deal in fantasy," Zeva corrected. "That's a different thing altogether."

"Well, it's a powerful thing nevertheless," Dahlia brushed off. "And surely somewhere fantasy begets reality."

"*You* could do with a fantasy now and then," Veronique

said, casting a cynical eye over the couples before them. "You should take one of the men up on their constant offers."

Dahlia had been running the club for the better part of six years, having decided that there was absolutely no reason why the ladies of London shouldn't have the same access to pleasure as their gentlemen—without shame or fear of harm.

After hiring Zeva and Veronique, the trio had built 72 Shelton into a ladies' club, specializing in meeting the expectations and desires of a discerning clientele. They'd hired the finest cooks, the best staff, and the handsomest men they could find, and they'd built a place that was known for discretion, respect, safety, and high wages.

And pleasure.

For everyone but Dahlia.

As proprietress of the club, Dahlia did not partake in the benefits of membership for a number of reasons, not the least of which was that the men employed by the club—no matter how well paid—were employed by her. She slid an irritated glance at her lieutenants. "You two, first."

It would never happen. Even if they did not ascribe to the same rules as the club's owner, Veronique was happily married to a ship's captain who, though he was too often at sea, loved her beyond measure. And, while Zeva was never without companionship, she was easily bored, and kept her relationships far from 72 Shelton Street so as not to complicate their inevitable end.

"Dahlia doesn't need fantasy," Zeva added with a smirk in Veronique's direction. "She barely needs reality—though Lord knows she could use it now and then."

Dahlia cut the other woman a look. "Watch it." Over the years, she had taken a lover or two—men who, like her, weren't interested in anything other than easy, mutual pleasure. But one night was often plenty—and none of the arrangements had ever been difficult to leave—for Dahlia, or for her companions. Still, she couldn't resist rising to Zeva's bait. "I've had plenty of reality."

Both women turned to her, brows raised. Veronique spoke first. "Oh?"

"Of course." She took a sip of champagne and looked away.

"When was your last dose?" Zeva asked, all innocence. "Of reality?"

"I'm not sure it's your business."

"Oh, it's not." Veronique grinned. "But we do like the gossip."

Dahlia rolled her eyes. "I don't know. I'm busy. Running a business. Paying your salaries."

"Mmm." Zeva did not seem convinced.

"I am! Some might call it an empire, considering the number of girls we've got on the rooftops." The club at 72 Shelton was the central location for a wide network of informants and spies that kept Dahlia in knowledge and in business.

"Two years," Veronique said.

"What?"

"It's been two years since your last dose of reality."

"How would you know that?" Dahlia asked, ignoring the heat rising in her cheeks.

"Because you pay me to know."

"I absolutely do not pay you to know about my—"

"Reality?" Zeva offered.

"Could we stop calling it that?" Dahlia said, dropping her glass on a passing footman's tray.

It did not matter that Veronique was right, or that it had been two years since she'd sought out . . . companionship. It wasn't as though there were any particular reason for it.

"Wasn't it two years ago the Duke of Marwick returned to London and began wreaking his havoc?"

"Was it?" Dahlia asked, ignoring the jolt that came with

his name. "I wouldn't know. I don't keep tabs on the Duke of Marwick."

He was gone, anyway.

"Any longer," Veronique said under her breath.

Dahlia narrowed her gaze. "What was that?"

"Just remarking on how long it's been," Veronique replied.

"Not long enough, I'd say," Zeva added, with a waggle at her brow. "Else she'd have been better satisfied."

Veronique snorted and Dahlia rolled her eyes. "And to think, this is supposed to be a place of discernment."

On cue, a squeal sounded from nearby, punctuated by a loud "Yargh!" and Dahlia turned to discover that the pirate Tomas had hefted his lady over his shoulder. Her skirts were hiked in all directions, revealing gossamer silk stockings tied with elaborate pink silk ribbons.

As she watched, the masked countess let out another delighted screech and promptly began beating Tomas about his broad shoulders. "Let me down, you brute! I shall never give up the location of the treasure!"

The Frenchman slid a hand up the back of the lady's thigh, high enough that Dahlia imagined he'd reached ample, secret curves when he growled, "I already know the location of your treasure, wench!"

As the rest of the room cheered and clapped their amusement, the countess dissolved into giggles and Tomas started up the stairs, headed for room six, where a large bed awaited whatever sport was in their future.

"Oh, yes. Very proper," Veronique retorted.

Dahlia smiled. "As I was saying earlier, if the ladies of London wish to play at being better off for having a queen, we shall aid them in their pursuits. And this month, the windfall we've received from the ladies will be shared with the staff—you two included, if you stop irritating me."

"I shan't turn it down, to be sure," Zeva said, stopping at the edge of the salon, where a discreet exit led through a dark hallway to the front of the club, and a receiving room sat ready for additional guests. "However . . ."

"Come now, Zeva," Dahlia said. "You're the only person on earth who can find fault with the near doubling of our profits."

"Your queen has increased profits, yes, but she's also increased membership." Zeva was all business, turning down the hallway and leaving Dahlia no choice but to follow. "There have been nine unexpected members tonight, all arrived without appointment."

At the words, one of Veronique's security appeared at the doorway nearest the entry to the club, indicating a situation that required the woman's expertise. With a nod, she looked to Dahlia and Zeva. "Let's see what kind of trouble they're getting into."

It wasn't uncommon for a member to arrive without notice. The dual promises of the club were discretion and pleasure, and members often came and went as they pleased, eager to try the wide offerings of 72 Shelton. But nine unannounced women was a larger number than usual—and one that would strain the club's resources.

"Remember, an increase in membership is an increase in power," Dahlia said as she and Zeva moved quickly down the hallway. Every member of the club became a potential asset for Dahlia and her brothers—often at odds with Parliament, with Bow Street, with Mayfair, and with the London docks.

"And will there be an increase in rooms abovestairs?"

"There are other ways to be entertained than in a bed," Dahlia said. Members had access to card rooms and dining rooms, to theaters and dancing. Whatever they liked, it was there for the taking.

A black brow rose in reply. "Are there, though?"

Granted . . . most members came for companionship. "Who is here?"

Zeva rattled off the list of women in attendance that evening: three wealthy wives and two younger women—spinsters—joining them for the first time. "Those all have appointments. But they're not alone."

The trio had arrived in the receiving room before Dahlia could ask who else was in attendance. And then she didn't have to ask.

"Dahlia, darling!"

Dahlia turned toward the delighted greeting, smile already growing as she accepted the embrace of the tall, beautiful woman who approached. "Duchess." Pulling out of the embrace, Dahlia added, "And without a mask, as usual."

"Oh, please." The Duchess of Trevescan waved a hand in the air. "The whole world knows me a scandal—I should think they'd be disappointed if I didn't frequent Shelton Street."

Dahlia's smile became a grin. The duchess had not overstated her reputation—she was pure merry widow, but instead of a dead husband, she'd been gifted an absent one—a disappeared duke who had no taste for sparkling London life, and instead lived on a remote estate in the wilds of the Scilly Isles. "I am always surprised to see you on nights that are not for Dominion."

"Nonsense. Dominion is for show, my dear," she said, leaning in close. "Tonight is for secrets."

"Unmasked secrets?"

"Not *my* secrets, darling. I'm an open book, as they say!" She grinned. "Everyone *else's* secrets."

Dahlia smiled. "Well. Whatever the reason, we're grateful for you."

"You're grateful for the business I send your way," the duchess said with a laugh.

"And that," Dahlia allowed. The duchess had been a vital early customer—someone with access to the brightest stars in Mayfair, and wild support for women who wished to explore themselves, their pleasure, and the world that was offered without hesitation to men. She and Dahlia held each other in the mutual respect that came from two women who understood each other's immense power, a respect that could have been the seed of friendship but had never been cultivated—for no other reason than that they both held too many secrets for honest friendship.

Secrets that neither woman had ever tried to divine, a fact for which Dahlia was regularly grateful, as she knew without question that, with the right motivation, the Duchess of Trevescan would be one of the few people in the world who could uncover her past.

A past she had no interest in revisiting ever again.

The memory came from nowhere, like a runaway carriage, with eyes the color of twenty-year whisky and a fall of dark blond hair and a stern, square jaw that had taken her blows like it had deserved them.

He *had* deserved them.

She stilled, for a moment losing her easy smile. For a moment losing her place.

The duchess's dark brows knit together. "Dahlia?"

Dahlia shook her head, simultaneously clearing it and waving her off, taking a beat to turn to the quartet of women—masked and draped over a silk-upholstered chaise behind the duchess. She found a bright smile of greeting. "And you've brought that business tonight! Welcome, ladies!"

No one in 72 Shelton Street would ever breathe the name or title of a member, but Dahlia immediately catalogued the quartet who often came to Shelton Street unannounced in the wake of the duchess: Lady S__, a notorious scandal who enjoyed Covent Garden more than Mayfair; Miss L__, a bluestocking who routinely said the wrong thing and landed herself in peril with the *ton*; Lady A__, a quiet, aging spinster whose keen eye was worth that of a half dozen of Dahlia's rooftop spies; and finally, Lady N__, daughter of a very rich, very absent, very accommodating duke, and lady love to Dahlia's brothers' second-in-command.

Dahlia met Lady N__'s smiling eyes. "I see you are without your lady."

She waved a hand in dismissal. "Your brothers have a ship in port, and a late night ahead of them. You know as well as I that, without her, they'd all drown in the ship's hold. But that's no reason for me to stay home and rend my clothes, is it?"

The Bareknuckle Bastards smuggled goods wildly taxed by the Crown into London on ships laden with ice; the cargo, moved quickly and always under cover of darkness, provided income that was both perfectly legal and exceedingly illegal. Such was the business of Covent Garden.

"Well, we are more than happy to have you with us tonight, my lady." Dahlia laughed, before turning back to the duchess. "I assume you are not here for companionship?"

The duchess inclined her head. "In fact, no. We are simply here to read the news."

To collect whatever gossip they could. "You'll be happy to know we've a wide assortment of material this evening, then."

The women—whispered about in ballrooms as a hodgepodge of ineligibility—were more than welcome at 72 Shelton, where they rarely took advantage of the more sensual perks of membership, instead choosing to languish in receiving rooms and attend the fights downstairs when they were scheduled. After all, private rooms did not deliver gossip, and this group traded in information above all.

"We've three fights scheduled for tonight, and an ever-expanding membership, which is making Zeva a bit grumpy."

Zeva looked up from a quiet conversation with a liveried footman in the corner. "You pay me to be grumpy."

The duchess laughed before lowering her voice with

Dahlia. "I confess, I expected that there'd be a higher level of security tonight—" She looked over her shoulder toward the door, guarded by a pair of the biggest Covent Garden brutes anyone could find. "Though I suppose those two do just fine."

Them, and a half dozen markswomen on the rooftops surrounding the club, but no one needed to know that outside of a select few. Still, "Why would we require additional guards?"

The duchess lowered her voice for privacy and turned, her gaze traveling over the women scattered throughout the room, richly upholstered in scarlet and awash in a decadent golden glow. "I'm hearing there are raids."

Dahlia's brows rose. "What kind of raids?"

The duchess shook her head. "I don't know. The Other Side was closed two nights ago."

The Other Side was the secret women's half of one of London's best loved gaming hells—much of the membership coming via women of the *ton*. Dahlia raised a brow. "It's owned by three of the most beloved aristocrats in London, who happen to be partnered with the most powerful man the city has ever known. You think the Crown would come for them?"

The duchess raised and lowered a shoulder enigmatically. "I think the Fallen Angel wouldn't close half its business for no reason. They've information on every man in membership . . . and those secrets alone are enough to summon a raid." She paused, then added, "But you . . . you've got plenty of those secrets, too, don't you? Collected from the wives."

A statuesque brunette entered on the far side of the room, elaborately masked, and Dahlia inclined her head to greet the passing baroness before replying quietly, "I find that women often know more than men think."

The duchess tilted her head. "More than men know, as well, no?"

Dahlia smiled. "That, too."

The words were punctuated by a wild laugh from across the room, where a collection of masked women conversed as they waited to be escorted deeper into the club. "I swear it's true!" one said with urgency. "There I was, expecting the usual suspects, and there *he* was! In Hyde Park, on a magnificent grey."

"Oh, no one cares about the horse," her friend retorted. "What did he look like? I hear he's *utterly* changed."

"He *is*!" the first replied, her red curls bobbing. "And entirely for the better. Remember how he was so dour, last season?"

Dahlia made to turn away from the conversation, but the duchess set an emerald-gloved hand on her arm, staying her movement. Dahlia slid her a look. "You can't be interested in whichever eligible bachelor they're on about—"

The duchess smiled, but did not move her hand. "I like a good transformation story as much as the next."

A new participant joined the conversation. "He was at the Beaufetheringstone ball last week—he danced every dance! One with me, and it was like dancing on a cloud. *So* skilled. And he's *so* handsome now. And that *smile*! He's not dour any longer."

A sigh followed. "So lucky for you!"

Dahlia rolled her eyes. "Whoever the poor man is, he's clearly in the market for a wife if he went from dour to dancing in a year."

"Mmm," said the duchess.

"My brother says he's been at the club for a week, introducing himself to . . . *fathers*!" came a breathless reply.

The duchess looked to Dahlia. "In the market indeed."

Dahlia offered the other woman a smug smile. "A tale as

old as time. And not in the least bit interesting, except to say that I'll fetch the betting book if you'd like to make a wager."

"I hear he's hosting a masquerade Wednesday, next." The young woman's slender hand touched the edge of her stunning golden mask as she tittered, "And here we are, already masked!"

"Well," came the reply. "That does it—everyone knows a mask is for dalliances. I wager he's already chosen her. There will be a new duchess before Christmas."

Duchess.

The word sliced through the air.

It wasn't he.

"Now *that's* interesting," the duchess in attendance said quietly. "It's not as though there are eligible dukes just lying about."

"No," Dahlia said, distracted. "You had to hie off to a secluded isle for yours."

"And he never comes when he's called," the duchess replied with a tsk. "But this one . . ."

Curiosity got the better of Dahlia. "Who is it?" One shoulder lifted, then fell in wordless ignorance, and Dahlia raised her voice to the women who had been speaking. "The duke you discuss," she prodded, telling herself it was idle curiosity. Telling herself it was simply because information was currency. "Does this paragon of manhood have a name?"

It wasn't he. *It couldn't be.*

The young woman in the simple black domino answered first, eagerness in her tone, as though she'd been waiting for the moment she could speak to Dahlia. Her lips curved into the kind of smile that came with a magnificent secret, slow and easy, as though she had all the time in the world to share it.

"Who is it?" Dahlia repeated, sharp and urgent, unable to stop herself.

What in hell was wrong with her?

The young woman's eyes went wide behind her mask. "Marwick," she said simply. As though she wasn't sucking all the air from the room.

Blood rushed into Grace's ears, a roar of heat and frustration and anger clouding all her better judgment. And that name, rioting through her. *Marwick.*

Impossible. They had to be wrong.

Hadn't she sent him away? Hadn't he left, into the darkness?

She turned to the duchess. "I don't believe it." He couldn't be back. He'd left a year ago and disappeared—there was no reason for him to be back.

Of course, it wasn't true. There was a singular reason for him to be back.

The other woman plucked a glass of champagne off a passing tray with languid, casual movement, unaware of the thunder of Grace's heart. Of the way her mind stormed. "And why not? Every duke needs a duchess."

I chose the title to make you my duchess.

You were to be duchess.

"He's here to marry," she said.

"What a bore," the duchess replied.

Grace was many things, but she was not bored. Christ. He was back.

He was back.

And like that, the storm quieted. She knew what she must do.

She met the other woman's eyes. "I require an invitation to that masquerade."

Chapter Eight

If she hadn't known that the Marwick House masquerade was hosted by the Duke of Marwick himself, she never would have believed it. There was nothing about the wild party spread out before her that appeared even remotely suited to the man she'd sent packing a year earlier.

That man would have found every bit of this event frivolous and unworthy of his time. Of course, that man had spent his waking hours chasing Grace, until he'd found her, and discovered that the girl he sought no longer existed.

In the week since she'd discovered his return, she'd done everything she could to understand it. What he sought. How, and why.

And *whom.*

Because there was only one option for the Duke of Marwick to have returned to London and presented himself in society—no longer as the mad duke they'd once imagined him to be, but now as something else, apparently?

The words of the women in the club echoed through her. *So handsome. That smile! He danced every dance. It was like dancing on a cloud.*

She knew the last. They'd learned together—part of his

father's silly contest. For just this purpose. Every duke needs his duchess.

And the Duke of Marwick was back to secure his own, finally.

You were to be duchess.

She resisted the echo of the words from a year earlier. Resisted the urge to dwell on them, on the ache in them as he called them across the ring—his last attempt to win her back, even as she'd made her point. He would never win her back.

Because she was no longer the girl he once loved, and she would never be that girl again.

But that did not change the singular fact that long ago, they'd made a deal. No marriage. No children. No continuation of the Marwick line—the only vow they could make beyond the reach of the boys' father.

And if he'd returned to marry? To produce an heir?

Grace had no choice but to put a stop to it.

And if he'd returned for something else?

Then she had no choice but to put a stop to that, too. Because every second the Duke of Marwick was in the public eye put all of them at risk. He'd stolen a title, and they'd all been a part of it. She'd be damned if he put any of them in danger for his own chance at something more—not when Devil and Whit had happiness in hand with their wives and young families begun.

He didn't get to return and claim a future.

Not when he'd risked all of theirs without hesitation.

She hadn't told her brothers that he'd returned, knowing that they would insist on joining her tonight. Knowing they might insist on worse—on meeting Ewan in the darkness and doing what they'd vowed to do years ago. What she'd prevented them from doing, for fear of what might come of them if they'd been caught—the death of a duke was not something easily swept beneath the carpet.

So it had to be Grace who met the Duke of Marwick on his turf, to divine his purpose and mete out his justice. After all, hadn't it been Grace who had told him never to return? Hadn't it been Grace who had delivered the blows that night? And not only the physical ones—they would heal and be forgotten—but the ones that she saw land. The ones that had stripped him of his purpose.

Had it been so easy?

She pushed the thought away. It did not matter. What mattered was that he was back, and with a new purpose, winning the aristocracy with his handsome face and his winning smile and his dancing. And she would stop it.

Grace scowled up at Marwick House, a home so elaborate that it spanned nearly an entire Mayfair block, taking in the happy, inviting windows, gleaming gold in the darkness, providing teasing glimpses of revelers within. She spied a Cleopatra with a Marc Antony, and a shepherdess lingering in the window, crook in hand, as though she was waiting for her sheep to arrive.

As she inspected the windows, a gaggle of people pushed by dressed as chess pieces, black king, white queen, black knight, white rook. Moments later, a masked bishop arrived, and for a fleeting moment Grace thought he might be a clever addition to the chess pieces, but things began to make sense when his companion appeared, dressed in the diaphanous garments of a nun.

London had arrived in droves for the Marwick masque—a fact that left Grace with twin realizations: first, Ewan must have changed, as most of London hadn't been able to stomach him last year—duke or no; and second, the crush of people would provide the perfect cover for her attendance.

She would get in, sort out this new, improved Ewan, discover his goals, and get out to set plans in motion to end them. And being shoulder to shoulder with the rest of the city could only increase the possibility of her success.

She straightened her shoulders and fluffed her emerald skirts before ensuring that her bejeweled silver mask was properly fitted to her face—large enough to cover three-quarters of it, leaving only her dark eyes and dark red lips visible. And then she entered the fray.

The crush of revelers swept her up the stairs and down the long, elaborate hallway of Marwick House, the movement slowing as the ballroom came into view. All around her, there were gasps and delighted sighs of surprise. One man somewhere to her left said, "Marwick just made enemies of every hostess in Mayfair."

The crowd parted and Grace saw the room, her heart stopping in her chest for a long moment as she took in the elaborate decor—until it began to thunder.

He'd recreated their place.

The copse of trees on the western edge of the Marwick estate that had been Grace's favorite spot—their favorite spot. The ballroom was an echo of it.

Jaw slack, Grace entered the massive, welcoming space, her gaze turned up to the ceilings, where the chandeliers glittered happily from a sea of green flora and exotic flowers. Whoever had decorated for the party had spared no expense, designing a full bower of leaves and live flowers that hung low enough over the cavernous space as to add an air of privacy to the raucous ballroom.

As if the canopy above weren't enough, there were three tree trunks rising up from the dance floor, massive and towering, breaking the flow of dancers as they moved around the room. They were made to be oaks, ancient and soaring, evoking the outdoors. *Their* outdoors.

Without thinking, she stepped out onto the floor—summoned to those trees as though on a string, and she discovered that the marble tiles had been covered in a soft moss that had to have cost him a fortune.

And that was before the fortune it would cost him to

have it removed. Staring down at her feet, at her jewel-green skirts against the moss, gleaming in the candlelight like summer grass in dappled sunlight, Grace's mind raced, distracted from her work and her plans for that evening—and by what she had discovered here, in his home.

Memory.

Unbidden and unwelcome and unavoidable.

She was thirteen again. It was a warm summer day, and the duke was away from the estate for some reason, and they were released to their childhood. Not that the boys knew quite what to do with childhood, or with freedom, but when their wicked father was gone, they did what they could.

Whit and Devil had headed straight for the stream, where they'd splashed and played and fought like the brothers they were.

Grace had watched them for a while, and then headed into the copse of trees to find Ewan, now more than her friend. Her love.

Not that he knew it. How could she tell him, when their life was in such upheaval? When they had every day only at the whim of his monstrous father?

He'd been seated on the thick, mossy ground, leaning back against the largest of the oaks, his eyes closed. Sound was muffled in the quiet, magical space, but it hadn't mattered. He'd heard her arrive.

He didn't open his eyes. "You didn't have to follow me."

She approached, Devil and Whit's shouts falling away. "I wanted to."

He looked at her then, his eyes glittering in the strange, ethereal light. "Why? I'm not like them."

He wasn't. The trio might have been born on the same day, to the same father, but each had been raised by a different mother. Ewan wasn't an orphan like Devil. Nor was he raised with books and a hope for education like Whit. He'd spent the first decade of his life in a Covent Garden brothel, raised by a cast-off mistress and a dozen other women who'd taken him in when his mother had turned up with her expensive gowns and her jeweled hairpins.

She hadn't kept them, but she'd kept him, and that was what had mattered, Grace knew.

Grace knew, and she thanked God and his mother for it every day.

It had been eighteen months they had all been together, long enough for them to have learned each other's stories. Or, for Grace to have learned their stories. She didn't have stories. None worth sharing.

She hadn't been allowed them.

The only stories she had were the ones that she'd written with these boys, and with this one, in particular—the tall, blond, impossibly handsome boy she'd always imagined was half magic for the way he could win her in a moment with a smile. For the way he masterminded their silent battle with the man who seemed to own their fates.

That day, though, he'd been different. More serious. And Grace had sensed what was to come, even if she hadn't known it with certainty. It was almost over.

She'd dropped to her knees in front of him, the rich, earthy scent of the glade cloaking them. "You're going to win."

His gaze went sharp. "You don't know that."

"I do." She nodded. "I've known it from the start. You're strong and smart and you look the part—Devil is too angry, and Whit is too uncertain. It will be you." The old duke wanted an heir, and it would be Ewan.

And it would be soon.

"*I* am angry," he said, fiercely. "*I* am uncertain."

"But you don't show it," she said, her chest growing tighter.

"I can't." The whisper was the kind that shouldn't have come from a boy. It was too grown, and Grace hated his father for it. "I can't."

She reached for him, her fingers traced the high arc of his cheek. "You can with me."

He'd gone stern, then—stormy enough for her to forget the sunshine beyond the trees. He'd grabbed her hand in his, pulling her touch away. "I don't want to show it with you. I never want you to see it."

Confusion flared. "Why?"

A pause, and then his touch changed, and he wasn't pushing her away anymore. He was pulling her closer, coming up to his knees to meet her. He set his forehead to hers, and they stayed like that for an age, Grace's heart pounding in that mysterious way that young hearts do, with a promise of something that cannot be named, and a hope for something that cannot be imagined.

And then he'd kissed her. Or she'd kissed him.

It didn't matter who did the kissing. Only that the kiss happened. Only that it had transformed them both in the way firsts did, making itself memory that could never be lost.

Memory that crashed through her now, twenty years later, in this room that felt like it had been designed as pure resurrection of that memory, which felt as though it had happened yesterday. As though it had happened only moments earlier. As though it was happening now.

She took a breath, grateful for the shield provided by the crush of people gathered around her, all agog at the elaborate decor, and for the mask and wig that protected her from discovery—not that anyone in the room who might recognize her would reveal her identity. After all, if someone knew Dahlia, then they had reason to frequent 72 Shelton Street, and that was a far more dangerous piece of gossip than Dahlia's introduction to society.

"Playing at being a brunette tonight, are we?" someone said close at her ear.

The irony of the intrusion at that particular moment, as Grace dwelled on her anonymity, was not lost, though the new arrival was a more than welcome intrusion, forcing her to stop thinking of the past.

She turned to the other woman—a woman whose dark eyes glittered behind an intricately worked peacock mask—all while ensuring that her own masks, physical and emotional, were well in place. She immediately recognized the Duchess of Trevescan—who had procured the invitation Grace had requested.

"Am I that easily identified?"

The duchess smiled. "I make it my business to know everyone." That much was true. The duchess had the farthest reach of any woman Grace knew—which made her a powerful foe and an essential friend.

"The wig is fantastic," the duchess said, reaching to tug on one of the mahogany curls artfully piled atop Grace's head. "French?"

"French." Brought in on one of her brothers' ships two weeks earlier.

"I suppose in your case, natural is a dead giveaway. It's gorgeous, anyway."

"I could say the same for you." Grace dipped her head, allowing surprise into her voice. "I so rarely see you masked."

The duchess laughed and shook out the skirts of her magnificent gown, sending a riot of silken teals and sapphires and greens and purples shimmering in the glow of the canopy, along with the explosion of peacock feathers that had been added to the costume. "You rarely see me masked because you regularly see me in a location that should not require masks, as you well know. Men never hide their identity when visiting their private clubs. Why should I?"

It wasn't entirely true, but Grace could not deny the double standard that existed when it came to gender and pleasure. Nevertheless, she could not stop herself from looking about to see who might be listening.

"Don't worry," the duchess said. "The masks ensure that absolutely no one is interested in what we have to say." She sighed. "You see why I much prefer to be fully identifiable?"

Before Grace could reply, the duchess continued. "I confess, having never seen you on this side of Piccadilly, I was rather surprised when you asked for an invitation." She flipped open her enormous peacock-feather fan and added, "Are you going to tell me why you took such a keen interest in this *particular* party?"

"I have always been something of an arborist."

The duchess burst out laughing. "What a tragic lie. I can only assume it has something to do with Marwick's obvious search for a bride."

Grace allowed one side of her mouth to rise in a little smirk. "No. As I said, I quite like moss, and where else can you find so much of it in city limits?" The other woman's laugh faded to a grin as she added, "And indoor oak trees—what a treat! Of course I angled for an invitation."

The duchess rapped her on the arm with her ridiculous fan and said, "I shall divine the truth, you know."

Grace offered her most secret smile. "No, you shan't, Your Grace, but I invite you to try."

The other woman's brown eyes twinkled behind her feathered mask. "Accepted."

Before Grace could reply, the air around them changed, heralding something new and exciting. Not something.

Someone.

She turned to look behind her, and a thrum of heat shot through her as her gaze fell on a tall, handsome man in perfectly tailored black trousers and coat, white cravat starched to perfection. A simple black domino that was a mere nod to the festivity and not designed to hide his identity—not that he could hide his identity in this room.

The Duke of Marwick, whom she had not seen in a year, since she'd put him to his knees and thrown him out into the streets, stood not ten feet from her.

Six feet.

Three.

She hated the breath that caught in her throat as she took him in, close enough to touch if she reached for him. Close enough to notice how he had changed. He was still tall and lean and handsome, but now, somehow broader than he'd been, more muscular, and with a face that held fewer hollows, even as his cheeks remained perfectly carved below his mask.

Not that she'd ever mistake his beautiful whisky-colored eyes, with their dark fringe of lashes. And if they weren't enough? That full, handsome mouth was his and his alone.

She'd marveled at his handsomeness in the club a year earlier, but tonight—he put the past to shame.

He'd been eating.

He'd been sleeping.

More than the physical, however, he seemed changed in other ways—his movements more languid, his smile easier—his smile existent.

He'd been *well.*

For a moment, Grace wondered if perhaps she was wrong, and it wasn't he, after all. Except of course it was, because she would never mistake him. He was written upon her, for better or worse. Etched with desire and sorrow and anger.

Seizing the last, she watched his gaze slide over the duchess's extravagant gown, taking in the wild costume even as she extended a hand. He accepted it with perfect manners and bowed low over it as she delighted in the treatment. "Ah! Another surprising discovery among the rabble."

"Did you think I would not stay for the revelry?" He offered a look of joking offense, so utterly unlike him, and the room around Grace began to tilt.

He'd heard her. He'd listened. He'd left her.

"I think you've never cared for revelry before," the duchess intoned, leaning in close—close enough for something in Grace to hesitate. "Why start now?"

"Perhaps I've never had such winning company," he offered, his lips curving in a magnificent smile, leaving Grace with the wild, momentary thought that she might be going mad. And then he turned and met her eyes, and the damn man winked.

He didn't recognize her.

He couldn't. Nothing about his response to her indicated that he recognized her in the slightest. *How could that be?*

It didn't matter. Indeed, it made things easier.

Still, shock wound through her, even as she should have been satisfied—after all, wasn't this what she'd intended? To be hidden from him in plain sight? Wasn't this part of the plan she'd worked on again and again as she'd heavily kohled her eyes and stained her lips? And put on Dahlia's mask?

She would never again meet him as Grace.

Especially not here, in his Mayfair home—the home of a line of dukes. And even if she did—even if he had expected her—he wouldn't expect her like this. Not elaborately turned out in the dress, the mask, the hair, the maquillage—all perfectly designed for a woman of the height of aristocracy. A woman who'd had the best education, a battalion of ladies' maids, wealth beyond reason, and a life of privilege, sparing no expense.

He'd expect her to come as she always had, in trousers

and topcoat, boots over her knees and weapons over her shoulders, ready to take prisoners.

And if she had come, he wouldn't have smiled at her.

They did not smile at each other any longer.

He bowed low, and for a moment, Grace was thrown back in time, or maybe not back. Maybe tossed sideways, into another time, another place, when they would have crossed paths not as once friends and forever enemies, but as a lady and a gentleman.

A duke and a duchess.

She rejected the thought and relished his ignorance as she sank into a low curtsy.

"Your Grace."

He tilted his head at her words. "You have the better of me."

She willed Grace away for now, letting Dahlia take the lead with a flirt. She was here for a reason, after all. "I am sure that is not true."

"It is." He leaned in closer. "Do you have a name?"

Only the one you gave me.

The response—which she would never say aloud—tore through her, but years of practice kept her from revealing it. "Not tonight."

That smile again, the one that set her back with confusion and something she was not interested in naming. Something she would never take for herself.

He looked to the duchess. "And you, lady, will you tell me your name?"

The other woman looked at the duke, and then Grace, and then the duke once more. "I'm not certain you wish to know my name, Duke." Grace's eyes went wide at the reply, even as the words dissolved into laughter, bright as bells. "In any event, I'm afraid I tire of conversation—no offense." She was one of the few people in the world who could say such a thing and actually offer no offense. "And

I see an empty swing hanging on the tree in the distance." She wiggled her full bottom beneath her vibrant skirts. "Waiting for a peacock, I'm sure."

Before a reply could form, the duchess was off, pushing between an elaborately dressed Marie Antoinette and a tall, forbidding plague doctor, and disappearing into the crowd, no doubt delighting in the idea that a duke and the owner of one of London's most exclusive brothels were conversing—and due to her own influence. Grace gave a little growl of disappointment that they'd been left alone, even as she knew that alone was the only way she had a hope of understanding why he'd returned.

"Is your friend always so . . ."

"Fleeting?" Grace supplied. "Yes."

"I was going to say eccentric," he replied.

"That, too," she said.

He looked to her then, "And you?"

She couldn't help the little, secret smile. "I, too, am eccentric."

"I was asking if you planned to be fleeting." Somehow, in the crush and cacophony of people, his words were low and lush, and they settled deep in her belly even as she reminded herself that she was not to derive pleasure from this man.

This man who had thieved everything from her.

Tonight was not about pleasure. It was about planning.

But he had designed a room and an event that was pure fantasy, and for her to understand why—to properly understand what he was planning and cut him off at the pass—Grace was going to have to play.

Which should not be difficult—did she not trade in play?

She was not a fool—she knew what he asked for.

From whom?

She ignored the insidious whisper, and the thread of unease that came with it. Ignored, too, the idea that he flirted with another woman. Let him flirt. Let him imagine a future of partnership, as though she hadn't vowed to take that from him from the start.

Grace would wear her mask and give him what he wished, and in the process, she would clarify the objective of his return. Of his change. Of his newfound entrance into this world they'd always sworn never to embrace.

This world to which he was never supposed to return.

That was why she was here. Reconnaissance.

In, then out. Here, then gone.

"Isn't everyone here fleeting?"

"Are they? They're the collective product of centuries of aristocratic breeding."

Not you, though, she thought. *Not I.* "I've never put much stock in aristocratic breeding, Duke." The title was a test. Would he flinch?

He placed a hand to his chest in mock disappointment, his winning smile widening. "You wound me, lady. Truly."

He didn't recognize her. Something loosened in her chest, relaxing her. Settling her into her role. "Look around you," she said, waving a hand in the direction of a Henry VIII and a Sir Thomas More nearby, in raucous conversation with an Anne Boleyn and a Duchess of Devonshire, wig so high it was a miracle she could keep her head straight above her scandalously low-cut gown. "None of you can bear to behave as you wish without masks. What is the purpose of the power you've amassed, if not to find delight?"

He tilted his head in her direction. "We? Are you not one of us?"

She shook her head. "I am none of you."

"And you found us how? Wandering lost in my gardens?"

She couldn't help the hint of smile. "I've an invitation."

"From me?"

She ignored the question. "There are whole swaths of

the city that would do anything for a chance at the joy you can take in an instant," she said, instead. "And still you hesitate, allowing yourselves a taste of pleasure only when you can reasonably deny you've ever had it. What a waste."

"What then? Take pleasure as it comes?"

The words washed over her like silk. That was precisely what she meant. She, who dealt in pleasure as it came.

Grace smiled. "I am nothing if not a realist."

"Tell me something real, then."

She did not hesitate. "I am fleeting. So is this evening." Her gaze flickered past him, to the massive trees soaring above the crush of revelers. "But you knew that already."

"Did I?" He was watching her carefully, and she resisted the urge to look away, afraid he would look too hard. See too much.

Instead, she pulled her masks tight to her and gave him a knowing smile. "You've turned your ballroom into the outdoors, Your Grace. If that is not fleeting, I don't know what is."

"Mmm," he said, and the low rumble warmed her, even as she knew she should not let it. "And so? What should we do with tonight?"

He didn't know it was she. The proof of it was there in his gaze—full of curiosity and playfulness.

She was a stranger. She'd planned to be, of course. But she hadn't expected him to be one, as well.

"The same as we should do with every night," she said, softly, suddenly more honest than she had imagined she would be with him. "We should savor it."

Silence—and then, "Would you like to dance?"

She was caught off guard by the question. When was the last time she'd been asked to dance? Had she ever been asked to dance? Once or twice, she supposed, in the Garden, by someone full of liquid courage. But the last time she'd danced like this? In a ballroom?

It had been with him.

And he was made for it. Handsome and charming and with a smile that could win the coldest of skeptics, standing in front of her, dressed like any woman's fantasy.

You could do with a fantasy now and then.

Veronique's words from earlier in the week whispered through her, and on their heels certainty and focus. Drive. Purpose.

This was not fantasy. This was *reconnaissance.*

She had a *plan.*

She placed her gloved hand in his outstretched one.

"I would very much like to dance."

Chapter Nine

He'd known it was her from the moment she'd stepped into the ballroom, in a dress that fell in lush emerald waves to the floor, despite the mask covering everything but her beautiful kohled eyes and the dark wine color staining her lips, and the wig that stole her flame-colored curls from him.

He presumed she was trying for disguise, as though he'd ever not sense her. Not feel her. As though there would ever come a time when she walked into a room and his whole body did not draw tight like a spring.

But disguise required something more than Grace would ever have—an ability to be unnoticed. And Grace would always be the first thing he noticed in any room, ever.

She'd come.

His heart began to pound the moment she'd entered—he'd been speaking to someone—a lord, about a vote in Parliament—something Ewan had been working on for months.

Or maybe it had been a lady, wanting to introduce her daughter to the Duke of Marwick? Maybe it had been an old friend from school. Ewan didn't have old friends from school, so it wasn't that, but he couldn't be sure about the rest. Because he'd looked up from the conversation and she'd been there, at the edge of the ballroom, her face tilted up into the canopy that he'd had designed for exactly this moment.

Her favorite place on the Marwick estate.

The place he'd never returned to once she'd left.

Once she'd run. Once he'd scared her away.

Not that he'd had a choice.

He'd built this masquerade for her, making the staff and the gardener certain he was still as mad as he'd always been, but this time with his wild requests for indoor trees and moss-covered dance floors. And he'd known it would cost a fortune and very likely be wasted—because she might not have come.

After all, the last time they'd been together, she'd made it clear she had no interest in ever seeing him again.

But he'd built it for her, knowing she would discover that he was returned to London—a duke did not rejoin society's circuit without people talking, after all—and hoping that she might not be able to resist her curiosity.

Hoping she might come to discover his plan. Hoping she might come to be a part of it. Therein lay the true madness, however.

You can never have her back.

He'd heard the words every day since that night, when she'd delivered the only blow that mattered. The one that had set him back, the proof that the girl he'd once loved, the one he'd sought and pursued and dreamed of, was gone.

Her fists were like stone, certainly, and they'd landed with noble force—punishment he well deserved for what he'd done. To her. To his brothers. To their world. But when she'd spoken—when she'd looked him straight in the eye, her beautiful brown gaze full of loathing, and told him that he'd killed her, she'd destroyed him.

Because in those words—he'd heard the truth.

So, he'd done as she asked. He'd left. And he would continue to do as she asked. And never chase her again. And that decision had required him to become someone different. Someone stronger. Better. More worthy.

A different man from the one who had betrayed her. Who had betrayed his brothers, and himself in the balance.

Her words from that night still haunted him.

You, who stole everything from me. My future. My past. My fucking name. Not to mention what you took from the people I love.

So, he'd built this mad ballroom and thrown this mad masquerade, with the singular vow that he would never chase her again.

But that, instead, she might chase him.

Or, at least, come through the door.

She had, and it was like breath after being under water for too long. He'd watched as she took in the room, as she tracked the tree trunks and the massive canopy, as she'd been surprised by the moss beneath her feet. He'd fallen away from his conversation, every inch the mad duke London expected him to be when he turned away and crossed the room toward her, unable to stop himself from cataloguing her movements: the way her throat worked; the way her lips softened, opening on a little gasp of surprise—surprise? Or memory? The way her eyes widened . . . in recognition?

Be memory.

Be recognition.

As he watched, she locked whatever it was away. He saw her cast off one layer of emotion and don something else entirely, her spine lengthening, her shoulders straightening, her chin rising in a little, defiant gesture.

Like that, Grace was gone. Another woman in her place.

He moved faster, eager to meet her, the woman the girl

he'd loved had become. Faster still, when that woman turned a smile the color of French wine on the Duchess of Trevescan—in herself, a bit of trouble. And then Ewan was there, and Grace was turning toward him, her beautiful brown eyes on his, but without any indication that she knew him.

The years had made her many things—a stunning beauty, a brilliant mind, a boxer with a fist like fury . . . and an actress, apparently. Because she was able to hide everything that had come before.

And so, they began with fresh lies, ignoring the fact that there had been a time when they'd known each other better than they'd known anyone, and instead starting anew—with his jokes and her teasing and both of their smiles, hers bright and beautiful enough to make him willing to do anything to witness it again.

Even asking her to dance, knowing that holding her in his arms would be a special kind of torture. Because it was—pulling her into his arms, but not as close as he wished. The scent of her wrapping around him—citrus and spice, but without the possibility of him burying his nose in her hair to breathe her in. And when she looked up at him with her cool, controlled gaze, and her cool, controlled smile, as though they had just met and had not spent a lifetime in a different kind of dance, he ached to pull her from this room and its crush of people and revel in her.

But that was not what she wished.

What did she wish?

"Why the trees?" The words took him by surprise, and he met her eyes behind the mask.

The trees were for her. What would she say if he told her that? If he yanked the mask from her eyes and said, *You know why the trees. The trees, because you loved them. This place, because you loved it. All of it. For you.*

Forever.

But he did not say that, because if he did, she would run . . . and she would never return. And so he kept his mask firmly in place and matched her coy question with an equally coy reply. "Why not?"

She cut him an exasperated look—a fleeting glimpse at *his* Grace, from whom he'd received that look a thousand times when they were children. He'd always been serious—their life was not one that was conditioned toward whimsy—but teasing Grace had been one of his purest pleasures.

"You don't wish to guess?"

She was gone, hidden away before she spoke. "Anyone with reason would guess that you were mad, saddling your staff with the mess all this greenery will have made in a few days."

"You must not know of me, in that case," he replied. "They all think me mad anyway."

"They have said you were mad for years," she said. "I would have thought your choice in decor would be the least of your problems."

"Perhaps I'm turning over a new leaf," he said, emphasizing the pun.

"Mmm," she said, ignoring the reply and instead giving herself over to his dancing. She was a magnificent dancer, easily moving with him, and he resisted the urge to ask her whom she had danced with to make her so skilled a partner.

"And you? What do you think?" he asked, wanting her to show herself—to show that she knew him. To tell him the truth of her identity and give them both the chance to talk.

"I think the signs point to you being rather mad, yes."

He laughed at the words, turning them in a circle as the tempo of the music rose. Her fingers tightened on his biceps, sending a thrum of pleasure through him. "I meant, why do you think I built an arbor in my ballroom?"

"Madness is not an appropriate answer?"

"No," he said, unable to stop himself. "I've turned over a new leaf on madness, already."

A heartbeat of a wait, and then she said, "I think you're trying to get people's attention."

Person's, he thought. *Yours*. "Do you think it is working?"

She gave a bright laugh—one he'd never heard from her before, and one he liked more than he could have imagined—and said, her gaze sliding over the room beyond his shoulder, "I think this particular ball will be remembered for years to come, yes."

"Will you remember it?"

Her gaze lifted to his, and she smiled—still not Grace. "It is the first time I have danced in an arbor, so I would say yes."

It wasn't true. He could remember her twirling in an arbor, as he sat against a tree, young and full of anger, desperate to keep them all safe from the man who would steal their future. The man who had stolen their future.

He could remember her arms outstretched as the sunlight dappled her skin, setting her on fire as she spun and spun and spun until she was too dizzy to spin any longer and she collapsed onto the soft moss, her laughter the only thing that could pull him from his thoughts.

She had danced and he had watched, and it had been the only thing he'd loved in that moment. Just as she had been the only thing he'd loved.

But he did not call her on the lie.

Instead, he spun her in another circle, faster than the last. She gave herself over to it, and a little inhale . . . of delight? He couldn't help himself. "You will remember the decor, then."

Those gorgeous eyes found his. "Do you fish for compliments, Your Grace?"

"Shamelessly."

She grew serious, as though the conversation had reminded her that they were at odds, and always had been—except when they weren't. "I shall remember you, too."

He refused to release her gaze—to lose her attention. He lowered his voice, letting something other than gentility into it. "That's why the trees. To give you something to remember." For a fleeting moment, he thought he had her. But she didn't move.

Instead, she turned her head to consider the trees in question, her lips curving just slightly. "And what of your gardens? Have they been picked clean?"

"Are you asking to see them?" he asked.

"No."

He nodded toward the wall of open doors on one side of the ballroom. "It's a masquerade—every reveler with a mask is ferrying unsuspecting ladies into the gardens."

"It is unfortunate for you, then, that I am never unsuspecting."

He coughed a little laugh at the words, surprised by the spar. She hadn't been like this when they were young. She'd been too sweet and too innocent. But now . . . she was something else.

Before he could mine the thought, she added, dryly, "Isn't that the joy of the mask? No need to feign unsuspecting. Instead, one has permission to pitch oneself forward into ruination."

The word—*ruination*—came with a riot of images that made Ewan want to make good on every one of them. "Did you come alone?"

She had. If she'd come with his brothers, they'd already have taken their pound of flesh.

She'd come alone.

A thrill shot through him at the thought. Whatever it

was . . . whyever it was . . . it was not disinterest. And he could work with that.

Her wine red lips curved into a little, knowing smile. "Are you offering to ruin me, Your Grace?"

He met the smile with one of his own. "Are you asking to be ruined?"

Her smile did not waver. Still not Grace, but Grace's mask, the kind that would not easily be moved. "Who says *I'm* the one who would be ruined?"

He almost missed a step. "Are you offering to ruin me?"

"Are you asking to be ruined?"

Yes.

She saw the answer. One would have to be addlebrained not to see the answer. She gave a little chuckle that threaded through him, making him hard as steel. Making him ache for this Grace-who-was-not-Grace.

"And if I said yes?"

The words escaped him without thought, but her lips were the ones that that parted, soft and surprised, for a heartbeat. "You don't know what you play at, Your Grace."

He wanted to know. He wanted to play.

When was the last time they'd played?

Had they ever played?

Not like this.

The music came to a stop, and so did they, her lush skirts wrapping themselves around his legs, the touch of fabric another temptation. He leaned forward, down the scant inches to her ear. "Show me," he murmured.

She did not retreat, holding her ground. "Do you not search for a wife?"

No. I have already found her.

"Are you interested in the position?" He forced teasing flirt into the words, when he wanted to rip their masks off, pack her into a carriage, and take her directly to a vicar. To make her duchess, as he'd promised all those years ago.

"No."

Why would I settle for duchess? The words burned into him, and with them, the singular truth that the girl who'd once loved him was gone, replaced by this woman, strong as steel, who would not be wooed. Would not be chased.

"That is an uncommon response to the offer."

"That's because most women see a title and think it is pure opportunity—a line to freedom."

"And you?"

Her lips curved, but the smile did not reach her eyes. "I know titles are gilded cages."

The words sliced through him, on a wave of the past. It was the truth—their truth more than anyone else's. And she did not even know the whole of it.

"Tonight is not for the future," he said, hating the lie on his lips. Hating the way she breathed it in. Knowing that he had to tell it to keep her there. Knowing, beyond all else, that if she left him then, she would never return.

Knowing that his invitation was an immense risk.

But risk was all they'd ever been to each other.

She turned slightly—just enough to meet his eyes. "Masks are dangerous. One never knows quite who one is when wearing one."

He did not hesitate. "Or, they make it easier for one to show his truth."

The wrong thing to say. He heard the bitterness in her little laugh. "Am I to believe this is your truth, Duke?"

The second time she'd used the title, and the second time he had to hold back a flinch. He rushed to keep control of the emotions roiling through him. "It's closer to it than you might imagine." He paused. Then, "No one will notice if we leave."

She laughed at that. "You have been away from society

for too long. *Everyone* will notice. They have noticed you flirting with scores of women tonight."

"Have you noticed that?" He liked that.

She ignored the question. "And they will notice you leaving with me, and they will wonder about me."

"They already wonder about you," he said, knowing he had scant seconds to convince her, before the orchestra began again and she would find a way to leave him. "The beautiful jewel who hasn't yet realized that I'm the worst choice in the room."

"That might be the first true thing you've said all evening." Damn her mask for hiding her from him.

The words stung. The tacit agreement that he was not for her. And still, she stayed.

He clung to that. "It's not the first, but it is true," he said. "So is this: they wonder about you, but will they know who you are?" They wouldn't, would they? She didn't live in this world. He might not know where she did live—what he would give to know her life!—but he knew she was not an aristocrat, and she could remove her mask without hesitation and no one in the room would know her.

But still, he would never deliberately put her in danger.

She gave him a small smile. "Someone might. I have an invitation, do I not?" He loved the teasing words—the way they warmed him. But that wasn't what he was asking, and she knew it. "They shan't know who I am," she agreed, thoughtfully. "They are too deep in their desire for the fantasy you have offered them."

He clung to those words, rushing to beat the first strains of the orchestra. "And you, my lady?" He met her rich brown eyes. *His* lady. "What of your desires? What of the fantasy I offer you?"

Time stopped as she considered the question, a single note of the violin seeming to hang in the air around them.

Perhaps he'd never have her without the mask. Perhaps

she'd never let him in again. But she was here, and she was in his arms, and if that was all he could have . . . it would have to be enough.

Never.

"Let me be your fantasy," he whispered.

Let me be everything you need.

"Tonight only," she said.

He sucked in a breath. She offered him one night. Masked. Pure fantasy.

It wasn't enough. But it was a start.

"Tonight only," he lied.

The words unlocked her. Her hand tightened in his, and she moved, magnificently, impossibly pulling him through the revelers and out into the gardens beyond.

Chapter Ten

What of the fantasy I offer you?

Perhaps if he hadn't framed it in such a way, using that word she loved so much—that word that had been tossed at her earlier in the week—perhaps she might have resisted it.

Perhaps if he hadn't been so tempting. Perhaps if he hadn't been so handsome. Perhaps if he hadn't had such a brilliant smile.

Perhaps . . . but not likely.

Because when he asked her, masked and all, about her desires, she realized that somewhere, deep inside her, she desired *this.* An evening of fantasy. An evening with this man, against whom she'd measured every other man for twenty years, like a curse. An evening with him, without any consequences—as long as she kept her mask on. As long as he remained in the dark.

An evening when she took from him, not the other way around.

He'd taken from her for so long. Her name, her life, her safety, her future. He'd promised her all of those things, and delivered on none. He owed her, didn't he?

So, what if she took the payment?

Just once. Just tonight. In the gardens. Masked and unknown.

Dahlia, collecting for Grace.

A woman, finally getting her due.

Tonight, and then she'd put this—and him—out of her mind.

And tomorrow? She'd find a way to exit him from London.

But tonight, she clasped his hand in hers and pulled him from the ballroom, through the writhing crowds and the soaring trees, the rich scent of moss that wrapped around them giving way as they walked out the doors and into the gardens, to the smell of flowers—evening-scented stocks, overflowing planters all over the balcony—and Grace stilled for a moment, letting the fragrance flow around her.

The orangery at Burghsey Hall had always had stocks in abundance, and it had been one of her favorite evening hiding places, because of the rich twilight scent of the flowers. And with the scent, another memory, Ewan and her, beneath a gardening table as the sun set through the western windows. His hand in hers. Their fingers intertwined. Surrounded by this exact scent.

She turned to him. *Did he remember?*

He smiled. "By all means, my lady," he said, his voice full of dark promise. "Don't stop now."

Who was this new man?

Where was Ewan? What had happened to him?

You sent him away. And now, this man returns in his place.

A whisper of suspicion came with the words. Something like doubt. Something that didn't feel right. Pushing it away, she laced her fingers with his and pulled him down the steps, passing a chess piece giggling in the arms of a musketeer, and another Marie Antoinette, who peered closely at them as they rushed by.

What was it with aristocratic women and Marie

Antoinette—had they all forgotten that she'd misjudged her power and ended up without a head?

But let them eat cake . . .

He squeezed her hand and she looked back, stilling, letting him pull her around toward him and redirect their movements—no longer headed for the main garden, but for a side path, poorly lit and winding through a collection of linden trees. She followed.

"I suppose it's true what they say," she whispered softly as he guided her away from the house and the light. "Unmarried gentlemen will always lead you down the garden path."

He did not laugh at the words. Instead, he cast a quick, scalding look back at her before stopping at a door, set into the wall to their right. She hadn't noticed there was a wall, let alone a door, until he threw the iron catch and pushed the heavy oak open to reveal a magnificent landscape—a small patch of green, surrounded on its edges by a stunning garden in what Grace was certain daylight would expose as vibrant flowerbeds. And at the center, a gazebo, beautifully designed and painted.

She swallowed, taking in the space. "It's magical."

"It's private," he said, pulling her up the steps and into the gazebo before turning to face her, his fingers stroking along her arm, up, up, magnificently up, until the cool leather of his gloves was tracing over her chin, the sensation drawing her to him. Her lips parted, her eyes, behind her mask, tracking his own mouth, full and lush—just as she remembered it. How many times did she think of that mouth? How many times had she dreamed of kissing it, late at night, when she could afford a dream that felt like betrayal?

How many times had she stopped the fantasy, hating that she still wanted this man who had betrayed her so fully?

Let me be your fantasy.

"Wait—" he said, pulling his hand away from her, the removal of the touch like punishment. He ripped his glove off with his teeth and tossed it to the ground. "Now. Let me—" and he reached for her, his fingers a hot promise against her skin.

The touch was urgent and gentle, as though he couldn't bear to wait for her, and still, he wished to do it right.

"Let me . . ." The earlier command became a plea. He was asking to kiss her.

She wanted it. *Yes.* And still—before she could speak the words, she hesitated. "Wait." He did, instantly releasing her with a little groan of frustration.

Was it a trap? Did he know her? She knew him—why did it matter if two played at this game?

And if he *didn't*—as he seemed not to—why did *that* matter?

She met his eyes, barely visible in the light of the moon. "Why the trees?"

He went still at the question. Nerves? Or surprise? Or both? "I told you," he said, "so you would remember me."

Remember him in the past? Or remember him now?

She would remember him. Like this, handsome and charming and wanting her, for the rest of time. "I will remember you."

I never forgot you.

He nodded, taking a step closer to her, pushing her to the edge of the gazebo, until she was up against the wooden wall, and he dipped his head, whispering at her ear, "I intend to make it impossible for you to do otherwise."

Heat thrummed through her at the vow. It didn't matter that it was meant to be fantasy.

She would remember all of it.

She would remember the feel of his breath on her neck, setting her aflame. And then the rest of his promise—"I will remember the smell of you, like cream and spice."

She would remember his fingers tracing down her neck and over her shoulder, down her arm, tugging at her glove. Removing it in a long, slow slide, and baring her hand to the late summer evening. More words. "I will remember the feel of your skin, like silk."

She would remember it, too, the feel of him, and the way she thanked God for the mask that kept him from her—because she didn't trust herself not to tumble back into his arms if she could see all of him.

"I will remember the sound of your breath in my ear. The way pleasure hitches in it. I would like to remember the taste of you," he said, softly, his mouth tracing over her cheek, barely there, like a promise. Holding at the corner of her mouth, like a breath.

She didn't trust herself not to tumble back into his arms anyway.

Just one night. Just one tumble.

"Yes," she whispered.

Please, yes.

He didn't move. "Tell me your name." She pulled back at the words, her eyes flying to his, and he watched her for a heartbeat.

Grace. She should say it. She was half certain that he already knew it. But if he did—would it be like this if he knew it? So simple? So easy?

She would have to end the game if she revealed herself. And she didn't want to end it. Not now. Not when she was so close.

This was the most she would ever have of him.

This would have to be enough.

She reached for him, her hand curving around the back of his neck, her fingers sliding into his hair, tangling there. Drawing him close. Their eyes locked, and she whispered, "No," a fraction of a second before she kissed him.

He froze as their lips touched, and for a moment she

thought he would pull away. *Don't*, she willed. *Let me have this.*

And then his hands came to her face, holding her still as his lips opened and he met her kiss with his own, and her world was collapsing around her—the night, the masque, and more than all that, the memory. The boy who had been her first kiss, fumbling and awkward and perfect . . . gone, and in his place, this man—strong and sure and perfect—and something whispered through her that was at once immensely powerful and utterly terrifying.

She didn't stop to think about which was more important. She didn't want to stop. She never wanted him to stop. A sound rumbled low in his throat as his thumbs traced the bottom edge of her mask, running under the structured silk, smoothing over her skin as he positioned her to take her lips more thoroughly.

And it was her turn to rumble, the pleasure of his kiss like nothing she'd ever experienced—it set her on fire. Grace came up on her toes, her arms wrapping around his neck as she pulled him closer, not thinking of the night, or the ball, or his plans for a wife or a life beyond her—thinking only of him, of them, of what they might have in this moment, with nothing else in the way.

Nothing but desire.

Offered and accepted.

He licked over her lips, the rough stroke of his tongue like a flame, and she gasped at the sensation, her eyes closing as she pulled away and he set his kiss to the line of her jaw, the column of her neck, the soft skin of her shoulder as he lifted her to sit on the edge of the gazebo, giving her no choice but to cling to him.

Not that she would have taken an alternate choice.

She had never wanted anything like she wanted this—pleasure and pain, desire and risk. A kiss that was at once the past and the present—even if it would never be future.

And a single thought, shattering through her: *Mine*.

There wasn't room for that, of course. He wasn't hers. He never would be. And she couldn't face the idea that he might still be a part of her. This was it. One night. One fantasy. As promised.

And him never the wiser.

Ewan pulled back as though he'd heard the thought, and they both gasped for air. She clenched her fist in his hair and pulled him close again. Enough for him to growl his desperation into another lush kiss before he remembered he'd had something to say. Tearing his mouth from hers once again, he whispered, "Wait."

"I've waited long enough." A lifetime.

He gave a little huff of laughter. "Another moment won't matter."

Except it would. It was one less moment from this collection—from the only moments she would ever have.

"Tell me your name," he said, before she could protest again.

"No." He opened his mouth to protest at the instant refusal and she reached up, putting one gloved finger to his lips. "Shh. You promised me the fantasy, did you not?"

He looked pained. "I did."

"You asked after my desires."

"Yes—" he started, and she placed her finger to his lips once more.

"This is what I desire. This is the fantasy. No names."

If he pressed, there would be memory. There would be the past. There would be Grace and Ewan. But tonight, there could be Dahlia and the duke, dark and mysterious and full of promises that could be kept in an evening, no lifetime required.

"You told me," she continued. "Tonight is not for the future."

She watched him, willing him to follow her lead, time

stretching out like an eternity. And then he opened his mouth and took the tip of her finger between his lips, sucking gently and setting her on fire. Her jaw slackened as she watched the movement—betraying the lush strokes of his tongue against the sensitive pad of her finger. At her gasp of pleasure, he released her, the scrape of his teeth over her skin making her ache.

"No names," he agreed, softly. "Then the mask stays, as well?"

She inclined her head at the question. Of course the mask stayed. Her rule did not stop him from reaching for his own mask and pulling it off, tossing it away, into the darkness, as though he had no intention of ever returning to his ball or his house or his life. Or, if he did, he had no intention of returning to those things in hiding.

She drank him in—unable to help herself now that he was finally bare to her—wishing beyond anything that she could see him clearly in the moonlight. To make up for it, she reached for him, her fingers sliding over his high, aristocratic cheekbones, testing the heat of his skin. He reached up and took her hand in his, pressing it to his cheek, as though he were an offering.

"Now I can see you," she said.

"You could see me before; you only had to ask." She marveled at the words, so free and without care. What would it be like to never have to hide? Grace was so expert at hiding, at playing a part—myriad parts—that she often forgot her truth.

Not that she could ever show it here.

He ran a hand through his hair, the dark blond hinting of gold in the moonlight. He leveled her with a look. "And so? Do you like it?"

So much. "You'll do," she allowed, giving herself up to the moment. "For tonight."

He smiled, crooked and familiar for its boyish charm,

and her chest tightened at the echo of memory that came with it. Not enough to chase her away. Just enough to make her wish never to leave.

He met her eyes. "What else, then, my lady? If I am to be your fantasy, where do I begin?"

Her heart began to pound, but she refused to be swayed. She lifted her chin. "Kiss me again."

"Where?"

Everywhere. "Wherever you like."

He growled, low in his throat, and then, "I like all of it."

She reached for him, whispering in the darkness, "Then kiss all of it."

They came together like a storm, crashing into each other as he tilted her chin up to the roof of the gazebo, exposing the long column of her neck and setting his lips to it, tracing it with his tongue. She sucked in a deep breath of pleasure, unbearably aware of his hands at her sides, caging her to the low wall of the gazebo, her own hands in his hair, half holding on, half guiding him down her neck and farther, over the skin rising up out of the low cut of the dress. And then one hand was there at her neckline, fisting on it, tightening the fabric before he ripped it, just enough to pull it away and release her breasts to the summer air.

It was mad and wild, and in only minutes reality would return and with it the truth about his actions and her anger and their irreparable past and their impossible future, but right now, there was this . . . mad and wild.

She sucked in a breath and he pulled back at the sound, to take her in. She skimmed her fingers over her collarbone, checking for the sleeves that still covered her shoulders before lowering her arms and letting him look his fill.

He did for long enough moments that she thought he might not touch her after all, and then he swore, dark and wicked, and for a heartbeat his perfect elocution slid into his past—into the Garden. The edge of slang sent heat pooling through her, a straight shot of desire, but she saw him hear his own words—words that dukes did not say with ladies, no matter how far down the garden path they were. The flinch was barely there.

Would he stop?

Surely he wouldn't. Not now.

Don't stop.

"This . . ." he whispered, the words low and lush. "This is what I wanted. From the moment you arrived, I wanted to pull this dress off you." His beautiful eyes, lit by the moonlight, met hers. "Tell me you wanted it, too."

She straightened, pushing her shoulders back, presenting herself to his hot gaze. Putting herself on display. And then she whispered, "All of it."

Another magnificent growl in his throat. "As my lady desires." He set his lips to where she ached for him, lingering strokes with his tongue before taking her gently into his mouth and sucking, slow and rhythmic, until she was moving beneath him, meeting his lush draws with her body, whispering encouragement as he stole her thoughts.

And there, beneath the stars and the roof of that secret gazebo, Grace turned herself over to fantasy and to this man and to his magnificent mouth and hands—hands that were sliding beneath her skirts, over her ankles, and up the length of her leg, higher and higher, bringing the fabric with them, until the summer air was kissing her thighs with the same lush promise as he made to her breasts.

When he released her, she nearly cried her frustration, until he blew a long stream of air over the puckered tip of one breast, and looked to her again, his fingers playing over the soft skin of her inner thigh, painting patterns that robbed her of her sanity. "Where else shall I kiss you, my lady?"

She bit back a curse at the teasing words, even as she spread her thighs a touch wider. She was a woman who dealt in pleasure, and knew that she wished to take her own. Knew that there was only one man she'd ever want that pleasure from—even if she could never admit it. Even if he could never know it. She met his eyes, grateful for the mask—both the fabric one and the one that was more complicated to remove—and replied as Dahlia, who would not hesitate to take what she wanted. "Did you not say all of it?"

He swore softly at the words, leaning in to steal her lips in a kiss once more, before pulling back and saying, "Mmmm. I shan't let you go until I taste all of it. Every inch of you."

Without hesitation, he slid to his knees before her, taking her sense with him.

He spread her thighs, and she closed her eyes to his touch, wanting it more than she could say, her fingers tightening in his hair, his name whispering through her—the name she could never use—Ewan. When he pressed a kiss to the soft skin at the inside of her knee, the edge of his teeth scraping there like a promise, she exhaled, long and trembling. His breath was hot perfection, and he whispered, "I feel like Apollo in the woods."

She opened her eyes at the words, staring up at the stars painted on the gazebo ceiling—another canopy that she'd never see without thinking of him. "A-Apollo?"

"Mmm." He turned and pressed a lush kiss on the opposite thigh. "Apollo, wandering in the woods, until he stumbled upon the most beautiful woman he'd ever seen."

Her surprised laugh turned into a gasp of pleasure as his lips moved higher and higher, closer and closer to where she wanted him. She held on to him, pulling tight at his hair, loving the grunt of pleasure-pain he offered even as she hated the way he lingered, close enough for her to feel his breath and too far away for her to feel anything else. "Was she naked in a swimming hole?"

He hummed his amusement, and she heard the distraction in the sound, as though he was too focused on something else. On her. On the place where she, too, was focused. "I shall tell you later."

He set his lips to the hot, straining core of her, and she cried out at the sensation—unable to stop herself from staring down at him. She was pure desire. Unleashed need.

And Ewan, controlling it, as he always had.

He licked long and firm over her, setting her on fire before lifting his mouth and moving back, pushing her skirts higher, tilting her hips forward to give himself a view. "You're so wet," he growled, dipping a single finger inside her.

She sighed, rocking toward him, eager for more of him—touch, words, gaze, whatever he would spare. Later she would hate herself for wanting him so much. But now, she gave herself up to him.

"You shine like gold here. The moonlight loves you."

Her fingers tugged at his hair again. "I'm more interested in you loving me, right now."

A pause, and Grace bit her tongue. He would understand she meant—

"As my lady wishes."

He understood.

Her fingers slid into his hair, clutching him close, pressing him to the open, aching center of her, using him as he tasted her again and again, losing himself in her. He licked and sucked and stroked with tongue and fingers until she rocked against him, her breath coming faster and faster, her hips working to find the rhythm that would give her release.

"Yes." He growled against her as she tightened her fist, pulling his hair tight. "Show me."

She did, taking her pleasure without shame. Knowing he took his, too. Knowing that this night would be all they ever had.

Knowing it was a mistake.

His tongue found a glorious spot, and she cried out, the sound giving him all the information he needed. He worked at that spot in rough, rhythmic circles, his tongue like a promise, over and over, her grip guiding him as she moved against him, seeking her pleasure.

He pulled back to stare up at her, his gaze hot on her, framed by the torn fabric of her bodice. She groaned her frustration, her hips tilting toward him, and he rewarded the movement with a slow, delicious suck where she wanted him. "You are a queen," he whispered.

She closed her eyes at the words. At the impossible promise in them.

And then he added, "Tonight, I am your throne." The words crashed through her, leaving a trail of desire. Her eyes opened, and her gaze crashed into his as he said, "What do you need?"

This was what she needed.

He was what she needed.

Tonight.

Not forever.

Just tonight.

Perhaps it would be enough.

She tightened her fist in his hair and pressed herself to him, loving the way his eyes closed with pleasure, loving the feel of him there, stroking . . .

"This," she whispered. "I need this." A delicious growl vibrated through her. "This," she repeated. "I need—"

You.

Miraculously, she didn't say it.

And still, it seemed he might have heard it.

He growled, his tongue stroking hard, in circles, firmer and tighter until he was working the place where she was desperate for him, and she was on her toes and she was shaking with pleasure.

She flew apart, hands in his hair, whispered words as wild as the sounds he made, pure sin at her core. He stayed there, on his knees, against her, gentle and firm, until she released the long breath she'd held at the end, her grip relaxing from his hair.

He caught her as she lost herself, coming to his feet and fitting himself between her legs, holding one knee in a strong hand as he stroked over her cheek with the other, pulling her to him for a slow, deep kiss. He rocked against her pulsing core, the hard ridge of him a delicious pressure, one she could not resist meeting with writhing movement.

He released her mouth, pulling back from the kiss, setting his forehead to hers, the silk of her mask between them as he panted, "Tell me your name."

Grace.

She bit back the word. The revelation. Shook her head.

He rocked against her again, sending another jolt of pleasure through her—almost too much. "Tell me," he growled in her ear.

Too much.

She opened her eyes, finding him a hairsbreadth away. And there, in his gaze, she saw it.

Longing.

It was gone almost before it appeared, but she saw it. Recognized it.

"Please," he said, reaching out to push a loose curl from her cheek. And with that touch—with his hands on her disguise, the fantasy was over.

Did he know? The thought sent a shot of fear through her, and she stiffened, pushing him away.

He stepped back, instantly. "Wait."

She did not respond, coming off the wall and shaking out her skirts and wrapping the silken wrap over the tear in her bodice. Straightening. Stiffening.

Returning to reality.

He saw the change in her. He cursed his frustration in the darkness.

She lifted her eyes to his, loving and hating the way he stared at her—as though there was nothing in the world he'd rather look at.

"Let me see you again." There was frenzy in the words. Something held tight that threatened to come unmoored.

Never. If they saw each other again, if he touched her again—she risked everything. She could never come here again. This was the end.

Grace took a deep breath, and Dahlia replied.

"No."

Chapter Eleven

Burghsey Estate
Twenty Years Earlier

"What have you done?"

Grace's words came like gunshot from the other side of the room, shock and betrayal in her eyes, as she crouched over his brother, curled in a ball on the floor, his arms wrapped around his midsection.

Ewan had broken a rib. More than one. He'd felt the bones crack beneath his knuckles. Of course he had. He was inches taller than Whit, and a better fighter by far than the other boy, the runt of the litter, according to their father.

Their father, the monster.

Size didn't make him better than Whit, though. It had been Whit who had stepped up to fight Ewan, knowing before everyone else what the monster had planned. Knowing, before everyone else, that Ewan would be the duke's weapon in the end.

And Ewan had proven him right, putting him to the ground—leaving him broken and bleeding, tears on his face. Tears on his face, and on hers, too, but Ewan couldn't look at hers, knowing that when he did, he would feel all the things he could not afford to feel.

Every moment the girl lives, you're one whisper from the gallows.

His father's words, spoken moments earlier, in the hallway beyond, as he'd pressed the knife into Ewan's palm, a perverted knighthood. Not Ewan any longer. Now Robert. Robert Matthew Carrick, Earl Sumner, heir to the Dukedom of Marwick.

But it wasn't his name. It was hers.

She's nothing. She held your place. Now, you must take it.

He should have expected this—his last test—a heartbeat from the future he'd been promised when his father had picked through the muck to the brothel on Tavistock Row where he'd lived with his mother and a dozen other women like her, and made Ewan an offer that no child would refuse. Money, safety, a new chance for his mother, and a life beyond the stink and sweat and brutality of the streets. A title—a dukedom—so impossible a future that it somehow felt like it was in reach.

And then it *was* in reach, and he'd been such a fool, thinking that he could take everything his sire offered and still keep the rest. Still keep his mother. His brothers.

Love.

He should have known the duke would see everything. Would plan for it. Would make it impossible. Evil rarely came with stupidity.

She cannot live, his father had said, no feeling in his voice. *None of them can.*

Ewan had balked, immediately planning to run. To save them all.

But the duke was ahead of him. And the die had been cast.

Now.

And when he had protested, the older man had said the

only thing that could have moved him to action. *You do it, boy. You do it, or I do—and she will suffer the most.*

Ewan had believed him. How many times had their father turned sadist? How many switchings from a misstep at a waltz, a fork misused at dinner. The nights threatening to kill them with the cold. The darkness threatening to steal their sanity. The beatings.

The sweets, the gifts, the pets . . . destroyed before their eyes.

And now, his final threat.

And Ewan, the only thing that might stop him.

Whit had been first, alone in the room, knowing, in that way that he always did, what was to come. Ewan had dropped him, and though Whit had tried to remain quiet, his cries had summoned the others, which of course had been their father's sadistic plan.

Devil had crashed through the door, immediately taking in one brother on the ground and Ewan standing over him, blade in hand.

Not Ewan.

Robert. Sumner. Someday, Marwick himself.

The names shattered through him. He didn't want them. Not any longer. Not at this price.

But he no longer had a choice.

"Get the fuck away from him, bruv," Devil had growled, coming for him with the pure hot rage that moved him through the world. Fists and fury. He'd driven Ewan back, across the room, and Ewan had taken the blows. Deserving them. Knowing that they'd make his own less powerful.

Needing to be less powerful.

They'd toppled a small table and upended a chair before Ewan had knocked Devil to the ground, buying enough time for him to focus on his real goal.

"What have you done?" Grace's voice. Soft. Disbelieving.

She was the most beautiful thing he would ever see.

The best person he'd ever know.

The only thing he'd ever love.

And he had no choice.

Robert Matthew Carrick, Earl Sumner, clasped the knife tighter, the bite of the steel hilt sharp in his palm, knowing he had one chance to make this right. Knowing what he had to do.

She stood, seeing what was to come. "Ewan—no!"

Devil moved at his feet, rolling to his knees.

Save her, Robert thought, willing his brother up.

They would, wouldn't they?

"Ewan, what the fuck—" Whit, from his place on the floor, trying to straighten. To ignore the pain in his ribs, tears in salty tracks on his face.

"Ewan—" Grace, her hair a cloud of fire around her, her brown eyes enormous and full of confusion . . . confusion and something worse . . . betrayal.

"Don't do it," Devil yelled from behind him. "Fucking hell, bruv."

The foul little bastards deserve what's coming to them. If he didn't, his father would.

I'll never let you all go. His fucking father.

Do it, and I'll bring your mother here. Ewan knew it was a lie. But he also knew he had only one chance to make sure that this man didn't destroy everyone he cared for.

Sacrifice. His father meant it for the title.

Sacrifice. Fuck the title.

He tightened his grip on the knife, willing his brothers to be what he knew them to be. Willing them to be more than he ever could be. He met her eyes, across the room. He could read her thoughts—he'd always been able to read her thoughts. She didn't believe he would do it.

Of course she didn't.

She knew he loved her.

She shook her head, barely a movement, but he saw it. Saw it, and heard the words they'd whispered to each other night after night: *We'll run. All of us.*

But she didn't know the rest. Didn't know his father would never let them go together. She didn't know that their best bet at survival was this—Ewan, staying.

He deserved to stay. He wasn't like them . . . he'd wanted the title. Which maybe made him as bad as their father.

But they deserved to live.

I'm sorry.

Behind him, Devil was on his feet.

Save her.

He went for her, unable to look away from her eyes—those eyes he dreamed of every night. The eyes he'd loved almost from the first moment he'd seen her. Those eyes that would haunt him, forever.

They went wide with shock. Then understanding. Then fear.

She screamed, and his blade met flesh.

A SHARP RAP on the door to his study yanked Ewan from the memory, and he nearly dropped the tumbler of whisky that dangled from his hand as he returned to the present.

He stood at the window, staring down into the quiet gardens that, a week earlier, had teemed with revelers. The night sky was clear and the autumn moon was nearly full, revealing the roof of the gazebo behind the secret wall in the distance. The place he'd last seen Grace. The place where she'd left him.

"Come," he said.

The door opened before the word was fully formed, and he looked over his shoulder at O'Clair, the impeccable butler who came with the London house and appeared never to require sleep or food or time to himself.

"Your Grace," O'Clair said, with perfect clarity, stepping into the room. The words set Ewan immediately on edge. Christ, he hated that title. "There are . . . gentlemen below."

The emphasis made it clear that whoever was below had not passed the inspection of the butler, and that was enough for Ewan at the moment. He had no interest in visitors. "It's the middle of the night. Whoever it is can return at a reasonable hour."

The butler cleared his throat. "Yes, well, they don't seem to—"

"We ain't the kind of men who show face in Mayfair at reasonable hours, Duke," came a voice from behind O'Clair, whose eyes went wide with a mix of shock and affront that would have amused Ewan if he wasn't so surprised himself by the new arrivals.

Devil punctuated his words with a kick to the door, sending it swinging back on the hinge and crashing into the wall. He entered the room as Whit took up residence in the doorway behind him, arms crossed over his massive chest, looking every inch the Beast London called him.

No longer runt of the litter.

Ewan narrowed his gaze on his brothers. He appeared to have summoned them with his memory. Bad luck, that.

"Sirs! I must insist—" O'Clair, for his part, was beside himself and still soldiering on. "The duke is not receiving."

"Oho! Is he not?" Devil tapped O'Clair on the shoulder with the silver handle of his ebony cane, his scar flashing white and wicked down the side of his cheek. "No need to stand on ceremony, good man—the duke's more than happy to see us." He didn't look to Ewan as he said, "Ain't you, bruv?"

"I wouldn't use the word *happy*, no."

"Too fuckin' bad," Beast said from the doorway, the words coming like gravel.

The butler blustered, and Ewan bit back a curse. He might as well save the man. "Thank you, O'Clair."

The butler turned wide eyes on him. "Your Grace?"

Tonight, of all nights, he chose to resist orders? "I shan't need you for the rest of the evening."

O'Clair didn't seem convinced, but still, he collected himself. "Of course." He bowed, shortly, and moved to leave the room, stopping when he reached Beast in the doorway. "I beg your pardon, sir."

Beast grunted and moved just enough to let him past.

"I'll thank you not to torment my servants," Ewan said.

"Beast ain't good wiv manners." It was a lie. They were all impeccable at manners. Their father had made sure of it. He'd delighted in playing abusive Pygmalion before he'd found other ways to entertain himself. Beast grunted as Devil rounded the desk and sat. "Was this the old man's desk?"

"Yes," Ewan said, moving to pour more whisky. He sensed he was going to need it.

"Good," Devil said, the word punctuated with the thunk of his great heavy boots, muddy and full of whatever filth he'd brought in from Covent Garden.

Ewan couldn't blame him. He fucking hated that desk, and everything else in the house that had belonged to their father. But he'd be damned if he'd show as much.

Had Grace sent them? Had she discovered the truth of the night in his gardens, in the gazebo, and decided to send her brothers to finish the job she'd begun a year earlier? Had he miscalculated?

His heart began to pound. No. She wouldn't send them to do her dirty work. She was not one to turn away from a fight. Certainly not one from him.

Why hadn't she come to confront him herself?

He willed himself calm and filled his glass in silence.

"What then, are you here for another round of Who Shall Kill the Duke?"

Every time he'd faced these two in the last two years, it had ended in battle. Every time he'd faced them in the last twenty years. And he'd always laid them out. But somehow, they were the ones who had won. They had homes and families and a whole world to bring them purpose and pleasure.

And they had Grace.

"It isn't the worst idea, innit?" Devil said, the sound of the Garden so thick that Ewan knew it was meant to grate when he added, "Come now, bruv, we ain't monsters."

It did grate.

He refused to let it show. "Are you not?"

"No," came the reply from the doorway. "That's always been your specialty."

Ewan did not look up, even as Devil whistled his admiration and tapped his walking stick on his filthy boots, ever the showman. "Look at that. You've got Beast out here giving soliloquies."

"What do you want, Devon?"

The name was a calculated risk, one that paid off with the silence that came in reply. Ewan turned to face his brother, who was staring directly at him. The lightness was gone from Devil's voice when he said, "I remind you that only one of us has a given name that sees him to the gallows."

Ewan did not respond. They'd had the means to reveal him an imposter duke for decades, and somehow had never used them. He didn't worry about it now.

Some days, he wished for it.

Devil tapped his walking stick on his boots again. Once, twice in slow succession, his gaze tracking Ewan from head to toe. "You've changed."

He knew what they'd seen in the ring a year ago—when he'd met Grace after an eternity of thinking she was dead. When he'd taken her hits. And when she'd laid him low with the worst of it—the knowledge that he would never be worthy of the girl he'd once loved.

That that girl no longer existed.

These men had watched his destruction.

He knew what they saw now. He was bigger than he'd been when he'd seen them last. Broader and more muscular. His cheeks shaven, less hollow. His body healthier—and his mind, as well.

Not always, but mostly.

He'd prepared for this, the biggest battle of his life.

"Told you," Beast growled from the doorway.

"Mmm," said Devil, thoughtfully.

Beast grunted his reply.

Irritation flared. "Did the two of you come here to converse without me, or . . ."

"Have you seen her?"

He stilled at the question, a thrill coursing through him at the words. She had not told them. They did not know that she'd masked herself and come to the ball. They did not know she'd danced in his arms. They did not know about the gardens. About the gazebo.

About the fantasy.

Which meant she'd wanted to keep it to herself.

He sat, hiding his thoughts, spreading his arms wide along the back of the chair that faced Devil on the other side of his desk. He drank, slow and steady. And he lied. "No."

A grunt, behind him, from Beast.

Devil watched him carefully, that infernal walking stick tapping like water on stone. "I don't believe you."

"I haven't seen her," he said, ignoring how the words conjured all the ways he had seen her—the way her lips curved in a smile just for him, the way her voice washed over him after so many years, the soft skin of her breasts in his hands, her thighs tightening around him, the taste of her.

"You mean to tell us that you haven't returned for her?" Devil said.

He didn't reply. He couldn't. The words refused to form. Of course he was back for her. He would always come back for her.

Another grunt in the silence.

He shot a look at the door. "Do you have trouble speaking? Too many blows to the head?"

"I think you might refrain from giving him too many ideas about blows to the head, Duke," Devil said. "He's itching to have a go at you."

Ewan narrowed his gaze on Beast. "That didn't go so well for you last time."

"You fucking bastard," Beast said, coming off the doorjamb. "You nearly killed my wife; I won't pull the punch this time."

Ewan resisted the flinch that threatened at the words. He hadn't intentionally harmed the lady—she'd been on the docks when the fool he'd been paying to punish his brothers had destroyed a shipment the Bareknuckle Bastards were moving under cover of darkness. The Bastards ran myriad businesses throughout London, some aboveboard and many below, but their income was largely through smuggled goods, and Ewan had set his sights on *that* business, knowing that its destruction would in turn destroy them.

"She was not my target."

"No, we were," Devil said from behind the desk.

Ewan turned to face him. "I had a score to settle." They'd told him Grace was dead, and it destroyed him. Turned him wild. Filled him with anger and vengeance. And he'd been willing to do anything to destroy them, in return.

But she was alive.

And with her, his hope.

He looked to Whit. "I quite like Lady Henrietta." He paused. "Not Lady Henrietta anymore, is she? Mrs. Whittington." He ignored the twist in his gut. "I am told you've a babe on the way. Felicitations."

"You stay the fuck away from my family." Whit came into the room, approaching him, but Ewan did not move, knowing he could not flinch.

"I've no interest in your family," he said. It was a lie. He was immensely interested in his brothers' families—something that had always seemed as likely to him as owning a unicorn or discovering a mermaid in the stream on his country estate.

They'd made a pact when they were children—in the darkness after their father had tormented them. Whoever became duke would let the line end with him, refusing to give their sire the pleasure of heirs.

Ewan had never allowed himself the liberty of imagining children. But now—his brothers—they had children, and he wondered about them. If they had the amber eyes they all shared. If Devil's daughter had a wide smile like her father. If she was as clever as her mother. If Whit's child would grow as loyal as its father was.

And what Ewan's would have been like, if he'd lost the dukedom instead of winning it.

He held all that back, however. "The point is, I came for what you loved because you came for what I loved," he said. "You told me she was dead."

"She might as well be for all the chance you have at winning her back."

Let me see you again. His words from the gazebo.

No. Hers.

He pushed away the memory and the threat that his hope might be misplaced. "She's not why you're here."

"No, she's not," Devil conceded. "We're here because every time you return to London, people die. And that's not happening this time."

"Unless it's you," Whit added.

Ewan looked to him. "And what, you intend to do it?"

"I've been aching to gut a Duke of Marwick for my entire life," Devil said from behind the desk.

"And yet, I live." He'd always wondered why they'd never returned to take their revenge. God knew, he'd deserved it.

"Yeah, well, when we make promises, we keep them."

Ewan did not misunderstand. He'd made them a promise when they were children. That they would run together. That they would protect each other. And he hadn't been able to keep it. Still, he leveled Devil with a sharp look. "Promises to whom?"

Devil's brows lifted. "I think you know."

"Grace." The word came unexpectedly, on a breath he should have held in. One that revealed too much.

She'd kept him alive.

Whit looked to Devil. "I told you."

"Mmm," Devil said. "We ain't here about that, though."

About what? What had she said?

He resisted the urge to ask the questions, instead settling on a frustrated, "What then? Get it over with."

Devil tsked at the tone. "Just because we agreed not to kill you don't mean we wouldn't happily rough you up, bruv."

Frustration flared into something else, and he worked to remain relaxed in the chair, despite itching for a fight. He'd been itching for one since he'd come to London. Since he'd vowed to be a different man.

Still, if anyone was to bring out the worst in him, it was these two. "I'm game if you are."

Devil's brows rose and he shot a wolfish smile to Whit, who pulled his fists—the size of hams—from his pockets.

"Me first, if you're offering. Or do we get the coward who met Grace in the ring last year—willing to take his licks like the toff he was trained to be?"

How he wanted to put a fist into his brothers' faces. Instead, he stayed distant, playing the role they expected. "I owe her more than I owe you."

Truth.

"Ah, so you gave her a gift? By not fighting her?"

"I'd never hurt her."

The words froze the other two men, and Ewan felt their surprise, looking quickly from one to the other before Devil shook his head. "My God."

"He doesn't see it," Whit said.

"See what?"

"That you've hurt her every day since we ran."

Silence fell in the wake of the words, and he watched Devil's jaw tighten, the scar that ran six inches down the side of Devil's face—the one Ewan had put there decades earlier—went white with the movement, and no doubt with the memories of Ewan's past actions. He'd a lifetime of threatening them. Their lives, their futures, their wives, their world.

And threatening them was the least of what he'd done.

Whit continued, the words hitting heavier because they came from the brother who so rarely spoke. "She's never been safe. Never not been in hiding. Never had a day when she did not have to look over her shoulder. For you. You've been chasing her since the night you chased her from Burghsey."

"Not chasing. Searching."

"Aye, searching so you could finish what you started." Devil, this time. "Eliminate the proof that you stole a dukedom and a life and a future."

He'd never intended to steal it. He'd meant for her to have it with him. "That's not true."

"Nah. I know that, now. But she don't and even if she did, it wouldn't matter."

Anger flared, irrational and full of indignation even as he heard the ring of truth in the words. "Tell me why you are here, or get the hell out of my house."

Devil watched him for a long moment, and then said, "Careful, bruv, you're starting to sound like a real Marwick."

At the suggestion that he was like their father, the facade of ducal disdain was gone, Ewan's vision clouding with rage as he moved with speed he hadn't needed in two decades. He was out of his chair and at the desk, his hands flat on the wood as he faced down Devil. And then, clear and strong, like a bell, "Say it again. Give me a reason to rip you apart."

Devil tapped that infernal stick against his boot again and again. When Ewan was ready to snap it in two, his brother asked, entirely casual, "Did you kill him?"

Their father.

For a heartbeat, he imagined that this was what it would be like if they'd stayed together. The three of them, late at night, with scotch and the past.

He swallowed back the hint of regret that came with the realization and lifted his glass. "Does it matter?" He knocked the whisky back.

Two sets of dark brows rose as his brothers shared a look—one Ewan could not read. The silent communication grated.

Devil replied. "Not really, no."

"Then why don't you two get the hell on with it?"

"No need to get angry."

"We're all angry," Ewan spat. "Always have been. Three brothers, born beneath the same angry star." On the same day, at the same hour, they'd been told. Cut from the same cloth, and somehow vastly different.

"Mmm." Devil tilted his head. "But it wasn't just us, was it?"

It wasn't. Grace had been born that same day. That same hour. To a different man, but to the same fate.

Did they think he didn't know? Did they think he didn't think of that fate every damn day? That she wasn't first in his mind in the morning and last in it at night and present in every dream that came in between?

Did they think he did not ache for her?

He wanted her. And he wanted them gone so he could go back to wanting her.

"Why are you here?"

For a moment, he thought this was why—to torment him. To force him to face the past and question the present and dread the future—alone. For a moment, he saw all of that in Devil's eyes.

And then Whit spoke from immediately behind him. "We came to discuss the blunt."

Cold, unpleasant surprise washed through him and he straightened, looking over his shoulder at his enormous brother—the handsomest man London had ever seen, despite his moniker—then down at the mahogany desk, which generations of dukes had called their own. He tracked the grain of the wood—perfectly straight, to a heavy, dark knot that had been unable to be hidden beneath the stain that finished the desk.

Staring at that knot, he said, "What blunt?"

"What blunt," Devil said, disdain in his voice. "You know what blunt. The case of coin you sent to buy forgiveness in the Garden. It ain't every day ten thousand pounds turns up at our warehouse."

Ewan's head snapped up. "I didn't send it to the warehouse."

Amber eyes gleamed. "It doesn't matter where you sent it, bruv. Money like that turns up in the Garden, it lands at our warehouse."

Ewan clenched his jaw at the words. "It's not for you."

Devil was insulted. "You think we'd take your blood money?"

Blood money.

He ignored the words, and the way they carved space in him. "I think that ten thousand pounds is enough to tempt better men into worse things."

Beast cursed softly. "We ought to put him into the ground for that alone."

Devil's gaze narrowed on him. "First things first, Duke—we're rich as kings. Why, Beast alone owns half of Berkeley Square. We don't need your money. And even if it weren't tainted with the past, we wouldn't take it."

"Good, as it wasn't for you."

"Nah. It's for the boys you killed."

Ewan forced himself to remain still. He'd sent the money to the Rookery doctor, after having heard that the man had saved two of the boys harmed in the dock explosion that had been the final act of violence perpetrated against his brothers at his directive. He'd sent it via three layers of emissaries, not wanting the money to be tracked back to him. Not wanting to attract attention. Never wanting this conversation.

It seemed that three layers had not been enough.

"You weren't supposed to know," he said.

"We know everything that happens on our turf," Devil said.

"What do you want—you want me to apologize for wanting to help?"

Devil laughed again, the sound without humor, his gaze flickering past Ewan to Whit, behind him. "You hear this?" He returned his attention to Ewan. "This bastard blows up the Garden, comes for our men—kills five of them and maims another half dozen during two years of mayhem, and thinks a few 'undred quid is enough to wave it away?"

Five.

He closed his eyes, the number vicious in his mind. He'd been desperate to find her, then desperate to avenge her. But it didn't matter. Those were lives. Snuffed out. He hadn't pulled the trigger but he'd hired the men who had, and he hadn't thought twice, because he'd been after bigger game—his brothers.

He'd wanted them dead, thinking of nothing but their destruction for years. Mad with fury and grief and a desire for vengeance that rotted him from the inside.

They'd told him Grace was dead, and he'd spiraled away from morality and ethics, with no sorrow and less intent of ever coming back.

But she'd been alive.

And with that discovery had come another—the return of his humanity.

So, yes, he'd sent the money and asked for it to be distributed to those he had harmed. He'd grown up in the poverty of the Garden—he could still remember it. The stench of the offal shops and dogs fighting over scraps and the fights in the darkness. Hungry bellies and empty eyes. His mother's silent tears in the quiet moments when the men left, and the sky turned pink with dawn.

Death of a child, of a partner, of a friend—it could destroy a future. A whole batch of futures. And these bastards thought to keep the money from those who suffered? To what, punish him? For what, pride?

Fury rioted through him. "What do you think you do? That kind of money changes lives," he said, staring down first Devil and then Whit. "It could buy food, let homes, give children education. A life. A fucking future! Think of what we could have been if we'd had a few hundred pounds."

"Nah. A few hundred pounds wouldn't've made you a duke, though, would it?" Devil smirked, and Ewan wanted to tear him apart.

In the past two years, he'd learned everything he could about the Bareknuckle Bastards and how they operated—how they'd done everything they could to bring up Covent Garden. Doctors. Schools. Running water. His brothers—who would never claim him again—had made good on his long-ago promise. And in the dark of night, when he allowed it, Ewan was grateful for it.

So this—whatever it was—didn't make sense. "You toy with their lives to toy with me?"

"No," Whit said, the fury in his voice matching Ewan's. "*You* toy with them by thinking you can pay them for their sorrow and sleep well at night."

"I haven't slept well in twenty-two years."

Beast grunted at that.

"You're not fools. You know as well as I that money can help."

"Aye," said Devil. "And it will."

Confusion furrowed his brow. "You're keeping it."

"Course we're keepin' it!"

Fucking hell. "Then why—"

"'Cuz it ain't enough," Beast growled from behind. "We'll give them your money, but they deserve more. They'll be gettin' more."

He did not pretend to misunderstand. "But not money."

"Not *only* money," Devil corrected him.

"What, then? My head on a pike in Seven Dials? Are we back to who gets to kill the duke?"

"It still ain't the worst idea," Whit said, looking very much like he was sizing up Ewan's head for a strong stake.

"These aren't aristocrats, Marwick. These are real people, with real lives and real memories. And they don't want you paying them to leave off their anger and grief.

And if you ever thought a moment about your life before you became a toff, you'd know that."

A memory flashed at the words. Grace, inside the copse of trees on the western edge of the Burghsey estate. Their place. Devil and Whit had been playing in the distance, shouting and tilting at each other, inseparable like they'd always been, and Grace had asked him for the thousandth time to tell her about London.

He'd told her about the Garden—the only part of the city he'd known. The only part that had mattered. He'd told her about the people. About how they fought for everything they had. How they did it with pride and determination, because they couldn't afford anything less.

They don't get what they need, and not what they deserve, neither, he'd said. *But we're going to change all that.*

He hadn't made good on that promise.

But she had.

He looked to his brothers, knowing, instinctively, that they understood what Grace hadn't the other night. They weren't here to keep him from taking a debutante bride and carrying on the family name. They knew he'd sooner drown himself in the sludge of the Thames than touch a woman who wasn't Grace.

And that's when Ewan knew the worst of it. Whit and Devil were here to tell him he was to leave the Garden alone. That he was to leave *her* alone.

Impossible.

"I owe you; I won't argue with that," he said. "But I won't leave."

"You misunderstand, Duke," Devil said. "You don't owe us. You owe them. You don't need our forgiveness. You need the forgiveness of the Garden."

He'd never get it. But he wanted it.

We're going to change all that.

"You need the forgiveness of Grace," Devil added.

He wanted that, too. More. "How."

Whit grunted, then said, "I told you."

Devil smiled, his scar—the scar Ewan had put there with his own blade—pulling tight on his cheek. "Come and see us."

For the Garden? Or for Grace?

"And what, you make me a gladiator and feed me to the lions?"

"High opinion of your fighting, bruv," Whit said, dry as sand.

Devil's smile turned into a rich laugh. "You've been away from us for too long, toff." He popped his hat on his head, pulling it down low on his brow, so all that was left was his scar and the lower half of his face. "Come and see us to make amends, or we'll come back and take them."

He headed for the door, Whit coming shoulder to shoulder with him. Once there, the brother the Garden called Beast turned back to face him. "You didn't ask us."

"Ask you what?"

"Whether Grace made us promise not to kill you."

He didn't have to ask. He knew she had. He lifted his chin, refusing to ask the more important question. The one that would haunt his sleep.

"You didn't ask *why* she made us promise not to kill you."

That one.

He almost kept quiet. Almost. "Why?" The question came out harsher than he expected. More urgent.

Whit looked to Devil. "I told you."

Tap. Tap.

Whit looked back at him, and in that amber gaze he knew as well as his own, Ewan saw fury and betrayal and something else—something like sorrow. "It's what you did to her. What you owe her."

"What?" The word was out before he could take it back.

Devil looked at Whit, then back at him.

"Tell me, or get the fuck out," Ewan said, desperation in his voice.

Whit answered. "You broke her heart."

The words sent pain straight through him, sharp and ragged enough to have him raising a hand to his own chest.

Whit watched him for a moment, seeing the truth. "We don't have to wreck you," his quiet brother, who'd suffered so much at his hands, said. "She'll do the wrecking. And you won't for a minute think you don't deserve it."

Chapter Twelve

"They say she won't last the year."

Grace looked up from where she was checking the line of debits from the monthly ledger as Zeva and Veronique entered.

Today, Zeva wore an elaborate aubergine gown, shot through with silver and worth a fortune, and Grace admired the ensemble even as she shook her head at the other woman's utter disregard for practical dress. Veronique, on the other hand, wore breeches and a crisp white shirt, crisscrossed with a holster that held a pair of pistols at easy access beneath her arms. Grace couldn't remember a time when the head of the club security had been without her weapons, though they were not always so visible.

She waved the duo—different as chalk and cheese and somehow the perfect team—into the chairs opposite her desk. "Who won't last the year?"

"Victoria," Zeva said, simply.

"I assume we discuss the queen and not a member?" Grace's weekly meeting with her lieutenants almost always began with Zeva's read on the latest scandal sheets. More often than not, some excitement relating to members was involved.

"Good God, yes. Can you imagine Queen Victoria, a member?" Zeva laughed, then said, "It would be good for business, I suppose."

It would be terrible for business, Grace was certain.

"Anyway," the other woman went on. "I read it in the news—and with Dominion coming up, it seems it should be added to the betting book. No one thinks a woman can last as monarch for any legitimate length of time."

"You mean no *man* believes that," Veronique snorted, crossing one buckskin-covered leg over the other and relaxing into her chair. "Women can easily remember that Elizabeth existed."

"And rode men into battle," Grace pointed out.

"Sadly, did not ride men in any other way, poor virgin queen," Zeva said. "A bit like you, Dahlia."

"That's not what I hear," Veronique said slyly.

Grace snapped her attention to her lieutenant. "What was that?"

Zeva's eyes went wide and she flashed a smile broad enough to be seen from the rooftops beyond the window. "Oh, yes, let's investigate! What was that?"

Veronique shrugged. "The girls talk."

"The girls shouldn't talk," Grace said.

"You pay them to talk."

"Not about me!"

Zeva's attention bounced between them as though she watched shuttlecock. "What about her?"

"She went to Marwick's ball," Veronique said, waving a hand through the air, as though that would be enough information for Zeva. Forgetting that no amount of information was enough for Zeva.

Grace looked back at her ledger, the numbers swimming

on the page as she willed the floor to open up and drag her to another, faraway land.

"Well, we knew she was doing that," Zeva said.

"Yes, but apparently she didn't spend all her time in the ballroom."

"So?" A pause. A weighty, information-filled pause. "Oh. Ohhhhh." Another pause, and a wolfish grin. "Where *did* she spend her time?"

"In the gardens," Veronique whispered, loud enough for the entire building to hear.

"Dahlia! I must say," Zeva said, putting a hand to her breast. "I'm really quite proud of you."

Grace rolled her eyes.

"Well, we did suggest she get herself some fantasy," Veronique said, smartly.

"Enough!"

"How interesting." Another pause. "This is the same duke you beat black and blue a year ago? The one who wanted to make you his duchess?"

Not just duchess.

You are a queen. Tonight, I am your throne.

Her cheeks flushed at the memory of the words. Perhaps they wouldn't notice.

"Oh, *interesting* . . ." Zeva said, noticing, of course. She paid Zeva to notice, as well.

"Tell me," Grace said. "How is it you both are so very certain that I will not sack you?"

"For what, doing our job?"

Silence fell in the wake of the question. Veronique wasn't amused. From the moment she joined Grace to build 72 Shelton Street, she'd managed the safety of the club's members and staff with unwavering commitment. The only time she was not at the club was when her husband's ship was in port—and even then, the captain joined her on the premises more often than not.

Grace should have expected she would have been followed. Over the years, she and Veronique had built a vast network of young spies throughout Covent Garden and beyond—housemaids and tavern girls and roof runners for messages. Criminals throughout London—throughout the world—used children as pickpockets and drunkblades because no one ever noticed children, but Grace found that girls were even more likely to be overlooked. Overlooked, and underpaid. And so she had made a point of giving girls good pay and even more power. They brought information to Veronique and Grace whenever there was news to be had—the more interesting the better.

Her donning a ball gown and heading into Mayfair was certainly interesting.

Still, Grace didn't like it.

What else had they reported? Had they seen what had happened in the gazebo?

Zeva cleared her throat and said, "Yes, well, well done everyone. What were we discussing?"

You are a queen.

It was Grace's turn to clear her throat. "Queens."

She shouldn't think of it. It had been a mistake. One night, lost to memory and nostalgia. To what might have been. He hadn't even known it was she. Of course, now it seemed that all of Covent Garden knew that it was she.

Christ. This was what she got for buying fantasy instead of selling it.

Zeva was still talking. "Well, I for one sincerely believe that Elizabeth Regina would have been a proud member of 72 Shelton."

"She'd have to get in line," Grace said, welcoming the change of topic, laying a hand on a stack of new membership requests. "We grow more popular by the minute. I've three duchesses and, from what I can tell, the leader of a small country in here."

"That's what I want to discuss," Veronique interjected. "I'm concerned about our growing popularity."

Zeva sighed, "Ah, Veronique, ever the raincloud."

Veronique shot the other woman a look. "We cannot all occupy ourselves with proper canapés." She looked to Grace. "All I am saying is we've signed twenty-one new member agreements in the last month—"

"Twenty-three," Zeva corrected.

"Fine. And there's no sign that interest is waning. So, if we intend to continue to increase membership . . ." Veronique paused, catching Grace's eye. "And I assume that we are?"

"I see no reason why we wouldn't," Grace said.

"Then we are going to require more security." The head of 72 Shelton's security detail spread her hands wide and sat back in her chair, on the opposite side of Grace's desk. Casting a discerning gaze over the haphazard towers of newsprint, member dossiers, bank documents, and bills, she added, "At the very least, we're going to need a dedicated guard outside this room to rescuc you when you become trapped beneath the avalanche of paper that will one day bring you down."

"Nonsense. I know where everything is," Grace said, as Zeva laughed from her place. "How many do we need?"

Veronique did not hesitate. "Five."

Grace's brows shot up. As 72 Shelton was both a women's club that prized discretion and a brothel that prized safety, it already had a fifteen-person security detail that worked in three shifts, round the clock. "Do you expect a run of murders?"

"There was a brawl three nights ago at Maggie O'Tiernen's."

"There is a brawl every three nights at Maggie O'Tiernen's," Grace said. The pub was legendary for its brash Irish proprietress, who loved nothing more than urging brawny sailors to fight for her honor—and the honor of keeping her company for an evening. "No one likes a spectacle like Maggie."

"I hear it wasn't an ordinary brawl," Veronique said.

"Incited by someone?" Zeva asked.

"No one can confirm it," Veronique replied, "but I don't like it. Not on top of Satchell's."

A gaming hell for ladies, Satchell's had been open for less than a year, but was already beloved of aristocratic women—in part because it was discreet, lushly appointed, and frequented by the Duchess of Trevescan, who was the kind of patroness any new business would do crime to have, a sparkling jewel with just enough scandal to make wherever she went seem worthy of time and funds.

Of course, Grace had known the duchess for long enough to know that she was interested in places where women congregated, full stop. "What happened at Satchell's?"

"It was raided."

Grace stilled. "By whom?"

"Could be competitors." Veronique picked at something invisible on her breeches.

"Could be," Grace repeated. Running a business based on vice didn't exactly put a body in league with the best of men. "The queen's got everyone looking to make money on women."

"We're proof it's good business," Zeva interjected.

Veronique shrugged. "Could be. Could also be the Crown. Could be Peel's boys." The newly minted metropolitan police force, eager to make a name for itself. "Men drunk on power and wielding clubs and fists and firearms all look the same."

Grace nodded, something twisting in her gut. "Could be."

"We don't do anything illegal," Zeva said. She was right. Prostitution wasn't illegal. Neither were private clubs. The most illegal thing they did was pour smuggled liquor—but so did every men's club in Mayfair.

Of course, they weren't a men's club in Mayfair. And that put them in danger. "No one likes it when women take their pleasure into their own hands," Veronique said.

"No one likes it when women take their *lives* into their own hands," Grace said.

If they were raided, no one would need to know what the members were up to in the Garden. The list of members' names alone would scandalize Britain.

"We've a thousand enemies, the Crown, the police, and our competition only the most visible." Grace looked to Veronique. "The Other Side was closed two weeks ago."

Veronique's brows rose. "That's three." She had the best sense for trouble Grace had ever known—something born of her time on ships. She knew when a match would burn out, and when one would light an inferno. If she believed something was happening, something likely was.

The Other Side. Maggie O'Tiernen's. Satchell's. Three places that catered to a female membership. All threatened in recent weeks.

"Peck?" Tommy Peck, Bow Street Runner. One of the decent ones, if his care for the girls in the Garden was any indication.

Veronique shook her head. "He hasn't been seen." She paused. "And there's another thing."

"Go on."

"I've reason to believe the building is being watched."

Grace didn't like that. "How? We've guns on the roof and spies on all the others."

Veronique shrugged. "Can't prove it. Strange faces havin' a wander. Boots awful shiny for Cheapside boys."

Better safe than sorry. "Hire the security. And make sure the tunnels are clear before Dominion." Before Grace had taken it over and turned 72 Shelton Street into an exclusive women's club, the building had been an old smugglers' hideout, with secret tunnels running hundreds of yards in multiple directions, in case of attack from other smugglers—or the Crown.

Nothing that happened inside the brothel was illegal, so she'd never thought too much about them, except in two instances—first, they were regularly used to bring guests to the club who were not trusted to know its location and, second, they were sometimes prepared for entertainment—periodically a member took an interest in the idea of a dungeon.

But she knew better than most that where there were women in power, there were too often men who would stop at nothing to snatch it from them, and she would do whatever was necessary to protect the staff and clients of 72 Shelton.

Veronique nodded, apparently satisfied. "Done."

"What's next?"

The rest of the conversation ranged over the inner workings of the club—the arrogant and brilliant chef that Grace had brought in from Venice, who was constantly at odds with the pastry chef with a streak of the perfectionist. The preparations for September's Dominion two weeks hence—the first of the autumn, and always the most elaborate. The arrival of a unique trio—two men, and a woman with a particular skill with ropes that filled a specific void in the services the club was able to offer members.

After three quarters of an hour, Zeva and Veronique were through with their reports. They'd stood to leave, and made their way to the door before Zeva turned back. "One more thing."

Grace looked to her lieutenant.

"There's a new bill in debate in Lords. Loads of good in

it—safety for molls, punishment for culls who do them ill, age restrictions for workhouses, fresh water pipes for the rookeries."

All issues directly affecting Covent Garden and the East End. Surprise flared. "Whose bill?"

"Lamont and Leighton."

Two of the most decent dukes in Britain. "Who is debating it?"

A little shrug. "The good ones."

Grace shook her head. "It won't pass. There aren't enough lords who care about our world." If one thing was true, it was that rich aristocrats steered wildly clear of taking care of the poor.

Zeva nodded. "Well. They talk, anyway."

"Let me know when they do more." She looked to Veronique. "And tell the girls that my private business is just that—private."

Veronique smirked. "What private business?"

Grace couldn't help her little huff of amusement, the sound lost to the tentative knock at the door. With a tilt of her head, she opened it, revealing the fresh face of a girl of twelve or thirteen. Her grey-green eyes slid from Veronique to Zeva, then behind, to Grace, when they rounded in surprise and flew back to her employer. "I—they told me downstairs to come up."

"Report," Veronique said.

The girl pulled off her cap, releasing a riot of black curls, and looked to Grace, her nervousness clear.

Grace smiled, remembering her own nervousness at that age—and how she had learned fast to push it away when with adults, for fear of revealing weakness that was too easy to take advantage of. "Go on then."

"'Ere's a visitor."

Grace stood at the word. A code.

"Where?" Veronique asked.

"The Rookery."

Grace came around the desk. For years, her spies had been tasked with watching Devil and Whit in the Rookery where they lived and worked—to ensure that her impulsive brothers were not dragged into hotheaded trouble. Since Grace had inherited sisters-in-law, however, news from the Rookery had slowed to a trickle. It seemed her brothers had turned their hotheaded trouble into the more valuable work of loving their wives.

But this report—a visitor in the Rookery—indicated that something uncommon was happening there . . . something that wasn't right.

A visitor wasn't as innocuous as it sounded. It meant a stranger. Usually someone out of place, asking questions that weren't his business. Often, it meant someone asking questions about the Bareknuckle Bastards. The girls were trained to pay close attention and immediately report whenever anyone came asking about two young boys and a girl who might have turned up years earlier.

But they hadn't been in hiding for a year—the freedom still fresh enough that Grace didn't take it for granted. "What kind of visitor?"

The girl looked to Veronique, who nodded. "Go on."

"He's a big brute. Haulin' boxes to the warehouse for the Bastards," she said.

A ship had come into port the day before, and would have been emptied the previous evening.

Evening.

She watched the girl, who shoved her hands in her pockets and shuffled her feet, clearly hesitating. Grace recognized the uncertainty. The girl had a hunch. A hunch Grace had, as well.

"That doesn't sound out of the ordinary," she said, approaching. "What made you come here?"

Those enormous eyes lifted to hers. "It's full sun."

Correct. The Bareknuckle Bastards didn't move cargo in the daylight. It was too risky.

What were they up to?

Grace nodded. "So it is. What's your name?"

"Victoria, mum." The girl bobbed fast as she could—an East End curtsy.

Surprised by the name, Grace looked to Zeva and Veronique, taking in their knowing smiles. "Well, I wouldn't lay odds against this one, at least." She reached into her pocket and tossed a coin to the girl, who caught it out of the air with a speed that rivaled her own as a child.

The girl would have made a great fighter—but she'd never have to prove that, because she'd have work with Grace as long as she wanted it.

"You did well, Victoria. Thank you."

Another bob, and the girl was headed for the door, almost there before she seemed to remember something and turned back.

"Oh, and there's another thing . . ." The girl paused, fiddling with her cap, then found her voice more quickly than before. "They say 'e's a toff."

Chapter Thirteen

She found her idiot brothers exactly where she expected to find them—on the rooftops overlooking the yard of the Bastards' warehouse, deep in the Covent Garden Rookery.

"Don't get too close," she said as she approached them, having used the vast network of the Garden's maze of interconnected buildings to get to them. "You wouldn't like someone with sense to push you right over the edge."

Devil looked over his shoulder at her, his brows rising in amusement. Of course he was amused. Devil liked nothing better than playing puppeteer with those around him. "Ah! You're here! And just as it's getting interesting."

Her heart pounded as she drew closer, tilting her head, expecting to hear jeers and hoots from the yard below, where a crowd had no doubt assembled to watch whatever elaborate scheme her brothers had concocted.

She was surprised to hear quiet instead.

Quiet made her heart pound harder. Quiet was more dangerous.

Grace came abreast of them, and they eased aside, making space between them for her as they'd done for two decades, since the night they'd run. And as unsettled as she was high on that rooftop, she was never so at home as she was with these men—brothers in name if not blood, and proof that family was found, not born.

But that did not mean they would not feel her wrath if they'd mucked everything up.

She took a deep breath and followed their gazes down over the edge of the roof, taking in the yard below, where the afternoon sun cast long shadows into the enormous rectangular space, flanked on all sides by the massive warehouse owned by the Bareknuckle Bastards.

A web of inside corridors connected the buildings, accessible only through the main entrance at the far end of the yard, where Annika, the tall Norwegian genius who ran the Bastards' business operation, stood framed in the great sliding doorway of the warehouse, against the pitch darkness of the interior. Nik was flanked by a quartet of men who hauled for a living, arms crossed over their broad chests, box hooks in hand. The five stood sentry, unmoving.

Watching.

As everyone else watched. The yard was packed with people, the crowd two deep—three in places—men and women, old and young. Grace recognized the Rookery's baker on the eastern edge of the crowd, towering behind a collection of the boys she knew hauled fresh water around the neighborhood. A few of the girls who worked the streets stood in the long shadow of the western wall. Even the doctor's wife had made an appearance.

It took Grace a moment to see what they all saw.

Lie.

She saw him the moment she looked over the edge, at the center of the yard, alone. He was in shirtsleeves, cuffs rolled to his elbows, revealing the muscles of his forearms, straining as he hefted a block of ice three-feet square, held by a length of rough rope over his shoulder.

Those muscles were the only thing about him that did not scream *duke*. He didn't have to speak a word for them to know where he came from. There was nothing about him that hid it.

Grace wondered where his coat was, as it was impossible to believe that he'd come without it, or a waistcoat. Or a cravat. Or a hat. As for trousers, they molded to his thighs and were not designed for the Rookery—their color too light to hide the dirt and grime of the Garden.

His face did not hide the truth, either. It didn't matter that his long nose had been broken when they were children—a well-placed blow on Devil's part—or that it was streaked with dirt and perspiration. The angles of it were all wrong, sharp and aristocratic, with even the bump on his nose seeming to have a Mayfair accent.

All that, and he was still the handsomest thing she'd ever seen.

No wonder the girls had sent word about him; he didn't belong here.

He looked every inch the duke he was.

Every inch the enemy.

And the Garden knew it.

All around the edge of the yard, they watched, reveling in his mistakes—the absence of a hook to haul the ice, the lack of a leather shoulder guard to protect his skin from the rough rub of the rope, the gloves that had been made for horses' reins and walking sticks rather than hard work and wear.

"Truly, it is a miracle you two lived to adulthood. And found women to marry you," she said softly. "It's a good thing they're brilliant, else I would dearly fear for your progeny. What sort of punishment is this? You've got him hauling ice? Has he seen the cargo that came packed in it? Because letting a duke near your smuggled goods is truly, madly stupid."

"He's not anywhere near the true cargo," Devil said.

"No?"

"Nah. He's just hauling the last of the ice."

"How much is the last of it?"

Devil looked to Beast. "What, eighty?"

Beast shrugged. "One hundred?"

One hundred blocks of ice, each one easily fifty pounds. And without a hook. His hands would be blistered from the ropes. His shoulders, too. He wore none of the protection that haulers traditionally wore. Her jaw clenched. "How many has he done?"

"Ten? A dozen?"

She shook her head. He wouldn't be able to do much more. He wasn't a hauler. He hadn't been born with a hook in his hand.

And still, it looked like he would never stop. Something tightened in her throat, watching him in the dirt, in this part of the city that had been his before it had belonged to any of them. "So you set a duke down in the middle of the Garden, and expect him to walk away unscathed?"

"I wouldn't say we expect that, no," Devil said.

"Mmm," Beast agreed. "I think we're rather hoping he wouldn't."

"I thought we agreed you didn't touch him?"

Devil looked at her and spread his arms wide. "I'm on the roof, Gracie. So far away it's like I was never even here."

"Still, you're starting something, and he won't stop till it's finished," she said. "You know that."

"*He* started it," Whit said.

She cut him a look. "What does that mean?"

He grunted. "He came looking to pay his debts."

"His debts."

"Wot, we weren't supposed to take him up on the offer?" Devil said. "Ten thousand and some sound work in the Garden is a lot to pass up."

Ten thousand pounds. "For the families?"

It was a fortune.

Beast turned on her, his amber eyes, usually so soft, turned hard, and his voice to match. "Five men, and it ain't enough." The words were clipped, tight on his tongue, and Grace felt the sting of them, like a wet lash. "He owes them, and you'd do well to remember that."

Her face went hot with his censure, and she spoke to his profile. "You think I don't remember?"

He did not look at her. "I think you've always had trouble remembering the truth of him."

She bit back a sound of frustration, hating the way her chest tightened at the words. What did she care one way or another what happened to Ewan?

Not Ewan.

She watched him cross the yard again, his back to her. The muscles of his back were visible through his now-wet shirt. They rippled beneath the weight, and her mouth went dry.

Marwick. That was the truth of him, whether he was dressed for dukedom or not.

Grace tore her attention away from him, instead fixing on the crowd that watched in near silence. There was nothing easy about the quiet—she'd lived in Covent Garden long enough to know the difference between calm and tension. And everybody below seemed to hang in suspension, waiting for the chance to take this duke and make an example of him.

Rich, powerful, entitled.

And for no reason but birth.

Except he hadn't had all that at birth. At birth, he'd been one of them.

But they didn't know that. No one did. No one ever would, with the exception of the Bareknuckle Bastards. Even if someone in the Rookery did remember the blond bean of a boy, whelp of a moll on Tavistock Row, they'd never match him to the duke before them—it didn't matter how much ice he hauled.

"They're ready for a fight," she said quietly. How many times had she seen them like this? On the balls of their feet, ready for a brawl.

Beast grunted his agreement.

"Of course they are. They love it," Devil said. "A duke in the muck? It's like watching a hound recite Shakespeare."

"And so? You expect him to give it to them?"

"He's smart enough to know the Garden wants its fight, and they won't settle for less. And if he wants forgiveness—"

"He wants forgiveness?"

Devil cut her a look. "Not from us." He lifted his chin in the direction of the yard. "From them."

She watched as he set the ice at the feet of one of the bruisers at the warehouse door, and a whisper of memory ran through her. *They don't get what they deserve.* He'd said it to her when they were children. About these people. About this place.

He turned to make his way back across the yard.

We're going to change all that.

As though he'd heard the words, he looked up to the rooftop, his gaze immediately finding her. For a heartbeat, he stilled—not long enough for anyone to notice.

Grace noticed.

He lifted his chin in recognition, and she resisted the urge to respond.

Whatever this was, whatever his plan, it was not enough.

It would never be enough.

She tracked him back across the yard, her gaze following the lines of him, over the shirt that clung to him, revealing his broad chest and the ridges of muscle that he'd developed in the year he'd been gone, the opening at the neck revealing a wicked patch of raw, red skin on his left shoulder, and a hint of the edge of the stark white scar that had been there since they were children.

The mark his father had left on him when he'd discovered Ewan's most prized secret—love. The old duke had found them curled together in the darkness on a summer evening, wrapped in each other's warmth—a warmth Grace could still remember if she allowed herself to—and he'd gone mad with rage.

No heir of mine will lie with the dreck that came from her bitch of a mother, he'd screamed, coming for her.

Ewan had defended her, but his father had been stronger, with six inches and a hundred pounds on him. He'd taken Ewan to the ground and left his sadistic mark on him, as she watched.

And the next day, everything had been different.

The boy she'd loved was gone.

He'd betrayed them days later.

"What's he doing here?" she asked, pushing the thought away. "Hauling ice doesn't win you and it most definitely doesn't win the Rookery. If anything, it riles them up."

"He's back for you," Devil said, simply, not looking away from Marwick's movement below.

The words ripped through her along with the memory of his touch in the gardens earlier in the week. Along with his whispered questions—urging her to tell him her name. Along with the whisper of doubt that had chased her away in the end . . . the sense that perhaps he had known it all along.

She shook her head, having no other choice but to disagree. "He isn't."

Why did the words feel like a lie?

What if he is?

She ignored the thought and spoke to the yard, "He's on the marriage mart."

"Yes," Devil drawled. "That would be a problem, if it were true. But it's not."

She looked at him. "What?"

Beast grunted. "It's a trap."

"A trap for whom?" she asked. "He can't think I would . . ." She trailed off, the words lost to the memory of the way she'd turned herself over to him in the gardens of his ball. "He can't think he can win me back."

Devil stared at her for a long moment. "Can't he?"

She stiffened. "No."

"All right then," Devil said, thoroughly agreeable, and utterly infuriating.

"It's a trap," Beast repeated.

Without thinking, she looked back at Ewan, letting her gaze track over the ridges and planes of his chest, down over his muscled thighs and then back up, slowly—slower than she should have been, over the beautiful planes of his face, more proof that the boy was gone.

This was no boy.

She met his eyes, not knowing what to expect. Definitely not expecting the knowing curve of his lips, the rise of one blond brow, as though he had witnessed every inch of her perusal. As though he'd liked it. He lifted his chin in her direction, as though to acknowledge her careful inspection, a knight in tourney, searching for his lady's favor.

Where in hell had that come from?

She was no lady, and he was certainly no knight.

"Oy! Duke!"

"There it is," Devil said, softly. "They don't like the way he looks at you, Dahlia."

Grace barely heard it, too busy watching the duke in question as he ignored the shout. Ignored, but heard—the proof of the hearing in the way his long strides slowed, just barely. Another movement that one would notice only if she was really looking.

Grace noticed it.

Ignoring the way the realization unsettled, she said, "I suppose you told them everything?"

"Nah," Devil said, casually, one hand in his pocket, rocking back on his heels. "If we'd told them everything, he'd've been dead the moment he showed his face. We just told them that he was a duke."

She slid him a look. "What sort of duke?"

Letting Covent Garden into his voice, Devil flashed her a grin, his scar gleaming white on his cheek. The scar Ewan had put there twenty years earlier. "The sort wot deserves what 'e gets."

It was true, she reminded herself. And this crowd would give it to him today.

"I didn't expect the O'Malleys out of the gate first, though."

Beast grunted. "The O'Malleys are always first out of the gate." He looked to the sun, creeping lower over the west edge of the yard. "And at this hour? Patrick O'Malley's already soused enough to go up against a duke."

Patrick O'Malley was a proper bruiser who was ever ready for a fight. He stepped out from the crowd. "You think you can just climb down into the muck wiv us? Slum it for a bit, until the work starts to sting, and then go back to polishin' yer knob wiv the rest of your kind, tellin' tales of yer time in the Garden? You think we're a lark?"

They didn't know Ewan had been born in the Garden.

They didn't know he had no interest in ever telling tales of his time here.

"If O'Malley starts it, the whole place'll finish it," Beast said. "The duke doesn't know what a boon he just got—men'll take his side just for the pleasure of goin' in against the O'Malley brothers."

She looked to her brothers. "You're asking for a riot."

Devil shrugged. "Nah. It won't be a riot. It'll just be a proper brawl. As God intended."

"And if he dies? Who'll hang for it?" she said, sensing that the whole thing was about to get far out of hand.

"Do you forget how he fights, Gracie?" Whit asked.

"Don't Gracie me," she snapped. "I'm not a child."

Whit looked to Devil. "I told you."

Her brows snapped together. "Told him what?"

Devil sighed. "So you did."

"Told him *what*?"

Beast looked back to the ground. "I'm only sayin' that the young Duke of Marwick fights like Lucifer himself. He isn't going to die."

"I'm talkin' to you, Duke," Patrick O'Malley shouted below. "You want the full taste of the Garden, I've got it for you."

Ewan didn't reply, except to rope another block of ice from the wagon immediately beneath them and head back to the warehouse, keeping his focus on the door where a man with a strong hook and a stronger back leaned against the jamb, arms like tree trunks crossed over his chest, waiting. Refusing to meet the duke halfway.

The crowd tightened, taking up more space in the warehouse yard.

Grace swore. "This is madness."

A clump of mud smacked Ewan on the back of the head. He stilled. Stiffened.

O'Malley approached, wiping his dirty hands on his already filthy trousers. "*I said*, I'm talkin' to you, Duke."

"He'll take that bait," Devil said.

Beast grunted his reply. "Can't help it. Never could back down."

Memory flashed, Ewan reeling from a solid punch when they were children. Turning instantly, swinging, coming back for more.

Far below, he rounded on Patrick O'Malley.

"Fifty quid says he's down in under two."

Grace turned surprised eyes on Devil. "You think Ewan goes down?"

He raised a black brow. "You don't?"

She didn't.

Beast removed two watches from his pocket, eyes still on the yard, seeing the way the people assembled fairly vibrated with excitement. The heat and the crowd making them ready for riot. "Two minutes? Or seconds?"

Devil laughed. "Be generous, bruv."

Beast looked down at his watches, then back at Ewan, turned to face them now, scanning the crowd . . . then up, over the buildings. To the rooftops. His gaze lingered on them. On her.

Beast saw it. "Aye, alright. I'll take your money."

"You think 'e's still got it?" Devil sounded surprised.

He still had it, Grace thought.

Beast nodded to Grace. "I think he's always had it when she's in the mix."

She shot him a look. "I'm not in the mix."

And in that split second, while she was looking away, hell broke loose below.

Chapter Fourteen

She'd come for him.

It had been a calculated risk—he'd known without question that whatever punishment Devil and Whit had designed for him would end with him battered and bruised, and likely by more than just his brothers.

But he'd also known that this might be the only chance he'd have of her coming to him. He'd made himself a promise, that he'd stay away from her. That he'd let her come to him. That he'd give her what she asked.

That's what he had done. He'd gone away, and he'd rebuilt himself a better man. A worthier one. Stronger. Saner. And he would wait for her to come for him, because that was what she needed.

It did not matter that all he needed was her.

But when his brothers demanded he return to the Garden and pay his debts with sweat and blood as well as money, he'd agreed, unable to resist the invitation to this world that had once been his and was now theirs. Hers.

It was a cheat, he knew. A way around the promise he'd made to let her come to him. To let her choose him, unmasked. It might be a cheat, but he was not beyond cheating to win her back.

So he'd taken the knocks and carried the ice, feeling every inch a spectacle, the sole focus of a crowd of people who were out for blood. They didn't know his truth—that he'd stood in countless similar crowds. That he'd watched men and dogs and bears fight, and he'd cut his teeth on the bloodlust that came from a world where cruelty was commonplace and inhumanity was armor.

He'd always imagined that his father saw that in him from the start.

The sheer want of a boy willing to do anything to survive. To thrive. To win.

And he hefted the weight for the crowd, hearing every shift in it, every quiet threat in it—the way some watched with admiration and others with anger and others with disdain, hating the fine lawn of his shirt, the polish of his boots, the clean shave of his jaw. The trappings of money and power, distributed at random. At birth.

They didn't know he didn't come by them randomly.

They didn't know they'd been hers at birth.

He'd dropped the dozenth block at the door of the warehouse and turned back to fetch another, knowing that the only way out of the exercise was through—it would end with fatigue or fighting. Those were the only options, and he would never let the first happen.

He'd learned his pride in the Garden, as well as any of them.

He slowed his pace a touch—only as much as he could without attracting notice—taking the extra fractions of seconds to stretch his shoulders—only as much as he could without attracting notice. His left shoulder was on fire, rubbed raw by the rough rope he used to carry the massive blocks of ice.

He didn't dare draw attention to the pain. Instead, he

stretched his neck under the guise of perusing the crowd, first on the ground and then up, on the rooftops.

She'd come for him.

She was flanked by his brothers, who had been watching from the start, Devil smiling like an ass and Whit looking like he was ready to do murder. But Ewan had no interest in them.

He didn't care, as long as she didn't leave. As long as he could drink her in, the long lines of her made longer by her black breeches, tight to her legs. By her black leather boots, wrapping up over her knees, by her long black coat, billowing back in the wind, lined in a glittering sapphire silk.

He liked that lining very much—the nod to her love of color. The proof that something was left of the girl he'd loved, even if she'd grown into this woman who looked down on him like a fucking queen.

High above on the rooftops, watching her warrior.

And him, ready to do anything for her favor.

The wind lifted her hair up and back behind her and the sun caught it, turning it to flame. Turning *him* to flame, as it revealed her face. Unmasked.

Unmasked and perfect, her eyes on him. Everywhere. He bathed in her scrutiny, wanting to spread his arms wide beneath it, loving the way she assessed his muscles beneath his damp clothes, loving the way her gaze lingered on his burning shoulder, somehow easing the pain. Loving the slide of her gaze up his neck and over his face.

Christ, he loved it.

He saw her throat work.

Saw her lips part on a breath.

And when she met his eyes, he saw that she liked it, too.

He lifted his face to her, acknowledging her attention. Wondering what she would do if he scaled the damn wall to get to her.

She'd probably push him over the side, but the idea had

merit, and for a moment he imagined an alternative—him coming up over the edge of the roof, lifting her in his arms, and stealing her away to somewhere private, where he could give her enough pleasure to make her forget all the pain he'd wrought.

"Oy! Duke!"

He was pulled from the thought by the shout from the crowd, his well-honed instincts immediately refocusing his thoughts. The bark had come from his left, and he slowed, turning his head just barely—not enough to look at the enemy, but enough to locate him.

He didn't have to do much to see him, a big, broad bastard who seemed like he'd never refused a fight. The crowd assembled seemed to spit the bruiser out, landing him several feet into the yard, a half-dozen yards from Ewan. Finding himself with an audience, the man did what men with a little strength and far less sense tended to do.

He blustered.

Instead of listening, Ewan roped another block of ice and focused on the crowd, knowing that if the Irishman started a brawl, the Garden would finish it. And Ewan would be in the thick of it. Pleasure shot through him at the idea. He was good for the fight.

He'd been good for a fight for days. For decades.

Hefting the heavy weight, he ignored the wicked burn at his shoulder and made his way back across the yard, this time able to see the man who would come for him first. Able to recognize the slur in his Irish brogue. Able to register his slight swerve—a need for balance, even as he stood still.

The man was drunk. Which meant a fight was on.

The crowd knew it, too. They circled, closing in on Ewan. Building him a ring. He kept his gaze on the far end of the yard, but watched the faces, a dozen screwed tight already. More willing to jump into the fray when there was one for the jumping.

How many would he have to fight?

A clump of mud smacked Ewan on the back of the head.

He stilled. Stiffened. Turned.

The bruiser approached. "I'm talkin' to you, Duke."

He was eight feet away.

Six.

Ewan looked to the rooftops, where Grace watched, riveted, just like the rest of the Garden. His heart pounded, and his chest broadened.

He wanted to show her what he was still able to do.

Four.

Ewan set the ice down.

Two.

When the blow came, he was ready.

He caught the other man's fist in his hand, startling him. Ewan's brows rose as the Irishman's jaw slackened. "Don't expect a duke to have a right hook, do you?" he said softly, letting the Garden seep into his voice.

His opponent's eyes went wide at the words, and then he scowled. "You ain't got nuffin' yet, toffer." He followed the words with a massive swing of his free hand—fisted to the size of a ham.

Ewan dodged the blow and straightened, planting his fist directly into the face of his attacker. "How about now?"

If there was a reply, it was lost in the roar that sounded from all around them, echoing off the brick walls of the warehouse. For a moment, Ewan thought perhaps it was the sound of the thrill of an audience—how interesting could his hauling ice have been for them? But then he heard the sounds of fists meeting flesh. Everywhere.

It wasn't the thrill of the audience. It was the thrill of the fight.

The whole yard had been watching, waiting, wanting a shot at their own blows. And now, they'd been gifted a proper brawl.

He landed a second blow—a sharp uppercut that knocked his opponent back on his feet, snapping his head properly back on his neck, but before the other man could catch his balance and return to their fight, a hand grasped Ewan's raw shoulder, sending fire through him as it pulled him around to face him.

He roared the agony of the touch, his blows already launched as he came to face another man, who happily took a punch to the nose before setting his own fist firmly into Ewan's gut.

The Duke of Marwick hunched over the blow, but recovered quickly, coming back to his full height and the admiration of his new opponent. "You ain't like any duke I've ever seen," the man said.

"I ain't like any duke anyone has ever seen," he replied, and the two were back at it—sparring until another man launched himself into the fight, wanting his own chance to bring down the duke who'd come into the Garden.

And so it went for seconds, minutes, hours—time was lost with dodging blows and throwing his own, making sure they were soft enough when they landed that they didn't do real damage. He knew why he'd been brought here—to take his knocks. And he would do just that.

Proving to the Bareknuckle Bastards that the money wasn't all he offered.

Giving the Garden the fight they wanted—on equal footing, no titles or power or money or privilege changing the outcome of the game.

And giving her a look at the man he had become.

Grace.

Just the thought of her was enough to pull his attention from the fight, just enough to miss a dodge and take a strong punch directly to the nose. Pain knocked his head round, and when the stars subsided, he couldn't help himself—he looked to the rooftops once more.

She was gone.

He froze. A mistake, as another bruiser leapt into the fray to have a go at him. He blocked a swing, pushing the man into another crowd that happily swallowed him up for their own fight.

She was gone, but his brothers remained. Whit watched with intense scrutiny, as though he was learning how to exploit any weakness in Ewan's strategy for his own purposes, and Devil observed with a smirk that made Ewan wish he could scale buildings for the second time that afternoon—this time to wipe the smile off his arrogant brother's face.

Where had she gone?

Why hadn't they gone with her?

Was she safe?

Another round of sparring pulled him away from the rooftops, a half-dozen fighters coming from all directions. Fighting dirty. A hand grabbing his hair, another at the waist of his trousers. A third with a club of some sort. He raised a brow. "Unsportsmanlike, that."

The brute grinned—revealing a handful of missing teeth, and took a swing. Ewan dodged the blow, just barely, but was not out of danger. Someone grabbed him from behind, slipping one arm beneath his own, and a second around his neck. Holding him tight. Choking him. He struggled, the other men closing in, taking leisurely shots at his torso.

The blows were enough to take the breath from him, and he looked up to the rooftop, meeting first Whit's eyes, then Devil's. Neither of his brothers moved to help.

Neither of them would save him.

The arm around his throat tightened, and Devil reached out a gloved hand, extending his thumb. Ewan understood instantly.

And what, you make me a gladiator and feed me to the lions?

Devil snapped his thumb down, to face the earth.

As though waiting for the emperor's ruling, the arm at Ewan's neck tightened. He reached up to grab it, unable to get a decent grip. He shouldn't have pulled his punches with this one.

He looked back at his brothers, high above. Whit was talking, his eyes on something beyond. Devil's attention followed.

They didn't even care to watch him die.

The roar of the crowd had lessened, replaced by a different roar, this one in his ears. He was losing consciousness. The air around him was stilling, the brawl seeming to quiet. He leaned his head forward in a last effort to break the hold. He snapped his head back, connecting with the nose of the man behind him, who cried out in pain and released him.

Ewan pulled loose and turned. It was the original Irishman. No. A different one, but with the same face. The same meaty arms. Brothers?

How must that feel? he thought as he stumbled back, gasping for breath. *To have brothers who stand with you?*

He'd known how it felt once.

Ignoring the blood that streamed from his nose—it seemed Ewan had broken it—the man came for him once again, no doubt to finish the job that had been interrupted.

He backed away, slowly, expecting another set of hands and fists to come from another direction. They didn't. Instead, silence came.

And it wasn't in his head.

The fight had come to a stop, all around him.

No. The fight had *been* stopped, all around him. He looked to the rooftops, where his brothers remained sentry.

Broken Nose's attention flickered to something in the distance, over Ewan's shoulder, and whatever he saw there had him coming up short. Whatever it was, it brought restraint to the Garden—a place where restraint was virtually unheard of.

Not knowing what to expect, Ewan turned to look.

And there she was.

Their queen.

No. Not theirs.

She didn't spare the crowd a look as she parted it like the sea, her hair a riot of flame around her shoulders, her black coat, perfectly tailored, blowing back to reveal the sapphire lining somehow pristine in the dirt, a match to the pristine sapphire corset she wore, designed, clearly, to be worn just so, above trousers, without shame. Everyday wear.

And at her waist, the scarlet scarf he remembered from a year earlier—not a nod to frivolity or a whimsical belt . . . a weapon.

There was nothing hesitant about her movements—her strides even and certain. She neither sped her pace nor slowed it, knowing, with the certainty that came of royalty, that her path would clear.

And it did with each step, her gaze fixed on her destination.

Him.

His heart pounded as he watched her approach, as he read the beautiful angles of her face, the gold of the setting sun on her cheeks, the firm set of her jaw and those lips, full and soft like sin. She was magnificent, and regal, and he'd waited a lifetime for this moment—for her to come to him.

She'd come for him.

On the heels of the realization, a single word ripped through him.

Mine.

Pure pleasure curled through him as she reached him, her gaze impenetrable as she took him in, looking over his face, where he knew a half-dozen bruises must be forming, down to his chest, where his white shirt had gone dark with fight and filth, the open V of the neck ripped to display a wide swath of his chest. Her lips pressed together in a line that could have been distaste or displeasure, and she lifted her eyes back to his.

She was mere inches from him, tall enough that he would not have to bend to kiss her—and for a wild moment he considered it, desperate for another taste of her. For the feel of her breath against his skin. For the softness of her skin.

He wanted to touch her here, in this place where she reigned, unmasked and more beautiful than she'd ever been because here she called every shot, ruled every corner, knew every move, before anyone made them. She was all-powerful, stopping a Garden brawl with sheer will, and that power made him want her more than he'd ever wanted anything.

She saw the desire in him—he let her see it, loving the recognition in her beautiful brown eyes, exactly as he remembered—the only thing left of the girl he'd loved. They quickly narrowed, and he did not back down, refusing to look away from her. Not after all these years of looking for her.

He stiffened, defying the pain in his shoulder, in his ribs, in his nose. Refusing to show it to her even as his heart pounded as he prepared for whatever came next, knowing that whatever the game they were about to play, the outcome would change everything.

Who would she be when she spoke? The masked woman in his gardens? Or Grace, finally revealed?

Neither. Someone new. Masked in a different way.

She spoke, the words for him alone. "I told you not to return." A year earlier, when she'd left him in her ring, and gone on to live her life, without him.

"I was invited."

She tilted her head. "You could have refused."

Never. "That was not an option."

She held his gaze for a long moment. "My brothers brought you here for sport."

"And I gave it to them, though I would have preferred they come down from their perches, up on high."

A tiny muscle in her cheek twitched. Was she amused? Christ, he wanted that smile—the one that had come so easily to him when they were young. "They prefer the spectacle."

"And you?" he asked, softly, his fingers itching to touch her. She was so close. He could snake an arm around her waist and pull her to him in seconds. In less. He could give her the pleasure she'd begged for in his garden here . . . in hers. "What do you prefer?"

"I prefer peace," she said. "But you've only ever brought us war."

He did not miss the reference to the havoc he'd wreaked on the Rookery when he'd been mad with loss and anguish. The pain he'd delivered to this place that he'd once vowed to keep safe.

But today, she kept it safe. She kept *him* safe.

And there was immense pleasure in that. Because keeping him safe meant she hadn't forgotten. Keeping him safe meant there was hope.

She'd stopped them from killing him.

"You shouldn't have come," she said.

"I would not have missed it," he replied.

"Why?"

You. "Would you believe I came for penance?"

"Penance is sport in the Rookery," she said. "But you know that better than any of us, don't you? You cut your teeth on it." She lifted her chin, defiant. Angry. "You also know you haven't come close to getting your due. You don't know all you've done to this place. You don't know what it owes you."

"And you? What do you owe me?" The question should have been smug, but it wasn't. Instead, it was honest.

Grace met it with the same. "All they will give you and more."

He did not release her gaze. "And yet you stopped the fight."

She narrowed her gaze. Ewan didn't speak. He didn't have to.

"You were pulling your punches," she said.

It was the truth, but she was the only one who would have seen it.

"Stupid, that. If I'd let it go, they'd've killed you." She made a show of inspecting his face—his nose and jaw throbbing from the blows he'd taken. "You're half there already."

He raised a brow. "Careful, or I'll think you prefer me alive."

She didn't like the suggestion that she'd done it for him—that much he could see. But Christ, he liked it very much. If she didn't want him dead, she wanted him alive. And that was something he could work with.

"Dead dukes tend to attract attention, and I don't like the Crown in my business."

"No place for it here," he said. "The Garden already has its queen."

He heard the echo of the night earlier in the week, when she'd come to him masked and free of their past.

You are a queen. Tonight, I am your throne.

She heard it, too. He saw her breath catch for a moment. Watched her pupils dilate a touch—just enough to reveal the truth. She heard it, and she remembered it. And she wanted it again.

She'd come for him.

As though she could sense his arrogant pleasure, her lips flattened into a thin line. "I told you not to come back."

She was angry, but anger was not indifference.

Anger was like passion.

She straightened and stepped away from him, leaving their intimacy and returning to her subjects. She lifted her voice to the assembled masses. "I think we've doled out enough Rookery medicine this afternoon, lads." She looked to the brute who'd started the fight. "Your kind ain't for dukes, Patrick O'Malley. Careful next time—I may not be here to save you from the hangman."

"Aye, Dahlia." The Irishman gave her a sheepish smile that made Ewan want to set him into the ground for the familiarity of it.

Until that very moment, it hadn't occurred to him that she might have a lover. That one of these men, born of this place and built by it, might be hers.

He sucked in a breath at the thought. It was impossible. Not a week earlier, she'd come apart in his arms. Against his mouth, her hands in his hair and her cries in the air between them. She'd chosen him that night.

Tonight, only, she'd whispered.

One night. That's what she'd promised him. Fantasy for one night.

No. He resisted the thought. One night was not enough. Would never be.

Mine.

While he was planning the bruiser's demise, she turned away, leaving him, her leather-encased legs devouring the yard. Frustration flared at the idea that this might be all there was.

"And you, Dahlia?" he called out, using the name this place had given her. "What of you? Is your kind for dukes?"

A ripple of surprise tore through the crowd at the bald question. She froze. Turned back. *He had her.*

"I'll 'ave 'im if you won't!" a woman shouted off to his left.

For a moment, she was still as stone. But he saw the anger flash in her eyes just before she turned to address her subjects. When she spoke, her words ricocheted off the buildings, ensuring that everyone assembled heard her.

"This toff wants to come to scratch, and Lord knows we're all itching to give him the fight he's asking for. But he ain't for you."

Anger flared, and he took a step toward her, the movement sending a sharp pain up his side, licking through his shoulder like fire.

She looked up to the rooftops, to where he knew his brothers watched. She repeated herself. "He ain't for you."

What was she doing?

And then she looked at him, something in her eyes that he wasn't expecting. She held his gaze for a long moment, and he would have given anything—paid anything—done anything—to know what she was thinking.

"He'll get the fight he wants," she said, her voice a clarion call. "But hear me now—this fight is mine." The words thrummed through him as she turned to the Garden. "Understood, lads?"

Around the yard, a chorus of grunted agreement.

She met his eyes.

"He'll get it from me."

His whole body drew tight at the words and the underlying promise in them. That they weren't done with each other. That she wasn't through.

That she'd come for him.

And then she turned away, and a thrill of pleasure rioted through him even as she disappeared into the crowd.

She'd come for him, and now it was time for him to go to her.

Chapter Fifteen

Grace left, knowing what she had wrought.

Knowing—even as she slipped from the yard and its crush of people, even as she increased her pace, half wanting to lose him, half wanting him to follow—that he would follow. She moved more quickly, eager to get into the web of labyrinthine streets, away from him and the way he made her feel. Away from the fact that he made her feel, at all.

She turned down the nearest alleyway, and then another, then down a long, curving Garden street, past half a dozen children playing skip the stones and a gaggle of women around a metal washtub, gossiping over the last of their laundry in the late afternoon sun.

The women smiled as she passed—the two she recognized lifted hands in greeting—but no one wavered from the conversation. "I ain't never seen a duke lookin' like that," Jenny Richley said. The appreciation in the words sent a lick of memory through Grace that she didn't care for.

"Cor, you ain't never seen a duke, t'all, Jenny," came a retort from Alice Neighbors.

Jenny laughed. "Do you think they're all so handsome?"

No, Grace thought. *They weren't.*

They shouldn't be. They should be old and horse-faced. Soft and with a stink of privilege and a touch of gout. And he wasn't.

Because he was never meant to be a duke.

She clung to that: the duke's son who had stolen the dukedom. And he'd done it by leaving her to the wolves. And then he'd kept it by making sure the wolves stayed on the hunt.

Hadn't he?

Doubt, fresh and unsettling.

Past the women, at the far end of the alley, there was a spot to take to the rooftops, footholds built into the side of the building, and Grace headed for it, knowing it was the surest way to lose him.

She wanted to lose him.

Didn't she?

"I don't know, but I'd be very happy to 'ave a second look at that one—really be certain he's as pretty as he seemed."

Grace reached for a brick protruding from the wall, ready to begin her climb, when the reply came—and not from the women. "I'd be more than happy to give you a second look, ladies."

"Good God!" one of the women she did not know squeaked. "It's 'im!"

Grace froze, clinging to the wall, the tails of her coat billowing out behind her, admiration flaring before she could stop it. He'd found her more quickly than she'd expected. She turned her head just enough to see him at the entrance to the alleyway, the blood from the gash on his cheek now dried, his once-white shirt now stained beyond repair, torn at the shoulder, clinging to the taut muscles of his chest.

Not that she noticed.

He raised a brow, noticing her not noticing.

Grace lowered herself to the ground and slowly turned

around. "Lookin' a bit worse for wear if you ask me, Duke."

The women tittered.

"That much is true—the men in your Rookery know how to throw a punch." He lifted a hand and touched the bruise blooming beneath his left eye.

"The women, too," one of them said with a low, throaty laugh.

Ewan smirked at that, but did not look away from Grace. "Aye, I've experience with that, as well."

She lifted her chin. "Seems like you've crossed the wrong crew, if you ask me."

"It takes me time to learn my lesson."

The women assembled laughed at the self-deprecation. "Well, he ain't done nuffin' to cross me," Alice said as she reached for a nearby basket. "Are you hungry, my lord? Would you like cake?"

"He doesn't want cake," Grace said.

"Nonsense. Of course I want cake," he said, approaching the women. The words were barely made before a tea cloth was extracted from the basket and unwrapped, a treat passed in his direction.

With a thank-you, he turned and fetched a nearby crate, flipping it upside down. She saw the tiny wince as he hefted the box with one hand. Barely there.

He was in pain.

She ignored her response to the realization, instead gritting her teeth as he joined the circle of women around the tub as though he'd spent every day of his life marauding through Covent Garden, availing himself of proffered cakes.

She crossed her arms and leaned back against the wall, watching as he accepted the cake and took an enormous bite, nothing polite or mannered about it.

"Now *that's* a man," Alice said with pride.

"Aye," Jenny replied. "I would've thought dukes would be more concerned wiv crumbs."

He smiled around his chewing, his jaw working like he was a cow in pasture. Grace ignored how the exaggerated movements underscored the angle of that jaw. The beauty of it. The fact that a body could draw a straight line with it.

She didn't care. She had a perfectly functional ruler in her office.

He swallowed. "I don't see how anyone could worry about crumbs with such a delicious bite in hand." He dipped his head and gave the full force of his smile to Alice, who flushed under the brilliance of it. Not that Grace could blame her. She'd flushed beneath the weight of that smile herself countless times. Jested and danced for it.

Spent ages trying to remember the exact curve of it. The precise way his eyes warmed with it. The way it felt against her skin.

She inhaled, and he turned to look at her. Alice's attention lingered on him, as she said, "It's nuffin', really. Just my mum's scones. Another?"

He rubbed his hands together like an excited boy. "You know, I believe I will, thank you."

Alice looked over at Grace. "And you, Dahlia? Will you 'ave one?"

She looked behind her, to the wall she should scale. To the rooftops that would lead her to 72 Shelton, far from this place and this man and whatever this new trap he laid was.

But before Grace could offer Alice a polite refusal, before she could head for the wall—she looked to him first. And she saw the dare in his eyes, clear as day.

Why shouldn't she accept the treat? This was her place as well as his. More than his. And that made the scones more hers than his, too.

She approached, and Jenny moved to one side of the low

block upon which she was perched, making room for Grace as she selected a scone and sat down across from him, making sure the washtub was between them, as though a metal drum of tepid, dirty water would protect her.

Not that she needed protection.

She didn't. Not even when the man who sat across from her was nothing of what she expected—he was neither the boy she'd loved for too long, nor the madman she'd feared for longer, nor the lover she'd given herself over to some evenings earlier . . . for not long enough.

But it didn't matter that she didn't recognize him. Grace was an expert at disguises, and she knew without question that the man before her was ephemera. He remained the Duke of Marwick, and didn't Grace make a living giving aristocrats a chance at playing pretend?

So this duke had chosen a Covent Garden fighter.

So he had the fists to back it up, and the heroic smile to win ladies as well as bouts.

It didn't make it true. It made it fantasy. Not even his eyes, on hers, glowing like amber, could change that.

"Your shirt is covered in blood," she said.

He licked crumbs from the corner of his mouth and she worked not to look. "Badge of honor."

"That wound on your face won't be when it goes bad. It's time for you to head back to Grosvenor Square and send for your toff surgeon to come 'round and mend you."

"If ye need help mendin', I've some balm for ye, Duke," Alice said.

"Oho!" another crowed. "Careful! Alice ain't usually so generous!"

Alice laughed. "Any excuse to get a closer look!"

Grace expected Ewan to recoil from the bawdy jokes—the Garden was too harsh and too changeable for anyone to have time or inclination for the delicate sensibilities of the aristocracy. But instead, he grinned, the look sheepish and young. She ignored the way her stomach flipped with recognition of the boy she could glimpse in that look.

She didn't want to recognize that boy.

Didn't want to remember that there had been a time when she'd loved him.

When he loved her, and he'd held her in his arms and whispered about this place—*his* place—the place where they would one day reign together . . . until he'd changed his mind and decided to turn his back on it.

"Thank you for the offer, Miss Alice"—Grace resisted the urge to roll her eyes at the way the women fawned over the use of the polite title—"but I've other plans than mending right now. After all"—he rolled his shoulders back all long and lazy—"Dahlia promised me a fight."

Their audience turned in unison, to where she sat. Four separate sets of eyes going wide. Grace bit back a curse—there was no way this interaction wouldn't get back to her brothers.

"You're done with cake," she said.

His eyes went wide. "Am I?"

"You are," she said. "You've interrupted these women's work. And they've lives that extend far beyond this place and you."

"Nah, miss," Alice protested. "The two of you are more excitement than we've seen in ages."

"Truth. My girls won't ever believe a duke came and sat with me while I did the wash," Jenny said, shaking her head and leaning over to collect more of her wash from the basket at her feet. Tossing the grey linen waistcoat into the tub, she bent to fish a rock from the bottom and used it to rub the dirt from the clothing.

"Would they be more likely to believe it if you told them I helped?" Ewan looked down at the basket between them and lifted another clump of fabric from within, shaking it out to reveal a large billowing shirt before he plunged his own hands into the tub and came up with a rock of his own.

Grace's eyes went wide.

The women around the tub froze, and truly, it felt like the whole Garden did—the children in the street, the clock at the market hall.

"Your Grace." Jenny found her voice first, and it was full of shock. "You can't."

He looked to her. "I can, in fact. I wasn't always a duke."

He was mad. Grace's eyes grew wider at the words—a revelation and a confession and a threat to everything he held dear. She couldn't stop herself. "You were an *earl* before that."

He met her gaze and she heard his words as though he'd spoken them aloud. *I didn't mean that.*

She raised a brow. "Earls don't do the wash, either, Your Grace."

"I do," he said, simply, turning back to his work, rubbing the stains on the shirt with his rock as the entire world gaped at him.

Finally, Jenny spoke again. "Please, Your Grace. Don't. It's terribly . . ." She trailed off and looked to Grace as if to say, *Help, please?*

She moved to stand. To call him off. But instead, he said, "Do you always travel by rooftop?"

She stiffened instantly at the question. She did not answer.

"Since she was a girl," Alice replied instead of her, with a deep, rich laugh. "My boy was the one who taught her to climb."

"She needed to learn, did she?"

She hadn't needed to learn.

Ewan tilted his head at that, his eyes on Grace as he continued to work the stone over the fabric he washed in quick, practiced movements, like he'd done it before.

And he had. He'd done it here. In an alley much like this.

After all, he'd been a Covent Garden boy long before he'd been an Eton man.

Though the muscles of his arms did not seem very Etonian to Grace.

Thankfully, he interrupted her thoughts before she could linger on them. "Tell me about the boy who taught you to climb."

You taught me to climb. She couldn't count the number of times they'd sat in the treetops together.

But she wasn't about to say that, and so, instead, she said, "Asriel," refusing to look at him. She collected a pair of trousers from Alice's basket and dunked them in the basin. She smiled at the older woman as she grabbed a broad brush from the water and began to scrub. "He showed us all the footholds in the Garden."

Alice laughed. "That child stopped my heart weekly, with the way he climbed."

"Like a cat," Grace said. How long had it been since she'd thought of that? "How is he, Alice?"

The black woman smiled, and Grace recognized a mother's content. "Oh, he's very well. Very well. Still with that casino over on St. James's, but he finds his way home for supper now and then." Asriel had been one of the few to leave the Garden for work, finding it as security detail at the Fallen Angel, one of the most desirable men's clubs in London.

"You tell him Dahlia sends her gratitude for those long-ago lessons."

Alice nodded. "I will."

She looked to Ewan, not liking the way he watched her. Or, perhaps, liking it too much. "Don't. Don't look at me like that."

His brows rose. "Like what?"

"Like you like me," she said, returning her attention to her work.

"I've always liked you," he said, simply, and she couldn't

help but peek up at him, finding his bruised and bloody face open and unsettling.

They weren't supposed to like each other.

Her eyes flickered across the circle to rest on Ewan. "And you, milord—who taught you your skill?"

One side of his mouth kicked up. "I don't expect you're referring to laundry."

All the women laughed, and Jenny crowed, "I wouldn't mind hearing that story, too!"

"My mother taught me," he said, simply.

She couldn't keep herself from looking at him at that, knowing that there was nothing simple about it. His mother, once mistress to one of the most venerated dukes in Britain, then cast off, with child, here.

"Your mam!" Alice said, eyes going wide. "A duchess, doin' the wash?"

"Not just the wash," he said, deftly manipulating the conversation. "What would you say if I told you she taught me to throw a punch, too?"

"Cor!" the third woman said. "I'd say she sounded like a proper Garden duchess!"

"She was that," he said with a smile, and everyone laughed. Everyone except Grace, who couldn't stop watching him. And when he looked at her, she saw everything he was not saying, and hated it.

But then he said the rest. "Maybe I ought to find myself another Garden duchess."

The laughter stopped immediately, silence opening up in the washing circle like a secret. Grace's chest tightened with something close to panic.

It was panic, wasn't it?

Whatever it was, this ended now.

Grace set the wet trousers she'd washed on the pile of clean laundry, cleared her throat, and stood. "That's enough."

He looked up. "Is it? Why?"

She studied him for a long moment. Did he really not know?

Perhaps he was the madman he'd once been. But he wasn't dangerous.

Wrong. Like this, covered in blood and doing the wash, he was more dangerous than he'd ever been.

"Because you don't belong here, Marwick."

He flinched at the words before he stood, moving with a hint of stiffness that he tried to hide, but she saw anyway. When her eyes met his, something flashed there, and she recognized it from their youth. Defiance.

He knew the score—knew that if he showed weakness here, the Garden would eat him for supper. He'd been weaned on that lesson, in this very place. He did belong here, he would argue if given the chance. Had he not been born here? Had he not learned the maze of streets to the east of Drury Lane before the rest of them had even known Drury Lane existed?

But he'd left it. And she'd come and taken it.

And now it was hers and she understood it—and the pride of the people who lived there—better than he ever would. And he made them all feel like fools when he brought his fine cloth and his pristine speech and his manicured hands here.

And Grace, most of all.

"You're awful deep in the Garden to be headed for Mayfair, Duke," she said, tilting her chin to the west. "Follow the sun and find yourself home, before you meet a dangerous someone on the streets."

She forced herself to turn away, to head back to the wall, to climb to the rooftops and get back to work. She'd be damned if she'd watch him leave.

"I am safe on these streets now, aren't I, Dahlia?" he called out, and she couldn't help it. She turned back, the name on his lips, where it didn't belong.

He wasn't leaving. He was coming for her, slow and easy, as though his thigh wasn't aching and his shoulder wasn't aflame and bruises weren't blooming all over his smug face—how was it possible it was still so handsome? No one should be handsome as they turned black and blue.

"Haven't you just claimed my protection your own?"

She came off the wall to her full height as he neared. "I wouldn't say protection, no."

"No? I heard it quite clearly," he said, his voice lowering so it went liquid and dark, but not quiet enough to exclude their audience. "I heard you say I was yours."

She ignored the way the words curled through her, narrowing her gaze as the women watching vibrated with excitement. He was performing, and she didn't like it. "The blows to the head addled your brain then, because I said nothing of the sort."

"No?"

"No. I said your fight was mine."

"And if I told you that I was all fight?"

A little sigh came from beyond, and Grace ignored it. Ignored, too, the way the words wanted her sigh, as well. "I would tell you that you've been a toff too long for that to be true."

He watched her for a long moment. "And what if being a toff has made me a fighter? What if it has filled me with anger and venom and made me into the kind of bruiser you would have?"

She stilled.

"What if I'm all fight?" he whispered. "What if that's all I have to give?"

The sun was low now, nearly over the rooftops, casting golden light through the alley, turning his golden hair, dusted with soot and mud from the Rookery, to the same color as his eyes, burning into hers. Those eyes that she knew as well as her own. Better.

The ones that haunted her in her dreams—the only place she could allow herself to remember them.

He lowered his voice. "What if you cannot claim my fight without claiming me?"

She couldn't breathe for the images the words wrought. For the memories that came with them.

She didn't want it. She didn't want the whispers of their past. Didn't want the confusion of the present. She didn't want the taste of him on her lips or the memory of the way he unraveled her with his touch and his mouth.

He was close enough to touch. "Are you going to eat that?"

What?

He nodded between them, and she followed the line of his attention to the scone, still in her hand, half eaten. "The cake," he said. "Do you intend to eat it?"

She clasped it to her breast. "Are you asking me for it?"

"'Twould be a pity for it to go to waste."

She narrowed her gaze on him. "Are you deprived of treats, Duke?"

The question wrought an instant change. "Yes." His voice was suddenly low and dark. "Christ, yes. I've had a lifetime of treat deprivation."

Her jaw slackened at the words.

That half smile again. The one she knew so well from their youth. "But, I don't want the scone."

He lifted his hand to her face, tucking a lock of hair behind her ear, and heat shot through her at the touch. She sucked in a breath. "What, then?"

"Only what you want, as well." He changed his grip, and he was tilting her up to him. Then his lips were on hers, the hotly contested scone tumbling to the ground, and she was lost.

It was different from the kisses the other night—when she'd been masked and wigged and kohled beyond recognition. When he'd given her private pleasure for the sake of just that—pleasure. No past, no future, just present.

Of course it was different. Because this kiss was all time. This kiss was promise and threat, history and speculation. And it was the summation of twenty years of wanting him even as she knew that she would never have him.

It was aching and sweet and delicious and awful and it laid her bare there, in the golden light of the setting Covent Garden sun, where she'd never been bare before. Where she'd never been safe enough to be bare.

But now, as his arms came around her, collecting her against him, he was home. And she was safe. At least for as long as they kissed.

Don't ever stop.

The thought raced through her as she lifted her arms to encircle his neck, to keep him there, against her, pure pleasure.

Please, don't ever stop.

He didn't seem interested in stopping. Instead, as she came up on her toes to even their height, his arms wrapped tight around her waist, pulling her into him, pressing her along the hard length of his body, all muscle and strength. She rocked her hips into his, the soft, aching part of her pressing along the straining length of him.

He wanted her. As much as she wanted him.

She sighed at the realization, the sound lost in their kiss even as he growled his pleasure and pulled her tighter, his large, warm hand coasting up her back and into her wild curls. There was nothing gentle about the caress, his fingers tightening . . . fisting around a mass of her hair, holding her still.

Good. She didn't want gentle.

He deepened the kiss and she opened for him, his tongue sliding over hers as her hands mirrored his own, clenching in the silken strands of his hair as she licked across his lips and met him movement for movement. He couldn't get enough of her. She couldn't get enough of him. And then he was turning her, lifting her, walking her back behind a tall stack of crates and barrels.

He set her to the wall, barely out of sight of the washwomen, and planted his hands on either side of her head, caging her in for his kisses—more and more drugging, more and more desperate, threatening to pull her deeper and deeper into whatever it was that had brought him back.

Threatening to make her beg for him—

Don't ever stop.

And then he fit his strong thigh between hers, the heavy weight of it against her aching flesh pulling a little cry from the back of her throat—only loud enough for him to hear, and still it seemed to set him aflame. She slid her hands down his chest, splaying her fingers wide across the broad expanse of him—so different now than a year earlier, when she'd mapped the lean contours of him.

There was nothing lean about him now. He was all muscle, fresh topography, worthy of a new map.

Her fingers traced over a rib, and he sucked in a breath. *Pain.* An iron Rookery fist. A broken rib. And still, he'd found time to flirt and tease. He'd found strength to follow her.

I'll follow you, Gracie. Always.

A promise, echoing over the years.

One of his enormous hands slid inside her coat, clasping her hip to hold her still and tight to him as he pressed that glorious thigh higher, firmer. When she rocked into him, he released his hand, sliding it up over her side to palm her breast.

They were in the middle of the Rookery. Yards from an audience. She should stop him.

But she didn't want to.

The feel of his hands on her was unbearable. Grace was

not a stranger to pleasure, but had she ever felt such? Had any man ever touched her with such fire? With such certainty?

The questions were gone before they came.

There were no other men.

As his thumb slipped beneath the edge of her corset and traced a rough circle around the straining nipple there, Grace lowered her own hand, setting it to the wicked, wonderful length of him. He was hard and hot and perfect, and when he offered her a deep, delicious grunt, she returned it with a throaty laugh—his pleasure hissing through her as keenly as her own. The fingers of her free hand fisted again in his hair, and she gave his lower lip a long, delicious suck, reveling in the rich taste of him, in the lush fullness of that lip.

His grunt turned into something else. Something predatory.

But she was not prey any longer.

Today, now, they were equals.

Hunting each other.

How would she ever stop herself.

"Everything all right back there?" The excited question came from a distance. Miles away, it felt, but loud like cannon fire, and followed by a cacophony of devious, delighted laughter.

She pulled away from him, gasping for breath, returning to the Garden. Her gaze tracked over the alleyway, over the stones growing darker by the second, the sun now turning the western sky into an inferno.

She pushed past him, straightening her coat, rounding the stack of crates to face the collection of women, wide-eyed, bold, unapologetic, deeply knowing smiles on their lips.

He spoke from behind her, calm and at ease, as though everything were perfectly normal. "Beg pardon, ladies."

She stiffened at the words, at the tittering from their audience, and looked at him, resisting the urge to put her fingertips to her lips, to settle the buzz in them, the delicious sting he'd left with his kiss.

No. It wasn't delicious.

She shouldn't have kissed him.

It didn't matter that he'd made it difficult not to, with his newfound swagger, as though Covent Garden brawls were his daily bread.

It didn't matter that those brawls seemed to suit him.

She didn't have to touch her lips. His dark, penetrating gaze found them anyway, and in his throat rumbled a little growl that sent heat straight through her, her eyes immediately finding his. Recognizing the want there.

Want?

Need.

It didn't feel like want in her. It felt like need as he snaked an arm around her waist and pulled her in tight, leaning down and kissing her again, lazy and lingering, as though they had a week for it, and weren't being watched.

Before she could protest—*she would have protested*—he released her again, lowered his lips to her ear and whispered, "Grace." Her name, like a benediction. Again. "Grace." And then, "Christ, I've wanted that for so long."

So had she.

"Take 'im home and give 'im a nice wash, Dahlia!" Jenny called out, and the rest of the women hooted and cheered from where they had unstuck themselves, their chores and their voyeurism finally finished, lifting baskets to hips and preparing to head home.

For a moment, Grace imagined it. Taking him home. Calling for a bath. Washing the day and the dirt from him, until he was clean and the sun was gone and they were cloaked in darkness and the permission it gave people to take what they wanted.

For a moment, she reveled in that fantasy.

For a moment, she forgot that he was not safety.

He was not home.

He was the enemy—hers, and her brothers' and the whole of Covent Garden's.

She pushed at his shoulders, and he went more readily than she would have expected. More readily than she wished.

She pushed the realization aside, hating the questions that followed. Hating the answers more. Anger and frustration coursed through her. "That was a mistake."

He shook his head. "No, it wasn't." He said it like it wasn't a discussion. Like they discussed the time of day. Or the color of the sky.

"Of course it was. This is the game we play," she said, letting her exhaustion seep into her words. She was tired of running from him. Tired of hiding from him. "We make mistakes." She paused. "*You* make them."

The words struck true, wildness flooding his gaze. A hint at the mad duke Mayfair thought him. "Then tell me how to pay for them."

How many times had she imagined him saying those exact words to her? She shook her head. "There is no paying for them, Duke. Not with money or power or a lifetime of washing clothes."

The women behind tittered their interest.

"What, then?" He pressed on. "I take my knocks from the men in your yard. From your brothers. From *you*."

"*Your* brothers," she said.

"What?"

"They are *your* brothers."

He shook his head. "No. They ran with you. They protected you."

"Yes," she said, lifting her chin. "They protected me from you, but they are *your* blood."

He ignored the truth of the words. "You still haven't given me a reason. One good reason, and I'll leave. One reason why I cannot pay my dues. Say my prayers. Do my penance."

"There are a thousand reasons!"

"One would imagine you could give me one, then." He paused. "Instead, you lead me on a merry chase through the Garden."

"You followed me," she retorted.

He raised a brow. "Yeah, but you wanted it."

She had. Damn him for saying so.

Frustration and anger flared, making her want to scream. Instead, she closed the distance between them, reached up and grabbed the already threadbare neck of his shirt—the place where the rope from earlier had torn a hole in the fine lawn. She yanked, finishing what the earlier fight had started, tearing it open to reveal his raw shoulder and on it, the M his father had put there—white and raised against the angry red skin, a wicked scar.

"There's your reason!"

He rocked back on his heels as she let the shirt go.

"You'll always be his. And I don't care what song you sing to the women of the Rookery. I don't care how skilled you are at doing the wash. I don't care that the map of the Garden is inked on you, or that you were born in its muck. You walked away from it all the moment you betrayed us. The moment you chose him over us."

She stopped, resisting the heavy fullness in her throat. Resisting the prickling pain behind her eyes. The mourning for the boy she'd once loved. The one who'd sworn never to leave her. Never to hurt her.

That boy had lied.

"You'll *always* be Marwick," she said, staring into his face, dark with the bruises of the day and the shadows of the evening. "And that means you'll always be a mistake."

And maybe, one day, she would learn it.

Grace swallowed around the ache in her throat, turning

away before he could say anything, but he reached for her, clasping her hand before she could leave him. Pulling her back around to face him.

"I never chose him."

She shook her head, but he refused to let her dismiss him, his hand sliding down her arm until he was holding hers. She should have shaken him off. But she didn't, even as she hated the feel of him there, against her skin. Rough. Strong. Hot.

Lie. She didn't hate it.

And she hated it even less when he tightened his grip and said again, "I never chose him. I have done terrible things in my life. Things for which I will surely spend an eternity in fire. Things for which you may never forgive me. And I bear them all. But that is one I will never bear." There was anger in his voice. No. It was not simple like anger. It was hotter. It was fury. "I never chose him."

She wanted to believe it. God, there was nothing she wanted to believe more. But when she closed her eyes, she could still see him, years ago, coming for her, knife in hand. She could still see him in the darkness last year, watching the London docks burn.

But now . . . who was this man? So different?

He looked to the rooftops. "I swore I would wait."

Confusion flared. "Wait for what?"

He leveled her with a gaze. "What do you need?"

That question again. He'd asked it before. In her ring. In his gardens.

What do you need, as though he existed solely for her pleasure.

No. Not pleasure.

Purpose.

For her whole life, she'd known her purpose. She'd been placeholder, prize, protector. She'd been an employer and a friend. She'd been businesswoman and negotiator and fighter and spy. And there had never in her life been a moment when she hadn't known precisely her purpose. When she had not had a plan.

When she did not know the answer.

But there, in the hush before her city turned from day to night, Grace Condry, bareknuckle fighter, unparalleled businesswoman, and queen of Covent Garden, found that she did not have an answer.

She didn't know what she needed.

She didn't know what she deserved.

And she was terrified of what she desired.

"I don't know," she said, the words too quiet. Revealing too much.

The confession changed him, his gaze hardening, his jaw tightening. He took a step back and somehow, impossibly, she hated the distance he put between them.

But didn't she want distance? Didn't she want infinite distance between them? Didn't she want him to leave and never return?

Didn't she need that?

Of course she did.

Didn't she?

He stopped, and two yards might have been two miles.

And then, over the riot of her thoughts, he spoke. "Come see me when you know."

Chapter Sixteen

Waiting for her was torture.

Ewan stood at the center of his bedchamber later that evening, aching from the bout with the Garden and from the bout with Grace, knowing that only one set of those aches was guaranteed to heal.

He'd seen the way she wanted him. He'd felt it, when they'd kissed there, in the open alleyway. He'd heard it in her little sighs, as she'd clung to him and pressed herself against him, making him wild.

And worse, he'd seen how she struggled with that desire when he'd asked her what she needed.

She needed *him*, dammit.

Just as he needed her.

And he might have convinced her of that, as the sun set over the rooftops. She might have let him follow her as she scaled the wall and made her way to her home, where she might have let him stay.

She might have let him kiss her again, and finish what they started.

She might have told him what she needed. And let him give it to her.

But that wasn't enough. He didn't simply want to be allowed to be with her. To touch her. To kiss her. He wanted her to want it too, with the aching, gnawing desire that he wanted it.

And that meant letting her choose him. Come to him.

Take him.

So, he'd left, instead of pulling her into his arms and keeping her there until she revealed all of it.

Come see me when you know.

He growled his irritation at the memory, frustration making him yank his trousers up and button the falls with a roughness that sent pain shooting over his ribs. "You fucking deserve that," he muttered to himself, stopping before he finished buttoning, and turned to the looking glass on the far side of the room, still in shadow, despite the candles lit all around it to give him the best look at the damage he'd taken earlier in the day.

If he hadn't left her, would he be with her still? Would she have tended his wounds? The question came with the memory of her fingers on his chest earlier, sliding down, over his ribs, gentling when he'd sucked in a breath at the pain. The first indication that she hadn't liked him hurt.

As though her touch could ever hurt him. Even as she'd delivered his punishment in the boxing ring, even as he'd taken her fists and then the silken scarf at her waist that a lesser man would have underestimated, he'd reveled in her touch.

She was alive.

A year later, and the revelation still threatened to break him.

She was alive, and if he was right, she wanted him, so he'd taken the risk and left her wanting, leaving her there, in the Garden, and returning to the house in Mayfair, his attempt to sneak through the kitchens failing the moment the cook saw his battered face and screamed for O'Clair, who immediately transformed into a mother hen, insisting they call a doctor, Scotland Yard, and the butler's brother—who was a priest, apparently.

After convincing the butler that he was bruised but not broken, that no crimes had been committed, and that he had no need for last rites, Ewan had called for a bath, a bottle of whisky, and a basket of bandages.

He made liberal use of the first two items before settling in with the third, wincing as he inspected the spots that mottled his torso. It was dark, and the candlelight in the room was not ideal for wound care, but he wasn't about to ask O'Clair for more candles, lest the butler return to panic, so Ewan was left with what he had—a looking glass and a dozen flames casting shadows across his skin as he gingerly tested the ribs within.

He didn't think anything required a surgeon, but the pain was considerable—scotch notwithstanding.

Cursing roundly, he worked to wrap the bandages around his midsection, irritation making the task more difficult than it should have been. He was tired and in pain, and tied in knots from the events of the afternoon—the bout as much as the chase she'd led him on, through the crowd and deep into the Garden. And from the control he'd had to hold tight.

Christ, he'd wanted her. He'd wanted to toss her over his shoulder and take her to the nearest private corner to give her the opportunity to give him the fight she promised.

But when he'd found her, halfway up a wall, headed for the rooftops, returning to dominion over this world he'd loved so well, he had realized that he didn't want her in private. He wanted her in public.

He wanted to be the one who knew her secrets and her stories. He wanted her to show him all the ways they could take to the rooftops together.

He'd hated that there'd been another boy, teaching her to climb. Hated that he'd never realized she would need to know more than trees to survive. Hated that she'd had to survive—and all because of him.

He wanted to learn her maps—over slate tiles and around smokestacks—and hear every tale she had to tell about the last twenty years. He wanted to make new maps. New tales.

And he wanted the world to see them together.

I don't know, she'd said, and he'd heard the layers of the confession. Felt them in his soul. Because he did not know, either. The only thing he knew was that he wanted to learn with her. He wanted a future, and all they had was the past.

You betrayed me.

With a grunt, he yanked on the long strip of linen he wrapped around his ribs, pulling it as tight as he could, gritting his teeth against the pain.

"You'll never get it tight enough on your own."

He nearly dropped the bandages at the words, the movement sending a screaming pain through him, and he exhaled it harshly as she stepped into the room, closing the door behind her.

Heart pounding, he drank her in, relief and pleasure and no small amount of pride coursing through him. *She had come.* Would there ever be a time when he wasn't consumed with thrill at the idea that she had sought him out, of her own will?

And this was her own will.

His, as well.

She wore her uniform—the clothes that made her a monarch. Black trousers and leather boots that threatened always to do him in, encasing her long legs up over the knee like sin. Above the trousers, an ice blue corset, embroidered with gold thread. At her waist, another scarf—her weapon of choice—the foil of the corset, gold with threads of that blue. Over all that, a black coat, perfectly tailored. On another woman he would have thought the coat a disguise—something to hide her from prying eyes and turn her into a gentleman on the street. But Grace did not hide. The coat hung open to reveal the stunning corsetry beneath and the matched lining beyond, the same blue, the pale blue color of a winter's sky.

Buttoned, the coat would make for perfect stealth, a hood pulled up over her wild red curls, the only evidence that they existed a small errant one, loosed from hiding. He wanted to knock that hood back and let it all fall down around her shoulders, as it had been earlier in the day.

He reveled in the look of her—steel and silk, like the woman herself, even as frustration flared. She'd come to him masked again. It might not be the silken mask she'd worn the night she'd come to the masquerade, but she wore a mask nonetheless, the same one she'd donned earlier, when she'd commanded her Covent Garden army—this one made of strength.

Gone was the woman he'd glimpsed after the bout—the one who'd told the story of learning to scale walls. The one who gave her smiles easily to the bruisers in the muck and the women at the wash.

He wanted those smiles, easy, for himself.

He wanted *her.* Honest.

But he would take this over nothing.

"How did you get in?"

She gave him a little smile. "I'm a hardened street criminal, Duke. You think a thing like Grosvenor Square would prevent me from a bit of breaking and entering?"

"It's not the address I would have expected to stop you," he said. "I am, however, surprised to know that my overbearing butler didn't meet you on the stairs."

She crossed the room to a small table where a collection of glasses sat with a heavy ship's decanter, and Ewan could not look away from her swagger, her coat swinging around her long legs. She pulled the stopper from the decanter and sniffed at the brandy inside. Her brows rose. "French. Very expensive."

"I understand there are ways to get it more cheaply," he said as she poured herself a glass.

She did not miss the reference to the Bareknuckle Bastards' less than legal enterprise. "I haven't any idea what you're talking about." She drank and then said, "There wasn't a single butler in nightcap, armed with antique dueling pistol, to be found. Disappointing, really."

"Mmmm. What's the point in having an overbearing butler if not to ward off interlopers?"

Her eyes glittered in the candlelight. "Aren't all ducal butlers overbearing? How else can one be sure there is always a starched shirt and a pressed cravat, ready for donning?"

"I don't know. I don't spend much time on ducal estates." It wasn't precisely true. He spent most of his time on the Burghsey estate, but he lived in a small cottage he'd built on the western edge of the land. It ran on a skeleton staff, just enough to keep the place from falling down around him.

"Hmm," she said. "Well, either way, your butler failed in buttling when I arrived, to be sure."

"I shall bring up your concerns with him at his next performance review. Did not stop strange woman from entering house: demerit."

Those beautiful lips curled again. "I'm not sure it counts as a demerit. Truthfully, I'm very good at getting where I need to be without being noticed."

He didn't know how that was possible, considering how intensely he noticed her. How he knew the shift in a room when she was present. Twenty years, and he still noticed her like she was cannon fire.

"Would you like me to leave?" she asked.

"No." He never wanted her to leave.

She poured a second glass and closed the distance between them, offering it to him.

He took it. "And so?"

She tilted her head in question.

"Have you decided?" he asked, hearing the frustration in his tone, the reveal that he was losing patience.

She took a step closer and he sucked in a breath, imagining what would happen if he caught her in his arms and carried her to the bed, and stripped her bare—and made love to her as he'd wanted to every night since he'd been old enough for such thoughts.

Would he be able to strip her of her mask then?

And what would she do?

She would run.

He knew it, because she'd run from him for years—every time he'd ever come close to finding her in the twenty years since they'd parted. She'd run from him, and he deserved it for the way he'd betrayed her, and broken her heart, and broken his own in the balance.

She would run, and he would do anything to stop that, so he remained statue-still, and let her come to him.

She stopped a heartbeat from him, and she pulled a sack off her shoulder—he hadn't noticed it when she'd entered. He could not see her eyes, the hood low enough that it cast the upper half of her face in shadow. All he could see were her full, pink lips when she said, "They did a fair bit of damage to you."

He did not hesitate. "I did plenty of my own."

She smiled in that way that made her look like she had a secret—was it possible she was proud? Christ, he wanted her proud. He wanted her to have watched him fight and admired his skill. He knew it made him an animal, but he didn't care. He wanted her to know he could destroy worlds at her bidding, if only she'd ask for it.

Whatever she needed.

"Why haven't you called a doctor?" she asked, softly.

He couldn't stop the little thread of offense he took at the question. "I don't need a doctor."

She lifted her chin, and the candlelight caught her face, washing it gold as she met his eyes with disbelieving amusement. "Men and their ridiculous rules regarding medical care. You go on and on about how you're perfectly fine, despite the bruises blooming all over you—it looks like Patrick O'Malley broke your nose."

"Are you here to nursemaid me?"

She did not reply, instead reaching up to lower her hood, letting her mass of red curls loose like an inferno. Christ, he loved her hair. It was a force of nature, threatening always to lay him low. Like the woman herself.

The darkness tightened around them. "Why are you here?"

She stilled.

He hated that stillness and the way it settled her mask once more. He'd miscalculated in the Garden. He'd lured her into showing him something of her truth, and then he'd left, and he might never get it back.

You can never have her back.

He couldn't have the girl he'd known, but was he never to have even a glimpse of the woman she'd become? Was she to hide from him forever?

"Tell me the truth," he whispered, and he couldn't hide the urgency in the tone.

She stayed quiet, instead lifting her hand to his face, her fingers gentle as they traced the swollen skin beneath his eye, the yellowed bruising on his jaw. The line of his nose, somehow miraculously unbroken despite her suggestion.

"If I said I was here to mend you?"

He released a breath at the words, somehow filling him with more pleasure than her touch. "I would say you have a fair bit of work on your hands."

He did not tell her he was not certain mending was an option.

She hovered on the edge of movement, as though she knew it.

Stay. Please.

It took everything he had to wait her out.

Choose this.

His heart threatened to beat from his chest until finally . . . finally, she reached for the linen strip he'd used in his attempt to bind his own ribs. He relinquished it without hesitation, standing so still he barely breathed as she circled him, investigating him, her touch soft and strong, sliding over his ribs and testing the damage that had been done.

He sucked in a breath as she traced over the muscles of his abdomen, and she looked up, her rich brown eyes inspecting his for pain. "Too much?"

Never enough.

He shook his head. "Go on."

"This one could be broken," she said softly.

"It's not."

"How do you know?" she asked.

"We both know I've broken them before." The memory unfolded between them. Ewan had taken a boot to the rib and she'd mended him then, too.

"Whit was always better with his legs," she whispered.

"And now?"

She smiled at the question, and jealousy flared at her clear adoration of the man Covent Garden called Beast. "Now he's good with everything. He grew big and brutal. And he doesn't lose."

Something filled him at that—the fact that the smallest and weakest of them had become the strongest.

"The summer he grew—we were ten and five, maybe six," she said, amusement in her words. "It was like witchcraft. We couldn't keep him in shoes. One week, we were out of money and he put a toe through the front of one, and I had to steal a pair."

"From where?"

She shrugged. "A cull in a brothel on Charles Street.

Greasy git who liked to agree to one price and pay another. The sweaty bastard deserved it."

"Was he—" He swallowed the rest of the question.

She tilted her head at him. "A customer? No. I was more use to Digger Knight as a fighter than I was as a moll."

"I wouldn't judge if he were." Born in a brothel on Tavistock Row, Ewan knew better than most that women had few enough choices in life for men to decide they owned that one.

"I know you wouldn't," she said. And the truth in the words gave him pleasure.

She finished bandaging him, tucking the end of the linen in on itself, her lips flattened into a straight line as she inspected the rest of him—the bruises above the bandages and on his face, and his shoulder, rubbed raw from the ropes he'd used in the yard earlier that day.

The shoulder she'd bared for him earlier, revealing the scar he wished every day he could erase, along with the past that came with it.

But erasing the past would erase her, too.

With a little nod, she bent to retrieve the bag she'd come with. Setting it on a nearby chair, she fished a small ceramic pot from within and opened it, lifting it immediately to her nose. He couldn't stop his smile as he watched the movement, an echo of the girl she'd been, who was first to smell anything—pleasing or otherwise.

"Is something amusing?"

"You've always done that." She immediately dropped her hand and approached. "What is it?" She extended the pot toward him, and he leaned down to inhale. "Lemon."

"And bay, and willow bark. It's healed worse than this."

"For you?"

"And scores of others." She dipped her fingers in the salve and reached for him, and he let her, breathing deeply as she anointed him with it, every touch a glimpse of heaven.

"You've done this before."

"Tended wounds?"

"Tended my wounds." He paused, then, "I thought I dreamed it last year. Your touch." In the darkness. In that little room where he'd realized she was alive. Where he'd realized he might be, again.

Grace didn't look up from her work, and he took her rapt attention as a chance to drink her in, the spray of freckles across her nose, her enormous eyes, the scar across one brow, barely noticeable for the years that had passed since he'd wiped the blood from her forehead and the tears from her cheeks. He couldn't stop himself from reaching up and touching the crooked half circle.

She sucked in a breath and shot him a warning look.

He lowered his hand, and returned to his inspection, taking in the stitching of her coat and the rich sheen of the silk of her corset—which should have scandalized but instead set a body back with its strength.

"Do you ever wear gowns?" he asked, knowing it was a risk.

She hesitated. Then, "I'm familiar with the concept," she replied, the corner of her mouth twitching, making him want to kiss the spot.

Her fingers traced over his skin, passing from one shoulder, marked with a bruise, to the other, red and angry. She returned to the pot of salve, and when she touched him again, the cool balm soothed more than his shoulder.

"You wore one to my masquerade."

It was a risk, revealing what he knew, and she stilled, her fingers on his shoulder pausing. He could hear the calculations in her mind—could she convince him it hadn't been she?

No masks, Grace. Not tonight.

"How long have you known?"

He waited for her to look up at him. "I will always know you."

"You do not search for a wife."

He shook his head. "No."

"The mothers, throwing daughters in your path?"

"Unsuccessful."

She watched him for a long moment, and then, "The masque was not for Mrs. Duke of Marwick. A woman who liked mossy earth and towering trees. It was for me."

One and the same.

He was keenly aware of her fingers on his shoulder, stroking over the markings of his past. Of theirs. And as they stroked, he heard his brother's words.

You broke her heart, Whit had said.

She did not trust him. And all he could do was trust her, instead.

"I heard you liked elaborate parties."

Her fingers stuttered as she painted the salve over his skin in wide sweeps, around and around, avoiding the place he knew she watched. The scar his father had put in his shoulder the night he'd discovered that Grace was the only thing that mattered to Ewan. "I am not available for the position," she said, softly.

"I know." But it didn't make him want her any less.

"I would die a thousand deaths before I'd let that monster win."

The old duke, who had only ever cared about the line. He gave a little, humorless laugh at her anger. "And you think I feel otherwise?"

She met his eyes, and he let her see the full force of his anger for his father—that man who had made the continuation of the Marwick line a singular goal. And then, when Ewan had become duke, it had fallen to him to ensure his father never received that which he had deemed so paramount.

Which meant no children for Ewan, ever.

Not even beautiful, red-haired little girls.

Oblivious to his thoughts, Grace spoke again. "You came back despite my telling you to stay away."

I will always come back.

"But not for a year. Where did you go?"

"I went back."

To Burghsey, where he'd found an estate in ruin—one he'd left to crumble when he'd inherited and walked away. An estate he'd resurrected as he'd resumed his place there, restoring the lands and attending to the tenants, even as he took his place in Parliament and attended to an end he'd promised her a lifetime earlier.

He'd rebuilt himself, as well, into a new man. A man healthier and stronger and better than the one he'd been; worthier, too, even as he knew that he would never be worthy of the woman she had become—a woman who was strong and brilliant and powerful and so far above him he didn't deserve to look at her, let alone reach for her.

Nevertheless, he looked. And he reached.

"And why are you back now?" she asked, no longer touching him, and he could hear the edge in her words—anger. Frustration. "Do you think to convince me you regret it?"

"I do regret it. I regret turning my back on my brothers," he said. "And Grace, there is not a moment I don't regret turning my back on you."

Years of practice kept her from revealing that she was moved by the words, but he was watching her intently, his gaze riveted to the pulse point at the base of her neck, and he saw her heart race.

She did look at him then, her beautiful brown eyes wide and glittering in the candlelight. "And so? You thought a masquerade and a Garden brawl would make good on the past?"

"I have been to battle every day since I chased you away," he said, wanting her to hear it. "What is one more fight? What are a thousand of them?"

He would suffer the blows of Covent Garden every day if there was a chance for forgiveness there. For it here.

She ran a thumb over his scar, finally, and he went cold with the sensation, not knowing what she would do in the face of his words.

Another risk.

"Why did you come here, tonight?" he asked again.

She pointed in the direction of the chairs at the far end of the room, where a fireplace might have been lit if the night wasn't so warm. "Sit."

He did, lowering himself into the chair, wincing as he did so, hating to show her his weakness even as he reveled in the intimacy of it. In the history of it.

All the times when they were children, and the days after the explosion on the docks—she had cared for him, then. He knew it. He'd felt her there, even as she'd prepared to send him away forever.

As though he could stay away.

They were planets, drawn to each other.

No. He was a planet. She was the sun.

Keeping the little ceramic pot in hand, she collected her bag and his basket of bandages and came for him, her long legs claiming the carpet as she approached. He watched her, the sound of her boots on the floor filling him with pleasure and warmth and want—a desire like nothing he'd ever felt before, for this to be a commonplace occurrence. For them to tend to each other.

To know each other.

More.

She set her items down on the low table next to his

chair, her gaze taking in the assorted things collected there: a bottle of whisky and an empty glass atop a tall stack of books. A smile played over her lips.

"What?" he asked.

"Nothing," she said. "Only that I feel as though I'm catching a glimpse inside the lion's den."

"Mmm," he said, lifting a hand to rub the back of his neck, something like embarrassment coursing through him, though he couldn't say why. "This lion is very exciting, what with all the drink and books."

"So this is what you do when you are not out, doing ducal duty?" She turned away, crossing the room toward the mirror.

"I don't do ducal duty," he said, grateful for the change in topic, watching as she selected a candelabrum and returned.

She watched him for a moment, and then, as though standing above him like royalty, tall and stunning in her regalia, wasn't enough, she lowered herself to her knees before him, and set back to work.

The picture of her there, at his side, threatened to destroy him with the pleasure of it. He willed himself still, forcing himself not to reach for her. Resisting that singular word that coursed through him as he watched.

Mine.

She reached into the basket, removing another long strip of linen, and guided him forward to bandage his shoulder. "Next time you haul crates in the Garden, use a hook."

"Mmm," he grunted. "Do you know where I might find one?"

She chuckled at the words, and he turned to catch the glimpse of her amusement—like sunshine and air. "They don't issue dukes box hooks?"

"Nor ice tongs. Would you believe it?"

"You should take it up with the House of Lords." She

pulled the bandage tight over his shoulder and he sucked in a breath. "You'll need a fresh one tomorrow."

"And will you come back to give it to me?"

"No."

He turned to look at her, their faces scant inches apart—and he said, softly, "Why not?"

She met his eyes. "I shouldn't be here tonight."

"Which brings me back to why did you come?"

"I don't know," she said.

And the words, the echo of the ones she'd spoken earlier in the afternoon, unlocked him. He knew why she had come. He knew what she needed.

What they both needed.

He reached for her, touching a beautiful red curl, clasping it between two fingers and pulling it straight. "Why did you come here, tonight?" he repeated, the whispered question coming soft and aching.

Show me, he willed her. *Trust me.*

She met his eyes. "Why did you come back?"

He answered, knowing that he took a risk. As ever. He would never not take risks for her—that much was clear. "For the same reason I have done everything, from the start. For you."

She reached for him then, her hand sliding along his jawline, her touch still like heaven. She drew him close with her gentle, perfect touch, hovering a hairsbreadth from his lips, as though she was not sure if she should close the gap. "I told you not to."

"What do you need?"

She didn't answer. She acted.

Chapter Seventeen

He was back for her.

It shouldn't matter *why* he was back, or how he was changed, or that he was changed at all. And it should not matter that when he kissed her, she lost all capacity for reasonable thought.

But he hadn't kissed her. She'd kissed him.

And the low growl of pleasure in his throat had sent a matching thrum through her, feeding an already burning flame. Bandaging him had made her wild, fairly vibrating with want, especially as she'd felt his muscles tremble and tighten beneath her touch, his breath quickening—as though he were a predator, ready to spring. But he hadn't.

He'd held back. For her.

Waiting. For her.

Wanting her.

And once she kissed him, she'd freed him. He was turning to capture her, to pull her up and into his lap, his hands at her hips and then inside her coat, running up along the sides of her body to her breasts, encased in layers of silk and steel, straining for him.

Had his kisses always been so well crafted? Had he always been able to steal a woman's thoughts? Or had he spent two decades preparing himself to deliver the precise kind of kiss that made Grace forget where she was and with whom, along with every sensible reason why she should absolutely not kiss him back?

It was not an impossibility, she thought as she met his kiss with equal desire. With equal enthusiasm.

Just this once, she lied to herself. *Just this once, and then never again.*

She pressed deeper, wanting the kiss to go on forever, and he sucked in a breath that was not pleasure, but pain. She pulled back at the sound to study him, her own breath coming fast, as though she'd just scaled a wall.

His lower lip was wickedly swollen, and she immediately reached to touch it, gently. She stroked the bruise there, then ran her fingers down the line of his nose, equally bruised and certainly painful, and the high bones of his cheeks. "You'll be black and blue for an age. They got you, and well."

"I don't care," he said, his hand sliding up over her shoulder, pulling her back down toward him. "Come back and kiss me again."

The low command licked through her, and she nearly obeyed—she wanted to, but instead, she leaned over to fetch her sack from beside the chair, his hands coming to her bottom as she moved against the steel ridge of him, large and impossibly warm through her trousers.

"Mmm," he grunted as she sat up, and she looked to him, his gaze on her, lids low, the look capturing her for a moment.

Ewan had always been handsome, tall and blond and with the kind of flawless face that didn't seem possible outside of marble. Devil had broken his nose during a bout at Burghsey, and the imperfection had only made him more perfect. But now, bruised and battered, with a swollen lip and a collection of scrapes beneath his eye, he looked like a gift, delivered to her from that place that had been his before it was hers.

Ignoring the hot thrum of desire within, Grace focused on the task at hand, opening her bag and extracting a clean white cloth and a small metal box. His heated look turned curious, and she opened the box to show him the contents.

He raised a brow. “One of the blocks I hauled today?”

She gave him a little smile as she filled the cloth with ice and tied it off neatly before placing it to his eye, her other thumb stroking over his bare cheek.

“I don’t need it,” he grumbled.

“You do, though.”

“You did that very well,” he grumbled. “Made the ice pack.”

“I’ve made them before.”

“I gathered that from the special box.” His eyes found hers, serious. “How often?”

She swallowed, knowing what he was really asking. She shrugged one shoulder. “When we got to the Garden, one of us was fighting every night. Even if you’re good—like us—like *you*,” she added, remembering the way he’d fought, working to quiet enemies without destroying them. “Opponents get their knocks in.”

The muscles of his jaw tensed beneath her palm. “I hate that you had to fight.”

“Don’t,” she said, and she meant it. “Fighting is like breathing in the Garden, and I had enough rage in me to make me good. We were lucky we were all good, and we were even luckier we could get paid for it.” She looked to him. “You made sure we were good, you know that, right?”

“I shouldn’t have had to.”

No, he shouldn’t have. They should have been able to

have childhoods, with their mothers who loved them and fathers who were proud of them. And instead, here they were, battered and bruised in a thousand different ways.

Grace did not linger on the fights. "That's how Devil and Whit got involved in ice. We quickly learned the difference between a fight with it and without it, and they found a way to make certain we were never without it."

One of his blond brows rose. "I suppose the smuggling is just for fun, then."

She gave a little laugh at that. "No, the smuggling is for money, and to stick it to the aristocracy." She paused, then, "Which is a bit fun, I suppose."

He huffed a little laugh, and lifted his hand to press it against the back of hers. "And you, the resident doctor."

She nodded in the direction of the books on the table. "I'm no Dr. Frankenstein."

"Do not underestimate yourself."

"Shall we bring you to life after I am through? See what kind of monster has been made?"

Was it a flirt? Or was it a nod to their past? To the night he'd become the monster from which she'd run? To the years of her looking over her shoulder, worrying about the monster she believed him to be?

He took the ice from her hand, lowering it as he reached for her. "Grace," he whispered, pulling her close, sending warmth and something she didn't dare name spiraling through her. He pressed his forehead to hers and closed his eyes. "Whatever monster I have become . . . It is not you who made me."

She heard the anguish in the words and hated it.

And then she hated the confusion that came with the realization that she was beginning to think, perhaps, that he was not the monster they had all believed him to be.

It was becoming increasingly difficult to resist the way the memories of the past were colliding with the realities of the present—memories of him, on her turf. Taking his knocks in her club. Doing the wash with the women of the Garden. Paying his dues to the men of the Rookery. His humor.

And then, this afternoon, the way he fought, like he'd been built for it. *So he had.*

The way he'd come for her, like he'd been meant for it. *So he had.*

But most of all, she hated how much she ached for him, this new, changed man she had not expected to find when he came to. Hated how much she seemed to want him, despite the fact that he had given her a lifetime of pain.

Hated how, even now, as he suffered the effects of the bout earlier in the day, all she wanted to do was care for him.

Even though he did not deserve it.

She'd made the decision to come here to tell him just that—that he did not deserve her attention, or her protection in the Garden, or anything else he wished from her. He certainly did not deserve her care—she'd given him more than enough of that and watched him toss it away.

She'd only intended to answer the question he seemed so keen on asking her. What did she need? She needed him gone. She needed him to find the future he was looking for or the penance he required, and live his life. Far from her.

She'd only intended to leave the salve.

She'd only intended to know what she needed, finally.

And then she'd arrived in this dark room full of candles and mirrors and the scent of him, tobacco and tea, that combination she'd never been able to smell without aching for him.

Even as she hated him for his betrayal.

She should have left then. Should have ignored this room that seemed ripe for sin and sex. Should have ignored *him.*

But instead, she'd been lost to another memory, made without her consent. A memory that did not come with fear or pain or heartache, but with desire. Him without clothes—his trousers not even properly buttoned—not looking a thing like he did the last time she'd mended his wounds, doused in candlelight, fresh from a bath and covered with the badges from his earlier bout—a bout he might have won if he'd fought the way he should have.

He hadn't. Because he hadn't wanted to hurt the Garden any longer.

She loved and hated that in equal measures.

And so, now, when she thought of telling him what she needed, the most pressing need was no longer his leaving and never returning. Now, it was infinitely more dangerous, because it was the same thing she had needed the last time they had met in the darkness.

It was another kiss.

Another touch.

Another night.

One more.

And it did not matter that he might be a more terrifying monster than anything one could find in books.

He sensed the change in her as she took his face in her hands and stared down into his eyes—those amber eyes she'd loved so much and so well and so long, until she'd closed herself off, for fear that they'd haunt her forever.

But they were here, now, and for this night, they were hers.

"Take it," he said.

Everything you need.

She kissed him again, her hands moving, no longer healing. No longer soothing. Wanting. Claiming. He sucked in a breath as she smoothed her hands down over his chest, gentling as she tracked past the bandages on his abdomen, his muscles rippling and tightening enough to remind him of his wounds.

He hissed at the ache, and she lifted her hands as though he'd burned her. "Did I—"

Ewan shook his head instantly. "Don't stop."

She watched him for a moment, unmoving. Uncertain.

"Don't stop."

She didn't want to stop. She wanted to start and never stop. And hold this moment, this night, forever, keeping the past and the present and the impossible-to-ignore truth of them at bay.

A single word shattered through her.

Mine.

He reached for one of her hands and set it to the flat plane of his stomach below the bandages and above the line of his trousers, where muscles cut deep in a V and a trail of dark brown hair disappeared.

She swallowed at the image they made, her fingers on his skin. "I shall be gentle."

"I don't want gentle," he said. "I want you."

She gave him what he asked, her fingers grazing over him, toying and tracing a path down to the place where the falls of the trousers remained unbuttoned, forgotten after his bath. He sucked in a breath as she lingered there, transfixed by the shadowy spot and the thick, impossible-to-ignore ridge directly below, knowing that all she had to do was slide her fingers a touch farther and claim him.

Mine.

What a word. What a wicked, wonderful word.

Ewan lifted a hand to her hair, stroking over it, his fingers tangling in the riot of red curls. "Tell me."

Her lips parted, plump and perfect. "Tonight."

His throat worked, and she knew what he wanted to say. It wasn't enough. She knew it. But she would worry about that tomorrow, when she would reinforce the walls she had built to keep him out, and return to the world she had built without him.

He nodded, the movement stilted, an agreement she knew he did not want to give. And one that freed her nonetheless.

She took it. And then she took him, sliding off his lap to come to her knees before him, loving the way his head tipped back on the chair as he let her go, his eyes going dark and hooded as he watched her, the straining muscles of his neck matching the straining muscles in his hands where he clasped the arms of the chair with white knuckles, refusing to reach for her.

Letting her lead.

And below, his straining cock, hard and glorious.

Mine.

Her hands traced down the placket of his trousers, measuring the outline of him, and she reveled in the way her touch undid him, the way his whole body drew tight like a bow. He was desperate to touch her. She could see it. But still, he held back. He took a deep, shuddering breath, and in that moment—in the revelation of his sheer will to let her control the moment, to let her claim it for her own—something woke inside Grace. Something that she knew would bring pain as much as it brought pleasure.

But tonight was for pleasure.

She came up on her knees, the movement adding pressure to her touch as she leaned in and placed a kiss on his pectoral muscle, turning her face and sliding her cheek over the warmth of him before setting another kiss at the base of his neck, where it met the long line of his collarbone.

She pressed one at the center of his chest, his heart pounding beneath her kiss.

Another, a few inches lower.

He cursed, low and dark, the filthy word sending desire pooling through her. "I've waited for this for so long," he whispered as she followed the line of his bandages with soft, full caresses that set them both aflame.

"Tell me," she repeated his words to his skin as her fingers worked the buttons of his trousers, spreading the fabric wide, revealing the stunning length of him.

Even here, he was perfect.

Especially here.

She sat back, not touching, but staring, long and smooth and hard like stone, rising up from a shadowed thatch of dark brown hair.

"Fuck," he whispered, and it wasn't a curse. It was a prayer.

With difficulty, she drew her attention away from him and met his eyes. "More."

One of his brows rose at the word, and he released his grip on the arm of the chair to reach for her, to cup her face and hold her gaze, the fire in his own impossible to deny. "You like it."

She returned her attention to her prize. "I do."

"I can see it. I can see you want it." He paused, his hips shifting, barely moving. "Christ, Grace . . ."

"Ask for it," she whispered. "Tell me what you like."

"Your touch," he said. "Let me feel—" His hips jerked the moment she gave him what he wanted, her fingers on his hot skin, and he swore again, the wicked words like gunshot in the quiet room. "Yes. Fuck. Yes. I've waited forever for you to touch me like this."

"Like this?" she asked, growing bolder.

He lifted his hips toward her, his fingers sliding deeper into her hair. "God, yes. Like that."

"But not just this," she said, moving, gripping him. Sliding her hand from the thick base of him to the beautiful head, topped with a single drop of liquid. She repeated the movement, and he groaned. "This, too."

"All of it," he said, his voice like sex.

"Show me," she whispered.

His hand was on hers, instantly, and the image—his big, rough hand surrounding hers as he taught her to give him pleasure—was pure need. He tightened their grip. Moved his hips.

Another drop of liquid.

"Don't be gentle," he said, the words coming like gravel on stone. "I don't want it. I want you to—" He bit back the end of the sentence, and she would have done anything to hear it.

"What?" she prompted, her mouth watering at the heat of him. At the portrait they made. "What do you want?"

"I want you to take from me," he said. "I want you to know that whatever you want, whatever you need, I can provide it. I *will* provide it."

The words were almost too much to bear, and Grace leaned forward, her lips coming to their hands, pressing kisses along his bruised knuckles, and he froze at the caress, refusing to move, his breath coming ragged. She lifted her lips and looked at him, the want in his eyes impossible to ignore. "Will you provide me this?"

He closed his eyes, his jaw clenching as his free hand came to her hair. He whispered her name low and dark and wonderful. "Are you—"

She was sure. "I am your queen," she whispered to the back of his hand, giving herself up to the fantasy. Willing him to do the same. "Let me have this."

He released her hand.

Free, she stroked him again, reveling in the smooth size of him—hers to do with as she wished. She worked him, spreading his trousers wide and reaching inside to find the heavy sac within, taking it in hand with a gentle firmness that had him thrusting up off the chair. Another wicked curse. Another droplet.

Too much to resist. She whispered his name and licked over the tip of him, her tongue barely there, just enough to taste the salty sweetness of him. His hands shot to her hair, but landed like feathers, cradling her with care—even as she felt his whole body straining to keep him from taking her. From pressing into her mouth and taking the pleasure she offered.

The pleasure she wanted.

The pleasure he had turned over into her keeping. She reveled in it, and in the power he had given her, and a small part of her wanted to test him—to see how far she could push him until he lost control.

But the other part of her wanted to lose control with him.

"Look at me," he whispered. She did, instantly, and one of his thumbs came to her lower lip, stroking over it. "You don't have to—"

She stopped the words. "Does it ache?"

He exhaled a heavy breath. "More than you can imagine. Or maybe you can imagine it. You ache, too, don't you, love?"

She did, and she did not deny it. "I do."

"Let me take care of you," he said, low and lush like a promise. "Let me strip you bare and spread your legs and lick you until you scream. Let me taste you again. Christ, I've been thinking about the taste of you for days." His thumb stroked again, setting her lip on fire. "Let me ease that ache, where you are hot and wet for me."

The filthy words rioted through her, hot temptation as he pulsed in her hand. She was all those things—hot and wet and aching. She pressed her thighs together to ease the sensation and only served to enhance it.

"You want it, too," he whispered, as though he had sensed what she'd done. "You want me there, between your legs. At your hot core."

She did. She wanted that—God, how she wanted that. But not now.

She opened her mouth and sucked the tip of his thumb into her mouth, her tongue slowly stroking over it once, twice. Giving him a taste of what she intended to come. He swore again, the curse sending pleasure coursing through her, pooling at the heavy, aching spot at the center of her.

She released him and smiled, pure satisfaction. "I want this more."

The words hit him like a weapon, and he leaned down, tilting her face up to his, stealing her mouth in a wild, wanton kiss that stole her breath before he pulled back and whispered, "When you are done, I'm taking what I want."

She nodded. "I shall allow it."

One side of his mouth lifted in stunning masculine amusement. "Queen is right." And then he sat back again, letting his head hit the chair once more.

"Tell me what you want." Not question. Command.

"Suck me." The command was rough and sweet, just as everything that had led to it. His fingers tightened in her hair, firmer now. "Go on."

She parted her lips and took him slowly, learning the size and feel of him. The hard steel of him. The taste of him. The way he held himself perfectly still as she delivered his pleasure. As she took her own, her hand still wrapped around him, stroking.

Grace had spent years running a sex club, making certain that every woman's desire was met to exacting specifications, and in all those years, she'd considered her own, of course—but she'd never once imagined the pure revelation that came from this act. From giving a man the kind of pleasure that threatened his sanity.

And one's own.

Because in her lifetime, Grace had never experienced such pleasure or such immense desire for her partner's pleasure. But now, as she licked and sucked and drew him deep, reveling in his taste and his strength, she was driven by a singular purpose. To give him release. To make him come. To taste it. To know that she was the one who had drawn it from him.

She'd never felt so powerful.

She worked over him, finding the precise speed that made him mad, the precise sensations, the precise spots that drove him wild, loving the sounds he made, and the half sentences he spoke, and the blasphemy he whispered, and the way he said her name like a prayer. And then his hands tightened in her hair and he gasped, "Grace. I'm going to . . . I cannot stop . . ."

Don't you dare stop, she thought to herself—to him. She sucked a touch deeper, moved a touch faster, feeling him grow against her, the head of him pulsing. *Give it to me.*

Mine.

His fingers tightened and he growled a wicked curse, and Grace drank in her power as he called her name to the room and gave himself over to her and to his release. She stayed with him, until he returned to himself, his body relaxing into the chair for the first time since he'd sat. His hands lifting her hair up off her shoulders, the cool air of the room running over the hot skin on the back of her neck.

It was her turn to groan, because it did not soothe, that air—instead, it set her nerves on fire, and the ache she'd held at bay while controlling his pleasure was enhanced and now turned too impossible to ignore.

He knew it, and he leaned down, and he said those words that had tempted her from the start.

"What do you need?"

You. I need you.

No. She couldn't say that. It gave away too much.

"I—" She couldn't find the words, the hot ache in her too much. "I need—" She looked up at him. "Please."

Instantly, he was moving, lifting her, pulling her back into his lap, not caring about his bruises or his bandages—not caring about anything but taking her mouth and cupping the place between her legs, sliding one glorious hand to where she needed him. He broke the wild kiss. "I know," he whispered, a hot promise at her ear. "Here."

"Yes," she whispered back, as he stole the sound with his lips, spreading her wide until she was straddling him, even as she reached for the falls of her own trousers, yanking at them. She fumbled and he was there, unbuttoning them deftly, the magnificent man, even as she realized she had a different problem. She broke the kiss. "Boots."

He nodded, and together they moved with lightning speed, divesting her of boots and trousers until she was bare, except for her corset and coat. He watched her, rapt, as she turned to wriggle out of her coat, leaving her more beautifully bare in an elaborately boned corset, blue the color of the summer sky, with wide straps that covered her shoulders. And when she came back to him, to straddle him once more, the ache was worse and she whispered, desperately, "Do it again. Touch me again."

He obeyed instantly, pressing his hand to her, tight. Strong. Steady enough that when she rocked against it, it set her aflame. She reached down to where he touched her, his gaze following her movement, watching as she clasped his wrist and held him steady.

"Wait, love." She didn't want to wait. She had waited long enough. She wanted this. Now. She grunted her disapproval at the words and worked herself against him, pressing him more firmly.

He groaned a little laugh and said, "Grace." She looked at him, ready to do battle for her own pleasure. Out of her mind with want. With his free hand, he pulled her in for another kiss, and as his tongue slid deep, one of his fingers parted her folds, finding purchase.

She gasped at the lick of pleasure, so acute.

"You may always use me, love," he rumbled in her ear, his finger sliding against the spot where all her desire seemed to have pooled. "But when you use me, I wish you to use me well."

Pleasure rioted through her and she rocked her hips against him, working herself, loving the way he stroked and pressed and moved against her. "Show me," he whispered, dark and lush. "Show me what you ache for."

And then her fingers tangled with his, and she was rocking there, against him, learning the rhythm of her pleasure, teaching it to him, and ultimately ceding it to him, rising up over him, her hands on his shoulders as she panted her need and worked herself against him, knowing she shouldn't, and not caring as he watched her and moved against her, and guided her into a flood of pleasure, until she was crying out in the quiet room, and he was saying the most sinful things, like *harder* and *faster* and *take it* and *yes, love* and *you're the most beautiful thing I've ever seen.*

As she lowered herself back to his lap, he pressed a kiss to her cheekbone, and another to her temple, and he held her in place as she trembled with the aftershocks of her orgasm—giving her his body and his time and making her wish they would never leave this place.

When she returned to thought, she stiffened, instantly lifting her weight from him. "Your bandages."

"You think I feel pain right now?" He pulled her back into his lap and pressed another kiss to her hair, the caress so natural that it warmed Grace in places she had never been warm.

She smiled. "I only wish you to feel pleasure."

His hand slid down her arm, the touch sending a shiver through her as it changed from lazy to purposeful. "Then we must do that often."

Her smile disappeared.

It couldn't happen, of course. There was no *often* between them.

There was no future between them, because all the space had been filled with the past.

This had been a mistake.

She moved to leave his lap, and he grasped her hand. She froze, expecting him to hold her there. He didn't. But he did hold her, the warmth of his hand in hers a lure and a promise and a temptation that she did not need. She pulled away, hating the feel of her hand sliding from his.

He didn't resist. He didn't pull her back.

Frustration flared, and Grace knew it was irrational. "I must go."

He did not move, watching as she pulled on her trousers, then picked up the items that had dropped to the floor, leaving him the salve and the ice box, and the cloth. Setting the basket of bandages carefully on his table.

She looked down at him. "I must go."

He nodded. Was he not going to stop her?

She didn't want him to, did she?

This made it easier, did it not?

It did. But it didn't make it better.

Swallowing around the knot in her throat, Grace turned away to collect her coat from where she'd tossed it to the floor, interested only in the pleasure he offered, every part of her wanting to stay. Wanting him to ask her to stay.

And then he did. "How did you get past the servants?"

Knowing she asked for trouble, Grace turned her head, giving him her profile as she said, "I do, in fact, always travel by rooftop."

He stood at that, slow and deliberate, and her heart began to pound. "I wanted to follow you today. Up that wall."

She turned to face him. "It's not as easy as it looks."

He gave her a half smile. "I believe that."

She watched him for a moment and then said, "Instead you left me."

"And you came to see me."

The echo of his words from earlier. *Come see me.* She was supposed to have come to see him to tell him what she needed and instead she'd simply come to see him, this man she did not know, so different from all the other hims he'd been. So different, and so much more dangerous.

"Show me," he said, interrupting her thoughts.

She shouldn't. It was a mistake to spend any more time with him than this. To spend any more time learning him than this.

She shouldn't. But she wanted to. She wanted to bring him to the roof and give him a taste of the freedom she had claimed for herself.

To make a new memory.

An idea teased through her.

She crossed the room to his wardrobe in silence, opening it to pull a fine white shirt from inside. Holding it to her chest, she turned back to find him buttoning his trousers, his amber gaze glittering in the candlelight.

Shamelessly, she watched him work the fastenings, and immediately she missed the ridges and shadows before the buttons were even seated. There were members of 72 Shelton who requested their consorts in full, elaborate dress simply to watch them take the clothes off and put them back on, and though Grace rarely questioned the desires of her clientele, she had never quite understood the pleasure of watching one's lover disrobe.

But right now, as his strong arms worked and the muscles of his forearms flexed, her mouth dried, and she found she was coming to see its merits. She could watch him work at his trouser buttons for hours.

He finished. "Are you going to dress me now?"

She tossed him the shirt, admiring the speed with which he snatched it from the air before pulling it over his head in a smooth movement that belied what she knew were the protesting aches and twinges in his muscles. There was an intimacy to it, the idea that she'd just held the soft linen that was now sliding over his skin like a caress.

Once he was wearing the shirt, the tails hanging loose around his narrow hips, he raked his gaze over her, taking in her corset and trousers, his gaze lighting with interest.

At another time, with another man, she might have been amused by the rapt attention, so soon after they'd both found release. But here, now, she was not entertained by the desire in his eyes. Instead, she reveled in it.

He was hers.

How far would he follow her?

Tomorrow, day would come, and with it the truth of their past and their present, and the impossibility of their future. But there was tonight, and if coming of age on the streets had taught Grace anything, it was that planning was for business and not for pleasure.

Decision made, she lifted a candle and extended her hand to him. "Come with me."

Chapter Eighteen

They climbed the dark back stairs to the roof of the Marwick ancestral home as though they were in the wilds of Scotland, miles from the nearest person, and not in Grosvenor Square, where any number of London's most revered aristocratic families could see them.

And perhaps Ewan should have cared about that, but he'd never cared about the dukedom and that night . . . all he cared about was Grace.

Grace, topcoat in one hand and his hand in the other as she led him up, past the second floor, the third, until the stairs grew dark for lack of wall sconces and narrow enough to fit only one person. Once at the top, she turned and pressed herself to the wall, lifting her chin to indicate the door inlaid above their heads. "Go on, then," she whispered. "Open it."

He reached up, surprised to find that his heart was pounding. Hesitated.

"Nervous, Duke?"

He met her eyes, the candle between them bathing her face in flickering light, and gave a little self-deprecating laugh. "I don't know why—it's not as though we shall find a collection of critical aristocrats on the other side."

She grinned. "Ah, but imagine if we did. We'd empty London of smelling salts. Though, to be honest, I'm not sure what they'd be able to critique," she said as he pushed the door up and open, sending it slamming down on the roof. "My bottom looks superior in these trousers."

Leaving him with that incontrovertible fact, Grace climbed up and through the hatch, that same bottom full and beautiful, making him want to pull her back inside, take her to bed, and show her all the ways it was superior—roof be damned.

But she was already gone, climbing through to the outside and turning back, the silver thread of her corset gleaming in the candlelight as she made a show of looking about. "You are safe. Not a single roving aristocrat with a discerning eye."

The teasing warmed him—and he loved it even as he knew better than to believe this more than a heartbeat of happiness. Wasn't that always the way with him and Grace? Always chasing happiness, never catching it?

He climbed out onto the roof, following her into the unseasonably comfortable autumn night. She was already headed to the southern face of the house, where it bordered the square. He watched her for a moment, amazed by her ease here, above the city.

"Someone might see you."

She turned on him with a smile. "Afraid the Marquess of Westminster has a spyglass in the window across the way?"

"Good God. I wasn't, but now that you've said it . . ."

"Westminster isn't a voyeur. He's far too austere for such a pastime," she said casually, as though it were perfectly common for a girl who'd kept a roof over her head by bare-knuckle fighting to know the personality traits of one of the wealthiest aristocrats in Britain. She kept going. "And even if it weren't too dark to see anything worth seeing, the only things he'd be looking at through his spyglass are your horses." She looked to him. "Do you have horses?"

The question took him aback. "I do."

She waved a hand. "Not carriage horses or the grey you've been known to ride in Hyde Park. I'm talking about racing horses. That's what Westminster is interested in."

"How did you know I ride in Hyde Park?"

She shrugged, returning her attention to the square below. "The same way I know Westminster likes horses."

"What way is that?"

"It's my business to know things."

"Such as affinity for horses."

"Such as whether or not Westminster's affinity for horses has anything to do with an affinity for gambling. Such as why Earl Leither is lobbying for looser penalties for opium traffic. Such as why the publisher of the *News of London* is so devoted to the idea of women's suffrage."

His brows shot up. "And how do you know these things?"

She lifted a chin toward the square. "You toffs think the whole world is built inside the buildings of this perfectly manicured square, where no one with less than ten thousand a year is welcome, but the truth is, the world is built on trade, and trade, while banal, bourgeois, and boring to the aristocracy, is a business worth being in."

"What kind of trade?"

"Information and pleasure. Sometimes both. Never neither."

"And you deal in those commodities?"

She shrugged one shoulder and looked toward Westminster House. "The point is, Westminster isn't interested in our location or the state of our dress, or lack thereof. It's dark, Ewan. No one can see us. And if they do, they shall simply think that Mad Marwick has found his way to the roof with his most recent paramour."

"The paramour shall be the most surprising part of that story," he said, dryly.

She stilled, and he cursed himself, not wanting this conversation. Not now, just when he'd convinced her to unlock for him. Turning to him, she said, softly, "No mistress, waiting in the wings at Burghsey?"

Was she jealous?

"*I'm* barely in the wings at Burghsey."

"That doesn't mean you can't find pleasure there."

"There is no pleasure there." The words came out colder than he intended. Harsher. He cleared his throat, not wanting that place here, between them. Not wanting it close to her ever again. He cleared his throat and said, "Honestly, pleasure is not something with which I have experience."

She turned back to him. "How very sad. What is the point of title and money and power and privilege if not to use it in nightly ducal bacchanal?"

He laughed. "I'm afraid I have never received an invitation to a ducal bacchanal."

"Hmm," she said. "I think you should count yourself lucky on that front. I know a number of duchesses, and their husbands are largely deadly dull or absolutely disgusting; neither quality makes for a good party."

"I shall endeavor to avoid both, in that case, and leave all my bacchanals to you."

She smiled at that. "I am very good at them."

"I have no trouble believing that," he said, wanting to return to her life.

She inclined her head. "My business is pleasure, as I said."

"And information."

"You would be amazed what flows along with pleasure."

"I think I can imagine." He paused, then said, "What have you learned about me?"

"Who says I've asked about you?"

He smirked. "You have asked about me."

A moment, then, "No one knows you."

You know me. He didn't say it.

"The most anyone can tell me about you is that you have a grey horse. And you like to ride in the park."

"I don't like to ride in the park, as a matter of fact."

"Of course, you don't," she said, as though everyone knew that. "You like to ride in places where you can ride far and fast."

He looked to her. "And pretend I never have to return."

"But you always have to, don't you? Return?"

He always had, tied to his father and the dukedom like he'd been on a chain. Tethered to Burghsey House. To this one.

"And no one can tell me where you've been for the last year," she said, softly, to the night.

He looked to her. "No one knows."

She waited. "And so?"

"You told me to leave," he replied, looking away, back to the rooftops, shadowed in moonlight.

"And yet, you returned," she said.

"A different man than I left," he confessed. "A better one."

Silence, the autumn wind the only movement between them. "I think you might be," she said.

"The man who left didn't have a purpose."

"And now you do?"

He looked directly at her. "I do."

The words should have scared her and sent her running over the rooftops, back to the Garden. And perhaps they would have done in the past. But tonight, here—Ewan had the distinct feeling that he was not the only one who had changed.

As though she'd heard the thought, she swallowed and looked away. He followed her gaze, looking down into the square, where the tops of the trees were barely visible in the moonlight. "It never occurred to me that I had a roof."

"That's what comes of never having to worry about having one."

He looked down at her. "I have had to worry, you know."

Worrying about a roof was what had thrown them together in the first place. Fear of loss. Fear of uncertainty. Fear of hunger and want.

"I know," she said, softly. "We all have."

He didn't think she meant it as a barb, but it struck true as she pulled on her coat and turned away from the edge, moving to the chimney stacks at the center of the roof. She perched herself on the brick step that led to the chimney block, extending her booted legs, watching him.

"Christ." He shook his head, turning back to the darkness. "Grosvenor Square. It still feels impossible."

He felt this way every time he came to London to this house that had never felt like his, in this city that no longer felt like his, in this world where he had never felt like he belonged—it did not matter how many tutors, and years at Eton and Oxford, and dancing lessons and land management tutorials he'd had. It did not matter the tailors and valets and butlers and cooks he'd had. When he walked the hallways of Marwick House, he always felt like the fraud he was.

"It shouldn't." She pulled him from his thoughts. "We always said you'd end up here, Duke."

He gritted his teeth. "I wish you wouldn't call me that."

"It is your title, is it not?" When he didn't reply, she said, "Would you prefer Your Grace?"

"No," he said instantly. "Christ. No. I've always hated that." It was a never-ending memory of her, like torture, ensuring that she was always with him and still never there.

She tilted her head. "So you don't like the name, you don't like the title, you don't like the honorific. You don't like the butler or the neighbors or the house or the attire or the privilege." She paused. "Is there anything about the dukedom that you do like?"

Instead of answering, Ewan turned to look over the dark roofs, the light from the waning moon barely enough to see the next house, let alone across the square. "I don't see how it's possible for you to travel London like this."

She flashed him a grin. "You mean by sky?"

"Is that what you call it?"

"I've always rather liked the poetry of it," she said. "The truth is, the sky would be easier. But when the moon is out and the street lamps are lit? I know the way."

The words echoed through him, something strange about them. He met her eyes. "You know the way?"

The air between them thickened with the question. It didn't make sense that she would know the way. It didn't make sense that the girl who had been raised on the streets and become Covent Garden royalty, running information and spies and pleasure like she did, would have the time, interest, or inclination to learn the way from the Rookery to the northern edge of Grosvenor Square.

It didn't make sense that she would know the wheres and hows to get herself to the rooftops here, in Mayfair, where the city was more manicured, less labyrinthine, and teeming with people who would send round to Bow Street without second thought if they saw someone skulking about on the roof.

It didn't matter how beautiful she was, or how commanding.

Unless she'd been doing it long enough that she knew all the ways to avoid being seen. Ewan caught his breath at the idea, immediately closing the distance between them, knowing that the question was a risk. If he was right, it could scare her off.

But was this not their life? Did they not risk?

As he drew close, she deliberately did not look at him, picking at something invisible on her trouser leg. Even if there was something there, it was the dead of night—there was no way she could see it. She was avoiding him.

"How do you know the way, Grace?"

"It's only a mile," she replied, and he heard the caution in her tone. "It's not like knowing the way to Wales."

They both knew Mayfair might as well be Wales for as far away as it was from the Rookery. He was close enough to her that he could see her a bit, her face glowing gold in the flickering candlelight, and her hair shot through with silver from the moon.

"Tell me," he said softly, moving toward her and suddenly very eager to know the truth. "Tell me how you knew this was my roof."

She fidgeted, the movement so shocking that it set him back. Had she ever fidgeted? He reached for her, his fingers pushing a lock of her red hair behind one of her ears—how had he never noticed her ears were perfect?

"It's Grosvenor Square, Marwick. There aren't that many homes, and I can count chimney stacks as well as the next girl."

He shook his head. "Not Marwick. Not now, dammit."

Her eyes went wide at the steel in his tone. "Careful," she warned.

Ewan didn't care. There was something there, and he would know more. "Tell me how you know there's an opening in my roof, Grace."

Her gaze snapped to his, defensively. "There's an opening in everyone's roof. Toffs don't know, because they don't sweep chimneys and they don't tar roofs, so why should they spend time here?"

"Tell me how you knew how to get inside."

"I've never been inside," she said, not liking the direction of his questions. "With the exception of the ball, I've never been inside."

He believed her. But something was off. Something had happened here.

There was something else.

"What, then?" he asked.

An eternity passed while he waited for her to speak. Finally, "I used to come here."

"Why?"

"I knew a duke who needed a good fleecing."

He shook his head. "No, Grace. Why?"

It was his turn to wait an eternity. More.

"I came to wait for you," she said.

The confession nearly put him to his knees. "Why?"

She looked away. "It doesn't matter."

It was the only thing that mattered.

"I thought I could—" She trailed off.

She didn't need to. She couldn't have. Whatever Grace had thought she could do if she'd seen him in those years after he'd run them off—whatever she'd thought she could convince him to do if only she'd seen him . . . she wouldn't have been able to.

Finally, she said, "What happened after we left?"

He shook his head. "It doesn't matter."

"It does, though. Where did you go? You were never here."

"School," he said. He'd gone to school, mercifully, and there, he'd found something like solace—even as the rest of the boys thought him mad. Even as they might have been right. "Eton, and then Oxford, and then away—to the continent. Wherever I could go and be rid of him and his threats."

"He never stopped hurting you," she said, softly.

Of course he hadn't. But not in the way she thought.

His father had hurt him again and again by promising that if Ewan ever misstepped, Grace would suffer. Devil and Whit, too. Ewan would play the part of doting son. Of Earl.

And if he didn't, the people he loved would pay.

Of course the whole world had thought him mad. And if he'd known she'd come here? To this rooftop, to wait for him? He would have razed the building to keep her safe.

And then, a worse thought. One that terrified him. "Did you ever see him?"

It was the only thing that mattered. Ewan did not think he could bear the idea of her coming face to face with his father—even now, even as a Covent Garden queen who could more than easily hold her own against the dead duke.

She shook her head. "No."

She could have been killed.

"You should never have had to find your way here. You should never have had to count chimney stacks," he said, anger flaring. "This was supposed to be—" It was supposed to be she who was the child of this home, and instead, in a wild twist of fate, it had become he. "This should have been your house. You should be the one with the coveted address, the warm bed waiting below. The servants and the carriages and the money beyond imagining."

"I have a warm bed waiting," she replied, her eyes dark and unreadable. "And servants and carriages and money beyond imagining. I've even a coveted address, as far as addresses go in the East End." She paused. "Don't wring your hands. I never wanted the title, the pomp, or the circumstance. And I've done quite well on my own."

"Who is Dahlia?"

She smiled. "You're looking at her."

He shook his head. "No, I'm not. I've seen her. At my masquerade. In the warehouse yard, ending a riot. Downstairs, for a heartbeat, until you gave me access to Grace."

She fidgeted beneath the words and he knew he was right. "But who is she?"

She met his gaze. "She's the queen."

He hated that she wouldn't tell him. Hated that she didn't trust him with her truth.

But he couldn't blame her.

He took a deep breath, his gaze tracing over her corset, the gold thread gleaming in the barely-there light from the candle at her feet, an echo of a memory. "Do you remember what I promised you? When we were young?"

"We promised each other a thousand things, Ewan."

He nodded, loving the sound of his name on her lips. "You remember, though."

For some reason, it mattered that she did, and he let out a long breath when she said, "You promised me gold thread."

Relief shot through him and he nodded, watching her. "At the time, it was all I could think to promise you. My mother . . ." He paused, and she watched him so carefully, her beautiful eyes so full of understanding, even now, even as he'd betrayed her. Even as he'd betrayed them all. "She'd talk about gold thread like it was currency. I thought it was the most extravagant thing I could give you."

"I never wanted extravagance."

"I wanted to give it to you, nonetheless. I promised you—"

I would make you duchess.

She heard it. "I never wanted that, either," she said, softly, before coming to her feet and approaching him. "I only ever wanted the world you offered me." She stopped in front of him and looked up, her eyes black with the darkness, the light from the moon and the candle she'd left behind barely enough to see her. "Do you remember that?"

He remembered everything.

"Much of it is the same, you know. The carts on the

cobblestones still clatter and clang, and there's never a moment when a brawl isn't ready in a tavern. And the market square is full of farmers and broad tossers, all looking to sell you something."

When they were young, he painted her countless pictures of the Garden, full of life and freedom, glossing over the bad bits and giving her the good, convinced that she'd never have to face the first.

"And so? Have you learned all the curse words?"

She grinned, her teeth flashing white in the darkness. "Every last one. I've created some of my own."

"I should like to hear them."

"I don't think you're ready for them."

That tease again, a hint of what could be. He clung to it. "And now you know the best part," he said, softly.

"The rain turns the streets to gold."

He reached for her at that, thinking she might flinch from him, but she didn't. He touched the side of her face, pushed a lock of her beautiful hair behind one ear, loving the memory of it. There had been a thousand things they'd never done together—but this—a gentle touch, a stolen moment—it was all familiar.

"I never wanted the dukedom," she said. "I wanted the Garden. That was what you promised me. That we would give it what it deserved."

We're going to change all that.

"And did you?" he asked, knowing the answer. "Did you make good on my promise?"

She nodded. "We did."

Her. Devil. Whit. He hadn't been a part of it. In fact, he'd made it worse.

He looked to the sky. "I sent money. To the families."

"I know."

And back to her. "You asked me if there was anything I liked about being duke."

"And?"

"I like being able to pour his money into the Garden. I like being able to use his name to make change there."

"The bill in debate. It's not Leighton's or Lamont's. It's yours." Her gaze found his, sharp and understanding. Seeing more than he was ready for her to see. "For the Garden."

"I thought that if Mad Marwick introduced it, no one would consider it."

"No one will consider it anyway," she said. "No one in the Garden ever gets what they deserve."

She was right. There weren't enough in Parliament who stood with the men and women in London's poorest corners. Even now, he could not make good on his long-ago promise. Not like she had.

"I don't expect forgiveness."

"Good."

"But I wish it."

I wish it from you, as well.

She looked past him then, over his shoulder. "The sun is coming."

He looked in the direction she pointed, to the east, at first, not seeing anything but the black sky. And then he saw it, the barely-there charcoal edge on the horizon, a collection of angles. Rooftops.

"You never told me the best part of it."

He looked to her and shook his head. "I don't understand."

"You never told me that the Rookeries are the first to get the sun."

They had changed it.

The words, a simple observation that shouldn't have meant anything, stole his breath. Whether it was the words or the distant promise of dawn, he would never know, but he said, "I wish I had run with you."

The confession was a risk, and he immediately wished he could take it back. It would remind her of that night, when he'd ruined everything with the worst kind of betrayal. But it was suddenly essential she know the truth, even if it ended with her anger.

But perhaps it was the dawn that kept her anger at bay, because when she spoke, there was no vitriol in the words. Instead, there was something wistful there.

"Something else would have ruined us," she said to the rooftops in the distance—her country, awaiting her return. "We were too much each other to have ever really loved each other."

He hated the words. "I loved you," he said, knowing it wasn't enough.

"I know," she said. "And I loved you. But it was a springtime love. A summer one. Left alone to flourish until the cold came. Until the wind threatened to rip it apart and the frost killed it off."

He hated the image. Hated that he was the cold, when she had only ever been the sun.

She returned to the moment, her eyes finding his. "First love is not forever."

The words were another blow, harsher than the ones he'd taken earlier in the day. "And so? What now?"

She was close enough that he heard the breath she took, the slow, even inhale, giving her time to think. "Ewan," she said, softly, and for the first time since he'd returned and they'd begun this dance, or game, or whatever it was they did, he heard something in her voice like care.

He clung to it, and said, "What if we freed ourselves from it?" Confusion furrowed her brow and he said the rest. "What if we began again?"

"Began again?" she said, disbelief in her words. "How would we do that? I have never been able to live my life free from you." His heart began to pound as she spoke to the darkness, to this city that had been his and now was hers. "Not before I met you and not after. I was nobody before you, a placeholder, waiting for you, like a fly in amber."

"I, too, was nobody," he said, wanting to touch her and knowing he shouldn't.

"You weren't, though," she said, her eyes glittering in the flickering candlelight. "You were Ewan, strong and smart, and the one who swore you'd get us all out."

"I did get you out."

She stiffened at the words, like she was made of steel. "You *chased* us out. You scared us out. And you left us alone, living in your"—she waved a hand over the square, before she spat—"*palace* while we scraped and fought for everything we had."

It was true. And also false.

Tell her.

How would she ever understand?

"You lied to us," she said, her long, loose hair whipped up in the wind. "You—" *Christ.* Her voice cracked. He didn't think he could bear it if she cried. "You lied to *me*," she said, the words coming like thunder, crashing all around them. "And we can never begin again, because everything you were—everything *we* were—it remains. And it cannot be erased. And I should hate you for it."

It was time to tell her, and he might have. He might have explained then. Might have begun the work of telling her the truth—explaining what had happened on that long-ago night. And it might have been enough.

Except she wasn't finished. "And even if I could forgive the boy you were, what of the things you did as a man? Devil. Whit. Hattie. *Five* boys in the garden—you may not have pulled the triggers or lit the match, but they are gone because of you. You threatened our livelihoods. Our *home*." She narrowed her gaze at him. "You say you've changed."

He had.

"You say you are a better man."

He was.

Wasn't he?

"But I'm not sure it matters."

All that mattered was that he had harmed her.

"It *shouldn't* matter." She lowered her voice to a whisper, as though she was speaking to herself and not him. "It shouldn't matter . . . and I should hate you."

He clung to that *should*, reaching for her, telling himself that he would let her go the second she pushed him away. The second she resisted him.

But she didn't resist him.

"Who am I without that hate?" she whispered.

His heart ached at the question.

"Who are you without it?" she added.

"I don't know," he told her. Truth. "All I know is that I want to know." He put his forehead to hers and closed his eyes, and said the words that had haunted him every day since the day she'd left. "I'm sorry."

He'd never meant anything so much.

They crashed together like thunder, the kiss robbing them both of breath and threatening to rob Ewan of far more. As he pulled her close, she was already tilting up to him, her hands already coming into his hair to pull him to her, her lips full and open as they met his, breath and tongues tangling as they consumed each other.

Like fire.

And it was fire, hot and made nearly unbearable with the knowledge that she wanted him as he wanted her. That though she should hate him, whatever she did feel—wherever they stood now—was not hate. It was something else.

Ewan could work with something else, if only she would let him.

His lip stung with the force of the kiss but he did not care, not when her tongue was stroking against his and he was so quickly lost, a groan escaping as he tasted her again, pulling her close and lifting her to him until they were pressed against each other, like two halves of a whole.

Like they'd always been.

Though he could not tell where his ended and hers began, he could taste the emotion in the urgent kiss—sorrow and anger and frustration and desire, and something that she would not name but that he knew would always be there.

Her fingers sank into his hair, and he settled into her mouth, stroking deep until she sighed her pleasure, the sound rushing through him, straight to the core of him, where he was hard and aching once more.

The evening hadn't been enough.

It would never be enough.

It was a claiming. *He* was claimed. Hers forever.

And she . . .

Mine.

Christ. He would give everything to claim her in return.

As though she'd heard the thought, she stopped the kiss, pushing him away, taking a step back to put space between them, their breaths heavy and aching, shock and desire flashing along with wild frustration in her eyes.

But that wasn't it. There was something else.

Need.

She needed him, and Christ, he needed her, too.

She saw it. Saw that he would give her everything she asked. Everything she wanted. She took another step back, shaking her head, and held up an accusing hand. "No."

"Grace," he said, reaching as she turned, her hair, her coat, everything about her slipping through his fingers as she took off across the roof, and disappeared into the night.

Every ounce of him raged to follow her. To catch her and tell her everything. To make her understand.

I'm not sure it matters.

She disappeared from view and he stared after her, watching the eastern sky grow lighter, charcoal giving way to lavender and then the deepest red he'd ever seen, like the whole city was aflame.

And only once the blinding sunlight climbed over the rooftops did he let himself go. Around Grosvenor Square, servants climbed from their beds to the frustrated roar he let out to the dawn.

Chapter Nineteen

One week later, Grace went to Berkeley Square for dinner.

When they'd married, Whit had bought his wife a stunning town house on the western edge of the square, because she'd said she liked it, and he had set himself a singular life's goal—spoiling Hattie. The house sat empty most days of the week, because Hattie ran one of London's largest shipping operations and Whit was never without work at Bastards' headquarters, and they both preferred their more convenient home in Covent Garden.

But Whit didn't like visitors in his private quarters—even family—so they hosted family dinners each Friday in the town house, affording Whit and Devil the pleasure of doing their very best to "scare off the toffs" when they arrived, which usually involved making a racket in an ancient gig, complete with mud-caked boots and faces in dire need of a shave.

Suffice to say, the venerable aristocratic residents of Berkeley Square had a great deal to discuss on Saturday mornings.

The dinners were usually one of Grace's happiest times of the week, allowing her a heartbeat of time to cuddle with

Devil and Felicity's Helena, eight months old and perfect in every way.

But that night, a week after she'd fled the rooftops of a different Mayfair square, she dreaded the event, knowing that she would no longer be able to avoid thinking about the Duke of Marwick's rooftop.

Nor would she be able to avoid thinking about the evening in the Duke of Marwick's home. Nor the moments on the Duke of Marwick's lap, nor the afternoon with the Duke of Marwick in the Garden, blood and dirt on his shirt as though brawling was an everyday occurrence.

And she would absolutely not be able to avoid thinking of the Duke of Marwick himself, who was no longer the Duke of Marwick in her mind. It had taken her years to stop thinking of him as Ewan, and mere days for her to return to it.

Ewan.

And that change, barely anything to the rest of the world, was enough to send Grace into internal chaos.

Who am I without that hate?

Who are you?

The questions had echoed for a week, as she'd lived her life and run her business and planned the October Dominion. And for a week, the answers had eluded her.

Still, she attended the dinner, entering the house, shucking her coat, and accepting a gurgling Helena from her smiling nurse, grateful to have the baby as a shield for what she suspected was to come.

She wasn't the only one in Covent Garden with spies. She merely had the best. And it didn't take the best of spies to notice when a duke came kissing Dahlia in broad daylight with a bevy of washerwomen looking on in delight.

Her cheeks warmed as she entered the dining room of the home—one-half long, elaborately set table, already laden with platters of game and veg, as though Hattie had prepared for the queen herself, and one-half sitting room. It was a design choice that Grace had always rather liked, stemming from the fact that Hattie abhorred the trend of ladies and gentlemen separating after meals, and she prevented it by making the dining room comfortable for more than eating.

Grace had barely stepped into the room—was still having a nonsense chat with Helena, in fact—when Devil turned from the sideboard where he'd poured himself two fingers of whisky and said, "Ah, we wondered if you'd be too busy to join us tonight."

Ignoring the tightening in her gut at the words, Grace tossed a quick smile to her sisters-in-law, Felicity, by the high windows on one end of the room, and Hattie, perched on the arm of the large chair where Whit sat, and said, brightly, in a singsong voice to Helena, "Why would I be too busy to join you?"

"I don't know," Devil said, approaching her with a second glass. "We thought perhaps you'd be too busy catting about with Marwick."

"I see we're getting right to it, then." Grace's heart threatened to beat from her chest, and she wondered if others could hear it over the only other sound in the room—a babbling Helena, her little fist clapping against Grace's cheek.

She took the drink from Devil and looked into it. "Is it safe to drink?"

He smirked, his scar pulling tight on his face. "I'm not the one with a history of trying to kill you, Gracie."

Devil had never in his life pulled a punch.

"Oh, for heaven's sake." Felicity came over from her place by the window, the bright pink skirts of her gown rustling against the plush carpet. "Stand down, will you? Would you listen to this one," she scoffed. "As though he's lived the life of a saint."

"I haven't tried to seduce a woman I've nearly killed," he said.

"No," Felicity retorted, "you only tried to seduce a woman in an attempt to ruin her life."

Hattie coughed a laugh, and Whit and Grace's brows rose in the kind of unison that proved that siblings didn't need to share blood to share affect.

"That's different!" he declared. "I was going to get you sorted, proper spinster-like."

"Ah, yes. A widow's cottage in the Hebrides or some such." Felicity cut him a look before returning her attention to Grace. "So. Tell us."

"I don't know what you are asking."

Lie. But Felicity was not easily waved off. "We know he kissed you after—this part seems very strange—helping Alice with the wash?"

There was no point in denying it. It had been in broad view of half the Rookery. "It's true."

Silence again, and Grace felt four sets of hot looks on her as she pretended to be riveted to Helena, her only ally. The baby blew a bubble and laughed, completely unaware of her surroundings.

Devil turned to Whit. "Do you have anything to say?"

Whit shrugged. "I told you."

"As though we needed a fucking oracle to see it."

Grace turned to him. "To see what?"

He ran a hand through his hair. "That he was back for you."

The reason I have done everything from the start, he'd said. *For you.*

"Not just that," Whit said. "You're back for him, too."

"I'm not." She shook her head. And then, at the quartet of disbelieving looks, she said, "I shouldn't be."

"Damn right," Devil said.

"Devil," Felicity said, censure in her tone.

He turned away, grumbling, "She's not wrong."

"But what if she is?" Hattie interjected as she stood,

crossing the room and selecting a turned carrot from a platter there. "I'm assuming we are not sitting down to dinner, right?" She took a bite of the vegetable and after chewing thoughtfully said, "What if he's back and he's changed?"

Grace ignored the thrum that went through her at the question. At the idea that Hattie might think it possible. "Men don't change," Grace said. "That's the first rule of surviving as a woman in the world. Men don't change."

"That's true," Devil said.

"Bollocks," Felicity replied. "You changed."

"You changed me, love," he said instantly. "That's different."

"Of course, I did," she said, "just as you changed me." She approached him, sliding into the crook of his arm. "What if Grace changed him?" She paused, then said, "The man who came for you, for Whit, for Hattie . . . for me . . . he was all anguish. No hope."

They told me you were dead.

Felicity shrugged. "Hope changes a person."

Grace went still at the words.

What if he finally had hope?

What if she did?

Helena began to fret, and Grace walked her to her parents. Without missing a beat, Devil took the babe and set her in the crook of his arm, pulling a silver rattle from his pocket and handing it to her.

"What's your point, Felicity?" Devil asked once the baby was settled.

"I think you very well know what my point is," she said to her husband before looking to Grace. "My point is, don't listen to them."

"Hear, hear!" Hattie roundly agreed. "They haven't any idea what they're on about."

"It took them both near-death experiences to know what they wanted."

"That's not true!" Devil said. "I knew what I wanted."

"You did not," Whit said. "Grace and I had to knock actual sense into you to get you to see that Felicity was far better than you could ever dream of having." He turned a smile on his sister-in-law. "You know that, don't you, that you settled?"

Felicity smiled happily. "In fact, I do."

"I, on the other hand, knew I wanted Hattie from the first moment I saw her."

Hattie's brows shot up. "You did, did you?"

He flashed a grin at his wife. "From the moment you pushed me from a moving carriage, luv. How could I not?"

Hattie turned back to Grace. "A glutton for punishment."

"Yes, well, I'm beginning to think it's a family trait," she said, dryly.

"But the duke . . ." Hattie said. "He doesn't seem to have difficulty setting his sights on what he wants."

"No," Whit agreed, dryly. "He's so certain he wants you, you had to stay in hiding for twenty years."

Grace was no longer convinced that they had been running from Ewan, though. Something was changed.

Or maybe it was false hope.

Felicity tilted her head. "That is something of a black mark, to be sure."

"What in hell are we discussing here," Devil interjected. "Have you forgotten he kept us running scared for years? Have you forgotten that he knocked me over the head and tried to freeze me to death?"

"It's important to note, you *didn't* freeze to death," Felicity said.

Devil's brows rose in disbelief. "We shall have words when we get home, wife."

She shook her head at the group. "We never have words when we get home."

"That's because you are distracting, but I shan't be

distracted from this," he said. "I survived because you saved me."

She turned to look at Grace. "Not only me. The duke left London the night he left Devil for dead. He'd known that he was being watched. If I hadn't saved Devil, Whit would have—he would have come to tell Devil that Marwick was gone."

It wasn't an impossibility, Grace thought. But it was a gamble.

"I've never bought that argument," Devil grumbled.

"Never?" Grace's brows rose. "Is this a discussion that is had often?"

"It's Hattie's theory," Whit grumbled. "I don't like it"—he turned his attention to his wife—"as he *exploded* her."

"Again," Hattie said quite happily, "I was only *slightly* exploded."

Grace looked to Hattie, feeling a bit like she'd been given too little laudanum and was hallucinating instead of sleeping. "Slightly exploded?"

Whit grunted his irritation.

Hattie waved a hand through the air. "And only because he didn't get to me in time." She looked to Grace. "I believe he intended to get to me in time. To stop me from being hurt. He wasn't responsible for the second explosion. That was the one that hurt me and the others. We know that."

"And so? We give points for not lighting the match?" Whit said. "For not firing the pistol? Intent wouldn't have saved you if you'd been . . ."

Hattie gave him a little kiss on the cheek. "Yes, love. But I wasn't."

"And so, what, we forgive him simply because you survived?"

She looked to Felicity. "I don't think he's gone without punishment, do you?"

"Hell, no," Devil said. "But I wouldn't object to him being packed into the ice hold for a decade or two. Cold storage would do him well."

They told me you were dead.

"And if he'd succeeded in killing Hattie? In harming Felicity? What would you have done?" Grace asked.

Devil looked to Whit, and she saw the answer pass between them. Recognized it, because it was her answer, too.

Devil answered. "I would have burned Mayfair to the ground to get to him."

She nodded. "The three of us, baptized in revenge."

"No," Whit said, softly. "Four of us."

Devil cursed softly, and looked down at his daughter, happily drooling on his sleeve. "As unlucky as we were, we were the lucky ones. I have Felicity and Helena, and the Garden. The business." He cut her a look. "You, I suppose."

Grateful for the levity, Grace put a hand to her breast. "Really, it's too much flattery."

He flashed a smile, and then said, "But what did he get? The estate? The house in Mayfair? The title and all the responsibility that comes with it? And the memories."

"We own the memories, too," she said.

"Yes, but our memories come with the present." He stopped. "With the three of us. Grown. Changed. Survived. What does he have but loneliness and regret?"

Whit grunted.

"I don't know," she said softly.

Devil continued. "Don't matter, because what he has ain't the question, Gracie. What *you* have is the question."

She shook her head. "I have the same as you."

Another grunt from Whit. And then, "You have worse."

"Why?"

"Because my ribs healed. And Devil's face. And the other breaks—" He reached for Hattie, who slipped a hand into his instantly. "We've had a chance to mend. But you—your break can't mend."

He'd broken her heart.

"And because it never mended, you were never able to love again. Which is why you've spent your whole life caring for the Garden. For the employees in your club and the girls on the rooftops and for us—never once taking a moment to think about how you might care for yourself. Never once being willing to take a risk and love again. Instead, you serve up love without ties over on Shelton Street, and pretend nobody notices that at the end of the night, you're alone."

She hated every word, for its truth, and hated that Whit, silent and stoic, always knew precisely the problem. "I like you better when you don't talk."

He grunted.

"I love," she replied, defensively. When her brothers looked to each other, she said, "I do! Against my will, I love the two of you. And your wives. And Helena." She pointed to Hattie, already sitting at the foot of the dining room table. "And the babe in Hattie's belly—when is that babe coming, anyway?"

Hattie rubbed a hand over the enormous swell of her pregnant belly. "Never, it seems. He wants to stay in."

"*She's* not stupid. The world is a perilous place," Whit said, tipping his chin at Grace. "Aunt Grace is thinking of taking up with a fucking madman."

"I'm not taking up with him."

One black brow rose. "What then?"

"I don't know."

"You've said that more in the last hour than you have in our entire life together," Devil said.

She shot him a withering look. "Don't think I don't hate that."

Silence fell for an age before he replied. "Grace, if there

is one thing I know . . . one thing I have learned in the last year . . . it is that this business—love—is the only thing we cannot know."

"So, take up with the madman," Whit said.

I'm sorry.

"He's not a madman," she said.

"No, he's not," Hattie said, looking to Whit.

"What does that mean?" Grace asked, looking from one person to the next, all of them looking as though they'd taken the last Christmas sweet. "What?"

Hattie sighed. "He came to me several days ago, at the Sedley-Whittington offices."

"He did?" Sedley-Whittington, named for Hattie and Whit, dominated the business at the London docklands. What did Ewan want with them?

"He's lucky Whit didn't drop him in the Thames," Devil said, taking another drink.

"Why?" Grace asked. "To give the docks more money?"

"No," Hattie said, curiosity in her voice. "He asked for work."

"What?"

Whit grunted. "My exact words."

Grace ignored him, all her focus on her sister-in-law. "What did you say?"

"Yes, wife, what *did* you say?"

"I gave him what he asked."

Surely she wasn't hearing right. "You gave the Duke of Marwick work."

Hattie nodded. "I'm not a fool—I heard he's a brute with a block of ice. Imagine what he can do with a hook."

Grace's eyes went wide. "You gave him a job hefting boxes?"

Hattie shot her a wry look. "He did try to explode me, Grace. I wasn't about to be kind."

The words shocked a laugh from her. "What does he want?"

"Well, it sure ain't a job," Devil said.

"He's damned good at it for someone who doesn't want to do it," Hattie said. "I've a mind to give him a promotion."

Whit cursed at the reply. "Of course you do."

Grace ignored the banter. "But why?"

Hattie shrugged one shoulder. "Maybe it needn't be complicated. Maybe he wants another chance. Maybe he wants hope."

Hope.

Helena offered a little, slobbery coo, and Grace looked to the babe, who had happily traded her rattle for one of her father's knuckles. She spoke to the child. "He's the reason there's a bill in Parliament to help the Rookery."

Silence. And then Beast knocked back his whisky. "It is to fail. He tilts at windmills."

Didn't they all?

"Grace," Felicity said quietly. "What do *you* want?"

What do you need?

The words echoed, over and over.

Come and see me when you know.

She looked up at her brothers. "Perhaps I want hope, too."

"Goddammit."

"Fuck."

Felicity grinned at the men's united response. "Well, then. Isn't *this* exciting."

Chapter Twenty

There was a fire-eater outside 72 Shelton Street.

She'd said she was an expert at parties, Ewan thought, watching the flames dance in the night as his driver trundled off down the narrow cobblestone street. *And this is a party, if ever there was one.*

If he'd given it much thought, he might have expected the raucous laughter, and the windows lit up like the sun, pouring golden light into the street, turning the cobblestones to gold. He might have expected the crush of masked women in elaborate dress, all reveling in the freedom of being far from Mayfair and recognition, but when she'd boasted her skill, he'd never imagined it was the kind that came with fire-eaters.

There was a fire-eater, however, flask on his hip and torch in his hand, surrounded by wide-eyed children from the Garden and flanked on both sides by men on stilts that lifted them nearly to the first floor of the building beyond—a building Ewan had been inside only once before, when Grace had brought him here to end his attacks on her brothers, and deliver him a lesson he richly deserved.

One he remembered with crystal clarity.

You can never have her back.

He had left, that lesson firmly in hand. And returned, hoping that the reverse was not true—that she might one day decide to have him back.

He'd made himself a better man, and there had been moments in the past weeks, fleeting ones, when her lips had curved and her guard had dropped, and he'd thought perhaps she warmed to him. And when she kissed him. When she came apart in his arms and she cried his name in pleasure.

Then, he was almost certain that she warmed to him.

And then came the night on the rooftops, when he'd gone too far—revealed too much—and she'd run from him. And he'd been certain that he'd ruined it all. He'd gone to Lady Henrietta the next day, having decided that if he could not win Grace, he could at least pay his Garden debts, beginning with her. With the ships she'd lost due to his anguish and grief. With the docks she'd had to rebuild, and the men who'd worked alongside her.

He'd apologized, and miraculously, she had accepted.

Ewan had spent a week tarring decks and hauling crates, and going home to Mayfair to collapse into his bed, sleeping well for the first time since he could remember. He told himself it was the physical exhaustion that helped, but he knew the truth. It was the knowledge that he was building, and not destroying.

It was the hope that with enough penance, he might be forgiven.

If not by Grace, then by her people.

And then, a week later, he'd received the package, a thin ebony box, wrapped all in black, with a gold 72 on the outside. He'd known instantly that it was from her.

Inside, on a bed of white silk, lay a black domino, like

the one he'd worn at his masquerade. He lifted it to discover a card, bearing a single line of text.

Come see me.

The back had indicated a precise date and time, and an address: 72 Shelton Street. Below, at the center of the ecru card, a pink dahlia.

Her signature.

Come see me, he thought. The same words he'd used with her after he'd left her in the Garden. But she'd left off the bit he'd included.

He knew what he needed. Did she?

Was that what this was?

Whatever it would be, he was not about to lose an opportunity to be with her. Especially here, in her element. He'd asked her to tell him about Dahlia, and now, she offered to reveal her secrets.

But he had not expected a fire-eater.

The man in question took a swig from his flask, held out his torch, and lit the night, the column of flame easily four feet high. The children who crowded the performer let out a collective wild cheer that became even more cacophonous as the stilt walkers lit their own torches and began to toss them back and forth, the performance creating the illusion that the door to 72 Shelton sat under an arc of fire.

Ewan slowed his approach, waiting for the performance to end, but the fire-eater had already seen him. "Welcome, milord!" He doffed his high hat and bowed with a tremendous flourish. "Please! Go right in."

When Ewan returned his attention to the stilt walkers with their torches, the fire-eater laughed a great laugh and said, "They're perfectly safe, good sir. And if *they* interest you, just wait until you discover what's in store . . . inside!"

On another night, at another time, for another man, the words would have piqued his curiosity enough to propel him through the door, but Ewan did not need the promise of extravagant performance and feats of strength. The knowledge that Grace was inside was enough.

She was inside, and she wanted him with her.

And so he walked through fire to get to her.

The metal door to the club opened without a knock, as though it had been waiting for his arrival. Inside, a tall black woman with elaborately kohled eyes that shimmered in the candlelight whispered in the ear of another woman, who immediately disappeared through a set of heavy velvet curtains.

"I am—"

"I know who you are," the woman said quietly. She leaned back and opened the curtain, just enough to look through it to something happening inside the building beyond. Satisfied, presumably, with what she saw, she returned her attention to him. "You'll recall that masks are designed to preserve anonymity, sir."

Sir. Not duke. Not here. Here, he was without title, and the pleasure that came with the loss was immense.

Ewan looked over his shoulder to discover two enormous men, each with a pistol strapped beneath his arm. Security. Where another man might have been uncomfortable with the show of brute force, Ewan was glad of it. It meant Grace was safer within these walls than he'd hoped.

He nodded at the men. They did not reciprocate.

And then he looked to the woman who had barely acknowledged him. "And so?"

She reached for the curtain and pulled it back, far enough for him to pass through, the movement filling the small entryway with the raucous noise and wild color of the party within. "Dominion awaits."

Dominion.

Of course it was called Dominion.

And she'd invited him here. To revel in it. To revel in her. Grace. Dahlia. *Both.*

Excitement thrummed through him and he looked to the woman who held the portal to Grace's world open for him. "Where is she?"

Her gaze narrowed on him, assessing. Good. He liked the idea that Grace had people who cared for her, even here, where she reigned.

"I don't know to whom you are referring, sir."

He nodded once. He was on his own, apparently, so he did the only thing he could; he pushed through the curtain, and into Grace's bacchanal.

It was like nothing he'd ever seen—a riot of color and sound, of laughter and shouts and music, bright and celebratory . . . there was no staid orchestra or string quartet here—instead, there were roving musicians. A young woman with a high powdered wig fiddled in one corner of the large open receiving room, playing faster and faster as a masked woman dressed in a cloud of pink gauze whirled with impossible speed, the fabric of her gown spread wide as she twirled, a circle of onlookers clapping in time with the music.

On the other side of the room, a collection of masked women draped over a large circular seat upholstered in lush sapphire velvet, watching the performer above them, who used the center of their seating as a stage. She was an acrobat, in diaphanous trousers and a shirt that wrapped tightly about her body, and she bent and twisted, inverting herself in impossible ways, with a slow speed that only served to underscore her remarkable strength.

As she held herself up by one hand, her legs pointing straight to the ceiling, the women watching burst into applause, and Ewan struggled to resist joining in.

A tray laden with champagne passed in front of him, a half-dozen gloved hands in myriad silks and satins reaching out to lift glasses from it, and the woman holding it didn't miss a step, delivering precisely what the partygoers asked. Once they were all satisfied, she turned to look up at him, a welcoming smile on her bright face, as though she'd known he was there the whole time.

"Champagne, sir?" she asked.

He shook his head.

"What then?"

She disappeared the moment he asked for bourbon, and Ewan wondered if he'd ever see her again; certainly the wild crush of people would prohibit anything like her finding him.

He turned away, heading for a small antechamber, door open. Inside, an unmasked woman stood behind a table in the corner—a handful of other revelers lingering, watching. She smiled and beckoned him closer. "Join us, good sir," she said in a thick Italian accent.

He approached, unable to contain his curiosity as the woman, who introduced herself as Fortuna, extracted a stack of cups from beneath the table, each painted with Venetian masks.

She named the empty cups as she set them to the table.

La Tragedia.

La Commedia.

Gli Innamorati.

And then, using tight red rosebuds, she proceeded to dazzle her audience with a collection of impossible tricks, passing the flowers through the ceramic, all while telling the story of star-crossed lovers, who found happiness and sorrow and ultimately, each other.

The cups flew across the table. ". . . fated to be . . ."

The buds appeared and reappeared. ". . . taking love for granted . . ."

And then, disappeared altogether as she showed the audience the empty cup bearing the portrait of two lovers in wild embrace. ". . . heartbreak," she said, softly, before setting it to the table, upside down.

"But!" Fortuna said, after letting disappointed silence hang around her. "Tonight is not for heartbreak, is it?" She looked to a woman nearby. "Is it, my lady?"

The woman shook her head. "No."

Fortuna looked to him. "Sir?"

He couldn't help his smile. "No."

"Allora . . ." she intoned with glee. "Perhaps, it is true what they say. In love, *hope*."

She lifted the seemingly empty cup, to reveal a rose, blooming vibrant red. A collective gasp rose from the audience, and Ewan's smile widened, even as Fortuna lifted the rose, bright and beautiful, dipped her head, and extended it to him. "For *your* innamorata. Piacere."

He reached for the rose, but before he could take it, her gaze passed by him, over his shoulder. "Unless . . ." She paused. "A rose is not correct?"

And then, before the eyes of everyone assembled, she waved a hand over the bloom in her palm, and damned if it didn't become something else altogether.

A stunning pink dahlia.

He laughed, knowing what he would find when he turned around. "As a matter of fact," he said, loud enough that she would hear him. "*That* is perfect."

Fortuna's secret smile turned wide, and she tipped the bloom into his hand. She said something else in Italian, but Ewan was already turning to find Grace, and his breath was gone from his lungs at the sight of her.

She was in gold.

The spools of gold thread he'd promised her as children, they were here, woven into her magnificent gown, a rich dupioni silk that glittered in the candlelight. To an outsider, the dress was no doubt considered demure—particularly in relationship to the other frocks in attendance—perfectly fitted to her shoulders and down her arms, where the silk ended in a crisp point at the back of her hand.

But there was nothing demure about the neckline—low and scooped, revealing the swell of her breasts, and a stunning expanse of smooth, freckled skin. Her copper curls tumbled down around her shoulders, catching on the fabric and teasing at the line of the frock, one errant curl caught inside the fabric like a wild temptation.

The combination of gold and copper turned her into the sun, and surely, that was the reason he was so damn hot all of a sudden.

She ought to take it off or she was going to set this building ablaze.

A smile passed over her lips, and something flashed in her eyes, as though she knew what he was thinking. She nodded in the direction of his hand, where he had barely refrained from crushing the magician's bloom.

"Fortuna's favorite trick."

"It's an excellent one," he said, his voice coming out low and graveled, as though he hadn't used it for weeks. "I particularly enjoyed the bit where she manifested you."

"That bit doesn't always happen." Her smile widened, and he had a wild urge to puff out his chest. He would make her smile forever if she'd let him.

"Even better," he said. "She's very good."

"What is a circus without a magician?" she replied. "Shall we trade? My prize for yours?"

She extended a glass toward him, two fingers of bourbon within, and he raised a brow, his gaze tracking over the room, looking for the servant with the tray of champagne. "How did she . . ."

"Dominion is designed to provide you with your pleasure, sir. You think a bit of bourbon is a challenge?" He heard the triumph and pride in her words, and they made him want to kiss her.

"To provide me with pleasure, is it?"

"To provide attendees with pleasure," she laughed.

"And what of you?" he asked. "Do you partake in it?"

She shook her head once, instantly. "No."

"Why not?"

She paused, and he saw the answer go through her, but she didn't speak it. And he'd never wanted an answer more than he wanted this one.

He waited. *Tell me.*

"Because it is business," she said, finally, and it might be true, but it wasn't the answer she'd wanted to give. "Because it is my building and my business and my commodity. I don't partake because my pleasure comes in giving others access to it."

He nodded. "Like me."

She looked down at that. Was she blushing? Christ, he loved that. He wanted that blush forever. "If you would like it, tonight, yes."

Tonight.

"I would like it, tonight and every night."

She was blushing.

"I only offer tonight."

He was through with one nights. He wanted them all. "Then I shall take it. And spend the evening convincing you to give me more."

She raised a brow. "We shall see."

"It's not a no."

She rolled her eyes, but he saw the smile playing across her lips as she turned away, leading him out of Fortuna's room, back through the larger space, where a second fiddler had joined the first, and a collection of couples had joined the original dancer, twirling and twirling in abandon.

Grace paused to watch, her gold skirts swirling around her as she stilled. He followed her gaze. There were three couples dancing, each pressed close enough to their partners that it made the dancing feel like something far more. An older masked woman danced with a tall, fair-haired man, the two of them locked in each other's eyes as they moved. Closest to Ewan and Grace, a dark-haired woman spun from her lover's arms, offering her a wide, winning smile before beckoning her from the dance . . . and presumably somewhere more private, for how quickly the women disappeared through the crowd.

And next to him, Grace smiled, her utter delight impossible to deny.

"Would you like to dance?"

She looked to him, confusion on her face, as though he'd spoken a language she didn't understand.

He turned and set his glass on a nearby table, and when he turned back, extended his hand to her. "This time, no masks."

"You're wearing a mask."

He shook his head. "Not the kind that matters."

Not tonight. Not ever again with her.

She stepped into his arms, and the crowd around them cleared a space, and they danced, quickly finding the rhythm of the music. She gave herself up to his arms and the movement, and they were soon swaying and rocking and turning again and again, faster and faster with the music, until he grew tired of the infinitesimal distance between them and lifted her clean off her feet, high against him, and her arms and legs were wrapping around him and she was laughing down at him, and the crowd went wild with excitement.

When the music ended, they were both breathing heavily and laughing, and her beautiful brown eyes were on his, and everything was easy and simple and real for a moment, and Ewan felt something strangely like peace for the first time in an age . . . perhaps ever.

He couldn't stop himself from leaning down and stealing a kiss, quick and soft and perfect, because she gave herself up to it immediately, and sighed when he pulled away.

"No masks," he whispered. "Not tonight."

Not between us.

"Why don't you take pleasure here?" he asked her again, softly. "Why not make space for your own alongside everyone else's?"

"Because pleasure is for sharing," she said.

And sharing was too much trust. He understood that better than anyone.

But he wanted to give her all of it. The trust, the sharing, the pleasure. Whatever she wished. "Let me share it with you. Tonight."

She was still for a long moment, not breaking his gaze, their breaths still coming fast and harsh, mingling together. Finally, she nodded. "No masks."

And Ewan wasn't sure he would ever feel a pleasure as keen as the one she gave him then. They separated, but he laced his fingers through hers, refusing to let her go as they fetched his bourbon and Grace led them to the door.

He drank as they walked. "This is some of the best I've ever tasted."

She inclined her head. "I shall inform our providers."

Devil and Whit.

"Or perhaps you'd like to tell them yourself," she added casually. "I hear you are hauling for Sedley-Whittington now."

So. She knew. "Lady Henrietta was kind enough to let me join the crew."

"Why?"

Purpose.

He didn't say it, but she seemed to hear it anyway. "And so this is your plan? Monday, Wednesday, Saturday, hauling cargo? Tuesday, Thursday, House of Lords?"

"It's honest work," he said, adding dryly, "Unlike Parliament."

He liked it. He liked the strain in his muscles at the end

of the day and the way the people he worked alongside took pride in it. He liked the taste of the ale that came at the end of the workday.

"In my experience, aristocrats don't care much for honest work."

He didn't want to talk about aristocrats. "This place is for my pleasure?"

She met his eyes. "Yes."

"No aristocrats tonight." He gave her a small smile. "But you knew that would be my first request, didn't you?"

Her lips turned up. "Indeed, sir. I did."

"Thank you," he said, softly.

"And what would be your second?" she asked.

His reply was instant. "I want to know Dahlia."

A beat, while she considered. While he held his breath. And then she waved a hand toward the door of the next room, one level deeper into this magnificent world she'd created.

An invitation to explore.

An invitation to know her.

He met her eyes. "Show me."

"With pleasure."

Chapter Twenty-One

He loved Dominion.

She could see it in him, in the way he eased into the space, letting the lush delight of it wash over him. When she'd found him watching Fortuna, she'd had trouble looking away from the way he was so riveted to the magic. He knew it was a trick, but he gave himself over to it nonetheless.

And in that moment, as she experienced Dominion through his eyes, she knew she would never regret inviting him. Because in the very act of accepting her invitation, of coming to the club, of delivering himself over to it, he gave her hope.

And that was what she wanted, wasn't it?

Wild and ridiculous and implausible and painful.

But also, rather perfect.

When they'd danced, he'd lifted her high in the air and given her the pleasure she'd so often denied herself. Freedom. Joy. Happiness, even in the tiniest sliver.

Didn't they deserve that? After all these years?

They took it, walking through the door from the receiving room to the central oval room of the club, which had been transformed into a circus tent of sorts—the lushly upholstered furnishings moved to the outer edges of the room, and a large trapeze hung from the ceiling, upon which an aerialist performed with unimaginable strength for an audience of—Grace calculated quickly—nearly fifty people.

"Your club," he said, softly.

She looked to him, unsurprised that he knew something of this place—he was no fool. But few knew the truth of it. "How much do you know?"

"I know it is for women," he said.

"It is, on all nights but Dominion, and tonight, no man is here without a chaperone."

He raised his brows. "And how do you keep the men at bay once they've experienced it?"

"An excellent question. Men are curious beasts, are they not? They at once wish to keep us out of their spaces and also loathe the idea of us making space for ourselves."

"You know that better than anyone."

His meaning was clear. She had been blocked from title, and threatened for her very existence even once she'd made it clear that she had no interest in that title. She swallowed, her thoughts clearly with his, and returned her attention to the room. "Guests are only allowed to attend with my express permission."

"And you have them researched."

She nodded. "Thoroughly. And once they are approved, they are ferried, blindfolded, from locations around the city by my own staff, and brought in through underground tunnels."

He looked to her instantly. "I wasn't."

"No," she said, softly. "You weren't."

Veronique had wanted him brought in with the rest of the men, insisting that of everyone who would be in attendance that night, Ewan was the one who was most dangerous—after all, hadn't he always been?

"Why not?"

Grace had refused, laying her trust on the line. Her hope.

And she did not believe it was a mistake.

Please, she thought, *don't let it be a mistake.*

"Because you are *my* guest."

Something flared in his eyes, something like satisfaction. "And the show out front? Why, if everyone is entering in secret?"

She smiled. "Is it even a circus if there are no children to see?" He laughed at that, and she added, "Are they enjoying it?"

"Things are on fire; they are positively gleeful."

"The more satisfied customers, the better," she said, turning back to the room. The evening's attendees were some of the most powerful and likeable people in London, Grace was proud to admit. The Duke and Duchess of L__ and the Marquess and Marchioness of R__ were both in attendance, husbands happily doting on wives. Lady N__ was back, this time with her partner; apparently there were no ships to be unloaded into the Bastards' warehouse that evening.

But, as usual, the audience was largely female members of the club and their companions.

Grace watched the aerialist pull herself up to stand on the moving bar, then carefully balance on one foot and tumble over herself before returning to a seated position, petticoats high and wild and frothy, like those of the lady in the delightful Fragonard painting.

"Dahlia, you've outdone yourself!" Grace turned, smile on her face even as irritation coursed through her. Tonight was not hers—it was the club's. Several feet away, the Duchess of Trevescan approached, champagne in one hand, and Henry, a very large, very accomplished companion, in the other.

"As ever, unmasked, I see, Duchess?"

The other woman waved a hand. "I don't like how they smear my kohl."

Grace tilted her head. "Well, if you are unconcerned, then so are we."

The duchess looked past her, taking in a masked Ewan, long and lean, with his impossibly full lips and impossibly square jaw. The woman's lips opened just slightly, her eyes going wide in surprise, and then something like . . . understanding. "I see you've a companion tonight, too, Dahlia."

Grace ignored the wave of heat on her cheeks. "Even I am allowed a guest at times."

"A *guest*," said the Duchess, her eyes not leaving Ewan, who was looking down at her, the combination of the shadow of his mask and the dim lights of the room making it difficult to read his expression. "Well, how delightful to see you both." She paused. "Together."

She toasted them, sipped from her glass, turned a knowing look on Henry. "Shall we, darling?" When her companion grinned, she took hold of his arm and led him through the crush, toward the stairs to the rooms above.

Grace returned her attention to Ewan, who watched their disappearance, thoughtfully, before looking back to the trapeze at the center of the room. They watched the performer for a few minutes before Grace said to Ewan, "It took a week to install the trapeze for her, but I think it was worth it, don't you?"

He grunted his agreement, and she looked at him, noticing for the first time that he was not watching the aerialist. He was watching the audience, most of whom were club members, many of whom were enjoying the more salacious offerings of the club, as often was the case at Dominion.

Around the perimeter of the room were a variety of couples—and one triad—in various states of pleasure—nothing outrageous—there were rooms abovestairs that afforded privacy, and several rooms on this very floor that would provide the absence of privacy, should participants' pleasures lean in that direction. But couples dotted the furniture, curled in on each other, women sitting on men's laps, skirts hiked to the knee for easy caressing. Directly across from them, Tomas whispered into the ear of a giggling Countess C__, draped artfully over his lap. Grace had enough experience to know that the two would be leaving momentarily for a room.

Across the room, Zeva stood in the doorway, ensuring that all was well and welcoming, and all in all, there was nothing out of the ordinary for 72 Shelton Street.

But Ewan seemed unable to look away from it.

What was he thinking?

Her stomach flipped at the possibilities, not all of them good. "You are staring, my lord," she offered, hiding her concern behind a teasing tone.

He did not look to her. "The men are not all guests."

She watched his profile as he realized that 72 Shelton, besides being one of the finest clubs in London, was also one of its finest pleasure houses. "No."

"And when you say pleasure . . ."

"However it comes."

A little grunt. Understanding? Distaste? Disdain? Something else? "And when the men who are neither clients nor staff see what this place has to offer, how are they persuaded to keep it a secret?"

She heard it then. Fascination.

Something loosened within her. He wasn't displeased. He was *intrigued.* And something else. He sounded . . . *impressed.* She smiled. "Once they are here, they quickly reveal their particular pleasures . . . which makes it easy for them to keep secrets."

"Particular pleasures like what?" he asked, turning to her.

She exhaled, part relief, part shock. Because there, in his eyes, she finally saw what he was thinking, the dark centers of his amber eyes blown wide with desire.

He liked it, this world she had built.

He wanted a taste of it.

And *that* was something she understood.

"Pleasures like the one you are experiencing right now," she said, softly, now more than willing to accommodate him. "Would you like to find a room and explore it?"

"You misunderstand," he said. "I don't want to watch them."

"You don't?"

"No."

Her brow furrowed. Nearly a decade of working in and around sex had made her something of an expert in knowing what clients wished. She was not usually wrong. "Would you prefer to be watched?"

He shook his head. "Not unless you would like that."

A thrum went through her at the invitation. At the willingness to explore it with her. At the desire in his darkening eyes. She lifted her hand, brushing a lock of blond hair back from his brow. "What, then?"

Something shifted in him, freeing him, and when he leaned in, his voice was low and dark at her ear. "Watching these women take their pleasure here in this place that you have built . . ." He wiped a hand over his mouth, and Grace thought that she might never have liked anything more in her life than that. "It makes me want to watch you take yours."

The words struck deep in her core, and she suddenly wanted that, too.

Needed it.

She didn't hesitate.

She wove in and out of the rooms, where more acrobats

and musicians and bawdy songstresses performed, and a teeming mass of people drank and ate and writhed in revelry. They pushed down a long hallway where two separate couples were locked in embraces, and into the theater space, where Nastasia Kritikos had taken to the stage, rolling and trilling an aria that would have made her the muse of Mozart himself.

She looked back, expecting to find Ewan watching the diva, but instead, he was watching her. The moment her eyes met his, he tugged her around, pulling him to her. Stealing another kiss along with her breath and her thought. When he released her, she was clinging to his lapels.

"Show me what else you have built here."

There were a dozen places for them to go: elaborately appointed rooms upstairs, each designed to evoke a particular fantasy; the catacombs beneath the building, wine cellars and cheese cellars; the hot house on the roof.

But she didn't want to take him somewhere that belonged to the club.

She wanted to take him somewhere that belonged to her.

So, she pulled him through a small card room; a collection of aristocratic ladies was gathered round a table where a Frenchwoman Grace had discovered in the market square turned elaborately decorated cards and divined their futures. The cards were hand-painted and beautiful, but they were no match for the woman herself, who seemed able to look directly into her audience and read their deepest desires.

Rapt, not one of the women in the room looked up as Grace pulled Ewan past, heading for the corner, where she pressed the hidden latch on a barely visible door, and pulled him from Dominion into a back stairwell.

She closed the door behind them, and they were instantly shrouded in quiet, the sound of the wild celebration beyond immediately muffled. The stairwell was dimly illuminated, candles lit at distant intervals, and she was instantly aware of the sound of their breath. She looked to Ewan, now so close that if she leaned just an inch toward him, they would touch.

He took in the small, crowded space and then gave her a crooked smile. "I was thinking something a bit larger, but—" And then he took her face in his hands and kissed her, pressing her to the wall at her back as she gasped, wanting nothing more than his touch.

She let him kiss her, deep and thorough, reveling in him—his broad shoulders, the low growl of desire in his throat, the scent of tobacco threatening to consume her.

He pulled back, just enough to speak. "Mmm. This will do."

Before she could respond, he was kissing her again, one hand sliding down to her bodice, stroking over the straining skin of her breasts above the suddenly too-tight gown. He dipped a thumb beneath the fabric, finding her nipple, straining for him. She cried out, and he kissed over her jaw to her ear, repeating that single, maddening touch over and over as he spoke to her. "This gown is sinful."

She opened her eyes, struggling to find words. "I chose it for you."

"Mmm," he said. "I know." He stroked again, and her eyes began to slide closed at the delicious touch. "Ah—" He stopped and she opened them again. "Watch me." Another stroke, this one a bit firmer. "I want to lay you on a bed like a feast, and take you in. I want to memorize the way this gold shimmers against your skin."

She pushed her head back to the wall and took a deep breath, unthinkingly exposing her neck and chest to him like a sacrifice.

He let out another little growl of pleasure and took it, placing delicious, sucking kisses down the column of her neck, then over the sloping skin of her breasts. Her fingers slid into his hair, guiding him lower and lower, until he hit the line of her bodice and they both groaned.

Grace cursed in the darkness, and she felt the curve of his lips there, on her skin.

"That makes me want to tear this from you," he said, running a tongue along the line of the gown. "And you deserve better than that."

Her fingers tightened in his hair. "I don't care."

He lifted his head, setting one finger to the skin at the edge of the fabric, tracing over one breast and up the side to her shoulder. "I do," he said. "I promised you spools and spools of gold thread. And I won't take it from you. Not ever."

She watched him. Saw the truth in his words. And in that moment, in the dark stairwell of her club, as the most scandalous set in London laughed and drank and reveled in reckless abandon mere feet away—as this man she'd spent a lifetime hiding from refused to rip her bodice—Grace fell in love for the second time in her life.

And the realization was so terrifying that she did the only thing she could think to do. She clasped his hand, and took him to bed.

They ascended the back, secret staircase of 72 Shelton Street, up past the rooms used by the club's patrons, and then past the floor where, a year earlier, she'd nursed him back to health, only to take him to the ring and send him away from her forever.

Thank God, he had returned.

But on the top floor, she threw a little latch and opened the door, revealing her rooms. More than that. Because this particular stairwell did not simply lead to Grace's outer office, with its desk piled high with papers and ledgers. It did not lead to her sitting room—where no one ever sat—or to the little library beyond, where she read most evenings. No, this door led to her inner sanctum. To her bed.

He followed her into the room, and this time, it was he who closed them in, the quiet snick of door against jamb setting her heart pounding. She turned back to him, expecting him to come for her again, hot and wild. She wanted that, so unsettled by the realization that she had tumbled into love—that she was willing to do anything to prevent herself from having to think about it.

Ewan appeared to have no such concern.

He came for her, but with the lazy certainty of a predator, as though he knew he had all the time in the world for what was to come, and that she wouldn't leave him.

Watching him, tall and handsome, his jaw square and perfect beneath his black mask, his eyes on hers, as though there was nothing in the world he'd rather look at, Grace realized that she wouldn't leave him.

She wasn't sure she could.

And then, from nowhere, she wasn't sure she ever had.

She took a step back, unsettled by her thoughts, anticipation coursing through her, and she was suddenly off balance. Gone was the slow predator; he caught her to him instantly, one arm around her back like steel. "I've got you."

She caught her breath, not at the sensation, but at the words, unable to resist her own. "I know."

He searched her eyes for a long moment. "Do you?" he whispered, lifting a hand to her hair, pushing a wild lock behind her ear. "Do you know that I will always have you? If you'll let me?"

She went warm with the words.

"I will always be what you need," he said.

"And what of your need?" she asked.

"Right now, I have it." She took a deep breath, and he added, "But I warn you, I do not think I can take it in half measures."

What if I want to give you all of it?

She held the question back, instead raising her hands to his face and removing his mask, revealing him to her. "No masks," she whispered.

He smiled. "No masks."

Grace didn't know how she would ever wear a mask with him again.

"Turn."

She did, instantly, his to command.

Gently, he gathered her hair and brought it forward, over her shoulder, giving himself full access to the back fastenings of her gown. The predator returned, slowly and methodically working the long line of buttons down her spine, each one loosening the golden fabric. She held it to her breasts as he leaned down, pressing a kiss to the curve of one shoulder, knocking one strap away.

His tongue touched her skin, and she was seared with fire.

And then he spoke. "That night . . . in my gardens."

"You pretended not to recognize me." She should be furious about it. But she wasn't. There was a part of her that was grateful for it, because he'd freed her from the riot of conflicted thoughts she had held that night, and given her something else—the fantasy that they were simply lovers.

There had never been anything simple about them.

And tonight, they grew ever more complex.

"I recognized you," he said. "Of course I recognized you."

A kiss to the back of her neck, soft and perfect, sending a shiver of desire through her. Another lick of fire.

"I will never not know you," he whispered, hot and perfect against her skin, and she was at once grateful not to be looking at him and desperate to see him as he confessed what should be a sin and was instead something far closer to heaven. "There will never be a time I do not know the shape, the sound, the scent of you, like sweet, spiced cream."

She swallowed as he continued with his worship, one kiss after another, as though it hadn't occurred to him that he might go faster.

As though it hadn't occurred to him that she might lose her mind if he didn't go faster, dammit.

"That night," he told her shoulder blades as he worked the ties of her corset, loosening her, freeing her. "I told you that when I am with you, I feel like Apollo."

"I remember," she said, the words coming on a barely-there breath as he loosened the last ties, and his fingers found purchase inside, sliding over her skin, flushed and uncomfortable from the binding stays. She gasped at the unbearable pleasure of the touch. "He—" One hand tracked around her body and came to the underside of her breast, full and aching. He stilled, as though waiting for her to finish. "He turned a corner in a forest and saw a woman naked in a swimming hole."

A rumble of amusement sounded at her back, the sound only amplifying the pleasure of his touch as he lifted her breast in his hand and rubbed his thumb over her nipple in a slow, languid circle. "She wasn't naked in a swimming hole."

She shook her head. "You didn't tell me that."

"I was distracted, if I recall."

"And is it possible you could be similarly distracted now?" she asked.

He gave a little tut of concern at her ear. "I'm telling you a story." His other hand came to join the first—to lift the opposite breast. To stroke the opposite nipple.

"I'm sorry," she said, writhing against him. "Go on." He pinched one nipple, just enough to sting. And she gasped, "Please."

"Mmm—" That rumble again.

Grace tried to focus on the story. "What was she doing then?"

"She was killing a lion."

He released her, pushing the dress and the corset down over her arms and her hips, until the golden fabric pooled at her feet, the slide of silk against her skin a wicked tease, making her want to step back into his arms, and let him have his way with her. Every way he could think of.

Before she could make good on the desire, he clasped her hips in his hands and pulled her tight to him, the magnificent hard length of him against her bottom. She pressed back, and he lifted one of her arms, wrapping it around his neck, one of his hands returning to a breast as the other slid over the curve of her belly.

"Touch me," she said, softly. "Please."

He growled, his fingers sliding into the thatch of hair that covered the most secret part of her, one finger teasing at the place she ached for him. She turned her face toward him, finding his glittering eyes. "Ewan." She sighed.

"Cyrene."

"What?"

That magnificent finger moved. "Cyrene, the lion killer."

"Mmm." She tilted her hips, loving the little brush of pleasure he gave her. "Tell me."

"She was born delicate and beautiful, the only child of a great warrior," he said, that hand working so lightly—too lightly—against her. "And no one believed she was worthy of battle."

"Ah. Taken for granted," she said, her fingers tangling in the hair at the nape of his neck.

"Exactly that," he said. "She wanted the battlefield, but she got a different kind of field—left home to tend sheep, always, as her father went to war."

"Tasty treats for lions, them."

He nipped her earlobe, sending a shiver of pleasure through her. "Exactly. And one day, as she was tending her flock, a lion came, and Cyrene, the great warrior, slayed it."

"Enter Apollo," she said, breathless, rocking her hips against him. "Faster."

He stopped.

She swore.

"You learned that curse word here." She could hear the wicked smile in his voice—the pleasure he took in directing hers. She turned to face him, wanting to see it. She'd spent a lifetime imagining the way he would smile in this moment, as he toyed with her pleasure and they pretended the world beyond did not exist.

His gaze tracked over her body as she turned, over every inch of her, each swell, each curve, every scar left from the fights of her youth.

She watched him catalogue them, following her legs down and back up, settling for a long moment on the dark thatch of curls that hid the most private part of her.

When he returned his attention to her face, he said, dark and delicious, "Apollo was laid low."

And Grace, queen of Covent Garden, who could stop riots with a single word, realized she had never felt more powerful in her life than she did in that moment, as this man, strong and handsome and powerful in his own right, was lost in her.

He pulled her to him, lifting her high in his arms and taking her to the bed, where he laid her down, letting her pull him to join her on the rough silk coverlet. Letting her kiss him, long and lush, with a slow sweep of tongue and a slow suck of lip, until they were both aching.

This.

This was her pleasure. Being wanted. Being desired. Not for her money or her power or the position she held, but for herself.

But it wasn't all. It wasn't enough.

The pleasure was in the reciprocity. In being wanted and wanting in return. In giving and receiving. In needing and providing.

There was the pleasure for which she had spent a lifetime searching.

And here it was, in Ewan, her first love. And now, she suspected, her last.

He pulled away from her and pressed a kiss high on her cheek. Another at the corner of her eye. Another on her jaw. "She was the most beautiful thing he'd ever seen," he whispered, and she was suddenly desperate for the rest of the story.

With a sly smile, she said, "Everyone loves a girl who can fight."

Those amber eyes tracked over hers, taking her in. "Truth." And that single, soft syllable threatened to set her aflame. Before she could explore it, he continued, his fingertips lightly tracing over her arm, to her hip, where she shivered in anticipation for more. "Apollo had been a god a very long time, you see, and he'd seen many beautiful women, but never one who was so fierce and so committed to her path. A warrior. He fell instantly in love, proposing to her on the spot."

"What then?" she said, breathless. "Did she tumble into his arms and they lived happily ever after?"

Another one of those small, knowing smiles. "You are not paying attention. She did not care that he was a god. She was one of the most skilled fighters the world had ever seen. She knew her power and was not about to relinquish it. Not even for an immortal."

"Clever girl," she said, her own hands on him now, stripping him out of his coat and untying his cravat as he spoke.

"Did I not tell you that she was brave *and* brilliant?"

She tossed the cravat away, spreading her hands over the fine white linen of his shirt, low, lower until she pulled it from his trousers. "And beautiful, you said."

He caught her chin in his fingers, tilting her to him. "Incomparable."

Another kiss, hot and delicious.

"But she did not want a second life like the one she'd lived with her father. She didn't want to sit in idyll, the wife of a god. She wanted to rule a kingdom—a warrior queen."

Grace was watching him now, hanging on every word, knowing the end of the story. The only way it could possibly end. "She refused him."

He nodded. "And so the great god—god of the sun, of truth, of light, of prophecy—he did the only thing that was left to him."

"He stole her," she whispered. And the words, part of a silly story, horrified her. The idea that there was always someone with more power, who would stop at nothing to lay claim. How many times had she looked over her shoulder, terrified of that power, in the hands of men?

In the hands of this man?

"No." He held her eyes, watching her carefully. "No, Grace. He didn't steal her. He begged her. The son of Zeus, the great deity of the Trojan War, he lowered himself to his knees and begged her to join him. He offered her wealth, jewels, immortality . . . if she just let him love her."

She shook her head. "She refused again."

"Why?" The story was fading, and there, at the edge of that single question, she heard reality. "He wanted nothing more than to give her the world. To love her and keep her safe, and give her everything she wished."

"But not everything she needed," she replied. "He couldn't know what she needed—with him a god, and her a mere mortal."

With him a duke, and her, nothing at all.

"She didn't want the world," she said softly. "Not from him."

He nodded, urging her to continue.

"He wanted to gift her the future," she said softly, "but she wanted to claim it."

He paused for a long moment, until she wondered if he was going to speak again, one finger tracing the line of her jaw, over the soft swell of her lips. "What do you need?"

The question brought her such comfort. Such joy.

And hope beyond anything she'd ever experienced.

"I need you—" she said.

He waited. Ever patient.

And finally, she continued. "I need you."

His eyes darkened at the words.

"Now," she whispered. "Tonight."

She didn't say the rest—the bit that would change everything.

She didn't say *forever.*

He might have heard it anyway, for how he kissed her, deep and thorough, rolling her to her back and coming over her to kiss her jaw, her neck, the slope of one shoulder, her breast, easing closer and closer to one straining tip. His lips softened over her and she sighed at the way he worshipped her, her fingers sliding into his hair, her back arching toward him, pressing closer to him.

Aching for him.

Not just for his touch, but for all of it, the intimacy of the caress, the care, the pleasure.

So much pleasure.

He followed her touch, his lips closing tightly around her, and he sucked gently, working at her until she was fisting his hair and whispering his name, holding him at her breast, full of heat and want, and slowly unraveling beneath his long, rhythmic sucks.

His hand was sliding over her hip, down the skin of her thigh, teasing her legs apart until she was open for him, lifting her hips to meet his touch, rocking against him. She ached with need, not just for the caress he promised, but also for the rest, for his eyes on her. For his lips on her. For his words around her. For him.

And then he parted her folds and stroked, finding her wet and wanting, only made wetter by his growl of satisfaction. He lifted his head from her breast and met her gaze. "You like this."

She nodded, moving her hips in time with his strokes. "I like you."

He stilled at that, and for a mad, fleeting moment, she wondered if she'd said too much. But if that was too much, what would happen if she told him the rest?

He stroked again, and her eyes began to slide closed. He stopped. "No, love," he said, the word warming her as much as his touch. "I want you to watch."

His fingers moved in lazy circles, there right at the heart of her.

She spread her legs wide. "Go on, then."

They both looked down her body, at his hand, working her, and she slid her own over his, their fingers tangling, their breath coming heavier. Neither of them looked away when he said, "Take it." He leaned down and took her nipple again, in long, lovely sucks that made her pant, his touch steady and strong, then faster, and she was arching up to him.

"Ewan," she whispered. "Please."

And then it was there, cresting, and she was rocking against him as he guided her through the pleasure, lifting his head to watch her claim it for her own. "There," he growled. "Take it. Everything you need."

She did, his watchful gaze a gift, a promise that he would always be there to hold her pleasure. To provide it.

To revel in it. To guide her through it, as it threatened to unravel her.

When she was sated, he lifted his head, his hand now cupping her tightly, ensuring she received every last moment of pleasure.

Finally, she looked to him and raised her hand to the side of his face. "This was supposed to be yours," she whispered. "I was to give it to you."

"And you think you haven't?" he said at her lips, stealing kisses between whispered words. "I feel nothing but the kind of pleasure that steals one's sanity."

She shouldn't like that, but she did. "That good?"

"Impossibly good," he said. "Christ, Grace. Pleasure with you—it puts pale to every other pleasurable thing I've experienced."

"Have you experienced much pleasure?"

She didn't know why she asked it. It shouldn't matter what had happened in the twenty years that had passed. It didn't matter if he had had lovers. It didn't matter who they'd been.

She shouldn't have asked.

He did not seem to mind. "No."

She ached at the reply. At the truth in it. He'd been alone for as long as she had. Longing for something, just as she had.

Longing for her.

"I missed you too much," he whispered, the words so soft that if they hadn't been entwined, she wouldn't have heard them. But she did, along with the truth in his voice. "Every day, every hour. I missed you." A pause, and then, "To say I have missed you—it's not enough. The word . . . it implies a natural occurrence. It suggests that if only I'd been home the day you called . . . if only you'd been on St. James's the last time I bought cravats . . . then I'd have had a chance not to miss you. But what do we call the aching emptiness that I feel for you? All the time? Every day?"

Tears stung at the words, at the way he put voice to the emptiness that lived inside her, as well. An aching sadness, like a part of her was gone.

He kissed her again, urgent and full of that ache. "What do we call the loneliness, as though my other half has gone, never to return?" he asked. "What do we call that?"

Love.

"Ewan," she whispered. Not knowing what to say. Not knowing what to think. Knowing only that she wanted to give him something to ease the ache.

To ease her own.

And then he froze, his breath stopping in his throat. Her eyes flew to his, but he wasn't looking at her face.

Chapter Twenty-Two

She had a tattoo on her left shoulder.

He hadn't noticed it before then—it had always been covered by straps and bodices and sleeves and, when he'd stripped her naked earlier, by her riot of red curls. And then, he'd been so riveted by her eyes and her face and the way she gave herself up to desire that he hadn't noticed.

But now he did, on her left shoulder three inches down and six in from the outer edge of her arm, a tattoo, in black. One he recognized because it was the foil of the mark he carried in the same spot on his own body. His, a white scar—one she'd tended mere nights ago—twenty years old and still raised and puckered, the punishment he'd been given for loving her.

The punishment he would have taken again and again, if it meant keeping her safe. And it had.

She had run, and she had built herself a kingdom and a palace alongside his brothers, whom she now claimed as her own. And he'd imagined that she had done everything she could to forget him, from the moment she fled, believing him the monster he had made himself to be.

But she hadn't forgotten him.

She'd carried him with her.

Because there, on her shoulder, three inches down and six in, was his mark, the M his father had carved into his own flesh, turned ninety degrees.

No longer an M for Marwick.

Now an E.

For Ewan.

His breath caught in his chest, heart pounding, and he couldn't find the words to speak—the heavy weight of that mark suddenly proving that everything he had done, everything he had been, everything he had sacrificed, had been worth it, because she hadn't forgotten him. She had carried him with her.

He reached for the mark, and she turned her head, to watch as he stroked his fingers over it, smooth on her perfect, soft skin. He covered it with his palm. "Did it hurt?" His words came out ragged, like his thoughts.

"Yes."

He looked to her. "You don't mean the tattoo."

She shook her head. "No."

"No masks," he whispered.

"It hurt," she said. "Everything hurt. For days and weeks." He closed his eyes, his chest tightening at the words as she went on. "I missed you like air. I would wake up, in the dark, in the dank, in the rain, in the cold. And I missed you. And I climbed those fucking buildings in Mayfair, and counted the fucking chimneys, and imagined that one day you would leave him. And leave that place. And leave your title, and come back to us."

Her eyes were full of tears, glistening in the candlelight. "No. Not us. *Me.* I imagined you would come back to me." One tear spilled over, dropping on the hand he held over her tattoo. Searing him. "And you didn't."

I wanted to.

Every fucking night. He'd lain in his bed in that godforsaken house in the middle of nowhere and he calculated the exact path he would take to get to them.

"I hoped the tattoo would ease the pain. Like drawing out the poison."

Christ, he hated being poison to her. "Did it?"

She met his eyes then, holding his gaze for a long moment, so he could see the truth when she said, softly, "No."

The word was a weapon. A needle, inking his heart. "Grace."

"God, I hated that name," she said, the words coming more freely now. "I hated the way it invoked you every time Devil or Whit used it."

"I have had the same curse—to be haunted by you every time a bowing servant or mincing dandy or matchmaking mama addressed me as Your Grace, I ached with fury. It was a constant reminder that my Grace was nowhere to be found."

She looked to him. "And is that what I was? Your Grace?"

"It is all I have ever wanted."

"Tonight?" she said.

"Always," he replied. "Forever."

He lifted his palm from where her skin seared him, leaning down to brush a kiss over the mark there, before finding her eyes again. Reaching up, he covered her hand, on his own shoulder, with his, and he said, "You told me that my mark made me his forever."

She went soft at the words, as though she wished to take them back.

"No." He didn't want her regret. There was enough of it between them for both their lifetimes. He shook his head. "If that is true," he said, "does your mark make you mine?"

She slid her hands into his hair then, pulling him down to

her. And in the heartbeat before she set her lips to his, she whispered, "Yes."

And with that single word, she set him free. He levered himself up, over her, letting her command the kiss, letting her explore him thoroughly. And then he was exploring her, sliding his bare leg between her own as she wrapped her arms around his neck and lifted herself to meet him, and gave herself up to him.

He growled at the feel of her against him, so warm and soft, the strong muscles of her thighs coming around his waist as the kiss turned rough and carnal, as though she had been waiting for it for as long as he had. Grace matched his desire; lifting against him, pulling him closer, opening for him, giving him everything he asked for. And then, as if that weren't enough, she broke the kiss with a little sigh, and said, "Make me yours."

On more than one occasion over the last years, Ewan had thought it possible that he was going mad. But that moment, when she whispered those words, delivering herself to him, he was the closest he'd ever been to it. Mad with desire. Mad with hope. Mad with need.

He tore his lips from her, giving her scant space to breathe. "If I do that . . . if you allow it . . . it's not just tonight."

She stilled, her beautiful brown eyes on his. "I know."

Did she? He didn't dare hope.

"It's not just this week, or this year, Grace." He took her face in his hands. She had to understand that. Had to make her own decision. "I want to start again."

She nodded. "I know."

"I want to be everything you desire."

She smiled, and he nearly stopped breathing at her beauty. "I thought you wished to be everything I needed."

"That, too," he said, kissing her. "That, too."

"In that case," she said, her gaze going dark and languid

as she lifted her hips against him, pushing the hard length of him against her softness once, twice, until they both groaned. "Make me yours."

Mine.

His control snapped with the single word and they were both moving, hands and mouths exploring, his hands on her skin, her fingers raking through his hair as he made his way down her body from her lips, down the column of her neck, worshipping again at the tattoo on her shoulder, and then over her breasts, giving each pretty brown tip a lingering suck until she was arching up to him.

He continued his exploration, painting kisses across her torso, reveling in the strength of her, the ridges of her muscles—honed over the years with fighting and scaling the rooftops of London. He paused on the soft, barely-there swell of her belly, and she giggled as he ran his cheek, rough with an evening's growth, over the skin there.

Ewan lifted his head at the magnificent sound, simultaneously familiar and foreign. "Covent Garden's queen is ticklish," he teased.

She smiled to the ceiling. "Don't tell anyone."

"Never," he vowed, repeating the movement and reveling in her laugh—and the way it quickly turned breathless—and she placed her hands at his head and lifted him to stare up at her, across the beautiful planes of her body. "It's my secret."

She smiled. "Keep it well."

He would—and he realized in that fleeting, magnificent moment that he would spend the rest of his life keeping her secrets.

Just as she had spent so much of her life keeping his.

He pressed another kiss on her sensitive skin and moved again, in a slow slide, until her legs parted and he was between them.

"Tell me another secret."

She sucked in a breath at the words, spoken to the core of her. Satisfaction thrummed through Ewan at that, and he leaned forward, parting her gently with his thumbs, to look at her.

"Christ," he whispered, the sensation of words on her hot, wet flesh clearly enough to make her wild. "I've never seen anything so pretty as this."

"Ewan," she gasped. "Please."

He let out a long stream of cool air, straight to the core of her, and she shouted her frustrated pleasure at the sensation. "Tell me another secret," he said.

"I want you," she whispered, and the words came out so graveled and distant that it felt as though she'd given him a gift.

"Good girl," he said, pressing a kiss to her thigh, high up, where she was all sensation. She lifted her hips, rocking into the air, searching for purchase, and he thought he might die from the stunning look of her, pink and wet and hot as flame. He moved, setting one finger to the top of her folds, and she sighed, the sound so remarkable, it took all his energy not to spend then and there. "Yes, there," she said, frustrated. "Do it."

She was so ready for him. Slick and wet and perfect.

He moved that single finger down the center of her, loving the hitch of her breath, the little cry she bit back as he circled the straining nub at the very top of her folds. He rubbed gently, up one side and down the other, and she finally released the cry. "You like that," he said, softly, more to himself than to her.

She swore again, the language coarse and powerful and perfect proof that she was coming unraveled. He lingered there, at that spot, stroking and rolling, exploring her until she was doing the work, using his touch to find her pleasure.

"That's it, love," he whispered, pressing a kiss to the soft skin of her thigh. "Show me what you like. Show me what will make you scream."

The words set her aflame, and he slid another finger into the hot, wet center of her, up to the first knuckle, just far enough to feel her pulsing around him. She widened her legs and thrust up. "More," she gasped. "Please."

"You ache here, don't you?" he asked. "Poor love. Does it hurt?"

"God, yes. I want . . ."

"Tell me what," he said. "Tell me what you want."

I shall give you everything.

"I want . . ."

My mouth, he willed her.

He was going to die if he didn't have his mouth on her soon.

She didn't say it. She did one better, threading her fingers into his hair, fisting tight, and putting him precisely where she wanted him. "That," she panted, as he settled his lips to her, holding her wide and licking her in long, thick strokes. "Oh, yes." She sighed. "This."

She tasted like sweet and sin, and he feasted on her, reveling in the taste of her, in the way she rocked against him, taking her pleasure, unashamed of it, her hands in his hair, holding him tight to her as she moved. And all the while, she spoke, his filthy love, telling him all the ways he was doing right. "Yes," she gasped. "Right there." She gave direction and he took it, eager for it, for all the ways he could drive her wild.

Slow circles became gradually faster, his tongue working in time to the rhythm of her hips, and then she called out his name, and he could hear she was nearly there. He continued on his course, reveling in the taste of her as he gave them both pleasure beyond anything he'd ever experienced.

And then, just as she reached the point of frenzy, she

looked down at him like a fucking goddess and said, "Shall I tell you another secret?" His eyes met hers across the length of her body, and he nodded, not wanting to leave her for a moment.

"I want you to touch yourself while I come."

A pure thrill rocketed through him, something like gratitude as well as want.

And need. That, too.

He took himself in hand, never so hard. Never so hot. Never so fucking needy. And he stroked himself in time to her movements, the pleasure of her taste on his lips, the vision of her moving against him, and his own hand making the experience unbearably good.

Her fingers tightened in his hair.

Her thighs trembled.

And, with the filthiest curse he'd ever heard, she found her climax, shouting his name to the dark room as he worked her with hands and mouth and tongue until all she knew was pleasure.

As she came down from her pleasure, his tongue gentling, his fingers stilling as she pulsed against him, she pulled him up to her, his name hoarse on her lips, eager for more.

Eager for all of it.

He lifted his head after the last ripple of pleasure coursed through her, and he moved to lie beside her, wanting to do nothing but hold her, to press kisses to her temple and urge her to sleep.

But Grace had other plans, immediately reversing their positions and climbing atop him, pushing him to the bed. "You didn't come," she whispered, giving him a long, lingering kiss that threatened his sanity for the way she lapped at his lips, the taste of her still there.

He shook his head. "I didn't want to," he said. "It was for you."

"Mmm," she said, low and sinful, leaning down to kiss

him again. "Would you like me to tell you what I want next?"

If he hadn't already been hard as iron, the lazy, satisfied question, and the soft weight of her against him, would have ensured it. "Very much."

She ground her hips against him once, twice, until he groaned, and then she sat back on his thighs, and took him in hand. He sucked in a breath at her touch, her stroking fingers sure and strong. "I want this. I want you."

"Everything you want," he said, every muscle straining to keep from pulling her to him, rolling her to the bed and taking control.

She seemed to know it, her touch shifting to stroke up his arms and down his chest, ending, once more, at the hard, straining length of him. She moved, rubbing against him again, both of them exhaling harshly as he knocked against the center of her pleasure.

"I like that," she said.

"Mmm," he replied. "I like you."

She looked up at him, her eyes glittering with pleasure. "Do you?"

How could she even doubt it? He lifted a hand to her face, capturing her cheek and holding her gaze. "So much," he said. He took a deep breath, memorizing this moment. "I searched for you for so long, thinking it would be the same when I found you. Thinking you would be the girl I'd loved."

Her throat worked at the words. "And instead, I found *you*, beautiful, yes, and bold. But strong and powerful—fucking glorious. You're glorious, Grace."

The words struck her and she took a deep breath, her chin lifting just enough for him to see her response. Pride. Satisfaction.

"I see you," he said.

"I dreamed of this," she replied, softly, the confession

searing through him. "Of you returning. And finding me. And wanting me."

He shook his head. "You cannot believe I would ever not want you."

"I am not the girl you loved anymore."

You can never have her back.

The words she'd hurled at him that night a year ago. The words that had broken him. The words that had reset him. "No," he said. "You are not. You are more. You are the woman I love."

She breathed in the words, her hands coming to his chest as her eyes filled with unshed tears. He reached up to pull her down to him, to kiss her again.

When he pulled away, he whispered, "You don't have to say anything. But I could not stay silent any longer. I love you. Not the girl you were. Not the woman I thought I would find. You. Now. Here." He tilted his head toward the windows overlooking the Garden. "Out there on the rooftops and below in the Rookery."

Her hands came to his face, and she kissed him again, long and lush, until they were both panting with pleasure.

He pulled away from her again. "Do you remember what I said to you that night in my gardens? Do you remember what I called you?"

A soft, secret smile played over her lips. "You called me a queen."

He nodded. "And I, your throne."

Fire lit in her eyes. "I like that."

He growled, low in his chest. "I do, too, love."

They came together again, his hand between them, parting her folds as she lifted herself, the tip of him settling at the opening of her, hot and wet and perfect. *No.* No heirs. "Wait . . ."

She stilled, understanding. She shook her head. "We don't have to wait. There is no possibility of pregnancy."

And then he, too, understood. There were ways to prevent the inevitable, and Grace was a grown woman who would know well how to use them.

She lowered herself a quarter inch. A half. Just enough for him to lose his mind as she sighed in his ear. "That feels—"

"Like heaven," he grunted.

She smiled down at him, "Do you think we can make it better?"

He gave a little huff of laughter. "I can think of several things we can try."

"Is this one of them?" she asked, coyly, and she lowered herself onto his straining cock, hot and glorious, slow and perfect, and the sensation threatened to ruin him.

"It's the best of them," he grunted, willing himself still as she lifted herself a touch and returned to her place, lower, taking more of him.

"God, it's so—"

He waited, watching her, knowing that it might be uncomfortable. Not wanting to hurt her, and desperately wanting to fuck her.

"Full," she whispered, and the word, all sin and sex, made him even harder. She felt it, her eyes flying to his. "You like that."

"Hah," he said, unable to find proper words for a moment. "Yes. I like it."

She kissed him again, rocking into him, until she found her seat and he met her sigh of pleasure with a groan of his own. And then she said, "You like it when I tell you how full you make me."

He couldn't stop himself from thrusting into her, just barely, just enough to make him mad with the tease of it. "I do."

"Shall I tell you more? Shall I tell you how hard you are? How you stretch me beyond imagining, until I cannot remember what it was like to not have you inside me? Shall I tell you how it feels, knowing that it is *you* there, Ewan?"

It was murder. She was destroying him.

And then she leaned down to his ear and said, "You, finally, where you belong."

His control snapped. His arms came around her and he flipped her onto her back in the bed, the sound of her delighted laughter the only thing that penetrated the haze of his desire. He met her sparkling eyes. "You think this funny?"

"I think this perfect," she said.

He kissed the words from her lips. "I wager I can make it more perfect."

She lifted her hips, teasing him. "Prove it."

And he did, moving, finally, starting with slow, shallow thrusts, until she was arching up to him, and he was suckling her nipples and her fingers were in his hair and she was begging him for more. He was happy to give her more, moving deeper, faster, with more power, until she was sighing his name and matching him, thrust for thrust, deep and smooth and then faster, until he was gritting his teeth to keep from spending.

Not without her. Never without her, ever again.

Not now that he knew what with her was like.

She was a siren, writhing beneath him, her wild curls spread over the bed like silken fire, and he was consumed with his love for her, this woman who had more strength and power and brilliant beauty than anyone he'd ever known.

And now, she was his.

As he thrust, she slid a hand down between them, and he made room for her to find her pleasure again, her fingers working the heart of her need as he thrust into her.

He leaned down to kiss her again. "Does that feel good, love? Your hands and my cock, together?"

"Mmm," she said, too distracted by her search for release. And then her eyes flew open, and he knew she was there.

"Ewan," she gasped.

"With me," he commanded. "Look at me as you take it. I want to watch."

She did, her enormous brown eyes on his as she fell into pleasure. Watching her proved his undoing. He followed her over the edge, shouting her name to the room even as he did all he could to draw her orgasm out, refusing to stop, refusing to slow, until she was spent.

And only then, when she fell back into the cushions, boneless, did he stop, turning as he returned to her side, pulling her with him until she was draped over his body, her soft skin pink with pleasure and her silken hair cloaking them both, their breaths coming in the same harsh staccato.

They lay there in silence for long minutes as their heartbeats slowed, her body loose and languid on his, as he traced idle patterns over her impossibly soft skin, marveling at the way the evening had twisted and turned, and landed them here, together, in sated peace.

Had he ever felt like this? A pure sense of satisfaction? As though nothing that had come before or would come in the future mattered, because in this singular moment, there was perfection.

He should have known it would be like this.

Grace, whom he'd always thought of as a missing piece, now so much more.

He stroked a hand down the bare skin of her back and she took a deep breath, the rise and fall of her breasts against his chest sending a low hum of awareness through him.

"I love you," he whispered to her, wanting to say it again, now, in this perfect moment.

She lifted her head at the words, her gaze searching his, finding whatever she was looking for, because she pressed a kiss to his chest, and then tucked herself back into the crook of his arm, as though she might never leave.

He tightened his arm around her, urging her to stay.

And then she asked for the thing he had known she would ask from the moment he'd woken up in the dark in this very building a year earlier.

Then, he'd been unprepared to answer it.

Now, he was ready.

No masks.

"What happened that night?"

Chapter Twenty-Three

He didn't answer immediately.

In fact, for a moment, she thought he might not answer at all. Or perhaps he hadn't heard her, as nothing changed after she asked the question—he did not loosen his grip on her, nor did his breath quicken, nor did the slow, steady beat of his heart increase beneath her ear.

Finally, he replied, the words a low rumble between them. "I have asked myself that question a thousand times."

She did not lift her head, knowing that whatever was about to happen between them would change everything. Afraid that the truth would make it worse.

"And so?"

Grace listened to his breath, slow and even, for a long stretch, willing herself to be patient, as though her whole world weren't in chaos at the idea that she might be in love with this man who had been her enemy for so long.

Over the years, she had imagined a dozen answers to the question. More. When they'd first escaped, she and Devil and Whit had spent hours trying to understand his betrayal. What had happened? What had turned him against them, so near to when they were planning to leave?

Devil, angry and bitter, had always believed Ewan had simply decided that the money and power was too good to pass up. He'd been the old duke's choice for heir from the start, hadn't he? Why throw his lot in with them, empty bellies and empty pockets on the dark, dank streets of the Rookery?

They'd likely die before they grew old.

Whit had been more empathetic. She could still remember him wincing as she wrapped her petticoats around his broken ribs, even then arguing that Ewan had always been the one with the longest game. *There's a reason*, Whit had said. *He didn't betray us.*

He'd said it for weeks. Longer, as they disappeared into the Rookery, hiding from the old duke, who they feared would come for them—the only people in the world who knew his plans to steal the dukedom for his line, rather than dying without heir.

And then, one day, Whit had woken with a changed mind and a different heart. A harder one. And from that day on, he'd done everything he could to keep them safe from even a whisper of the dukes of Marwick—young or old.

But Grace, she'd never had the benefit of cold disinterest. She'd never found it. She'd loved him and hated him. Raged at him and wept for him. And wished him back more times than she could count. More times than anyone could count.

And even when she'd closed herself off, she'd never been entirely able to forget him.

So it was impossible for her to find casual interest in his answer now, as they lay naked in her bed—so close to revealing everything to each other.

Especially not when he finally answered. "I would never have hurt you."

She had no choice but to lift her head at that, meeting his eyes, searching and finding the truth. And still, suspicion flared. Her brow furrowed with the memory of the night.

"I remember it," she said. "You—"

His whole body tightened at the invocation, and she stopped herself, for a moment considering not saying the rest.

No. If they were to move forward, the truth had to come out.

"You came for me," she said. "I saw the blade in your hand. I saw the rage on your face."

"It wasn't for you," he said. "I don't expect you to believe me, but it's true."

"Something happened."

"Yes, something happened," he said with a humorless laugh. "He made his choice."

"We always knew it would be you," she said. "From the start, it was you. Devil and Whit—they were decoys."

"They were there to train me to be a Marwick," Ewan said, his gaze on the ceiling. "To remind me of what was important. The title. The line. They were there to train me to be ruthless."

And he had been, that night.

Or had he?

He gave a little ironic laugh. "He taught them to be ruthless, too. He would be proud of them now."

"They couldn't care less about his pride." She didn't break stride.

"They never could," he said, "and that's why he hated them more than he hated me." He looked at her. "But he didn't hate us nearly as much as he was terrified of you."

Her brow furrowed at the words. "Me," she said. "What did he think I could do to him? He was a duke, and I was a child. I lived on the estate by his benevolence alone."

"Don't you see, Grace, that made you even more terrifying—a mere girl. An orphan who should not have mattered. You should have been easily disposable. But that was not your destiny. Instead, you hated him with fiery passion and cold calculation. You were brilliant and beloved by everyone who met you, even without them knowing the truth . . . that you were the babe baptized duke—" He cut himself off for a moment and then, after consideration, he said, softly, "And you fought alongside us with a fierceness that he could not control.

"From the moment we arrived at the estate, he pitted us against each other. Mind tricks and games and battles of will and physical brutality. And he could not break us. We were three, together. Locked in a battle not to win, but to beat him. And he loathed it, because he could not understand why he could not separate us."

"You were brothers," she said, simply. She had spent two years with the trio and twenty with Devil and Whit, and she knew that they'd been forged in the same fire—made as a set.

"No," he said, his hand stroking over her back. "He lorded over us with the promise of money for our mothers and wealth for ourselves. Food in our bellies and knowledge in our brains. Roofs over our heads. Whatever we wanted, if only we'd fight each other."

She shook her head. "You never did. Even when he put you in the ring together. You always pulled your punches." She paused, then, "A lesson you still carry with you. I saw you do it in the Garden the other day."

He rubbed a hand absently over his jaw, where a bruise still faded. "That was a mistake. If you hadn't stopped the fight, I might not be here."

Of course she had stopped the fight. She would never have let him die. "You'd do well to remember that, toff. We fight dirty down here in the mud."

"I shan't make the same mistake again." He paused, watching her carefully, and then he said, "I only ever pulled my punches for you."

She tilted her head. "What does that mean?"

"The three of us could have easily been broken. Separated. Manipulated," he said. "It wasn't blood that kept us together against him. It was you."

She caught her breath. "We all loved you. Whit and Devil like a sister—each of them willing to protect you without hesitation. And me . . ." He trailed off, and she reached for his hand, threading her fingers through his. "Like you were a part of me." He sighed. "Christ, you were so brave."

"No, I wasn't," she said, shaking her head. "I was nobody. I was nothing. No one noticed me."

"You were there, always. You think I don't remember all the times you rescued me? Us? Blankets in the cold. Food when we were hungry. Light in the dark. You mended us all again and again. And always out of sight."

"It wasn't brave," she said. Yes, she'd done everything she could to help them without the duke discovering her, but, "I never stood up to him. I could have done so much more to keep you all safe. I was proof of his crime. And I never—" She looked away, hating the memories of her time at the house—of the time they'd shared there. "I never stood up to him."

"Neither did I."

I did get you out.

The words from the other night, when she'd accused him of chasing them away. Of leaving them behind.

"Except I think perhaps you did." She watched him for a long moment, her eyes narrowing on him. "I think you stood up to him that night."

A candle on the bedside table flickered out. They'd been in her rooms for a long time. Two hours. Maybe more. She looked to the clock across the room. Half three. The party would still be in full swing below.

But here, time had stopped.

"Sometimes, I play that week over in my head. I remember every moment with such clarity." He looked to her. "Do you remember? We were planning to leave."

She nodded. "You'd decided it was time. Before winter came and he decided to make an example of one of you."

"It had been two years there," he said. "Two years, and we were all old enough for school, and Devil and I were already growing taller."

She remembered. "You wouldn't soon be easily hidden."

"That, and we knew that if we could just get to the Garden, we were able-bodied now. We could all work." He looked at her. "And we were big enough to protect you."

She smiled at that. "It turned out it was Covent Garden that needed protecting from me."

He stroked his hand over her skin again, pulling her tight against him. "I wish I had been here. I wish I had seen you take this place by storm."

She grew serious. "I wish that, too."

"Instead, he found us out." He lifted her hand and pressed a kiss to her knuckles. "You and me."

He set her hand to his left shoulder, where his scar still burned.

"I remember that night with crystal clarity," she said. "Chaste kisses and sweet words, and being wrapped in your arms." In the darkness, whispering their plans for a future. Together. Far from Burghsey and the dukedom.

"Do you remember what I said to you? Before he found us?"

She nodded, meeting his eyes. "You told me you'd find a way to make us safe."

"And what else?"

She smiled. "You told me you loved me."

"And you told me the same," he said, pressing a kiss to her temple and breathing deep in her hair.

"Then he found us, and he hurt you. And in hurting you, he hurt me, as well." She lifted her hand from where he'd been marked, and kissed the scar there once more. "I am sorry."

"Do not ever, ever apologize for that. I would take a hundred like it if it meant keeping those memories of you. The happiest of my life . . . until now."

She stroked her thumb over the raised skin of his scar. "And now? What is the happiest memory of your life?"

His hand came to her cheek, and she looked up to find him staring at her. "Tonight. In this place that you have built—a palace of pleasure and power and pride—this place you have entrusted to me, this world you have shared with me. This is my happiest night."

Tears sprang at the words, full of sorrow and regret—what might they have had if they'd run together? What might have happened?

"What happened, Ewan?" she asked again. "How did everything change?"

"He chose me. And in choosing, made it impossible for me to come with you." He brushed her hair back from her face, and whispered, "I couldn't come with you."

Confusion flared, the words not making sense. Why not? She shook her head, confusion and disbelief on her face. "Why? Because of the title?"

"Because of the man," he said, lifting her hand and setting it to his left shoulder, mirroring his own touch on his own mark. "Because of the monster."

"Tell me."

He took a deep breath, and then, softly, "He left my mother with nothing."

Grace didn't understand why he began there, but he did, and she would have lain in his arms and listened forever, if he'd asked her to.

Or, perhaps he chose to start there because it was where

he started. Where they started—like strands of silk, woven together by fate.

"She went out for a walk, mistress to the Duke of Marwick, and returned home to discover that her home had been emptied of its contents," he said, the words cool and easy, as though he'd heard them a hundred times before, and she imagined he had—a story burned into his memory by its heroine. "Everything was gone. Jewels, furniture, art. Anything of value. Gone."

Grace's fingers stroked over his chest, running back and forth through the dusting of brown hair there, his voice vibrating against them and in her ear. And as he spoke, she wished she had a healing balm for this—for the stories of the past that harbored anger and pain . . . and sometimes, the pain of others—always stinging, and never to be assuaged.

He gave a little humorless laugh to the room. "My mother talked about that day more than she talked about anything else. The day the duke had tossed her out. That day and the days before, with the parties and the privilege and the power she held over Mayfair—the Duke of Marwick's impeccable mistress." He paused, and then, "I don't imagine she took kindly to knowing that he had been consorting with Devil's and Whit's mothers at the same time."

She couldn't help her dry, "Well, his wife wanted nothing to do with him . . . what else is an able-bodied aristocrat to do?"

He grunted, and she thought she heard real humor in it. "Not able-bodied for long, though."

Scant months later, Grace's mother, the Duchess of Marwick, had used a pistol to ensure that the old duke never had the opportunity to take advantage of another woman.

"The Lord's work," Grace said. "One of the few things I know about my mother, and the thing of which I am most proud."

His fingers traced circles on her shoulder. "I imagine you take after her in strength and righteousness."

"And aim," she teased.

"And aim." She heard the smile in his voice, turned dry as sand when he said, "I imagine that my mother would have liked to have been her second in that gunfight. She would have liked to have punished him as he punished her." He stilled, and she did not move, except for her fingers, circling in light, languid strokes.

When he continued, he was whispering. "She hated him for betraying their contract. Ducal mistresses were to be paid handsomely in their retirement. They were to be given row houses in Earl's Court, and two thousand pounds a year, and an open account on Bond Street. But he gave her none of those things. Instead he punished her."

The old duke had punished every woman he'd ever interacted with. He'd been a brute. Grace opened her mouth to tell Ewan just that, to help ease the pain he clearly carried with him.

Before she could, he continued, "He punished her because of me."

"No." Her head snapped up as the word flew from her lips. "You weren't—"

He stopped her. "He left her a single trunk of clothing. And do you know," he said, not looking at her, "for years, when she would tell me this story, I thought she told me about that trunk to point to my father's sympathy. The dresses, decorated with pearls and shot through with gold—all sold by the time I could understand what pearls and gold meant.

"I always hoped she told me that story to underscore his humanity—knowing what life he was sending her to. One that she hadn't chosen."

She took a deep breath. God knew Grace had seen the best and worst of the Garden, but since the Bastards had started running the Rookery, they'd done their best to ensure that people who found their way there could make their own choices.

Choice made for honest work. And safe.

And it was too rare that women were afforded it.

Ewan went on, "But now, as a grown man, I know it had nothing to do with his humanity. He was furious. And he wanted her to live every day for the rest of her life with that trunk full of aging silks, and remember what she'd given up. Because of me. He wanted her to regret me."

She shook her head. "She didn't."

"You don't know that."

"I do," she said, forcefully, unwilling to let him win on this count. "I know it because I've lived in the Garden longer than you have, and I've seen more here than you ever did. And I know that women who don't wish to have children don't have to have them. I know your mother knew that—and how. And that is why I know she made a choice."

She put her hands to the sides of his face, willing him to hear her. "The duke didn't leave her with nothing, Ewan. He left her with *you*. Her choice."

"And what good was I?" he said, anger flooding his tone. "She died here, in this place with nothing but the memory of her choice. I wasn't even here."

Grace nodded. "She did, and I dearly hope your father is rotting in hell for that and a thousand other things. But you didn't die here." She had tears in her eyes. "*You* didn't die, Ewan, and that is the gift she gave you."

He was lost to thought for an age, until finally, Grace could not stop herself from filling the silence and telling him her own story, softly. "I went looking for her, you know."

His eyes snapped to hers.

"She was already gone," she said. "Fever."

"I know," he replied. "She died while we were at

Burghsey. He took pleasure in telling me that one night, not long after you'd left; I hadn't taken his beating with enough contrition."

She winced. "I'm sorry."

He shook his head, waving away the words. "Why did you come after her?"

"I thought if only I could . . ." she started, then trailed off.

"Tell me."

She could not have denied him anything in that moment. "I thought you might come back for her."

He swallowed at the words. "I couldn't." The same thing he'd said earlier.

Grace refused to let him look away. "You couldn't come with us. You couldn't come back for her. Tell me."

"You were all in danger," he said, his chest tight with guilt. "And I was the reason why. He knew where you were." The hate in the words was like ice, spreading cold through her. "At least, he told me he did, and I believed him. And he told me that if I ever left, he'd find you and do what I had failed to do." He stopped. "What I would never have done."

Understanding dawned. "He wanted me dead."

"Yes."

"And he wanted you to do it."

"My final task," he said. "To kill you."

The placeholder. "To eliminate any possibility of anyone ever discovering that you weren't the true heir," she said.

"Not just that," he said. "To make sure that I had no one left."

Grace's heart pounded at the words—confusion and anger and sadness warring within her, because that had been the result even though she lived. She and Devil and Whit had run, and what had happened to Ewan in the balance?

"Title first, last, and always," he said. "Heir, first, last, and always."

Her mind raced, playing over that moment, years earlier. Him coming for her, blade in hand. Whit on the floor, ribs broken. And then Devil, blocking him. Taking the blade.

Ewan had pulled the punch.

"Devil's face."

"I miscalculated," he said, the words barely sound. "It was never intended to be so long. He came at a different angle than I expected."

"Intended." She met his eyes. "Expected."

He did not look away. "I had to make it look real."

"For your father to believe it."

He shook his head. "For *you* to believe it."

Confusion flared. "Why did that matter?"

"Because I knew that if you didn't believe it, you'd never leave without me." He watched her for a long moment, and then added, "I knew that if you didn't believe it, you'd never stop trying to get back. And you would never be safe from him."

It was the truth. "I would have fought for you, Ewan. We all would have."

"I know. And he would have taken everything from you." He paused, his hands coming to her hair, toying with it as he said, "And in that, he would have taken everything from me. I could not be the reason he punished another person I loved."

His meaning flared, hot and angry and devastating. That monster of a duke had stolen his mother's future. Because of Ewan. And then he'd threatened Grace's.

"So you stayed."

He nodded. "I stayed, and I lived the life he asked of me, and every few months he would trot out some new piece of information about you."

She shook her head. "Why? Why not just kill us?"

"Because if you died, he lost his hold on me. Your safety was the only way he could keep me in line. To ensure that

I understood that you survived by his will. And my own actions."

"Because he knew what we all knew. That you were good." How often had they said it, she and Devil and Whit, as they sat in the dark, dank streets of the Garden and wondered what had happened that had turned him against them.

"I am not good."

He was, though. It had never occurred to them that he'd made a sacrifice.

"You came for me after he died." Not to destroy her. To love her.

"The moment he died. He drew his last breath and I cursed him to hell and came to London. He'd told me for years he knew where you were, but he'd never told me, and I tore the city apart looking for you. But you were already gaining power here, tucked away from anyone who was not part of the Garden. And this place did well keeping you all safe—and I grew more and more wild as the years passed, searching for you.

"I am not good," he repeated. "When I thought it was all for naught—when I thought you were dead . . . I, too, was a monster. I came for Devil, for Whit, for this place—wanting to lay them all low. To punish them for not keeping you safe."

Her chest tightened at the confession.

"I am cut from the same cloth as my father."

"No," she said, sitting up at the words. "Don't say that."

"It's true, though. Like him, I was willing to destroy for what I wanted. Like him, I am alone. And like him, I deserve it."

"*No*." The word was loud and furious. "You are nothing like him. You are nothing like him and I regret ever thinking you were. I regret believing that you manipulated and betrayed us. I regret believing that you were consumed with greed. I regret thinking you returned for revenge and not for something far more powerful."

She looked down at him, consumed with her own frustration and deep sadness that she had spent a lifetime believing that the boy she'd loved had been her enemy. Consumed by something else, as well. "No masks," she whispered.

His hand found hers where it pressed against his heart. "No masks."

"I love you."

The words hung between them for a long moment, and he went still as stone. But her hand was over his heart, and she felt the pounding there, instantly stronger. Instantly faster.

Her own heart in her throat, she elaborated. "And when I say that, I do not refer to the boy you once were, but the man you are now."

And then he laughed, perfect and wonderful and like nothing in the wide world.

There was nothing in the wide world like his laugh.

He pulled her close. "Say it again."

"I love you," she whispered, the words at once strange and wildly familiar.

"You do?" he whispered back, that beautiful smile in his eyes now, like perfection. And she wanted him so much—she wanted that smile warming her and wooing her for a lifetime. For longer. He repeated himself, amazed laughter beneath it. "You do."

She couldn't help but laugh, too, suddenly light and free. "Yes," she agreed. "Yes."

And he was sitting up and kissing her and she was kissing him, and he rolled her onto her back and she gave herself up to him. To *them*. To a fresh start. A second chance, without names or titles or history between them.

To happiness, ever after.

A knock came on the outer door to her chambers.

His lips were in the crook of her neck, whispering nonsense, making her giggle with the pleasure. "Send them away."

"It might be important," she whispered.

"More likely it is Devil and Whit, come to put their fists into my face for despoiling their sister."

"Pardon me, sir. If anyone did any despoiling tonight, it was me."

"That much is true."

A shout echoed up from Dominion, which remained in full celebration below, the sound punctuated by another knock, this one on the door to her private rooms. She stilled, and he lifted his head.

It was not a knock anymore. It was full-on pounding.

She was out of the bed immediately, heading to dress. Ewan just behind her, pulling on his trousers.

"Dahlia!" came Veronique's voice through the door. "It's a raid!"

Chapter Twenty-Four

"It's fucking mayhem down there."

Veronique spoke the moment Grace yanked open the door leading into her office, hastily dressed and heading for her desk. Veronique was flanked by two of the security detail, armed women whose job it was to keep the membership safe.

Grace looked from one to the other as she passed. "You two get back downstairs. We need to fight back and get the members out." From beyond the door, she heard shouts and screams, and an enormous crash. "Now."

"You need protection."

Grace shot her a look as she collected a stack of ledgers and journals.

"She's got it," Ewan said from the doorway, surprising everyone with his presence and his impenetrable tone as he followed Grace across the room.

She shook her head. "You cannot stay."

"Like hell I can't," he said, instantly.

"If you stay, you'll be seen. You'll be discovered."

"So?"

She looked to the ceiling, frustration flaring. "You're a

duke, Ewan. All they want is to be able to turn your power against you."

"No," he said. "I'm a duke. I hold all the power."

It was so arrogant. So arrogant and so wrong, here on the dark streets where a duke could be tossed into the river just as easily as he could find his way home to Mayfair, and she hated that he fell back on that title that had ruined so much.

But still, it mattered that he stood here with her.

She came back around the desk. She kicked the edge of the carpet spread wide across the office floor.

He didn't have to be told more, immediately bending down to pull the heavy rug back. Grace counted the floorboards and set her toe to one, throwing a hidden latch and revealing a secret door. If he was surprised, he didn't show it. Instead, he leaned down and opened it, revealing piles and piles of paper within. He backed away, making room for Grace to crouch and set an armload of books inside.

"Accounts," she explained, though he did not ask. "Membership rolls."

"He's on our side now?" Veronique asked.

Grace ignored the question and closed the door, throwing the latch once more. He extended a hand down to her, and she let him pull her to her feet.

Veronique raised her brows at the touch. "I hear the Garden boys nearly took you down a few days back, toff. And you expect to keep Dahlia safe?"

"I do." He returned the carpet to its original seat.

Veronique must have seen something in him, because she released the women who flanked her. "Go. Don't hesitate to do damage."

"Good fight," Grace said as they turned to leave, already turning for her desk, fetching her scarf and looping it around her waist.

Veronique reported the situation below as she watched.

"We're pushing everyone abovestairs to the roof, and everyone in Dominion to the tunnels."

"And the intruders?"

"A dozen, maybe fifteen. Strong bruisers. Armed with clubs and fists, and looking like the kind of gang you don't fuss with."

"How'd they get in?" Ewan again.

Veronique cut him a look. "Same way you did, toff. Through the front door, as though they'd had a fucking invitation."

Grace asked, "Who are they? Police?"

A shake of the head. "Not any police anyone's talking about."

But that didn't mean they weren't organized. And it didn't mean they weren't Crown. All it meant was that they were out for the kind of blood no one wanted proof of.

And Grace would be damned if she'd let them have it without a fight. She nodded, heading for the door. "Then we'd better get down there."

Veronique pulled a pistol from its holster under her arm and looked to Ewan. "You're sure he can fight?"

Grace met the eyes of the man she loved, in trousers and shirtsleeves, all muscle and strength, fury in his eyes and his jaw, looking for all the world as though he was prepared to walk through fire for right.

For her.

"I've never seen his equal."

She opened the door, and the trio headed toward the screams.

They ran down the center stairs to the main oval room of the club, where a half-dozen fights had broken out. The men who had come to destroy 72 Shelton were easily recognizable—dirty and ruthless. But they hadn't wagered on Veronique's security being equally ruthless and prepared to do battle.

Nor on the Bastards'. Across the room, Annika, who ran Devil and Whit's smuggling operation, pushed Lady Nora Madewell behind her and threw a wicked punch, breaking her opponent's nose, if the howl he let out was any indication.

"Not without me, you don't!" Lady Nora shouted, picking up a heavy crystal vase, laden with hothouse flowers, and cracking him over the head, setting him to his knees. With a grin, Nora looked to her love, pride on her open, pretty face. "Not bad, if I do say."

"Not bad," Annika agreed with a half smile—the highest praise a body could receive from the stoic Norwegian—pulling her lady close. "Very good."

Nearby, one of Shelton Street's army took a chair to a brute with a heavy club, and dropped him to the ground, summoning a collection of little shrieks from the members who were herding past, through to the back rooms, and the staircase that would lead to the underground tunnels that would take them safely from the club.

"That was a solid hit for Cate," Grace said.

"You've trained them well," Ewan said.

"Tell me that when we're on the other side of this," she said.

"Whoever this is, they'll never get away with it," Ewan said, looking over the crowd. "I recognized a dozen of the most powerful members of the House of Lords here tonight."

"They're not here for the men," Grace replied. "They're after the members; every woman here."

They looked over the crowd, scrambling to escape the men who were taking care to destroy everything in their path. Grace watched a brute with a club smash a stained-glass lantern in the corner of the oval salon before slicing a cushion open with a wickedly sharp blade.

On the other side of the room, someone had toppled a chaise.

They were after her club, dammit.

A couple peeled away from the stream of escapees and headed for them—Nelson, a cut on his forehead bleeding more than Grace liked, his arm lodged protectively around the Dowager Countess of Granville, a bloody handkerchief in her hand, her mask having been traded for a furrowed brow.

He met Grace's gaze as he pressed a kiss to the lady's temple. "We're for the roof."

"And for Mayfair," Lady Granville said, pointedly, worry and something else in her eyes.

They would never be back. Grace knew love when she saw it.

She stepped aside to let them pass. "Be well."

The couple was gone, a riot of sound following them up the stairs and into the night.

Grace looked back over the chaos before them. "They don't want to scare us," she said. "They want to end us."

"Why?" Ewan asked.

"Because," she said, watching. Lady Marsham and the Duchess of Pemberton pushed past, wild-eyed, and she saw the terror in their eyes as they peeked over their shoulders, looking for the enemy beyond. "They don't like that we are the future."

Even if they got everyone out that night, it would not be enough. The raid would do what it was meant to do—scare members off. Send them, frightened, back to their Mayfair drawing rooms and their Park Lane teas. Back to gossip on Bond Street and walks along the Serpentine. Back to the safety they enjoyed as the second sex.

And 72 Shelton would be made an example by the men who ran them back to ground.

Over her decaying corpse.

Anger flared, hot in Grace's throat, and she caught the eye of the aerialist, still high above the crowd, having pulled herself to standing on the trapeze for the best view in the house.

Grace lifted her chin toward the woman. "Where?"

Thankfully, the other woman did not misunderstand. She pointed in the direction of the front room, where Fortuna had been earlier in the evening. Where she and Ewan had danced, wild and free—a memory that would forever be tainted by this—these men, in her palace, leaving destruction in their wake.

Anger became rage.

Another scream sounded from the front room, and she was already moving, pulling the scarf from her waist and wrapping the ends around her fists with quick, economical movements as she pushed through the crowd.

She heard Ewan roar her name behind her, but she did not look back. This was her place. Her world. These were her people. And she would protect them at all costs.

ONE MOMENT SHE was with him and the next, she was gone, disappeared into the throngs of people fleeing in one direction, swimming upstream, running, as she had always done, into the fray.

Grace, always the first to save, no matter what danger she might face.

A glimpse of her flame red curls the only thing that retained his sanity as he followed her. She was moving too fast, lost almost instantly in the crowd. He roared her name, frustration and fear propelling him into the crowd—which seemed, blessedly, to understand his urgency and make space for him.

"It's Mad Marwick!" he heard at the back of his consciousness as he pushed through the crush, the moniker from his past, which he had worked so hard to overcome in the months since he'd returned—now back because he *was* mad. He was a wild animal, desperate to get to the woman he loved.

He looked over his shoulder. "You said fifteen?"

"Give or take." Grace's second-in-command was at his side. "Four in the center room, makes ten or so elsewhere."

"And your men? They can fight?" What was Grace headed into?

"My *women* are made of stronger stuff than you, toff."

He grunted, coming through to the room where the magician and the fiddlers and the acrobat had been earlier in the evening. He pulled up short as the woman with him cursed, under her breath.

The room had been destroyed. Curtains slit and furniture smashed, tables and chairs upended. Paintings ripped from the walls and slashed.

This wasn't sport. It was punishment.

They don't like that we are the future.

Around the room, the intruders brawled with club employees, and at the center of it all, Grace. As he watched, she clocked one of the brutes, setting him off kilter long enough to deliver a heavy kick to his midsection. He landed on the ground and she used her scarf to deliver the final blow, her quick actions inhibiting his movement as she knocked him unconscious.

She shook out her hand as he landed on the ground and turned around, her brown eyes finding Ewan's as he watched her, pride bursting in his chest at this view of her, in her element.

A queen.

Her brows rose in silent question as he went for her, unable to keep himself from it, from reaching for her, battle raging all around them, pulling her into his arms, and kissing her thoroughly, claiming her for his own—this Boadicea.

When he was through, she was loose in his arms, and

when she opened her eyes, he said, "I'm going to marry you." Another kiss, quick and lush. "I'm going to marry you, and we will keep this place safe, and you will never have to fight alone ever again. We shall fight together."

Her eyes went wide, but before she could say anything, movement came at the outer edge of his vision, and they both turned. The attacker was already lowering his club, aiming for Grace.

Ewan went wild, blocking the blow with a roar of fury, catching the club with one strong hand and planting his fist in the man's face once, twice. "No one touches her," he said on the third hit.

And on the fourth, "No one touches this place." He lifted the other man by the collar. "Do you understand?"

A nod.

"Who sent you?"

"Dunno. We was just told to make sure this place wasn't fit for usin' again."

Frustration flared. "Fucking hired dogs. You go back into the gutter you climbed out of and you tell whoever it is who hired you that this place is under the protection of the Duke of Marwick. Do you understand?"

Grace sucked in a breath at his shoulder, but he didn't look at her, too busy waiting for a reply.

"Y-yes."

"Good."

He lifted his fist to deliver another blow, but Grace stayed him with a touch, looking to the man. "Are you the same crew that went for Maggie O'Tiernen's?"

The bleeding man's eyes shifted around the room, and Ewan grew more irritated. "Tell the truth, bruv," he said, the Garden seeping into his voice. "You won't like the consequences of a lie."

The man's eyes widened. "Yeah. That were us."

"And Satchell's?"

Ewan looked to her. *What did she know?*

"Aye."

"What's your name?"

He hesitated, and Ewan shook him like a doll. "Mikey."

"I never forget a face, Mikey. Stay out of the Garden. You won't like it if we cross paths again."

He nodded, fear and gratitude in his eyes.

She indicated the rest of the room, where the fighters of 72 Shelton Street had dispatched the interlopers. "Take your boys and get the hell out of my place."

The man obeyed instantly—knowing with the keen sense of a hired gun that he had been bested. She watched the men as they left, looking far worse for wear.

And then she turned to him. "You proposed to me."

"I did," he acknowledged.

"You proposed to me in the middle of a brawl."

His smile was full of chagrin. "We've never been conventional."

She did not return the amusement.

"Shall I do it again, now that the brawling is over and we have emerged victorious?"

"No," she said, instantly.

He tilted his head. "Grace . . ." he began.

"Dahlia," she corrected.

"What?"

"I am not Grace here. I am Dahlia."

The air grew heavy between them, and Ewan did not like it. Did not like the harbinger it appeared to be, considering the steel in her words. "I would have thought that right now, of all times, you'd be Grace."

"Because you are proposing marriage?"

"Precisely."

"Because you want me for duchess."

"Yes." He wanted it more than he could say. More than he'd ever wanted anything, ever. "Yes. Christ. Yes. That's what I can do—I can make you duchess and make this place unbreakable. I can give you everything you have worked for. If you want this place? I want it for you. I want you safe in it. I want your employees safe in it."

"They are. We are," she said.

"Now, yes. But I can make you safe forever. You think those thugs were hired by Mayfair? By men terrified of their wives getting ideas about the queen? By men terrified of women having power?"

"I do," she said.

"Then let me fix it. Marry me. I'm a duke. This was what we said we would do." He reached for her, but she stepped away from him instead of toward him. "We said we would use the dukedom to win. This is how it begins. You marry me. And this place becomes untouchable."

This was the beginning of their future. The next part of their life. Their happily-ever-after. But something was wrong.

"Not even you have the power to stop whatever this is, Duke." He resisted the urge to flinch at the title—one she hadn't used with him in weeks. "This threat is vanquished from below, not above. Stopped by me, not you."

"Why shouldn't it be stopped by us? Together?"

A pause, and she went still. "Together."

"Yes," he said, and he would have given his entire fortune to know what she was thinking. "Together."

Grace watched him for a long moment, and there was something in her eyes, something he recognized from a long-ago night—twenty years gone.

Disappointment.

And then she said, softly, "You planned all this."

THE IRONY, OF course, was that the only time Grace had ever allowed herself to linger on the idea of marriage, it had been marriage to him.

It had been marriage to that boy she'd loved a lifetime earlier, who had made plans to be duke, and made plans to return to London, triumphant and powerful, and change the world from which he'd come.

And he had made plans for her to be duchess, and change the world by his side.

But she was no longer that girl of twelve, of thirteen, of fourteen. She was no longer the fifteen-year-old who shivered in the cold and dreamed of him coming back to her.

She was a grown woman who had saved that world and herself, without title or privilege. She'd built power from nothing. An empire from nothing. And when it came under threat, she fought. And she triumphed.

Had he not just seen it?

And now he offered her a title, as though it were a gift. As though it weren't the thing that had brought their whole world down around him.

And then that word—*together.*

The same word the Duchess of Trevescan had used earlier in the evening, when she'd been so delighted to see Grace and Ewan. *Together.*

Grace looked to him. "You sent her to me. The Duchess of Trevescan. That night. To tell me you were back."

He looked away.

"You did. You sent her, and she, what, planted the conversation about you? The revelation that you were hosting a masque and looking for a wife?"

That got his attention. "I wasn't looking for a wife. I'd already found her."

She ignored the pounding of her heart at the words, and the truth of them, glittering in his gaze. "All you had to do was convince me you'd changed."

"I had changed," he said.

"I thought that was true," she replied.

"It is!"

"No. I don't want to be your duchess. I have no desire to be complicit in your world—the world that ruined us. That ruined our mothers. My brothers. The world that threatens the Garden every day and tonight came for women because God forbid they should have a moment of their own pleasure. Their own satisfaction. Their own joy . . ." She paused, hating the words. Hating the rest. "And all that, before we even discuss how it ruined you."

Her anger grew hot as she added, "You think a title can save us from this?" She spread her arms wide to indicate the destruction around them. "It cannot," she said. "The only thing the dukedom of Marwick has ever done is threaten us."

He shoved his fingers through his hair and rounded on her, and she saw him come to the edge of his anger. "You think I do not know how it ruined me? You think I have not regretted that fucking title for twenty years? I *loathe* it. Every time someone speaks it into being, I hate it more. Tonight, in stripping me of it, you and this place gave me the most magnificent gift I've ever received—a taste of life without the fucking dukedom."

Her eyes went wide as he railed. "You think I don't remember the pact we made every day? No heirs. No future. Nothing that carries on the name." He stopped, his gaze wild on her face. "You think I don't remember that pact every time I look at you and think about what a life with you could be, if only I wasn't the fucking duke? Shall I tell you? What that life would be? What we could have?"

She shook her head, her heart tight in her chest. "No."

But he was already there. "You think I don't imagine days in the sun here in the Garden? Hauling on the docks? You think I don't ache for a life where I return to you, here, in this magnificent place you have built, and sleeping next to you all night, until I can kiss you awake in the morning? You deal in fantasy. Would you like to know how mine goes?"

No.

Yes.

"No."

He reached for her, capturing her face, tilting her up to him. "My fantasy is this. You, and me, here. With a collection of flame-haired babes." She closed her eyes. "My brothers. Their children. A *family*."

The last was a whisper.

"Christ. I cannot tell you how I long for a family—one built in our home. Yours and mine. The start of something new."

A fat tear fell at the words, at the ache in them, and the twin ache they set off in her own chest. He was there to catch it, his thumb tracing over her cheek in a wide arc, brushing her tears away. "But I can't have that. Because of that fucking title."

Her heart pounded in the face of his anger, decades-old, finally revealed.

"But the one thing I have clung to over the years was this—one day, I would use it as we'd intended. And here is that chance. Tonight, I take that filthy, stolen title, and I claim it to save this place. For you. Tonight, I give you that fight you've wanted."

She stiffened, terrified of what he would say.

"I love you."

In her years of bareknuckle fighting, Grace had taken countless unexpected blows, but never anything like that one—which pulled the air from her.

And he did not stop.

"Yes, I loved you the moment I set eyes on you a lifetime ago, but what that was—it pales in comparison to how I love you now. You are perfect—strong and bold and brave and brilliant, and the way I ache to be near you is only made worse when I am near you, because I cannot have you. Because every time I reach for you, you slip through my fingers . . . like fucking fantasy."

She swallowed, the knot in her throat impossibly tight as he spoke, the words an echo of her own feelings—her own desperate desires, impossible to sate.

"Yes—I asked the duchess to get you to the masque. And I stood at the edge of that ballroom, losing my mind, waiting for you to come in some kind of mad hope. And then you did, and I realized that what I felt before you arrived had not been hope, it had been fear. And when you arrived, *you* were hope."

A tear spilled over, down her cheek, and he reached for it instantly, brushing it aside with his thumb. "I would do it all again. I shan't ever not seek you, Grace. You are my beginning and end. The other half of me. And you always have been.

"Here is my fight," he repeated, softly. "Marry me."

She shook her head, sadness coursing through her, tears coming, hot and instant. "The story you told me. Cyrene and Apollo. He wanted her to leave with him. To live with the gods. She wanted to rule a kingdom. What happened?"

He hesitated.

"Tell me," she said, already knowing the answer.

"He made her Queen of Libya. And the land was lush and beautiful and prosperous, and ruled by a warrior Queen."

One fat tear fell, tracing down her cheek. "And what of him—did he rule by her side?"

He did not look at her. "Grace."

"No. What of Apollo?"

He turned his beautiful amber eyes on her finally, and she saw the sadness in them. "He left her."

She nodded. "Because she didn't want idyll, married to a god, playing at power. She wanted her own kingdom. Her love. Her life. All of it. Together. Equal. Or none of it at all."

"Was it worth it?" he asked. "A lifetime alone, when she did not have to be alone?"

"I don't know," she replied. "But the alternative was not enough."

He nodded. "And me? What of wanting me?"

Her throat ached at the question, painful and full with the truth of her answer. "I want you with my whole being," she confessed. "I want you with everything I am."

He reached for her then, his fingers sliding across her cheek and into her hair, his touch luring her closer, and she came, realizing even as she moved that it would always be like this between them. She would always come for him. Always be drawn to him.

The kiss he gave her was lush and heavy, full of aching desire and all the love that had gone unused in the years they'd been apart, and if it had been an hour earlier, a day earlier, Grace would have reveled in that caress and let it come as a gift, on a wave of future. Of hope.

But in that moment, it was not future.

It was the end.

Tears spilled down her cheeks when Ewan broke the kiss and lifted his head, opening those beautiful amber eyes and looking deep into hers. "And so my father wins."

The words stole her breath, and fear coursed through her. Fear, and love and a keen desire that she could not deny—not even as she knew what was about to happen. Not even as she knew he was about to give her what she had sworn she wanted, only after she'd realized she was terrified of it.

Terrified of losing him.

Could it be enough?

"I want you," he said, and she hated the way the words came, resigned. "I want you and I love you, and it isn't first love. It's final. And if you cannot see that—if you cannot find the courage to take it, and to revel in it, and to let me stand by your side, then it is not enough." He shook his head. "How many tests must I pass before you believe in it? Before you trust it? Before you trust me?"

"I want to," she said. It was true. There was nothing she wanted more than this man, with her, forever.

Silence stretched between them for an eternity, and she saw the riot of emotions play across his face. Frustration. Sadness. Disappointment. And finally, resignation. "Want is not enough," he said. "Not for either of us."

The words hung between them, a wicked blow. A punch he did not pull.

He left her then, and she knew, without question, that he would never return.

And Grace Condry, queen of Covent Garden, stood in her destroyed club and, for the first time in two decades, let the tears come.

Chapter Twenty-Five

The next morning, as the sun coated the rooftops of London in the bright light of a crisp autumn day, her brothers found her on the roof.

"Between us, we've, what—five houses?" Devil said, coming to stand at her side where she sat on a chimney block, arm draped over one knee, looking out over the rooftops toward Mayfair. He lifted the collar of his greatcoat and crossed his arms over his chest. "You'd think we could find somewhere warmer to meet."

Grace didn't look at him. "We've always preferred the roof. What was it you used to say? This was as far as we'd ever be from the muck?"

"Mmm," Devil replied, rocking back on his heels. "But Whit owns the southern edge of Berkeley Square, so look at us now."

No one laughed.

Instead, Whit came around into her field of vision, leaning back against the low wall marking the edge of the roof, crossing one ankle over the other, shoving his hands deep in his pockets and hunching his shoulders against the wind. "Club's a fucking mess."

And it was. Broken glass, curtains slashed to bits, furniture in pieces, not a single window remaining intact. At some point, someone had tipped over a candelabrum and burned a hole in the carpet. Thankfully, that had happened before every bottle of alcohol on the main floor of the club had been smashed and let to run out, or there would be no rooftop to be found.

Grace nodded. "And you're only talking about the inside. I'll be lucky if we ever see another member again."

"Nah," Devil said. "They shan't stay away. You promised them a circus, and didn't you deliver?"

"It's destroyed," she said. "I sent everyone home." She didn't want to face them.

"Well, a dozen of them are inside getting a jump on the clean, so I'd say your biggest problem is mutiny," Devil said. "Zeva and Veronique are barking orders like proper lieutenants. Maybe you ought to get them uniforms when you order new wallcoverings."

Irritation flared. "I told them to go home."

"It can be mended," Whit said, ignoring her. "You're rich and we've a line into every silk spinner, furniture maker and whisky distiller you need. That is, if we're still talking about the club."

Devil tapped his stick on the roof thoughtfully. "Well, the rest can be mended, too, truthfully. If anyone knows that, we do."

Grace looked to him. "The rest?"

He met Whit's gaze over her shoulder. "She plays coy with me."

Whit grunted. "She's never liked to talk about him."

Ewan.

"We hear he's broken your heart again, Gracie."

The words, soft and kind—kinder than anything she'd ever heard Devil say to someone who wasn't Felicity or

Helena—threatened to break her. She pressed her lips together.

"Can we kill him, now?" grumbled Whit.

"He loves me," she said.

"He's always loved you," Devil said. "That doesn't seem like it should be heartbreaking. Quite the opposite, as a matter of fact."

"He wants to marry me," she said to the rooftops. "I'd be Duchess of Marwick."

Her brothers were silent for a long moment, and then Whit grunted his acknowledgment.

"So. Therein lies the rub," said Devil.

Another long stretch of silence, then Whit. "What did you tell him?"

She snapped her attention to them, irritation flaring along with something like betrayal as she looked from one to the other. "What do you think I said?"

"Ah. So he didn't break your heart," Whit clarified. "You broke his."

"Who made you such an expert on hearts?" she snapped. "I thought you wanted to kill him."

His brows shot up. "Easy, Gracie."

"We don't *not* want to kill him," Devil said. "But we know what it's like to be laid low."

"I don't much care for feeling sympathy for the bastard, truthfully," Whit said.

"And so? What will he do?" This, from Devil.

Whit shook his head. "We've never been able to predict his movements."

A long silence, and Devil tapped his cane. Once. Twice. "Grace has."

She did not like the truth in the words, not as it was twined with the truth in her heart. The keen memory of him walking away—a new man. Changed, just as she was.

Forever.

She knew what he would do. It was over. "He's going to leave," she said, the ache in her chest nearly unbearable. "He's going to leave, and he's never going to come back."

The irony was, he'd finally done what she told him she wanted.

And now, all she wished was for him to come back and stay.

"He's already left," Devil said.

The words struck like a slap. "How do you know that?"

"Because we've been having him followed since he returned."

She shot him a look. "Why?"

"Well, first of all"—he turned and sat on the high ledge of the roof—"every time he's turned up in the past . . . how long?" He looked to Whit to fill the time frame.

"Forever," Whit supplied with a shrug.

"Right. Every time he's turned up *forever*, he's tried to kill one of us." He paused, then added, "You were the first one of us he tried to kill, I might add. But here we are—life is a strange, mysterious thing."

"He didn't try to kill me," she said.

Everything stilled on that rooftop—even the cold autumn wind seemed to pause to let the words seep in.

"How do you know?" Devil said.

"Because he told me," she said. "The old duke wanted me dead."

"Because you were proof of what he'd done."

She nodded.

"Not just that," Whit said. "He wanted you dead because he knew he'd never have all of Ewan if Ewan had any hope of having you."

Whit, always seeing what no one else did.

"Yes," she said. "But he never would have hurt me."

"We all saw it, though," Whit replied. "We all saw him come for you."

"No." This time it was Devil who interrupted. "He didn't come for her. He came for me. I always wondered why he looked me dead in the eye beforehand. I thought it was because he wanted the fight."

"He did," Grace said. "He wanted the fight with you, to give us all time to run."

Silence fell between them as they were all lost to the memory of that fateful night, when everything that had happened had somehow not happened at all.

"Christ." Whit was the first to speak. "He gave himself over to Marwick. To keep us safe."

"The old man had to have known where we'd gone," Devil said.

He knew where you were, Ewan had told her, *but he'd never told me.*

Grace nodded. "We were young and scared and no doubt left a dozen signposts along the way. But he never came for us."

"That doesn't mean he didn't threaten it," Devil said, understanding the manipulation instantly. How had they not seen what their evil father would have been willing to do? "God knows he'd used each of our safety to keep the others in line a thousand times before."

"And my safety, most of all," she said.

"Mmm," Whit agreed. "And no one was more susceptible to threats against Grace than Ewan."

Devil's cane tapped against the roof in an even, pensive rhythm. "Fuck," he finally whispered, awe in his tone. "He gave you up. Into our keeping. No wonder he was ready to blow up half of London when he thought we'd let you die."

"He gave up everything," she said, to herself as much as to them.

The brothers he'd just found.

Her.

I loved you the moment I set eyes on you a lifetime ago, but what that was—it pales in comparison to how I love you now.

"He gave us each other," she said, watching the rooftops.

For twenty years, she'd traversed this city from up on high, believing that the rooftops were the place she'd stolen from him. Claimed for herself. But they weren't stolen. They'd been gifted. He'd given her this place.

"All those years, we thought he chose the title over us," Whit said. "When he actually chose the title *for* us. It was a sacrifice for us."

"Not for us," Devil said. "For Grace."

He'd come to them for penance weeks ago. Vowed to make amends. When in actual fact, Ewan had been paying penance for twenty years.

"You said he left." Grace looked to Devil, tears in her eyes. "Where did he go?"

"Northeast." Toward Essex.

Back to the estate. To that place they all loathed, because it had stolen so much from them. And from him most of all. The answer made her want to scream. Instead, she came to her feet, looking from one of her brothers to the other. "He shouldn't be there."

"He's Duke of Marwick; where else should he be?" Devil asked.

Anywhere else. "He hates the title. Hates the house. It destroyed him," she said. "That place that was his ruin as much as it was ours."

More.

She looked at them. "He doesn't want it."

"The house?"

"Any of it," she clarified. "But he hasn't a choice, has he?"

I want you, he'd said. *I want you, and I love you, and it isn't first love.*

He could be happy with her.

They could be happy together.

It seemed at once impossible and like everything she'd ever wanted.

"He wants me," she said, softly.

"Then why would he go back?" Devil asked.

"Because—" she started, then stopped, hating the end of the sentence. Not wanting to finish it. *Because I was afraid to take what I wanted.*

Whit spoke. "Because he has nowhere else to go."

Because she'd pushed him away, again. She'd run from him, again. And this time, he hadn't deserved it.

Regret coursed through her—regret and something even more powerful.

Need.

She needed him. And there was no shame in it. Only promise. Only hope.

She came to her feet. "He shouldn't be there," she said again. "He should be here. With me."

She didn't know how it would work. But it would work. If the choice was a lifetime with him or a lifetime without him, there was no choice. Not one worth considering.

She was queen of Covent Garden, and she'd spent a lifetime making the impossible possible.

"I made a mistake. I have to go after him."

Devil's gaze snapped to hers. "Don't say it."

She did. "I love him."

"Fuck," he replied.

"I love him, and I have to save him."

Whit grunted. "I suppose we won't be able to kill him now."

"Pity, that." Devil heaved a dramatic sigh. "I shall get the carriage."

HOURS LATER, EWAN entered Burghsey House to face his past.

No one had been inside the manor house in a decade—since Ewan had assumed the dukedom and banned the staff from the main house, knowing that even if everything he intended went to plan, and he did find Grace and convince her to marry him, he would never again live inside these walls that had brought him nothing but pain.

The setting sun streamed through the western windows as he lit a long-forgotten candle and walked the halls of the massive house, along dust-covered, threadbare carpets and around furniture that had faded in a decade without use.

Ten years of dust and disrepair, and still, the house was the same: the massive entryway, rich mahogany and stonework covered in tapestries that had hung since the dawn of the dukedom; the familiar scent, of candlewax and history; the heavy quiet that had settled once Devil and Whit and Grace had left, slowly stripping him of his sanity.

Standing there, inside the house, Ewan was cast back with the force of a scarred fist on a filthy Covent Garden street.

He climbed the stairs, the map of the place a pristine memory. Passing portrait after portrait, the lines of dukes and marquesses and earls and lords whose identities had been drilled into him as a boy. All the venerable men who made up the unimpeachable line of Marwicks.

And Ewan, the next in line.

Little had his father known that Ewan had never wished it.

Little had his father known that Ewan would never give him that line. That there would be no more heirs to the dukedom. Not after Ewan.

Ewan, who had never been a real heir to begin with.

He climbed up to the first floor, then the second, where the sunlight faded into the darkness of twilight, and he crossed from east wing to west.

He did not need the candle in his hand, the map of the house remained etched in his mind, navigable in the pitch black if he wished for it to be, he counted the doors as he made his way down the hallway past the first two.

Three. Four.

Watch the squeaky board.

Five.

Cross the hallway.

Six. Seven.

Eight—his fingers trailed over the door that had once been his—a door Grace had found countless times in the darkness. He pressed his hand to it, resisting the urge to try the handle. To crouch down and look through the keyhole.

He didn't have to. He remembered every inch of that room. Every floorboard. Every pane of glass in the window. He did not have to revisit it. He was not here for the past, but for the future.

Behind the ninth door on the hall, a narrow staircase, climbing to the third floor, where the ducal chambers sat, triple the size of even the largest of the second floor rooms.

The master's rooms.

The duke's.

Ewan took a deep breath, turned the handle, and stepped inside to confront the enemy.

His father's rooms had been the first to be closed off, the moment the body was cold. He hadn't been inside them since, and he'd never imagined returning to this place—too afraid that it would be full of the man he loathed.

And perhaps, if he had returned before now, he would have found it such, thick with the memory of the man who had machinated and manipulated and threatened him again and again. The man who had stolen any hope Ewan might have had for happiness when he'd been taken from his mother's home, and forced to turn his back on the people he loved, to keep them safe.

But everything had changed.

Darkness had fallen outside, and Ewan raised the candle as he crossed the room—past the great bed and the long-empty fireplace with the massive wingback chairs that sat unused—the silence no longer ominous as it had been in this house for so long.

Instead, it was welcoming, as though the whole room, the whole *house*, the dukedom itself had waited for Ewan to return. For this.

He stopped beneath his father's portrait, a large oil painting that seemed, somehow, to have avoided the neglect and age that the rest of the manor had suffered, as though his father had sold his soul to ensure that he would forever be remembered like this—impeccably handsome and with the amber eyes he had passed onto all three of his sons.

Ewan had never liked looking at the painting; he'd never liked the similarities he saw in it. The eyes, the sweep of blond hair, the angled jaw, the long straight nose that would have been a similarity if Devil hadn't broken Ewan's and given him a gift in the balance.

For decades, Ewan thought that broken nose was all that set him apart from his father. The only thing that made him different—for hadn't he made the same choices as his sire?

"You bastard." The words were gunshot in that room that hadn't witnessed sound in ten years. "You used to love throwing that word at us. Like a weapon. Because we didn't belong to you. And you thought that was the pain of it. You never knew the truth, you feckless coward . . ."

Three boys, his brothers.

"You never knew that the word would knit us together. That it made us stronger than you. That it made us better than you." He stared his father down, through the darkness and the years. "You never knew that it would be your downfall.

"But you always knew she would be, didn't you?" he whispered, finally letting himself remember. Who he had come for. And why. "You feared her because of what she was to me, and that was *before* I understood what it was to love her. Before I understood what it was to stand with her, and see the future, and know that it did not have to be bleak. That it could be strong and smart and full of hope. And full of love."

He paused, breathing in the silence. Knowing this was the last time he would stand in this room. Knowing it was the last time he would give even a moment to this man. To this place. To the name that was never his.

Knowing that he would walk away from this estate tonight, and return to London, and make good on that long-ago promise he'd made to the place he'd always loved. To the woman he loved, who had already begun making good on it.

We're going to change all that.

Together.

Ewan lifted the candle, looked his father in the eye, and said, "You were right to fear her; but you should have feared me, as well."

And he set the portrait on fire.

The flames took hold instantly, the frame and canvas like perfect tinder, and Ewan turned to leave as the fire crawled up the wall, consuming this room, as though it were sentient, and knew the work he required of it.

Ewan left the room and found the next, knowing he had one chance to leave everything behind and return to London. To return to her and start a new life. Together. Away from this place and the specter of it. Quickly, methodically, he set more portraits aflame, the fire chasing over plaster and the woodwork, down the stairs—moving more quickly than he could have imagined.

It was a fire that would be talked about in Essex for years.

And with every moment, every new flame, Ewan felt more free.

Free to return home.

To her.

When the fire blazed to his satisfaction, hot enough to ensure the end of this place that deserved to be reduced to rubble, Ewan made for the door, the flames making quick work around him.

Good. It was time for it to end.

He didn't want to waste another minute dwelling on the past.

He wanted the future.

He wanted Grace.

He crossed the massive entryway toward the door, even as the flames licked over the first floor banister. Through an open door, he saw how they'd already chased through into the conservatory. Fast like fury. Hot like freedom.

Ewan set his hand to the door handle and pulled the door open, the cool air a welcome respite to the blazing heat inside. Before he could step through to the outside, an ominous creak sounded from above. He looked up to the first floor, where an overhang jutted out over the entryway, now swallowed by flames.

The hesitation was a mistake.

With a horrendous roar, the balcony peeled from the wall, and somehow, in the sound, he heard her voice.

Chapter Twenty-Six

Grace and her brothers rode the hours to Burghsey House in silence, the air inside the carriage thickening with memory as they returned to the place that had shaped them—Devil's vengeance and Whit's fury and Grace's power. And as the wheels clattered and the miles stretched into hours, they all lost themselves to the past.

Three hours into the ride, Devil cursed harshly in the waning light. "Christ. I don't remember it being so far."

"It took us two days to get to London," Whit said, rubbing a hand absently over his torso, an echo of the broken ribs he'd had on that interminable walk.

Thirty minutes later, Devil's fidgeting was nearly unbearable, his cane in constant motion against the toe of his boot. "I don't remember it being so fucking empty."

"I remember that," Grace said, softly, looking out the window, the sun setting in the distance in a blaze of yellows and oranges. "I remember how lonely it was, before you came." And then once they'd arrived, it was as though someone had lit the lanterns at the estate. "Though I suppose I should not say such a thing, considering what came of you being there."

"What came of us being there was finding each other," Whit said, his voice low and graveled, always sounding like he'd just begun to use it that moment. "What came of being there was the Bareknuckle Bastards." He met Grace's eyes in the waning light. "Grace, there are a thousand things I would change about that godforsaken man and that godforsaken place, but I would not change being there. None of us would."

Devil's cane tapped again.

"Though I would gladly change Devil's choice of a cane sword right now."

The tapping stopped. "Fuck off."

Ignoring their bickering, Grace turned back to the window, the sunlight barely there now, the darkness stealing any possibility of tracking their progress. How far were they from the house? How long before she could see him, and tell him the truth—that she loved him. That she wanted to be with him.

And that they would sort out the rest.

It had been twenty years without him, and she was through with it.

Grace stared into the darkness, lost to her thoughts as Devil and Whit squirmed and sniped at each other, the back-and-forth a comfort as she grew more and more desperate to see Ewan, playing over every moment they'd been together since he'd returned to London.

The club. His rooftop. The alleyway with the laundresses.

The fight in her Garden.

The kisses in his.

The masks they'd worn.

"How did he know?" she said softly.

Devil looked up. "How did he know what?"

"That it was me. In the darkness on that night when he woke up. In the ring, with the sack over his head. The night of the masque."

This time, it was Whit who replied. "He'll always know you, Grace."

I shan't ever not seek you, Grace.

And still, she'd pushed him away.

You are my beginning and end. The other half of me. And you always have been.

In twenty years, she'd convinced herself it wasn't true. That whatever they'd been—whatever she'd longed for—had been fantasy. A figment.

And she'd been half right. It had been fantasy.

But she should have known better than anyone that fantasy was often more real, and more powerful than reality.

And tonight, she wished to make it reality, full stop.

If only this carriage would go a touch faster.

She looked out the window again, the sunset still blazing red in the distance. It was only then that she realized that it was impossible. That it was far too late for sunset.

She wasn't looking at the sun.

No.

"No." She sat up and put her hands on the window. "What has he done?"

It wasn't sunset.

It was fire.

Burghsey House was engulfed in flames.

The carriage came to a stop one hundred yards from the inferno, as close to the flames as the coachman was willing to get, the gig rocking with his weight coming down from the driving block even as Grace scrambled for the handle and flung the door open, flying from the carriage.

What had he done?

Where was he?

"What has he done?"

"He's always been mad . . . but this . . ."

Whit and Devil were on her heels as she made her way

past the horses, already running, headed for the manor, ablaze in the night.

He was burning it all down. For her.

"Grace!" came Devil's shout behind her. "No!"

She didn't listen, tearing through the darkness toward the flames.

A great steel arm came around her, and she screamed, writhing against it. Whit. "Get the fuck off me!" she yelled as he hauled her back.

"Stop," he growled.

Frustration and fury came hot and angry, and she struggled against her brother's grip, wild with the need to get free. To get to Ewan.

She turned back, her hand already fisting, already flying, already landing directly on his nose and setting his head back. "Christ!" he growled as he took the blow . . . and she took off once more.

"Grace! *Stop!*" Devil shouted as *he* caught her, this time.

"I have to get to him!" she screamed, struggling against his grip. "I'll take you out, too!"

Devil was stronger than he looked. "And I'll take it," he said, in her ear. "I've taken worse for you, Gracie. We all have."

She turned back, ready to do more damage, but Devil was also ready, blocking her fist with one of his heavy hands. "Grace," he said again, calm and even, as though they were anywhere but here, on the ancestral lands of his father, where they'd all been through hell.

"Grace," Whit repeated from Devil's shoulder, where he'd caught up with them, nose bloodied, the red-gold glow of the fire making the worry on his face clear.

The worry on both their faces.

It was the worry that broke her. The softness in their eyes, those eyes that were part of a set. A trio. Her heart pounded. "He's inside."

"You don't know that." Devil.

She looked to him. "I do," she said, panic flaring even as she looked to Whit. "I *do*. He's in there, and he's alone, and I have to get to him."

She would be damned if she let this place have him.

Not after all they'd been through.

"Please," she whispered.

"We made a promise, all those years ago," Devil said, his voice ragged. "We promised him we would keep you safe. You ain't runnin' into fire."

"And how many times did he run into fire for us?" she cried. "How many times did he do it *here*? That night, a lifetime ago, he chased us from this building . . . and he has lived in its fire ever since."

"Grace . . ."

There was a beat of silence, and then, like a gift, Whit grunted.

Grace seized on the sound. "Please. I would know," she whispered to him. "I would know if he were dead."

Recognition flared in his eyes. A knowledge that came only from someone who knew the anguish she felt. "I believe you."

Devil's grip loosened.

Mistake.

Grace was already turning to run, smarter now. Her brother's wicked curse rent the darkness as she headed for the house, for the flames. For the man she loved.

And then he was there. The door of the great manor house opened, and he was *there*, in shirtsleeves, tall and magnificent and *alive,* framed by the fire behind him, like no duke she'd ever seen before.

He was alive.

Grace pulled up short at the look of him, hiccupping her relief, their last conversation playing through her. Thc confession he offered her. No. Not a confession.

He'd called it a fight.

His last battle for her.

Second to last.

Because when she'd pushed him away, he'd made one final choice. Thrown one final punch. And landed it perfectly. He'd come here and set this place they had all loathed so much on fire.

"Fucking hell," Devil said softly. "He did it."

This mad, magnificent man had burned down the past.

For their future.

She was already moving, toward him, desperate to get to him, when the wicked crack tore through the night. He looked up at the sound, and she knew what was to come.

No!

She screamed his name into the night, tearing toward the house, her brothers on her heels, as the windows blew out of an upper window and he was swallowed by flame.

No. This place did not win him.

He was hers.

And as though she had willed it, the flames parted, and he was there again, walking through fire, just as he'd promised, tall and beautiful, covered in soot and ash, the house burning like hell itself behind him.

And he came straight for her.

She flew to him, launching herself into his arms, and he caught her, lifting her high against him, and kissing her, dark and deep and perfect, pulling away eventually to look into her eyes. "What are you doing here?"

"I came to get you. I came to tell you that I love you. I came to tell you that you're mine, and I'm never letting you go again."

He kissed her again, long and lush, setting their hearts to racing before he set his forehead to hers and said, "I shall allow it."

Pleasure rioted through her at the lush words, at the promise in them. *Forever.* "What have you done?"

"What I should have done years ago," he said. "I should have destroyed this place from the start. This place that threatened to destroy us every day we were here. And threatened to destroy me every day after you left." He kissed her again, and she could taste the aching regret on his lips.

"It did not destroy you," she said. "It made you so much stronger."

"No. *You* made me stronger. Strong enough to free us. Strong enough to leave the past behind and build a new future. With you. In the Garden. If you'll have me."

Always.

She would always have him.

"Christ, Duke," Devil said as he and Whit approached. "This would have really set the old man off."

Ewan didn't release Grace as they turned to face the house, blazing in the night, and watched as an interior wall collapsed, sending flames shooting from the empty places in the stone facade where windows used to be.

He didn't look to his brother, not even when he answered, "Not a duke any longer."

Understanding dawned, bright and impossible, and they all looked to him. Grace shook her head. "You cannot mean it."

"But I do. I spent the last year restoring the estate. It thrives. Her Majesty will no doubt delight in its lucrative return."

He'd given it all up. For her. For them.

"You do not believe me?" He looked back to the inferno. "No one could survive that blaze. Not even the mad duke Marwick."

They all followed his gaze, his words settling as they watched the house burn.

Finally, after what seemed like an eternity, Whit spoke. "Duke's definitely dead. Seen it with my own eyes."

Devil's white teeth flashed in the glow of the fire. "Aye, lost to history as Burghsey House burned—all tragic like."

Ewan looked to Devil and Whit, watching them carefully. "And with him, all the ghosts that have haunted us."

And that was how Robert Matthew Carrick, Earl Sumner, Duke of Marwick—the duke who had never really existed—died.

"You're lucky you walked out of there, bruv," Whit added. "Else Grace would've been in there on your heels, willing the flames away and pulling you back from hell."

Ewan turned to her, pulling her close. "If anyone is strong enough to win that battle, it's you."

She reached up for him, letting her fingers tangle in his hair. "I've plans for you, yet."

That smile—the one that never failed to turn her inside out. "I've a plan or two of my own."

"Tell me," she said. *What was next?*

"A fresh start. A new life. Whatever it takes to be with the woman I love."

"What are you offering?" she asked.

"Honest work by day, and your fantasies by night."

Heat flooded through her at the sinful promise in the words. "Our fantasies," she whispered, coming up on her toes and kissing him again, her hands coming to his face. "So, what, then, we make you Duke of the Garden?"

"I was hoping for something higher."

"You can never go back to Mayfair," she said. "Not if you're killing off the Duke of Marwick. The whole world will know you there."

"I know, love. I don't want Mayfair. There's nothing there for me. All the work I've done—Mayfair can't make it right. Mayfair can't make good on my long-ago promise to the Garden. And it can't make good on the one I made to you." His thumbs traced over her cheeks. "I don't wish to be a duke any longer. Not when I might stand next to a queen. Not when I might be her king."

You are a queen. I am your throne.

The words sizzled through her.

He set his forehead to hers and whispered. "I do not want to be Your Grace ever again. All I want is for *you* to be *my* Grace." He kissed her again. "It's always been you. Every day. Every night. Every minute. Since the beginning. This is the sum of my ambition: To be worthy of you. Of your love. Of your world. To stand by your side and change it."

Yes.

"To live by your side. To love there and hang the rest of it."

The fire blazed behind him—the end of their past—the beginning of their future.

He'd set the seat of the dukedom on fire.

"I'll say this for it," Devil spoke up from where he and Whit watched the house burn. "It's one hell of a gesture."

Whit grunted his agreement, and Grace heard the approval there, too. Ewan had set them free as well.

She couldn't control the wild laugh that came at the commentary. "It's true what they say. You're a madman."

"Maybe," he allowed with a grin. "Mad about you, to be sure."

Devil groaned at the words and Ewan kissed her again, before adding, "You said I could never have her back. But what if I don't want her? What if I want you, instead? This isn't first love. This is next. This is last."

She nodded, tears in her eyes. "Yes."

He smiled—that smile, the one that never failed to lay her low. "Yes."

"I love you," she said, the only words that she could find.

"Good," he replied. "Tell me again."

"I love you."

He pulled her close. Kissed her deep. Smiled again. "Grace," he said, softly, like a litany. "My Grace. Finally here."

"Finally here," she whispered, pressing kisses across his face. Along his jaw, over his cheek bones, at his brow, where she could smell the fire. "What do you need?"

The echo of all the times he'd said it to her.

"Tomorrow," he said, his arms coming around her. "I need tomorrow. With you."

The Future

"There you are."

Ewan turned from his place at the edge of the rooftop to find his wife striding toward him, stunning gold corset over tight black trousers, beneath a topcoat lined with a matching gold thread. Her riotous red curls tumbled around her shoulders and her cheeks were rosy with the crisp air and a day in the sun.

He'd still never seen anything so beautiful, even now, after years by her side.

Before she could say anything more, he reached for her, pulling her close for a long, lingering kiss, stealing her breath and her pleasure before lifting his head and ending the caress, loving the way she lingered in his arms, her eyes closed in pleasure.

When she did open her eyes, it was with a dreamy smile—one he matched with his own, full of arrogant pride. There were very few things he liked more in life than the look of his wife in pleasure.

She laughed. "You look like a cat in the bin outside the fishmonger."

He recoiled at the analogy. "You know the saying is the cat that got the cream, do you not?"

She waved away the correction. "Have you ever seen the sheer arrogance of a cat with a bit of stolen fish? You're showing your not-so-humble beginnings, husband."

He pulled her in for another kiss at that, until she went loose in his arms again and he lifted his head, pressing his forehead to hers and whispering, "Say it again."

Pleasure lit in her beautiful brown eyes, the light from the setting sun turning them to fire. "Husband."

They'd been married mere weeks after the fire at Burghsey House, in the church of St. Paul's Covent Garden—where Ewan had been baptized thirty years earlier—not that a little thing like a falsified baptismal record would have stopped the Bareknuckle Bastards from a wedding and subsequent celebration. And afterward, Mr. and Mrs. Ewan Condry—the name his choice—had walked the streets of Covent Garden as king and queen, Grace showing Ewan every corner of the world where he had been born, and she had been made.

The dukedom had returned to the Crown after the fire, the old duke's plans for legacy fully thwarted. The land and tenants in Essex still thrived, and the staff in Mayfair had been snatched up by myriad aristocratic households—the mistresses of which were all members of a certain Covent Garden club.

The responsibilities properly handled, Ewan had never looked back to his title, too focused on his work, his love, and his future.

In the years since his return, 72 Shelton had been restored, the clientele growing along with the space—Ewan and Grace now lived in a handsome row house not far from Drury Lane, connected to the rest of the Bastards' homes by rooftop. Their daughters grew in the sun and shade of

Covent Garden, surrounded by hard working men and strong, smart women, and a world that their parents worked to make better every day.

"I will never grow tired of that word on your lips," he said, pulling her tight against him and pressing a kiss to her temple.

"You're missing the festival, *husband*," she said as they turned back to the edge of the roof, and looked down on the Covent Garden market square, where the barkers and hawkers of the day had given way to musicians and pie sellers and a fire eater who looked more than a little familiar. They watched as Felicity and Devil danced in a whirlwind to a wild fiddle, around and around until they were tangled in each others' arms and out of breath.

"I'm not missing it. I was just watching for a bit before I came down." After a day in the Garden, arguing about fresh water piping and the plans for new housing for the workers in the Rookery, he'd come to watch the rooftops turn gold in the setting sun and cast the market in gold.

And yes, he'd come to watch his wife as she reigned queen over it.

"I know," she said. "I've been watching you watching us."

"Oh?" he said.

"It's hard to miss such a handsome voyeur."

He grinned at the words, pulling her tight to him, again. "I see the girls are happy."

On the far corner of the square, beneath a torch that had been lit as the daylight faded, a half-dozen girls—cousins—crowded around Whit and Hattie. Felicity and Devil's Helena and her younger sister, Rose, each as clever as their mother and cunning as their father, were joined by Hattie and Whit's brilliant Sophia, who could happily take control of the shipping business at the age of nine. And with them, three flame-haired girls—seven, five, and four, each with a riot of curls to match their mother's, and amber eyes like their father.

"Whit's been doling out sweets all day," she said. "Lemon drops, raspberry drops, strawberry, his pockets appear to be bottomless."

"Hattie brings them in by the case," he said.

"She spoils him."

He looked to her. "He deserves it."

She grinned. "So do we all, I say." She paused, and then tilted her head and said, slyly, "Is there something sweet I can provide you, husband?"

The question sent a lick of heat through him. "I think I can imagine one or two things."

"Only one or two?" she said. "I'm disappointed."

He kissed her again, long and deep, until they both came away breathless. "I confess," he said, "I feel spoiled every day I am with you and the girls. I feel spoiled every day I stand with my brothers, in this place. I feel spoiled every night when I come home to you."

She leaned up to press a kiss to his beard-roughened cheek as he added, "Sometimes feeling so spoiled makes me wonder if it's all real."

"I've an idea," Grace said, pulling away from him, her fingers tangling in his. "Come down and play. Laugh with me and dance with me, and spend an outrageous amount of blunt, and let the broad tossers give you a good fleecing, and let Devil challenge you to a bout, and let Whit convince you to buy the girls a hound."

"No hound," he said, firmly.

His gorgeous wife grinned. "There's a little brown pup who might win your heart yet, husband . . . but I'm not finished."

"By all means," he replied. "Go on."

She approached again, pressing her long, lush body to his and wrapping her arms about his neck. And then she pressed kisses to his face and jaw and cheeks. "Come and play, until our feet are tired and our hearts are full . . . and then let's go home and tumble into bed. Happy. Just as we deserve."

And because they deserved it, that is precisely what they did.

Author's Note

Covent Garden holds my whole heart, even now, two hundred years apart from the world of the Bareknuckle Bastards. In the last few years, I've been lucky enough to spend days of research time in and around Covent Garden and the London Docklands; this series would not exist without the extensive collection of the Museum of London (particularly its magnificent work with Charles Booth's *Life and Labour of the People of London*), The Museum of the London Docklands, the Covent Garden Area Trust, the Foundling Museum, and the British Library.

A quick note on the raids that play a pivotal role in Grace's story. It would take time for the new young Queen to usher in the period of rigid morality with which her name has become synonymous—in those early years, there was a rise in social freedoms for women at all levels of society. But, as is too common in situations in which marginalized groups gain social ground, there was an enormous backlash. Between social disdain, political vitriol, and physical violence, the expanding role of women of all classes was hotly contested for the remainder of the nineteen century, resulting not only in commonplace raids like the one on 72 Shelton Street, but also in laws that criminalized sex work, refused women the vote, and widely set women back—all while Queen Victoria held the throne.

Of course, Grace and Ewan—and all the Bastards—fought these changes every step of the way.

When I proposed this story of historical romance featuring criminals and fighters and bordello owners who existed far beyond the ballrooms of Mayfair, Avon Books did not blink. I am keenly aware of how lucky I am to have Carrie Feron, who always knows the path I'm on, even when I don't, and the entire team there. Thank you to Liate Stehlik, Asanté Simons, Angela Craft, Pam Jaffee, and Kayleigh Webb, to Eleanor Mikucki for bravely suffering my absolutely abhorrent misuse of lay and lie, and to Brittani DiMare, who makes me look better with every book.

It's surreal to be writing the ending to the Bareknuckle Bastards—these four have kept me company for years, long before I started writing them. I'm so grateful to the Kiawah group over the years, from Sophie Jordan, Carrie Ryan, and Ally Carter, who helped develop the seed of the idea, to Tessa Gratton and Sierra Simone who cheered it on, to Louisa Edwards, who answered every call and text and late-night question I had. Thank you for helping to make my Covent Garden criminals real boys (and girl).

So many of my favorite women are a part of Grace. If you look closely, you'll see glimpses of my mom, my sister, Chiara, Meghan Tierney, Jen Prokop, Kate Clayborn, Adriana Herrera, Joanna Shupe, Megan Frampton, LaQuette, Nisha Sharma, Andie Christopher, Alexis Daria, Tracey Livesay, Nora Zelevansky, Julia Quinn, Kristin Dwyer, Holly Root, Eva Moore, Cheryl Tapper, and so many more.

As always, to my loves—V, my rebel girl, and Eric, who

would absolutely give up a dukedom for me—thank you for always letting me come home.

And finally, to you, dear reader: Thank you for believing in my bastards, for taking this journey with me, and for trusting me to bring Ewan around. I know a leap of faith when I see one. I hope you'll stay with me for what comes next—I cannot wait for you to meet my Hell's Belles in 2021.

Give in to your Impulses!

These unforgettable stories only take a second to buy and give you hours of reading pleasure!

Go to ***www.AvonImpulse.com*** and see what we have to offer.

Available wherever e-books are sold.

IMP 0811

At Avon Books, we know your passion for romance—once you finish one of our novels, you find yourself wanting more.

May we tempt you with . . .

- **Excerpts** from our upcoming releases.
- Entertaining **extras,** including authors' personal photo albums and book lists.
- Behind-the-scenes **scoop** on your favorite characters and series.
- **Sweepstakes** for the chance to win free books, romantic getaways, and other fun prizes.
- Writing **tips** from our authors and editors.
- **Blog** with our authors and find out why they love to write romance.
- **Exclusive content** that's not contained within the pages of our novels.

Join us at
www.avonbooks.com

An Imprint of HarperCollins*Publishers*
www.avonromance.com

Available wherever books are sold or please call 1-800-331-3761 to order.

FTH 1013